Duncan Campbell is a senior correspondent with the *Guardian*, where he has worked as the paper's crime correspondent and Los Angeles correspondent. Born in Edinburgh, he has written five non-fiction books. He previously worked for LBC Radio, *Time Out*, *City Limits* and contributed to *Oz*, *IT* and *The Rising Nepal*. *The Paradise Trail* is his first novel.

Praise for *The Paradise Trail*:

'The dialogue is the wittiest I have read in any work of fiction, including *Catch 22*. The fascinating historical and cultural context is unobtrusively drip-fed, and the whodunit suspense masterfully created. Admirably insightful and hilarious. [Duncan Campbell] is engagingly clever and writes like a dream. I can't recommend it highly enough' Howard Marks, *Guardian*

'*The Paradise Trail* is essential reading . . . enthralling . . . intriguing. If the wit of Billy Connolly, the game of cricket and works of Bob Dylan are also your thing, you won't be disappointed' *Scotsman*

'*The Paradise Trail* sparkles with humour, and has the edginess of a murder mystery; but its most bracing surprise is the acute irony with which it anatomizes a counter-cultural generation's youthful fantasies and middle-aged illusions' Pankaj Mishra, author of *Temptations of the West*

THE
PARADISE TRAIL

Duncan Campbell

headline
review

First published in 2008 by HEADLINE REVIEW
An imprint of HEADLINE BOOK PUBLISHING

First published in paperback in 2008 by HEADLINE REVIEW
An imprint of HEADLINE PUBLISHING GROUP

1

ISBN 978 0 7553 4247 1 (B Format)
ISBN 978 0 7553 4707 0 (A Format)

Typeset in Hoefler by Avon DataSet Ltd,
Bidford-on-Avon, Warwickshire

Printed and bound in the UK by
CPI Mackays, Chatham ME5 8TD

HEADLINE PUBLISHING GROUP
An Hachette Livre UK Company
338 Euston Road
London NW1 3BH

www.headline.co.uk
www.hachettelivre.co.uk

Prologue

18 December 1971

'COULD I SPEAK to the Consul, please?'

'And what is your good name?'

'J. K. Dutta. Calcutta Morgue. We have a body here that has been brought to us from the Lux Hotel.'

'Did you not ring last week about a body from the Lux Hotel?'

'This is another body.'

'Two bodies from the same hotel. That seems a little careless.'

Chapter One

Two weeks earlier

ANAND DESCENDED THE wobbly fire escape that led from his quarters to the Lux's courtyard with as much dignity as he could manage in cordless pyjama bottoms and tartan bedroom slippers. The latter were a going-away present from his landlady, Mrs Grodzinski, just before he left London for his return home to Calcutta. This was not how he had imagined the life of a hotelier when he inherited the Lux. He had pictured an elegant inn, perhaps like the French auberges in which he had holidayed during his early years at the London School of Economics. The description had said 'centrally located hotel, ten bedrooms, four multi-bed, elegant roof gardens, reception area, established clientele'. It had sounded promising.

The letter from the lawyer with news of his uncle's will arrived on the day after his finals. He read it out that evening, in Henekeys, over a port, with Vanessa, Nii and Vic. Vanessa said it was fate, he was obviously meant to be a hotelier and not an economist. They ordered another bottle of Sandemans and wandered off to Rules for dinner. Vanessa paid the bill because her father had promised her the first tranche of her inheritance if she graduated. They laughed over the pheasant about what kind of hotel it would be, whether the beds would be four-posters, whether he would have to ask couples for proof of marriage. Would there be a 'happy hour' at six for guests to mingle over pink gins?

He had had great dreams for it. It would be a literary haven, the kind of place where someone could stay while they worked on their poetry or polished their novella. Book discussion evenings. Authors invited to read from their work in progress. A decent library. There would be 'continental breakfasts' with croissants and airmail editions of the *International Herald Tribune* in the lobby. Copies of *Punch* and the *Listener* in the library. It would gain a discreet reputation, with flattering articles in the *Paris Review* and the travel sections of the *New York Times* and the *Observer*. Calcutta's Algonquin.

Then, after saying farewell to Mrs Grodzinski and his bedsit in Belsize Park, flying on BOAC back to Calcutta – the reality. A crumbling, three-storey tip behind two rusty old spiked gates down an alleyway off Sudder Street. The 'roof gardens' was a decaying mess with a large puddle in the corner where the drainage did not function properly. The bedrooms were infested with remarkably impudent rats, the reception area consisted of a shaky old school table with a dried-out inkwell. And the 'established clientele'? Well, there they were now, squatting beneath him in the darkness, not even waiting for dawn to get out of their hairy skulls on dope.

Anand had noticed that the hippy travellers – or 'heads', as some of them liked to call themselves – hung out in pairs or little groups. The only Indians they seemed to have dealings with were the money changers and dope dealers who lurked outside the Lux's gates. Two of his guests, one British, one American, had already been at the hotel for at least three weeks and had adjacent beds in the main dormitory room. The Briton, an anxious-to-please young man called Gordon, had long, straggly fair hair tied in a headband and the hint of a beard. The American, Larry, had a shaven pate, a bushy beard and the upper body of a wrestler. He delivered his remarks in a deadpan, corner-of-the-mouth way like the brash American comedians Anand had seen at the Establishment club in Soho. The pair were in the corner of the courtyard now, constructing a chillum for their first smoke of the day, a lighter flashing in the darkness. Since drugs were officially banned at the hotel, Anand was gratified to see that they made at least a pretence of hiding the evidence – cigarette tobacco, shavings of hashish on the top of a paperback book. He reached the bottom rung of the fire escape and joined them in the courtyard.

'I am afraid I must ask you to put that light out,' he told them. 'There is a blackout in force and they are bombing Agra.'

He had been rehearsing what he would say as he descended the steps. He was satisfied with the open-mouthed response from the pair. He noted that Larry was reading *The Glass Bead Game* by Herman Hesse. What was it about Hesse that they found so attractive?

'Mr Bose,' said Larry. He always addressed him formally, unlike most of the other guests, to whom he was clearly anonymous. 'This Pakistani pilot is flying over Calcutta, unaware of where he is, spots a Zippo sparking in a yard and it's "bombs away"? Is that what you're thinking?'

Anand liked Larry, despite his habits. He was not just here for the drugs and cheap living but was interested in Indian sculpture, forever meeting local businessmen anxious to sell him carved elephants or intricate models of the Q'tub Minar and then departing to the GPO to dispatch them, Anand presumed, to art dealers in America.

'Mr Anunziato,' said Anand.

'Larry, man, Larry.'

'Larry. You must not take things so literally. That is what you Americans do. You are all literalists. It is your Puritan heritage. No, I do not imagine that your lighter has put the entire city at risk but we are about to be a nation at war and we must show some sort of example here at the Lux. How is everyone bearing up under the blackout?' Do I sound incredibly pompous, Anand wondered, considering that I am only a year or two older than this ramshackle crew? Vanessa used to say, 'Oh, don't be so pompous,' in what sounded, to him, like a very pompous English voice.

'Look, we'll do whatever you say,' said Gordon, the British chap. 'Has the fighting really started?'

'Yes, it would seem that some skirmishes have already begun,' said Anand. 'The army sounds confident. But war is war.'

There was a silence between them. Were they waiting for him to go so that they could recommence their drug-taking?

'Well, here comes rosy-fingered dawn,' said Gordon, the wispy-bearded headband chap.

'My Scottish vagabond friend speaks eloquently,' said Larry, the shaven-headed American.

'Your Scottish vagabond friend has had a classical education and has been studying Homer at school,' said Anand, surreptitiously knotting the waistband of his pyjama bottoms so that they did not slip down any further. 'As I, too, was forced to do.'

'Where did you go to school?' asked Gordon.

'Right here, in Calcutta. Dalrymple Academy. And we had to imbibe all the same rich brew of imperial Britain that you probably did,' said Anand, 'courtesy of the Anglo-Scottish Educational Board.'

He felt suddenly tired. The insomnia that had plagued him since his teens had worsened since his return. Often he would find himself at three or four in the morning switching on his bedside light and reading until dawn, willing himself unsuccessfully to fall asleep. He read a lot. One of the few unexpected advantages of the hotel was a constant supply of paperbacks discarded by passing guests.

Were they all stoned all the time? Anand had smoked a few joints in his four years in London but they had not appealed. He preferred port but had briefly thought that cannabis might prove to be the elusive cure for his insomnia. It had not been.

Because he had been away in Europe so long, he had missed the early waves of the travelling band of hippies and wastrels, the boys and girls from Britain and Germany and America and Holland and Scandinavia and Australia, with their long hair and their hollow cheeks and their grubby kurtas and strange, buffet-style approach to the religions of the East – a Sikh bracelet here, a tin Tibetan Buddha pendant there, a Ganesh embroidered on their backpack. He noticed that they sometimes used their Sikh bracelets as bottle openers. Some affected a choti, the little pigtail that gave them the air of an earnest devotee, although he was never quite sure of what or whom. Anand's parents, both now dead, had been resolutely secular, scornful of their more devout Hindu friends and dismissive of their Christian neighbours who still attended St Paul's, Calcutta's robustly imperial cathedral.

Some of his guests he almost recognised. After all, the LSE had had its share of languid dopers and people who headed off to seek enlightenment in the East before settling down to a job at C and A or British Steel. But he had never pondered where they might stay, picturing them vaguely on the beaches in Goa or with unscrupulous gurus in caves in Nepal.

When his late uncle's lawyer, Mr Ganguly, first took him to the Lux, one of half a dozen properties around the world which the old man had left to nephews and cousins, he had suddenly realised: this is where the hippies come. I have acquired a hippy hotel, a home for 'heads' and 'freaks'. I go to London to learn about the principles of Keynesian economics and I return to organise the changing of the bedlinen of the detritus of empire.

For a few weeks, he contemplated selling it and flying straight back to England. But to what? His close friends at LSE had scattered soon after they all graduated, Nii back to Ghana, Vanessa to look after her father in Nottinghamshire, Vic to Harvard. His degree was a poor one – too many nights at Ronnie Scott's, too many days playing darts at the Dog and Duck – and England, under poor, portly Edward Heath and with the National Front marching with increasing frequency beneath the Union Jack, seemed a cold and unfriendly place. He did not miss the 'Fuck off, Paki!' cries that sometimes greeted him as he walked home late at night through Chalk Farm, nor the groups of young white men with angry, pinched faces and big boots; he could still feel that slight frisson as he hunched his shoulders in preparation for a possible attack. There had been, too, what his fellow students would have described as 'banter': the jokes about cat food every time they ate at an Indian restaurant, the sidelong glances in his direction to see if he was taking offence; the bad Peter Sellers imitations complete with beery repetitions of 'Goodness Gracious Me'. And stand-up comics at student bashes making jokes about 'the Pakis are arriving in England – disguised as an oil slick'. Ha ha ha.

So, back in Calcutta, he hired painters, spruced up the hotel's reception area, put in some framed photos of the Red Fort to replace the peeling Air India poster of the Taj Mahal, attempted to improve the plumbing, paid a bloody fortune for a neon sign that lit up at night – now, of course, subject to the blackout – and tried to make the best of it.

His sister, Uma, had come from Delhi to help him re-equip the hotel, organise the purchase of new sheets and pillows, but the new linen had been promptly stolen by guests or torn up to be used as headbands or sofis for their chillums so he had returned to the old system whereby the hotel just supplied a mattress on the bedstead. Guests had their own sleeping bags, which they often seemed to use as safes, squirrelling away their passports, rupees, traveller's cheques and dope. The newly painted walls were soon covered with graffiti about Jimi Hendrix and Jim Morrison – or was it Jim Hendrix and Jimi Morrison? – and bad renderings of the yin and yang symbols. Someone had just written on the bathroom wall, in quite neat handwriting, 'Dope will get you through the times with no money better than money will get you through the times with no dope. Discuss.' The rats returned, encouraged by the flakes of chapatti and banana peel left by the guests. The new mattresses were soon stained with indeterminate moisture. How can you tell spilled lassi from spilled seed? he found himself wondering.

And the guests, the guests.

Most were young white men like Gordon and Larry, the current longest-term residents. Some were fine, polite, if slightly distant, as though they were speaking and listening through a fog of hashish. Some were petulant, complaining, demanding, wearing their entitlement like a topi, as though the days of the Raj had never passed. Some seemed dreadfully ill and on more than one occasion he had to organise auto-rickshaws to take people to doctors or consuls to deal with the effects of hepatitis, dysentery, malaria, cholera even, broken ankles, septicaemia, ringworm, hookworm, hallucinogenic flashbacks and crabs. Even though he had spent the last four years mixing and studying and sharing (occasionally) beds and jokes with the European middle classes, he was still puzzled by these young men who abandoned good careers and loving families to lie on lumpy mattresses and exchange inanities about the *Bhagavad Gita* or Janis Joplin. The girls, of whom there were fewer, seemed smarter.

In any case, with the hundreds of thousands of refugees streaming across the border from East Pakistan into India, as they had been since June, there were other things to think about. The events there had taken him by surprise. In London, he had become used to thinking of 'the war' as the one in Vietnam, the one about which there were teach-ins and demonstrations. He had marched and even thrown an egg at a policeman in Grosvenor Square. (It missed, which half annoyed him, as someone who had once been able to throw a cricket ball from the boundary so that it arrived, one bounce, an inch above the stumps, in the wicketkeeper's gloves; but he was secretly relieved that he had not put himself at risk of arrest.) Now India was about to be at war too.

It was bewildering to be in a country preparing so self-confidently for battle after being in one where people were so vehemently opposed to fighting. Some of his Calcutta friends were positively looking forward to it. It was as if this was a cricket series and Pakistan was going to be beaten soundly and satisfyingly.

He had watched, the previous afternoon, the departure of two dozen army lorries packed with young troops. Headed for the border, off to fight. But for the style of helmet and the shade of khaki, they could have been any soldiers anywhere in the last half-century: the camaraderie, the noisy, cigarette-smoking bravado, the smooth chins that had barely 'shaken hands with John Razor', as his old Latin teacher, an Anglo-Indian much more Anglo than Indian, had had it. The streets were crowded with troops and refugees. Howrah station, never tranquil, was in chaos.

When the actual official shooting war would begin was another matter. There were daily rumours. More than once he was told by neighbours that the bombing had started and was being hushed up by the government. Only an hour ago, a night watchman had rushed past shouting that the Pakistani air force was bombing Agra, which had given him the reason to descend on his 'established clientele'. She would surely have announced it, he thought. (He had noticed that people referred to Indira Gandhi, the prime minister, simply as 'she'. Nothing more was necessary. Once sneered at by his Calcutta friends as a lightweight beneficiary of nepotism, she was now treated as a majestic leader.)

'Anyway,' said Anand. 'Since dawn now seems to have made her appearance, we need no longer worry too much about the blackout. Are you all as comfortable as can be – in the circumstances, of course?'

'Do you know how long this is going to last?' asked Gordon.

'Unfortunately, this is not a Test match,' said Anand. 'They do not have to conclude hostilities within five days. But I think the Indian army is confident so, with good fortune, it will be concluded in time for you to return to your loved ones by Christmas.'

'But we have no loved ones,' said Larry, eyebrow cocked towards Anand. 'We wander alone, feeble prey for the cosmic throat-cutter.'

Anand noticed a barely perceptible change in the atmosphere. An American couple, heroin addicts supposedly, had had their throats cut in a hippy hotel in Bombay a few months earlier and some crude sign had been left on their bodies. Another traveller had been killed in the same way in Kerala. Anand had been visited once at the hotel by a detective who asked him to report anything suspicious. But all of that had been overtaken by events to the north and it had been weeks since there had been any mention of the murders in the press.

Baba, the hotel's major domo, a small, elderly, white-haired, constantly bustling man, whom Anand had inherited with the establishment, came into the courtyard carrying a guitar at arm's length between index finger and thumb, as if it was a dead street dog that had started to rot.

'Hey, that's my axe!' said Larry.

'Here, let me have a go,' said Gordon, surprisingly assertive. He plucked, fiddled, tuned. Then launched into 'Oh, we don't want to lose you . . .'

He is almost in tune, thought Anand. He knew the song;

13

it was from *Oh! What a Lovely War* which he had seen in the West End with Vanessa and Vic. He remembered it clearly, the music hall songs, dripping with sentimentality, yet moving. Vanessa wept throughout. He had not known whether to offer a hand in comfort.

Gordon sang on. Larry smiled benignly. Anand ascended the fire-escape steps back to his room as more music floated beneath him. Larry took over the guitar and he and Gordon sang a song which Anand did not recognise.

'Established clientele,' he said aloud to himself as he reached his room and turned on the wireless for the news. 'Est-ab-lish-ed clientele.'

As he slumped into his armchair and felt the hint of one of its springs on his right buttock, he noticed on the floor a folded, lined sheet of paper, which looked as if it had been torn from a school exercise book. Someone must have pushed it under his door. He bent down and picked it up. The words were all in capital letters: 'PLEASE TREAT MY DEATH AS SUSPICIOUS.'

Chapter Two

HAD IT ALL BEEN a terrible mistake? Gordon wondered, as he stroked his unimpressive beard with one hand and surreptitiously checked, with the other, hidden inside his navy-blue loon pants, to see whether the rash – crotch rot? Something more sinister? – was spreading. It was. He had given up everything: Grace, who now seemed more and more retrospectively desirable with each passing week of celibacy; the job, which hadn't been that bad, had it; the comfy squat; the pub band with the vague possibility of a record contract – for what? For this?

He surveyed the courtyard of the Lux. There was Mr Bose, the owner, disappearing up the dodgy fire escape in his pyjamas, a boyish flop of jet-black hair over his forehead, a little premature paunch just visible above the knotted pyjama bottoms, having delivered the news that Agra was being bombed.

Was he serious? Agra? The Taj Mahal? Bombed? And there was Larry, shaven head shining in the dawn sun, shelling a cigarette on to a warped paperback of *The Glass Bead Game* in preparation for the day's first chillum. Well,

Larry was a good thing, a new friend. His first American friend. There was that.

'You know how they say that the darkest hour is just before dawn?' said Larry.

'Who says that?' asked Gordon.

'The Mamas and the Papas. You know . . .' Larry paused, delicately placed the ingredients for making the chillum on the ground, reached behind him for the guitar that was now leaning against the wall, put it over his crossed bare knee and sang, quite sweetly, about whispering a little prayer and the darkest hour being just before dawn.

Gordon joined in, singing the tenor part of the last line.

'Good harmony,' said Larry. 'But you came in too soon on "just before dawn".'

'Bollocks,' said Gordon. 'You were too slow.'

'Why do British people say "bollocks" all the time?'

'Why do Americans say "bullshit" all the time?'

'Shit is waste matter so, if I say something is bullshit, it means I think it is rubbish, of no worth, OK? If you say something is bollocks and you mean it's of no worth, then it means you have no respect for the male sexual organ. That's all.'

'Well, that is bollocks.'

'Shhhh,' came a voice from inside. Then more urgently: 'SSSSHHHHH!'

'Fucking Capricorns,' muttered Larry.

'I'm not a fucking Capricorn,' responded an Australian voice from the inner darkness.

'Fucking triple Aries then,' said Larry. 'Are you all still in bed? Morning has broken, for God's sake.'

Larry lowered his voice but continued singing: ' ". . . for the darkest hour is – just before dawn." It isn't, though, is it? We were out here just before dawn and it was much lighter than at midnight.'

Gordon looked at Larry, absorbed by his task. Having assembled a quorum of hash shavings, he was emptying a Scissors cigarette of its tobacco and mixing the two ingredients with the detached delicacy of the sous-chef he claimed to have once been.

'I don't think you're meant to take it literally, Larry,' he said.

'So why write it, droog?'

'Because . . . it's comforting. Because it's a song, for heaven's sake.'

Gordon pushed his long hair out of his eyes and into his red and blue headband. It was bleached almost blond now by a combination of Goan sun and slyly applied lemon juice. He persisted with his thought.

'Songs aren't meant to be taken literally. Mr Bose is right. You Americans are too literal.' Gordon slipped his advertising copywriter's brain into gear. 'Do you think that "people who need people are the luckiest people in the world"? Mmm? Or do you believe that . . . um . . . "electrical banana is going to be the very next thing"? Or do you think the Grateful Dead are really grateful?'

'Have you got my lighter?'

'Or the Incredible String Band are incredible?' countered Gordon. 'Does your warehouse hide my Arabian drum? Do jewels and binoculars hang from the head of the mule? Have sixteen vestal virgins really left for the coast?

Did . . . er . . . someone leave the cake out in the rain?'

'OK! OK! OK! Christ, I get your fucking point. Jesus! Now give me my lighter.'

'SHHHH!' came a voice from inside another of the bedrooms that adjoined the courtyard.

'Christ, it's like being in a fucking library!' said Larry.

'D'you actually like Hesse?' Gordon asked, glancing at the book on Larry's bare knees below his frayed lungi. Gordon found the writer frosty and unappealing. 'I find him a bit – ascetic.'

Larry paused from his chillum-making and stared at the book. 'I find him overrated and pretentious but, as you may have noticed, this tome is the perfect size for the job in hand. Pass the lighter, droog.'

'You should read Siddhartha. It's fairly painless.'

Larry shrugged. Gordon handed him the Zippo. It had inscribed ornately on its side: 'Yea, though I walk through the Valley of the Shadow of Death I will fear no evil for I am the evilest son-of-a-bitch in the Valley.' Such a lighter normally indicated that the owner had served in Vietnam; they were made in Saigon. Gordon knew that it was uncool to ask Americans on the road whether they had been in Vietnam. It was like asking people at ad agency parties in London what they earned. If Larry had been in Vietnam, he must have been demobbed or gone AWOL for some months now; his beard was thick and black, in contrast to his recently shaven pate, a tonsorial arrangement which gave the impression that his head had been put on upside down. The whole effect was accentuated by his thick, brooding eyebrows.

Tugging at his own wispy beard, Gordon felt mildly jealous. He had just noticed, during a rare and tepid shower in the Lux's modest latrines, that, at the age of twenty-six, he was starting to go bald. But why should that be a worry? Wasn't that why he was here, so that he did not have to concern himself with such samsaric vanities? Wasn't that why he had escaped the pointlessness of career and the chains of permanent relationships, the long narrow corridor with signs marked 'promotion' and 'mortgage' and 'family' and 'pension'? To be free of all that, that was why he was here. Or something.

Yes, had it all been a terrible mistake? But he could not go back now, not for at least a year – he had airily resigned from his job as a copywriter, abruptly informed Grace that their relationship had 'stalled' – had he really used that horrible, cold word? That he was 'fond' of her but not in love. Easy to be hard. He had headed for the pub as her tears rolled silently down her cheeks. He could not now write to her from Calcutta and ask for forgiveness, suggest she give up her job as a graphic designer and fly out and join him. He felt the stirrings of desire at the thought of her.

He watched Larry pressing the last traces of tobacco and hash into the chillum. It reminded him of the satisfied look on his father's face as he thumbed his St Bruno tobacco into his briar pipe in preparation for the single pipeful he allowed himself after supper every evening. Those rituals. His father's single glass of Amontillado sherry on his return from his chartered accountant's office, after he had changed from his suit into cavalry twills, fawn cardigan and – the one dash of bravado – cravat. The checking of his watch as the one o'clock gun went off in Edinburgh Castle. The switching-on of the news on the Home Service, followed, immediately after the headlines had been read, by the inevitable 'I don't think we need any more of this, do we?' regardless of whether the news was about a coup in Uganda or a protest about television standards by Mrs Whitehouse. He recalled his father's look of astonishment three months earlier when he had told him he was giving up his job and taking the Magic Bus to India. His parents had been less bothered about the end of his relationship with Grace; they thought her skirts too short and her hair too long.

Larry sprinkled water from a small copper bottle on to his sofi, the handkerchief-sized piece of red-and-white checkered cloth that acted as a filter against the chillum's harsh blast on inhalation. 'I guess, droog, if the Mamas and Papas had sung that "the lightest hour is just before dawn", it would have lost its paradoxical significance,' he said.

'You talk a load of bollocks sometimes,' said Gordon. 'Do you think when Bob Dylan sings about the Visions of Johanna—'

'Oh, no, not Deelan, PLEASE!' came a hoarse voice with a French accent from inside the dormitory. Remy, the French junkie, was conscious. 'You fucking Americans think he is God.'

'I'm not American, I'm Scottish,' said Gordon matter-of-factly.

'Dylan *is* God, you emaciated junkie,' hectored Larry. 'Do you think we should be discussing the fucking existential qualities of Maurice Chevalier?' He sang a mocking line of 'Thank 'eaven for leetle girls' while checking that the chillum was now ready to be lit. 'Or Charles Trenet?'

'I cannot believe you 'ave 'eard of Trenet,' came the response from the dormitory. 'You are not so stupid as you look.'

'SHHHHHH!' came another voice.

'Sounds like the Aussies didn't get to sleep,' said Gordon. An Australian couple, Kieran and Karen, both thin, weary and henna-haired, had arrived the previous day and been allotted the room where Gordon, Larry, Remy and an Englishman called Freddie Braintree were all staying.

'Shall we sing "Morning Has Broken" to them?'

'Christ, how does a bugger get any sleep here?' Kieran, bare chest highlighting protruding ribs, lungi slung low on his hips, toilet roll clasped tightly in one hand, emerged into the courtyard. 'Are you going to light that bugger up or just look at it?'

'Pull up a bollard,' said Gordon, an old *Goon Show* reference that he did not think any of his companions would get but which he found comforting. A family routine, the weekly gathering round the wireless to listen to the Goons, the collective chuckle when Minnie Bannister said, 'We'll all be murdered in our beds.' He felt a reluctant homesickness.

Kieran pulled up a short, three-legged stool and squatted on it between Larry and Gordon.

'Is that water OK, man?' he said, eyeing Larry's copper bottle.

'Sure,' said Larry. 'Where did you just come from?'

'Arrived from Bombay yesterday. Train.'

'Stay at Stiffles?' asked Gordon.

'The Rex.'

'Isn't that where—'

'The two American junkies got killed? Yeah.'

'They arrest anyone for that yet?'

'Nope. They think it may be the same bloke who strangled the Dutch guy in Benares.'

'I thought he was Belgian.'

'I heard German.'

'What's the difference?' said Larry. 'Some weird stuff going down anyway. Someone left a yin and yang sign with a line through it on the bodies. I heard it was an Indian guy who had a mission to cleanse his country and he was starting with all the hippies.'

'I heard it was a Vietnam vet who'd freaked out,' said Kieran. 'Can we not talk about this? My lady's feeling a bit ropey.'

' "My lady",' mimicked Larry. ' "My lady"! You one of the knights of the fucking round table?'

'Give him a break,' said Gordon. To Kieran, 'Got the runs? I've got some stuff if you need it. Mixture of chalk and opium. Got it from a chemist in Poona. It's magic. If it doesn't dry you up, it makes you not care about it.'

'I might have to. Whatever I eat, it just goes right through me. Train was a nightmare. One time all the toilets were full so I had to just—'

'We are not innarested in your lousy condition,' said Larry. It was a line from Burroughs that Larry had adopted.

He used it a lot now. 'But feel free to join our round table discussion on whether the darkest hour is just before dawn.'

'I'll settle for a hit of the chillum, mate,' said Kieran, tossing back his long, hennaed hair. As he spoke, the dormitory door opened again and Karen, his girlfriend, emerged. She was in what Gordon could now identify as a Rajasthani nomad dress, its tiny coin-shaped mirrors reflecting the half-light. Her hair was parted severely down the middle.

Gordon rose and offered her his stool. She almost demurred but weariness prevailed. She sat down gratefully. Gordon was unable to stop himself from peering down the embroidered V-neck of her dress. This is terrible, he thought. I should be getting beyond desire. It had been three months since he had touched a woman's bare flesh. He caught a glimpse of two small pale breasts and felt a stirring beneath the loon pants he had bought one Saturday from the Good Fairy market on Portobello Road. The stirring reminded him of his rash. From that dirty mattress in Calangute? He squatted down with his back against the wall and his knees up.

'Which way you headed?' he asked.

'Burma, but none of the planes are running because of the war.' Kieran shrugged. 'And if that manager guy's right and they're bombing Agra, I guess we're stuck here. What's this place like? Seems OK.'

'Well, the cockroaches are friendly,' said Gordon. 'Hey, it's not bad for seven rupees a night.'

'Seven rupees? We're paying ten.'

'Ah, supply and demand,' said Larry. 'No one can fly out of Calcutta so hotels are full which means they can charge what they like. It's called capitalism. It's what Gordon thinks he can escape by immersing himself in the spiritual bathtub that is Mother India. He has yet to learn that there is nowhere left on earth untouched by avarice. Still, he now knows that the darkest hour is not just before dawn.' And he started singing in a sweet, gentle bass. As he reached the last line, he was joined by another voice, its owner emerging into the courtyard singing in near-perfect harmony, an angelic expression on his face beneath its mass of curls.

Freddie Braintree, wearing just a pair of bleached-out bell-bottomed jeans, frayed where they had scuffed across a hundred Indian pavements, beamed at the gathering, tucked his sandalled feet beneath him and sat down to form a circle. Freddie seemed to be one of the many casualties, either mental or physical, whom Gordon had encountered on the road but there was something touching about him, the way that there seemed to be something sharp beneath all the acid-addled aphorisms.

'Swami, Freddie,' said Larry. 'What gnomic insights have you to offer us?'

'The darkest hour IS just before dawn.'

'Far fucking out, man,' said Larry, finally disposing of *The Glass Bead Game* on the ground beside him and brushing a strand of tobacco from the singlet he wore above his lungi. Addressing Kieran and Karen, who had pulled their stools close together and were leaning against each other, Larry announced, 'Freddie's an expert on the Incredible String Band – you know them?'

'Don't think I do, man,' said Kieran. 'Are they American?'

'Yes, you do,' said Karen, gripping her roll of toilet paper as though it was a baton and she was about to run the final leg for the Australian women's 4 x 100 Olympic relay team. '*The Hangman's Beautiful Daughter* . . . That song – 'The Half-Remarkable Question' . . . You know . . .'

'Oh, it's the haaaalf remaaarkable quest-tion,' quavered Freddie.

'NO, NO, not ze fucking String Band,' came the Gallic voice, followed by the sound of a body hitting the floor. A few moments later, wrapped in a crumpled, grey kurta with what looked like a bloodstain on its left sleeve, Remy appeared. He glared at the company.

'You talk sheet,' he said, eyeing the still-unlit chillum. 'First that crazy hotel manager tells us we are being beumbed and now you talk this sheet.'

'Remy, we are trying to elevate the discussion,' said Gordon. 'For we stand at a moment in history.'

'From the land of Rimbaud and Sartre, come these pearls –' Larry shifted into his French imitation – ' "you talk sheet". And did he really say "beumbed"? I am glad that Baudelaire is not alive to see how decadent his countrymen have become.'

'You Americans think you say a few foreign names and it make you an intellectual,' said Remy, eyeing the company. 'Fuck you.'

'Hey, droog,' said Larry, 'is that blood on your sleeve? Have you cut yourself?'

Remy looked at him sharply. 'Betel juice, man.'

Larry and Remy exchanged a look.

'Napoleon in rags,' said Freddie with a grin.

Gordon glanced round the group. It was still too dark to catch everyone's expressions accurately. Karen and Kieran were both frowning and curling themselves into semi-foetal positions. Kieran stood up suddenly and hastened off clutching the toilet roll.

'May your stools be firm, droog,' said Larry.

'Who do you think you are? Dr fucking Kildare?' Kieran shot back over his shoulder as he disappeared.

Remy was eyeing everyone with handsome, lazy disdain from beneath his tousled hair and through his opiated pupils. Freddie beamed, without guile, a child at a funfair. The previous day he had told Gordon that his body had become translucent and he could now watch a glass of lassi on its way through his digestive tract. 'Wow,' Gordon had said.

Finally, like a priest preparing to administer the sacrament, Larry handed the lighter to Gordon, said, 'Come on, baby, light my fire,' raised the chillum aloft, touched his forehead with it, intoned 'Boom Shanka' and, as Gordon flipped the Zippo into action, put the chillum to his lips and took a deep breath as though preparing to dive to a great depth, thus kindling the hashish and tobacco and lighting the group's faces with a flattering, rosy glow. Gordon looked at them. One of a pair of dehydrated Aussies, an angry French junkie, a damaged English elf and Larry. Had he given up Grace, his friends in the Clapham squat, his mates in the pub band, his pals at the ad agency for this? He tried to ignore the itch in his loins.

'Hey, you don't have crabs, do you, droog?' asked Larry. 'I once had crabs in my fucking eyebrows, man. God, that was a drag.'

'Fuck off,' said Gordon. 'God, I'm hungry. Anyone fancy breakfast?'

Ten minutes and four chillum hits later, Gordon and Larry were sailing down Chowringhee, a couple of beggars in their wake. The excitement in the street was almost tangible. Newspaper vendors were under siege. 'WAR DECLARED,' said the headlines. Small boys aimed fingers at each other and made the sound of guns firing. Now this is more exciting than writing a thirty-second commercial for shampoo, thought Gordon. Then, was he having a flashback? He looked again in the window of the taxi stalled in the traffic near the Oberoi Grand.

'Bogbrush?' he said. 'Bogbrush!'

Chapter Three

THE SAFARI JACKET had been a mistake, thought Hugh. He should have known that from the moment he took it home and Jackie asked if he was going off to bag some wildebeest in the Serengeti. Typical of Jackie, these days, to make some clever comment rather than be concerned about the risks involved in covering your first war. Now the jacket seemed too heavy in the morning sun of Calcutta and, he noted in despair, a Biro had leaked into the top left-hand pocket. On top of that, he still had a ferocious hangover from the night in the Bell.

'Better sup well, old man,' Henry had said, 'you're going to dry areas where you won't be able to get a drink for love nor money. They're of the Muslim persuasion in East Pakistan so I don't think you'll find too many hostelries serving Red Barrel.' Henry was the paper's most experienced war correspondent: Korea, Suez, Vietnam. It had been Henry who had told him to get a safari suit: all those pockets, handy for visas and pens and tobacco and so on. Henry wasn't going on this job, however; some unresolved business over expenses in Saigon.

Hugh leaned forward from the back seat of the cab

taking him from Dum Dum airport to his hotel in the centre of Calcutta. He glanced outside at the crowded street. Bullock carts and bicycle rickshaws, street sellers at tiny stalls, a poster ungrammatically advertising an English language school, a sudden pool of stagnant, muddy water in the potholed road. A rivulet of sweat rolled down his spine and hit the elastic top of his Y-fronts. 'No one wears Y-fronts any more, darling,' Jackie told him once, when she still called him 'darling'. 'Only people whose mothers still buy their underwear for them.'

That was typical of the way Jackie had changed since she started teaching at the new comprehensive in Hackney. Any excuse to have a go at his mother who, as she well knew, had given him a three-pack of Y-fronts in green, blue and red when he visited her for the weekend in Hove; his mother had, unbidden, gone through his clothes to see if anything needed washing and threw away his boxer shorts because they were 'just hanging together by shreds, dear. I'm surprised Jackie lets you wear them.'

'Got an up-to-date passport, Hugh?' Max, the news editor, had asked.

'Of course,' Hugh had said. He had been relieved to find it that evening in the top drawer of his desk at home, with its stamps from their honeymoon in Malta two years ago and their holiday in Corfu last summer.

'You're off to India then,' said Max. 'Looks like India will be properly at war with Pakistan in the next couple of days. You should be there just before it kicks off. Linda –' he indicated the new newsdesk secretary, who had the shortest miniskirt in the office and wore what appeared to be white lipstick and what his mother would have described as the contents of a coal scuttle round her eyes – 'Linda will arrange tickets to Calcutta. You're au fait with what's going on, are you, Hugh?'

'Oh, yes . . . er . . . Bangladesh . . . civil war . . . Sheikh, er, Mujib in jail . . . massacres and so on,' he flannelled. Henry had once said that you could become an expert on any foreign country in thirty minutes. Half an hour in the library and he would be 'au fait'. He went up to the fifth floor, asked for the 'Bangladesh' file and skimmed through the yellowing cuttings, jotting notes as he did so.

There was West Pakistan and there was East Pakistan and there were a thousand miles between them. Been partitioned that way since Indian independence in 1947. Mountbatten had given Pakistan to the Muslims and India to the Hindus. Bit of a botched job, it seemed. Now East Pakistan, part of Bengal before the partition, was unhappy. They felt West Pakistan was taking advantage. East Pakistan, population 75 million, produced all the rice and jute but didn't get the benefit of it. West Pakistan kept all the Western aid for themselves. Urdu-speaking West Pakistan had tried to make Bengali-speaking East Pakistan speak Urdu. East Pakistan had a charismatic leader. Hugh scrutinised the mustachioed face of Sheikh Mujib. He and his secular Awami League party had won the election, taking 167 of the 169 seats in the east. West Pakistan was unhappy about it. President/dictator Yahya Khan wouldn't honour the results. Sheikh Mujib locked up in jail. East Pakistan now fighting for its own independence. Wants to become Bangladesh ('land of the Bengalis'). Massacres carried out by West Pakistan army in Dhaka. Students slaughtered at the university. Hindus targeted and attacked. Lots of atrocities. Millions of refugees flee into India. International outcry. India hints it may go to war.

There were some bits Hugh didn't quite follow. He photocopied a couple of articles. By the time he had done that and phoned his mother, as he had every other day since his father died of a heart attack at his firm's annual dinner-dance the previous year, he was almost ready. The plane was at noon the following day. Time for a few pints with the chaps – envious, most of them. In a way, it was a relief that Jackie was away for a long weekend with her parents. He wouldn't have to phone her and listen to her saying, 'Again?' when he told her he was having a quick drink with the chaps before heading home to Crouch End. It seemed only polite to ask Linda to join them since she had done such a sterling job booking the air tickets and getting a hotel for him.

'Traffic very bad, sir,' said his taxi driver. He had great gaps between his teeth and the corners of his mouth were stained with something brackish. Could it be chewing tobacco? It seemed the wrong colour. He had his scarf wrapped round his head, top to bottom, as it were, like a character with toothache in a *Beano* cartoon. 'Emergency. You know emergency, sir? War coming very soon.'

'Yes, very much so,' said Hugh. 'I'm here to, you know, write about it. I'm a journalist.'

'Reporter, sir?'

'Correspondent . . .'

'What is difference, sir?'

'How much further is it?' said Hugh, ignoring the question, to which he did not really know the answer. Officers and other ranks? There was a throbbing pain behind his right eye which the constant peeping of horns did nothing to alleviate. 'How far are we from the hotel?'

'Not more than twenty minutes, sir.'

That's what you said twenty minutes ago, Hugh thought impatiently. The driver turned off the engine in even the mildest of traffic jams.

Linda had cheerfully come along for the drink-up. She had a good sense of humour, Hugh could tell: she got the joke about the two spinsters and the greengrocer which Jackie dismissed as 'infantile'. And she matched for drinks Max and Hugh and the rest of the half-dozen or so subs and reporters who gathered regularly at the Bell. Everyone bought a round and when Hugh looked down at the diver's watch he had bought half-price in the pub a few weeks earlier – it could tell the time at 20 fathoms, information which he doubted he would need but you never could tell what foreign assignments might flow if he had 'a good war'; he might well find himself with some crew excavating a wreck, for instance – it was nearly closing time.

Turned out that Linda's flat in Archway was pretty much on his way home so it seemed sensible to share a cab. As the driver took a sharp right at the Angel, Linda was thrown towards him in the back seat and they found themselves kissing. He could taste the illicit flavour of menthol tobacco on her breath. Jackie had given up smoking when she started her teacher's training course and now said,

'What's that awful smell? Have you been smoking?' whenever he came home after a night in the Bell.

'Want to pop up for a nightcap?' Linda suggested. 'My flatmate's in Gibraltar with her boyfriend and I've got some duty-free in.'

'Well . . . why not? Eat, drink and be merry for tomorrow we die.'

'Are you frightened about going to the war?'

'No, not really,' said Hugh, who was. 'Couldn't do the job if you were.'

Was it his imagination or had he seen, in the rear-view mirror in front of him, as the black cab headed through the damp London night, the taxi driver's eyebrows rising dismissively heavenwards?

'Sorry, traffic very bad,' said his current driver, who had beaten a field of at least twenty to wrestle Hugh's suitcase from him at Dum Dum airport and escort him to his cab. 'Five minutes away. Are you bachelor, sir?'

'Er . . . no,' said Hugh. A bachelor? Who speaks of bachelors in 1971? Only Cliff Richard, surely. Son, you'll be a bachelor boy. 'No, married. To a teacher.'

'Children, sir?'

'No, not yet . . .'

'I have three boys, sir.'

'Excellent. Good for you.' The eye was throbbing harder and the safari jacket was sticking beneath the armpits. He would have been better off with the old linen jacket that his mother had suggested he should take, the one his father used to wear when he sat in the deckchair in the Sussex summer, sipping his Robinson's lime cordial and identifying birdsong for the family: 'I think that's our friend, Mr Goldfinch.' But Jackie said the jacket made him look like a vicar at a summer fete so he had left it behind.

Linda's 'nightcap' was a half-bottle of Teachers. She poured two large measures into chunky tumblers, probably a free offer with four gallons of petrol. She told him how much she enjoyed her new job in the newsroom. That she had fancied him when she first saw him. That she had broken up with her boyfriend in Hull because he hadn't wanted her to come to London.

'He was so possessive! Any bloke that looked at me in the disco – God! My mum said being in the army had made him like that. You're married, aren't you?'

'Well, I suppose so, you could say,' he replied, trying to give the impression that his wife was either a helpless invalid or they were both swingers much too sophisticated to let a boring old thing like a wedding certificate interfere with a night of fun. 'But she's away at her parents' at the moment, she seems to spend more and more time there . . . Still, I suppose I should go back to my lonely abode.' He went for a pee. He lifted the toilet seat. 'Whoopee – there's a man in the house!' said a neat little handwritten sign Sellotaped on the base of the seat. It seemed to take about ten minutes to empty his bladder. Linda was standing in the chilly hallway smiling as he emerged. They kissed. She was wearing what he had heard Jackie call a 'skinny rib' sweater. He lifted it over her head. Her bra was black. He undid it. Jackie did not like him to do that any more. She said it was 'fetishistic'. Linda unbuttoned his unironed white shirt.

'Oo,' Linda said, patting his stomach. 'Someone's been drinking too much beer.'

He sucked his belly in and pulled her towards him. Her head was below his chin. He could feel her breasts against his chest. He undid his trousers but the left leg gave him trouble as he tried to get it off and he stumbled. Linda giggled. Maybe this wasn't such a good idea.

'Come into the bedroom,' she said. She was naked now. How slim she was, how desperately desirable she looked, lit only by the street light sidling in through the half-pulled curtains. She took him by the hand as he tried to shake off the trouser leg which had got caught up with the Argyll socks his mother had given him for Christmas. ('The Duke of Argyll advertised them himself, dear,' she had said.) He spotted a teddy bear propped up by the pillow of the immaculately made bed. His erection softened. The room was cold, warmed only by a three-bar electric fire, which gave off a smell of lightly singed dust. She pulled the covers back, slipped between the pastel-striped, flannel sheets and opened her arms to embrace him.

She was, as Henry would have said, like a tiger, clawing and biting. Jackie had been like that when they first met as students at East Anglia. She had told him she was on the pill the first night they had been introduced at a friend's birthday party and, two bottles of Bulmer's cider and a packet of ten Navy Cut later, they were in her single bed in the student hostel. But over the last few months, Jackie had made it fairly clear that she would rather read Simone de Beauvoir and eat wafer-thin mints in bed than respond to his beery kisses. He had hopefully bought *The Joy of Sex*, made a mental note about the importance of the clitoris and something called the 'buttered bun' and left the book suggestively in the bathroom. Only to see it three weeks later on the Oxfam pile with his old rugby shirts and the tie-hanger his mother had given him as a present to celebrate his getting a job in Fleet Street. The last time he had tried to initiate sex, when he had come home late and put his arms round her, Jackie had told him that she was not an 'ambulatory spittoon'. What on earth did she mean?

He felt Linda's teeth in his shoulder. Ouch! She cried out to him, 'Come on, Hughie, fuck me!' No one had called him Hughie since prep school. Hughie? They hardly knew each other. He kissed her hard on the mouth, ensuring at least that she could not call him 'Hughie' any more. They wrestled and licked and bit. He had seen an article in one of Jackie's magazines which suggested that it took women twelve minutes to reach orgasm. He surreptitiously looked at the luminous hands of his diver's watch. Only eleven to go.

'That was great,' he said afterwards. Linda was soon asleep. He dozed. When his watch told him it was 6 a.m., he realised that he had to get home, pack and reach the airport for the noon flight. He dressed gingerly. Linda was still asleep as he pulled the latch shut behind him.

Just as well he had left then. He was barely back to Crouch End when Jackie rang from her parents' house. She bade him look after himself. She sounded concerned. He wished she had been colder, it would have made the previous night's little betrayal easier. Changing his clothes, he noticed Linda's bite mark on his shoulder. She had almost taken a lump out of him.

He gazed now out of the taxi window. Closer to the centre of Calcutta, the bullock carts and pedestrians had given way to heavy traffic, cries of newspaper sellers, broken-down cars being pushed by their passengers. The taxi slowed to around five miles an hour as it tried to navigate its way into what his driver told him was Chowringhee Road, where his hotel was. Hugh stared at the people on the crowded pavements: thin men in vests and what he thought were called longis or lungis. Young men with Brylcreemed hair, short-sleeved shirts, neatly pressed trousers. Tiny children darting after them, dodging between the other pedestrians on the pavement like a rugby wing three-quarter dummying his way to the line. (Haven't played rugby since I left school, thought Hugh. At East Anglia, it had not been thought cool; he had gone to a practice match to find only himself and two chaps from Sedbergh there. They ended up playing darts in the student bar and that was the end of his sporting life.)

In the midst of this rush and bustle, walking along the pavement was a strangely familiar figure. He had a silly wispy beard and long, lank hair, looked British, like one of the hippies that filled the public gallery at the *Oz* obscenity trial Hugh had covered that summer at the Old Bailey. Obviously, it had been foolish to prosecute the three hippy journalists but he couldn't help but feel a mild satisfaction when he heard the jury foreman pronounce them guilty. 'I felt a "guilty" pleasure,' he told Max in the newsroom afterwards and they both laughed, as they had chuckled when they heard that the trio had to have their hair cut in prison. Richard Neville, Jim Anderson, Felix Dennis, those were the names of the accused. They had allowed schoolchildren to edit their magazine which had showed Rupert Bear with a giant penis. The judge – Judge Argyle, it was – obviously hated them, probably hated all the long-haired riff-raff in the public gallery and the unfairly beautiful girls in white denim hot pants and high suede boots who waited outside the court for the defendants to emerge. Why do girls like that go for hippies? Hugh wondered.

So was it someone from the trial? One of those louche witnesses who said how uncorrupting it all was? No, it was that bow-legged walk that was familiar as well as something about the face. The figure, accompanied by another white man with a shaven head and a W. G. Grace beard, seemed to pause for a moment as their eyes met. His taxi driver suddenly saw a gap in the traffic and stepped on the accelerator, throwing Hugh against the back of the seat. Was it just his imagination or did he hear a voice cry out what sounded like his old school nickname, Bogbrush?

'Here we are, sir,' said the driver a moment later. 'Oberoi Grand.'

A stately Sikh stood outside in an immaculately starched white tunic and crimson turban. Hugh handed over bundles of rupees to the taxi driver, his head throbbing too much for him to work out whether he had been heavily disadvantaged over the exchange rate. He hauled his suitcase and portable typewriter out, to the excitement of a group of small boys who had strayed into the forecourt. Solicitous hotel staff hurried to his aid.

'Where are you coming from?' asked one of the boys as he was shooed away by the commissionaire.

'Are you a hunter, sir?'

'Fuck off,' said Hugh under his breath.

The safari jacket was stuck to his back with sweat. He passed the boys with the same disdain he reserved for the Glaswegian he had encountered at Euston station the previous week, asking for 'huff a croon, pal', as though unaware that decimalisation had taken place weeks earlier. (He had covered the inquest of some daft woman in Gloucestershire who had committed suicide because, according to her relatives, she found decimalisation too hard to master.)

Other journalists were registering at reception. He recognised an Australian bloke who had won some foreign correspondent's prize the previous year and was gratified to see that he, too, was in a safari jacket, albeit one with short sleeves. As Hugh started to fill in the registration book, he noticed the heads of the reporters turn towards the entrance. A tall woman with short, blonde hair and dark eyebrows, wearing a white shirt, blue jeans and cowboy boots entered. She had a camera slung round her neck and a square suede bag over one shoulder. She placed her wallet and passport down beside the registration book. Hugh smiled at her despite his headache.

'Let me guess,' he said. 'Photographer?'

'Let me guess,' she said. 'Psychic?'

Hugh wasn't quite sure how to take that. He introduced himself. She was called Britt. She sounded American.

'How's about we all meet for a beer in the bar in half an hour?' he said, including the Australian and, inadvertently, the male receptionist in his invitation. Everyone smiled non-committally.

Hugh filled in the register: '10/10/44 . . . Hove, Sussex, England.' He paused at the box marked 'profession'. Then, in capital letters, with just the slightest glance to his right, he wrote: 'WAR CORRESPONDENT.'

Chapter Four

WAS THIS WHAT A war correspondent looked like? Britt wondered. That weird jacket with all the pockets. Did he know his ballpoint pen had leaked? That bushy, sticky-up hair, the sweat pouring down his forehead, dripping off his eyebrows, the faint hint of alcohol being expressed through the pores, a scent familiar from her dad.

She was conscious of his glance at her breasts. She was used to that; men seemed to lower their eyes almost unconsciously, like drivers on winding night-time roads in Marin, dipping their headlights politely for approaching traffic.

She started filling in the register beneath – what was his name? She glanced at the entry: 'Hugh Dunn.' Very WASP, as her mother would say. 'WAR CORRESPONDENT.' He was twenty-seven. How many wars had he corresponded about? The Australian guy, who was also checking in, looked more like a war correspondent, with his world-weary shrug, his dog tags exposed by the unbuttoned denim shirt, dangling in a cluster of grey chest hairs, a red bandanna knotted at his throat, just beneath a prominent Adam's apple.

She wrote: 'Britt Pedersen. 2/20 . . .' She scrubbed it out with the embossed Oberoi Grand pen she had been handed. They seemed to put the day before the month here. '20/2/42 . . . 29 . . . Athens, Ohio.' Then her address in San Francisco. 'Photographer.' She was not going to write 'war photographer'. This was her first war. What did she do now? Mok had said that he would fix up accreditation and bring it to the airport but then he had phoned at the last moment to say that the agency would telex it to the hotel. But there was no message awaiting her. Shoot.

'Anyone for that beer later?' came the Englishman's voice at her shoulder. He was hovering. Once she had been unable to tell the difference between Australians and New Zealanders and Brits but the influx into San Francisco of hundreds of young English guys, desperately seeking another Summer of Love, had changed that. Now the chances were that the person beside you in the line at the Fillmore, the psychedelic urchin asking for directions in the Haight, would be English.

The Beatles and the Stones made things easy for these English adventurers. They had that sort of cocky feel to them, as though they just had to talk to you with a Liverpool accent and you would be begging to go to bed with them – and probably pay for their Mexican meal on top of it. They did not like to hang out with each other, Britt had noticed, as though aware that there was only room for one tame Englishman in every crowd. They surfaced in larger numbers whenever a British band was in town. They didn't seem to wash much. Britt was a Kinks fan. She had taken their photo when they had played the Fillmore, young

English dandies with ruffled shirts and velvet jackets playing music with smart lyrics. 'Dedicated Followers of Fashion'. 'Sunny Afternoon'. 'Waterloo Sunset'. And there would be all these other young men, pretending to be music journalists or friends of the band or friends of friends of the band or even friends of friends of the roadies.

'Sure,' she said in response to Hugh Dunn's repeated request. 'Just give me time to have a shower.'

'Yeah, OK, then,' said the Australian, who had decided to have that beer after all. He cracked a grin in her direction. Another party of journalists bundled in through the revolving door, talking in loud, self-confident voices, greeting the Australian – 'Hello, Bob, you old bugger, might have guessed you'd be here' – leaning proprietorially over the registration desk, making demands she would never have dreamed of.

'OK,' said Hugh Dunn, pushing ineffectually at his springy hair, which reminded her of the scrub on her grandmother's farm, 'see you in half an hour.' He seemed deflated by the arrival of the new crowd, who were punching each other's shoulders, joking with each other, asking things like 'Where's Woolacott? Is Tomalin here yet?' She watched them as they checked each other out, like dogs sniffing each other's bottoms.

'Who you with?' asked one of the new crew, a grey-haired man who sounded English too. He knew the agency well, he said. Did she know – and he fired off the names of some of her colleagues. Most of them she had never met, they were based in New York or LA or were on assignment in Saigon for months at a time.

A porter in a white uniform took her luggage down the corridor, to the elevator. After the crowded chaos on the street outside, the hotel seemed other-worldly with its massive chandelier and grand piano, its palm-lined swimming pool and its sandy ashtrays that looked more like golf bunkers than a place to stub out a cheroot. There was a frangipani on her pillow beside a welcome written in elegant script on the hotel's crested notepaper. She looked in the mirror. Was that a zit? Surely not, she hadn't had a zit since film school. She changed the jeans she had worn since she left San Francisco airport for a pair of baggy pants and pulled on one of the Grateful Dead T-shirts that Mouse had designed and given to her dad. Perhaps not. Would war correspondents think a Dead T-shirt a bit hippyish? She replaced it with a plain blue denim cowboy shirt, pressing the studs up to the neck, then unbuttoning two of them, then buttoning them up and settling on just the one undone. The hotel telephone operator sounded like James Mason or one of those haughty British actors and made her connection speedily.

'Mok, I've arrived,' she said. Why had she phoned Mok before she called Josh? 'And while I remember, um, someone who was with you in Da Nang . . . yeah, could be . . . Australian guy called Bob . . . and an English dude called Nick, I think, yeah, said I should say hi to you . . . They reckon war will be officially declared today . . . yeah, I think so . . . Josh rang you? OK, I'll ring him . . . No, fine. Nice hotel . . . Well, I haven't eaten anything apart from Pan-Am plastic food since I saw you . . . OK, speak soon . . .'

Josh was not at home. He had not been wild about her coming. He had just introduced her to a friend who ran an architecture and design magazine and who offered her work. Josh had obviously hoped that this would keep her in the Bay Area. Then Mok had told her to come into the office.

'What you doin' this week, princess?' Mok had asked.

'Er, come on, Mok, if it's taking another picture of the Nixon girls visiting a Vets' hospital, I've got a major prior commitment . . .'

'Well, kid,' he said. (What was this 'kid', 'princess', occasionally 'goddess'? Should she challenge him on it? She had been reading and loving *The Female Eunuch* by Germaine Greer. It was like suddenly being given a map and compass. Mok was 'old school', part of the San Francisco Chinese community. Did that excuse him? He called his new wife 'baby doll'.) 'As you know, Jack is stuck in Saigon. Jefferson has got a hernia. And Al totalled that damn fool beach buggy of his and he's out of action till the new year. We need someone in . . .' He reached for the office atlas and pointed at East Pakistan.

Josh looked pissed when she told him she was going. He mentioned marriage again.

'Marriage?' her dad had said later that night. 'Holy moly! Why do you kids need to get married? Have I fathered a bourgeois daughter?' Her mother, living now in Ojai in southern California and sending her weekly packages of the writings of Krishnamurti and pressed flowers, had expressed no view on her going to East Pakistan. Her friends had been aghast.

She picked up the phone. James Mason took her details and moments later she could hear her dad juggling with the phone to get it to his good ear. Stoned, probably. He had cut down a bit on the booze but replaced it with large quantities of grass, mainly harvested from the crop produced by an old buddy in Mendocino County. She could hear music in the background. Dan Hicks and His Hot Licks? Asleep at the Wheel? Something like that. Van Morrison had recently moved in to the street next to her dad's in Fairfax so he liked to play some of that, too. 'G-L-O-R-I-A,' he would sing as he drove her home from the ferry at Sausalito.

'Hey, sweetpea.'

'How did you know it was me?'

'Who else would call at this godforsaken hour? How you doing? You in India?'

'Sure. Everything's fine. They think it's all going to start tomorrow.'

'What was that?'

'Turn the music down. Who is it anyway?'

'Dan Hicks. "How can I miss you if you won't go away?" Very apropos, yeah . . . hey, you haven't got Montezuma's revenge yet?'

'That's the same thing Mok asked. Montezuma never came to Calcutta.'

'He may have been astral travelling, honeybunch. OK, are you? Your mother called. First time she's spoken to me in months. She must be worried about you. Her daughter in a war.'

'Don't worry. There's lots of us here. Can you call Josh

some time and tell him I'm fine? I called him and he wasn't in.'

'Tom-cattin' already.'

'Hey!'

'Just kiddin'. He's devoted. Too devoted, poor sap. Take care, sweetpea. All the cameras in good shape? Look after my old Leica, won't you?'

Was that the tiniest hint of wistfulness in his voice? The sound of a 55-year-old photographer who had once wanted to be Richard Avedon and was now making a living taking photos for mail-order catalogues or for men's magazines like *Stud* and *Outlaw*? The love-ins and the body-painting and the stripping off at free festivals had been noted by the smart men in blazers who ran the gents' magazines. They had photo features now with titles like 'Hippy Chicks Run Wild' and 'Love-in at BARE Mountain'. It never occurred to her that her father would be involved until one afternoon she had come to visit and found a naked, stoned-out 'flower child', wearing nothing but a Janis Joplin straw hat with a poppy in its band and Indian ankle bracelets, sprawling unselfconsciously over the bed. The bed where her parents had once slept and where she and her little brother, Brad, had joined them for languid Sunday breakfasts of Danish pastry and fresh orange juice. Carefree days, hiking on Mount Tam with the dogs, giggling when her dad put up a sign in the bathroom saying, 'If it's yellow, that's mellow. If it's brown, flush it down.' So long ago it seemed now.

Brad had just quit his job at some fancy new coffee house in Seattle and headed for the nearest foreign border, avoiding Vietnam in Vancouver. Would he ever be able to come back home? And here she was looking for a different war in Calcutta. Her father had introduced her to the 'flower child' – 'Hey, Britt, this is Sunshine, Sunshine, this is my daughter, Britt,' and made a brief reference later – 'Just something I said I'd do for Harry, she's modelling to get through college, it's cool,' but the image of him with a naked woman younger than herself kept slipping back into her mind. Another time she had spotted a pair of ridiculous gold-spangled high heels and a garter belt under the couch and had not been convinced by his explanation that they were for a catalogue shoot. She was going to have to confront him about it when she got back.

'I'll take care of your old Leica.'

'And, more important, take care of your old self.'

She heard the intake of breath thousands of miles away in California and pictured her father, long grey hair pulled back, granny specs at the end of his reddening nose, tie-dye T-shirt riding up over his mighty belly, roach clip in one hand, phone in the other. For a moment, she felt lonely and far from home.

She blew a noisy kiss into the mouthpiece.

There was a self-confident knock on her door.

'Britt?' said an English voice. 'It's Hugh – we met downstairs. India has officially declared war on Pakistan. See you in the bar.'

Chapter Five

BREAKFAST WAS ANAND'S favourite meal, even if it was just two humble slices of toast and some milky tea. He pushed his plate to one side and looked again at the sheet of paper that had been slipped beneath his door. 'PLEASE TREAT MY DEATH AS SUSPICIOUS.' Was it a joke? Was he meant to do anything about it? Should he keep it? He had found other odd musings written on the lavatory wall but most of them were familiar, would-be clever aphorisms about Western civilisation or someone with the vaguely familiar name of Eric Clapton. He would ask Baba what he thought. Maybe he would look in the registration book and see if he could recognise whose handwriting it was. Later. First things first. He found some old cream writing paper in a drawer and started to compose a letter.

Dear Vanessa,

Many thanks for your letter. I write – if this does not sound too pompous – as war is declared. You said that you had found it hard to understand from the newspapers what was going on. Now I am in Calcutta

51

it seems very clear. I do not know exactly how many have been killed in East Pakistan – which will, I hope, soon be Bangladesh – since all this started. One hundred thousand? Half a million? A million? Who knows. A dreadful total, by any reckoning.

There are now more than five million refugees here on the outskirts of Calcutta and tens of thousands more come in each day. Some of them sleep in drainage pipes. Many suffer from cholera. By and large, people here are fairly sympathetic – so far. What would happen if similar numbers of desperate, frightened people started arriving in Britain? Would people be so friendly? I hope so.

The news we get sounds pretty grim. There have been stories about Biharis accused of being collaborators. Remember that discussion we had after too many bottles of that dreadful Rioja about whether or not we would join a resistance or become a collaborator? You said the only thing that would stop you from becoming a collaborator was the idea of having all your hair shaved off which you thought would be very unflattering. I am sure you would have been with the resistance from the start.

The local resistance in Bangladesh are called the Mukti Bahini. They have a sort of mythical reputation amongst some of the refugees I have met. There are terrible stories of Pakistani army atrocities against them. Women taken to army camps where they are raped and kept naked so they do not run away. One rumour has it that the West Pakistanis think the East Pakistanis an inferior race – shorter, darker and so on – and have decided to impregnate the women with the 'finer' genes of the West. Whole villages have been wiped out. Part of me is glad to be safe from all that in Calcutta, even if there is a blackout and a vague possibility of the odd Pakistani bomb, but part of me thinks how wonderful to have a cause to fight for – the liberation of your country. And the cause is noble, as noble as the fight for independence from Britain.

Mrs Gandhi is well aware that the war will be a popular one. There is much talk of giving Pakistan a bloody nose – even my gentle friends at the cricket club are talking like that. Everyone says it will all be over swiftly – by Christmas, my Christian friends say – and then there will be a free Bangladesh. Another country for us to beat at cricket!

Did your hasty politicians think for a moment in 1947 what might happen if they divided Bengal on religious lines, leaving us Hindu Bengalis in India and scooping up the Muslims and then announcing that they were the same country as West Pakistan more than 1,000 miles away?

I still find running the hotel hard work. As you know, it is about as far from my fantasy of the literary watering hole as could be imagined. It is full of your fellow countrymen who all have longer hair than you. They come out seeking enlightenment while all the bright young men in Calcutta are yearning to go to London to the LSE or Imperial so that they can become enlightened as to how to make £10,000 a year! Still, the place is packed and I had to turn away more than a dozen would-be guests yesterday. Already today there is a small line of young Western people outside hoping vainly that one of the current residents will leave – or die. No joke – sometimes this place is like a field hospital, lots of moaning in sickbeds. What happened to the old British stiff upper lip? Even so, the hotel barely breaks even. Oliver Goldsmith said that Calcutta was the place where wealth accumulates and men decay; for me it is the other way round. I should not complain, I know, particularly when people are existing in such hellish conditions in Bangladesh and in the refugee camps. Like a good boy, I remember my Milton: 'The mind is its own place and in itself/Can make a hell of heav'n, a heav'n of hell.'

I hope all is well in Nottinghamshire. I remember the lovely New Year we had with your parents and the games of charades. I treasure the memory of your father doing 'She'll Be Coming Round the Mountain'. And, of course, I have forgiven him for constantly referring to me as 'Mahatma Coat'.

Now I must go and arrange for a basin to be repaired because one of your countrymen, a chap with the memorable name of Freddie Braintree, stood in it to wash his feet and it broke. For this, I studied Adam Smith!

Your loving friend,
Anand

Was 'your loving friend' right? Did she know how he felt? There had been that moment on New Year's Eve when they had been dancing very closely and her father appeared to be asleep in an armchair. Then the old man had stirred and the moment passed. So chums it had been. Was it that they were both too frightened to cross the line and risk the comforting friendship? Everyone else was at it – 'like knives', as Vanessa would say. So why weren't they? Sex was less of an overt issue in Calcutta. He did not feel the constant pressure to be 'getting your oats', as the English put it. Not that that made his loneliness any easier to bear.

A tap at the door. The Australian woman with the nose ring – Karen? – was standing outside.

'There isn't any toilet paper, is there?'

He almost told her that the concept of toilet paper was both Western and wasteful but she looked so weary and drained that he did not have the heart.

'I am afraid not. How are you? Not too well? You are waiting for flights to resume? In which direction are you travelling?'

'Kieran wants to go to Burma but I wouldn't mind just heading home. I threw the I Ching this morning and it said, "There has been good fortune in the beginning, there may be disorder in the end." We did have a great time to start off with so I worry that disorder is coming. We've been travelling for more than a year, we don't have much money left . . .'

The I Ching. Oh dear, thought Anand. His guests seemed to trust the I Ching more than their own judgement. Some of them pronounced it 'Eye' Ching and some 'Ee' Ching. He did not know which was right. And was this a prelude to one of those not infrequent requests for a waiver of the rent? Some of the bolder guests even asked for a loan on the understanding, of course, that they would pay the money back the very moment they got home. But no, no request came.

'It's just that all the vibes here are a bit strange, you know. Perhaps it's the war . . .' She seemed anxious for him to continue the conversation but he had more letters to write before Baba arrived and he was too tired to engage. He nodded at her and pulled out another sheet of writing paper. When he looked up, she was gone.

Dear Vic,

I guess it must be the end of term at Harvard by now. How does it compare to LSE? Here LSE and the Dog and Duck and those nights at Ronnie's have never seemed so far away. War is about to descend and we can only hope it will be as short as all the old buffers say it will be. I have a vague memory that Vietnam and the First World War were meant to be over very swiftly, too.

Re your suggestion of coming here for a holiday – best to wait until everything is resolved. Commercial flights in and out of Calcutta are cancelled anyway for the foreseeable future and I am afraid that Americans are not terrifically popular here at the moment because Mr Nixon is backing Pakistan – as are the Chinese, an unholy alliance. On the street there is a lot of angry muttering and I see a lot of anti-American graffiti on the walls. A small mob set fire to the Pan-Am offices yesterday, that being the handiest identifiably American building they could find. By contrast, the Russians are our chums. We have just signed a 20-year long Treaty of Peace and Friendship with the comrades which means that the Soviet Union will have to last at least until 1991, whatever our old Trot friends in IS may say.

I hear periodically from Vanessa, as I am sure you do, too. I have not heard from Nii in months but I think he is still in Ghana. I told you all about the hotel the last time, I think, so I will not bother you further with descriptions of blocked drains and forged travellers' cheques but suffice to say that the Ritz it ain't.

Do let me know what you are up to. In love? In penury? In Boston for Christmas? Take care.

All the best,
Anand

He switched on the wireless. There was an upbeat bulletin about the Indian army heading for the East Pakistan border. He pulled the last piece of writing paper from the desk, filled up his fountain pen from the Quink bottle and started his third letter of the day.

Dear Nii,

Greetings from another corner of what was also once part of the British empire. It seems we are about to witness the birth of a new nation. Perhaps by the time that this letter arrives there will be a country called Bangladesh.

What is it like being back in Ghana? I find it strange to be home after four years in Britain, noticing all the remnants of empire here. The place names one took for granted as a child – Fort William, Dalhousie – now have echoes of that cold, grey country. I miss a few things – the bookshops on Charing Cross Road, the pub, Ronnie's, the *Listener* and *Private Eye*. Dare I say *Dr Finlay's Casebook* on Mrs Grodzinski's telly? But, beyond that, not much. I find Calcutta more vibrant, less cynical. The conversations here about politics have a rhythm to them that I never found in London, even when we were going to the IS meetings. By the way, do you remember that girl from the Workers Revolutionary Party you brought back one night? Whatever happened to her? Ah, happy days. Do I sound middle-aged? It must be that my 30th birthday is approaching. Downhill all the way.

What is your news?

The last I heard you were about to be poached by a merchant bank but I can't remember its name. Has it been odd adjusting to life back in Ghana? How they gonna keep you back on the farm now that you've seen Paree? Which reminds me – that record we looked for in Portobello Road that time, the Bix Beiderbecke, I found it in, of all places, a record shop here. I play it sometimes at night when I am up on the roof, after a glass of Sandemans – still my poison

– and I could be back in the front room of our place with that faint smell of the leaking gas fire and one of your goat stews in my nostrils.

I hear from Vanessa. She is well, helping her papa sort out death duties and leading the life of a woman of leisure. I expect she will be married to some Tory junior minister by the end of the year – unless we send him a photo of us all in Grosvenor Square!

Anyway, drop a line if you have a moment.

Best, your old friend,

Anand

Another tap on the door. Baba was there with a tall foreigner, shaven-headed and in a long saffron robe. He smiled at Anand and bowed. Baba, who clutched the hotel register in his hand, was in an agitated state. He gestured at the new arrival, who looked slightly older than the usual guest.

'I am asking him for his details and he is telling me nothing,' he said. He showed Anand the register.

The new guest appeared to have ignored the nationality, DOB, passport number and 'arriving from' columns. Under 'name', he had written in brisk capitals 'MUDD'. Anand sighed.

'I'm sorry to bother you but there is a government requirement that aliens give all their details,' he said, looking up at the serene figure. 'I can fill it in if you tell me – well, where have you come from?'

The man – was he a monk? – smiled back. His head was very smoothly shaven. Do you have to use shaving cream

59

Duncan Campbell

for that? wondered Anand briefly. The new guest reached over and gently removed the pen from Anand's hand, took a piece of writing paper from him and wrote in the same firm handwriting: 'Non-speaking order.' Then he smiled benignly, turned on his heel and set off downstairs, leaving Baba spluttering in his wake.

'He says he's from a non-speaking order,' Anand told Baba reassuringly. 'Ah, well, that makes a change. Most of the others are from a non-listening order, I think.'

From the courtyard came the sound of a guitar being strummed and a voice proclaiming, if Anand was hearing the words correctly, that the singer was 'just mad about saffron'. He shook his head, opened the window and emptied the cold contents of his teacup into the gutter beneath.

Chapter Six

THE HANGOVER HAD finally started to abate, aided perhaps by the cold Kingfisher which Hugh nursed at the bar as he picked at a bowl of cashew nuts and kept his eyes focused on the foyer. The comings and goings were now intense. Reporters and cameramen and photographers were arriving from everywhere. First, get your accreditation, Henry had told him, so that is what he would do. But on the other hand, it would be rude not to wait for – what was her name? Britt?

He spotted her as she came out of the lift and waved. She was wearing a large cowboy shirt. Was she a feminist? Maybe a lesbian. You had to tread so carefully these days. It had been so simple at East Anglia: every student there was happy to go to bed with everyone else. Sure, there were occasional problems, women not realising that, just because you spent a night together, it did not mean you were going to see them again. The odd bit of bother, too, when you had to tell a girl that you'd got a bit of a rash and the doc in the health centre said it might be NSU. All such a change from the chilly celibate cloisters of St Gregory's. (St Gregory's – was that where that bearded face, that

61

bandy-legged walk, came from?) But those easy-going days were over. Now it was almost a point of honour for women not to wear make-up. And they took offence so easily. He had even seen one of Jackie's teacher friends wearing a badge which said, 'How dare you presume I'm heterosexual.' What did that mean?

Britt let him buy her a tonic water. She seemed preoccupied.

'Where are all the others?' she asked.

'Getting accredited. We should do the same after we've knocked this back.'

Perhaps she wasn't used to hanging out with other journalists on these jobs, Hugh thought. He remembered his first experience of the pack, a murder case in Dorset. That feeling of wanting to be accepted, one of them. The routine maligning of their respective newsdesks far away in London and the groans at breakfast as everyone saw how badly their stories had been treated, how the subs had missed the point, how their puns and clever extended metaphors had been edited out, how the story itself had been relegated to page nine. Here the mood was different, a bit more, well, sophisticated. He felt a frisson of anxiety that everyone else must know what was going on and he did not.

Old Henry had often regaled the Bell with stories about conquests on his foreign assignments: bar girls in Laos who wanted to have his babies, bored diplomats' wives in Bangkok. What would he make of Britt? Even in those baggy trousers and cowboy shirt, she was very sexy. Did she fancy him? Hard to tell. He looked at her dark eyebrows and high Nordic cheekbones. Henry said that American women loved English accents.

'This is the first war I've covered,' he blurted out, slightly to his own surprise.

'Me, too.' She smiled.

This was going OK, he thought. Wonder if she's on the pill. Must be. Thank God the old days of the johnny were gone. What a bother that had been: packet of three for three and ninepence, then all the worry if they burst.

'Look, I think we should probably get down and pick up our . . . I think we need . . . Do you have a couple of passport photos? I guess that's a silly question to ask a photographer . . .'

Their taxi-driver was full of information. First Indian troops had crossed the border. Pakistanis running like hell. Indian army would be in Dhaka within days.

'Do you think the Indian army will teach them a lesson they will never forget?' asked Hugh.

'Oh, yes, sir.'

'Hmmm. Er, what is your name, by the way?'

'Deepak Lal, sir. And yours?'

At the accreditation office in Old Court Street, reporters clutching their little grey Indian army press cards were surrounding the press liaison officer, insisting on knowing when the first convoy would be leaving for the border. Hugh felt a shiver of nervousness. Should he have been quicker? Had he dropped behind in the race because he wanted to have a chance with Britt? There was Bob Whatsisface, the Australian, at the front of the queue. He did not return Hugh's nod. He overheard two other reporters saying that 'General Jacob' was the person to approach to make sure one was in Dhaka for the victory parade. Would it be over so soon? He nudged out an Italian journalist who reeked of eau de cologne and beckoned Britt to join him. He could feel the sweat at the base of his spine again. He shoved an arm across the front of his jacket so that Britt would not notice that damn Biro stain.

'Name, sir?'

'Hugh Dunn.'

'Publication or network, sir?'

He spelled it out. He saw his name on the list, there it was, below someone from *Le Monde* and a chap from the *South China Morning Post*. He was on the list. He was on his way.

'Convoy leaves four-thirty a.m. sharp tomorrow, sir.'

The Italian journalist was trying to edge in front of Britt. Hugh blocked him. He could feel the Italian pushing but he stayed firm. Like playing rugby again. Britt squeezed in and was signed up on the list below his name. That would mean they were part of the same convoy. On the way back to the hotel he tried to talk to her, glancing at her wedding ring finger, which was bare. So far, so good. Back at the Oberoi Grand reception, a sheaf of messages in his pigeon hole.

'Ring soonest, Max.' 'Linda called.' Linda? What could she want? 'Welcome to the Oberoi Grand. Enjoy our international cuisine tonight. Special rates for journalists.'

Nothing from Jackie. Probably at one of her reading groups. That was another new thing. Reading groups. Why did they have to read in groups? He enjoyed a good read as much as the next man and had, in fact, brought with him the new le Carré, *The Naive and Sentimental Lover*. He hoped there was some sex in it this time but he did not feel the need to go through a book paragraph by paragraph with a bunch of mates. What was the point? You read a book, you liked it, you told a mate, you swapped views on it. End of problem. Or else she would be at some fringe theatre or poetry reading. He had gone with her to one of those. Some bloke with a northern accent repeating the line 'Tell me lies about Vietnam' to an earnest audience of teachers and students with badges on their lapels. He shuddered at the memory.

But Linda had called. What, as Henry would say, can this portend? Surely she wasn't going to be trying to establish a Relationship? Oh, God, he thought. Let this war last two months at least. Three, preferably. Four would be ideal. And Lord, lest this seem selfish and uncaring, let the casualties be spread out thinly. Amen. God, when had he last been in a church? His father's funeral. He shuddered again at the memory of his grieving aunts and their snorting sobs outside the crematorium.

If he rang the newsdesk, as he had to, Linda would almost certainly pick up the phone. What would he say? He could promise to talk later, explaining that he had to knock out his story swiftly and then ring just after she would have left the office and leave a message. But that would mean leaving the message with someone else and that would lead to immediate gossip – 'Is Hugh getting his leg over with Linda?' He knew how it started.

By luck, Linda did not answer the phone. It was the night news editor, a long-winded young man who had just joined from the *Telegraph*. Hugh told him to 'say hi to Max and Linda'. That sounded casual enough, didn't it?

The newsdesk wanted nine hundred words in three hours. Moody stuff. Colour. Atmosphere. He had anticipated that he would be able to get by with six hundred words, 'eve of war' copy culled mainly from the wires. Max came on the line.

'How's everything?'

'Fine. Accredited and on the first convoy out in the morning. We leave at four-thirty a.m.' Would that impress him?

'Good. Everything else OK?' There was something about the tone of the question.

'Yeeees. Why?'

'Nothing, just making sure everything is hunky-dory – Hughie.'

Did he say 'Hughie'?

'What did you say?'

'Nothing. Must dash. Ted Heath is making a statement. Look after yourself.'

Hugh took his portable Olivetti out of its case, pulled out his photocopied cuttings, opened his Baedeker's guide at the Calcutta page and started writing.

'Calcutta, India,' he typed.

Was 'India' really necessary? The readers of the paper surely knew where Calcutta was. On the other hand, it was an extra word and he had nine hundred of them to knock off.

'Calcutta, India' it was.

Drop intro would be appropriate here. He had learned about the 'drop intro' while doing his training in Chester. Hook the reader in with some intriguing story about an individual, then move into the main story two or three paragraphs later. But he did not have much in the way of local colour. He had barely been on the streets. Even the taxi drivers, always a fall-back position, had not been much help. Ah, but that driver, the one who took them to the accreditation office, had agreed that the Indians would teach the Pakistanis a lesson they would never forget. Where had he scribbled his name? Colour, colour. What else? Oh, the blackout. Perfect.

'Calcutta, India,' he typed again. 'Cars with their headlights half covered with brown paper edge their way through the crowded streets of central Calcutta as dusk falls over what Rudyard Kipling once memorably described as "the city of the dreadful night".' Good stuff. A literary allusion and a telling detail in the first sentence. The telex was down and he would have to phone his copy through but even the copy-takers, a notoriously hard breed to please, would appreciate this.

'The blackout, part of the state of emergency declared by Prime Minister Indira Gandhi yesterday,' he went back to 'part of' and changed it to 'a key component of' to give him a couple of extra words, 'has fallen over Calcutta.' Perfect tense. 'Whatever diplomatic moves may be made now at this late stage . . .' No, no. '. . . at this very late stage, the xx million (SUBS PLEASE CHECK) souls in this city that has seen war and famine and pestilence' (what was pestilence?

Who cares?) 'are already prepared to fight what a young Calcuttan, Deepak Lal, told me would be "a war to teach Pakistan a lesson they will never forget", a war that could lead to independence for Bangladesh.'

This was going well.

'India is about to go to war for the third time in less than ten years,' he typed. His fingers skipped across the keys even though he had never learned touch-typing properly and worked in what his colleagues called the 'hunt and peck' style. 'In 1962, China was the foe; in 1965, Pakistan; and now, in 1971, it seems certain to be Pakistan again who is the foe.' (Too many 'foes'. He changed it to 'enemy'.) 'Conflict has looked inevitable since the mainly Muslim Karachi-based government made it clear that it would not accept the victory won in last year's elections by Sheikh Mujib's secular Awami League, which demanded autonomy for East Pakistan, separated as it is by 1000 miles from its western part as a result of the 1947 partition of the subcontinent.' (Was that sentence too long? The subs could cut it, that was their job.) 'Hundreds of thousands have died since then, mainly victims of the military. Sheikh Mujib himself lies in jail . . .' He paused and changed the last line. '. . . languishes in jail.' Another three hundred words or so. A paragraph of Mrs Gandhi's speech. Make that two paragraphs.

His paper had taken a sceptical editorial line on the war so far. The latest leader attacked Mrs Gandhi for being too close to the Soviet Union and suggested that an Indian invasion was unacceptable and probably part of a Cold War game plan of the Russians. 'India is not under attack from

Pakistan,' the leader said, 'so an entry into East Pakistan would effectively be a hostile pre-emptive strike. Such moves are unacceptable in the twentieth century.'

He daydreamed briefly about Britt. Maybe they would be stuck in Jessore tomorrow night. A Pakistani bombardment. Thrown together in the night in some darkened room they would have to share. 'Slowly, the shirt slipped down her shoulders and she smiled at him through the half-light of the distant explosions. "Oh, Hugh, I'm so frightened . . ." ' He forced himself back to the story and slung the typewriter carriage to its end as though whacking a cartridge into one of those Lee Enfields he had had to load on the shooting range in his school cadet force days.

The cadet force? Was that where he had seen that face, that bearded creature staring in the taxi's window? Was there, buried beneath all of that, a face from ten years ago, a younger, spottier face, contorted with fear?

The phone rang. Max. Only seven hundred words needed after all but could they have it sharpish. How about if he put him straight over to copy?

Hugh glanced at what he had so far. A good six hundred words. And he had not even had to mention the Black Hole. Could save that for the final par, busk it as the copytaker was taking it down.

'OK, shove me through,' he said. He looked at his watch. Only twenty-five minutes (at both sea level and 20 fathoms) had elapsed since he had started writing. His heart sank as he heard the soft Welsh tones of the copytaker. This was Ifor 'Is there much more of this?' Davis, notoriously rude when you rang in your copy. One day, perhaps, they would come up with some invention that would allow what you wrote to go magically from your typewriter to the page with no need for Ifor and his 'are you sure about that?' Ifor was also a keen union man, the father of the chapel, who always made sure that he finished work when his time was up, even if you still had another couple of hundred words to file.

'Calcutta, India,' he intoned down the phone.

'I think we know it's India,' said Ifor. 'I don't think our readers will imagine it's in Brazil or Yugoslavia . . .'

Oh, God, it was going to be like that, was it?

They rattled through the first half of the story. Only when Hugh came to his final paragraphs was there was a problem.

'It is more than two hundred years since the most infamous event in India's history that claimed the lives of 113 Britons in what became known as the Black Hole—'

'I would have thought the massacre at Amritsar was far more infamous,' said Ifor from thousands of miles away.

Hugh resisted the temptation, as he had half a dozen times since joining the paper, to tell Ifor that it was his job just to type out people's copy. He took a deep breath.

'It is more than two hundred years since one of the most infamous events in India's history that claimed the lives of 113 Britons in the Black Hole of Calcutta . . .'

Was that the sound of a barely stifled yawn at the far end of the line?

'Last night, the people of Calcutta, this city which grew up after Robert Clive bested the forces of the Nawabs of

Bengal and Oudh – that's O for Oscar, U for Unicorn, D for Delta, H – in 1774 . . .'

This time the noise of the yawn at the far end of the line was unmistakable. Don't react, thought Hugh. Concentrate, con-cen-trate.

'Last night, the people of Calcutta were looking out at cloudless night skies and wondering—'

'That's two "nights" there.'

'OK, then, "dark cloudless skies".' But what were they wondering? He had no fucking idea.

'Yes?' said Ifor. And then, more insistently, 'Yes?'

'Hang on a second . . . can't read my notes . . . Um . . . ah, yes, wondering what the morrow may hold.'

'What the WHAT may hold?'

'The morrow. The morrow. THE MORROW!'

'What the morrow may hold,' repeated Ifor. You could feel the disdain dripping from his voice even at five thousand miles. ' "What the morrow may hold." Is that it?'

'Yes,' said Hugh between clenched teeth. 'That's it. How many words is that?'

'Er . . . 699, six . . . hundred . . . and . . . ninety-nine . . .' said Ifor, stringing it out as though he was the returning officer in a Welsh mining constituency announcing the paltry number of votes for a Conservative Party candidate.

'Be a dear and pop that "India" back in at the top,' said Hugh. 'Thank you so much and goodnight.'

He replaced the receiver before Ifor had an opportunity to give him a further lecture on colonial history, dashed to the bathroom and emptied his bladder. He noticed, to his dismay, that splashes of pee were clearly visible in the fly area of his light khaki trousers. Bugger, he thought. 'No matter how much you shake your peg, there's always some goes down the leg,' as they used to say at school. He couldn't go down like this. He rummaged through his luggage, found his other pair of trousers, crumpled but unstained, slapped some Old Spice on his cheeks, checked his breath against his hand, spread some Crest over his toothbrush, gave his teeth a perfunctory brush, grabbed his room key and his wallet and headed down to sample the 'international cuisine' in what he trusted would be the company of a tall American blonde in cowboy boots.

Chapter Seven

'WHAT YOU SHAKING your head at, droog?'

Gordon only half heard Larry's question as they strolled along Chowringhee, battling their way through the crowds.

'Well, it's kind of strange . . .' said Gordon.

And it had been. For the months since his departure from London he had lived in a kind of limbo. Everyone from his previous life was part of a dimming memory. He had deliberately tried to block out thoughts of Grace and her tears as he left. Why was meditation so bloody hard? He could only concentrate for thirty or forty seconds before some unbidden thought, usually sexual, entered his head. Even getting the breathing right was difficult. But his sudden sighting of a slice of his past life made him strangely energised.

Small boys tugged at Larry's lungi, pointing admiringly at his thick beard, looking at the embroidered Mr Natural that Grace had stitched into Gordon's Good Fairy loons. 'What is your purpose?' they asked. 'From where are you coming? You bachelor, sir?'

These were the curious boys, different in style and tone

from the adult beggars with their wide beseeching eyes. Gordon carried a pocketful of paise to hand out as he went, to keep them at bay. The most persistent was a terribly deformed man, his legs collapsed beneath him and jutting at impossible angles. Larry called him Spiderman. When he saw Westerners he would manoeuvre himself with remarkable dexterity and match them pace for pace, tugging at their clothes at waist level. Should he give away more of his money? wondered Gordon. Was that something he should do if he was to advance in any way as a being?

'*Que?*' asked Larry. 'What was strange?'

'I'm sure I saw this guy I knew at school. Dunn – Bogbrush, his nickname used to be. I'm sure it was him. He was in a taxi . . .'

'Bogbrush?'

'You know, lavatory brush, toilet brush, what do you call it? His hair was all bristly. Very silly. But we all had silly nicknames.'

'What was yours?'

'Low Grady – because McGrady is my last name. I said they were silly.'

They arrived at the Star to be greeted by the owner, now aware of their breakfast rituals. Porridge and banana for Gordon. A lassi for Larry. Sweet chai. Then a cigarette, a gleaning of the daily paper and a stroll to the Maidan or the museum or Park Street cemetery. Sometimes Larry would disappear on his own. Today he seemed preoccupied.

'Sounds like a pretty weird school, man,' he said.

'Muscular Christianity, that's what St Gregory's practised. Stalag 17 with Latin. It was actually in quite a beautiful place in the Scottish Highlands although I don't think we noticed that.'

'Lot of sodomy?'

'If there was, it passed me by. Lots of crushes. Big boys and little boys. Lots of bullying.'

'Bogbrush a bully?'

Gordon ran by in his mind that moment that had been instantly prompted by seeing Bogbrush. Fear. Humiliation. Was this something he wanted to meditate on?

'More of a collaborator than an instigator, I suppose. I guess most of us were. Just happy not to be the one who was picked on. We had a suicide one year. Bloke who'd been bullied found with a noose round his neck in the gym, stood on a rugby ball and kicked it away.'

'What shape is a rugby ball?'

'Like your football, not our football.'

It was eight years since Gordon had left school yet the sight of Bogbrush – Hugh Dunn – was bringing it back vividly. The rules, the nicknames, the initiations, the jokes about spots and wet dreams. The realisation that the world could be a cruel place, divided into the bullies, the bullied – and the collaborators. He had read and re-read *Lord of the Flies*. Hugh 'Bogbrush' Dunn – Gordon saw him more clearly now, smirking as a new boy was put through the humiliating ritual of being stripped and covered in vinegar and boot polish. Smirking again in the shower room when Farquar-Fox was held under the water. Gordon winced at the memory. Could he have done something more? Run for a master? And then what? Join the bullied minority and face two or three years of being called a homo or a weed? Farquar-Fox hanged himself. The bullies escaped unscathed.

The café door opened. Larry looked up.

'Here comes the holy fool,' he said. 'We're over here, Freddie, O crazed droog.' Freddie beamed and joined them. There was something odd about his demeanour. His hair was damp as though he had just showered. The waiter arrived with Gordon's porridge and Larry's lassi.

'You have heard?' he said, clearly relishing the delivery of news of such import. 'War has been declared.'

'It's actually been declared has it now?' asked Gordon.

'Yes, sir. And what is your purpose here?'

Gordon found it hard to answer without being flippant. 'Can you never answer anything without making a joke of it,' Grace had said. There had been no question mark at the end of her sentence. He had half thought she might be relieved when he said he was leaving, going East, travelling, giving up his job. The relationship had not been faring well but she had wept against his chest that night in bed. 'D'you love me?' she asked. 'I'm very fond of you,' he had replied and did not understood why this made her weep great gulps of tears. He could not bear it, had got out of bed and made himself a joint in the sitting room, put on the headphones and switched on the Velvet Underground. 'Femme Fatale'. 'I'm Waiting for the Man'.

'Yeah, what is your purpose?' asked Larry.

'I wish I knew. Just felt I had to get away. The job was kind of heavy . . .'

'Writing ads, man?' said Larry. 'Doesn't sound too heavy to me.'

Freddie beamed across the table. 'Advertising signs that con you into thinking you're the one that can do what's never been—'

'Oh, fuck off, Freddie,' said Larry, lighting a cigarette. 'Good pay, was it?'

'Yeah, good money. Nice people, most of them. Yeah, there were some of the striped-shirt tosspots but, I dunno, after a while, all those meetings with account executives and clients . . . I was coming home one night – did I tell you this already?'

'Probably, man, but it's been washed away in the gutters of my unconscious.' Larry waved to the waiter. 'One more sweet lassi. *Gracias*. Pray continue, droog.'

'I'd been out for a curry with a bunch of the guys, someone's birthday. That day we'd been told we needed to come up with a new campaign for the Flour Promotion Board. Something to get people to eat more bread, to replace their slogan of "six slices a day is the well-balanced way". I was quite pissed, sitting in Goodge Street tube station waiting for the Northern Line train. Anyway, in front of me was this poster for Air India. A magic carpet, something like that, probably the Taj Mahal in there somewhere. I can't even remember the slogan. But it was something like "let us take you away on a magic carpet". And I just thought, yeah. Time to go. And there was this bloke, a panhandler, tapping all the people on the platform for money. He came up to me and said, "Got any bread, man?" I gave him a fiver for good luck.'

'Whooo,' said Freddie.

'That night, I decided I had to head off. Next day, I went into the agency and I told Adrian, the creative director . . .' The dope was having its effect. Gordon was not sure if the others were interested but he didn't care. Pleasurably zonked, he needed to tell his story. It had been so long since he'd spoken about himself rather than which guest house to stay in or whether Mandrax was really stronger than Quaaludes. 'I told him I had a great idea for the Flour Promotion Board, that they should have this slogan, "Got any bread, man?" I could tell he was not impressed. So I said –' I am rewriting this slightly, thought Gordon to himself – ' "Well, that's my last offer 'cos I'm hitting the road. I'll work my notice but I'm off to India." Adrian said, "Don't you think you're a bit old for that kind of thing?" '

'How old are you?'

'Twenty-six.'

'That's straights for you, droog,' said Larry.

'You know that something's happening but you don't know what it is, do you?' said Freddie. The waiter asked Freddie for payment. Freddie shrugged, displayed his empty pockets. Gordon produced a five rupee note, sighed and paid.

'Freddie, you're going to have to get more organised,' said Gordon. 'Don't you have any money left?'

Freddie beamed back and displayed his empty palms.

'You're right,' said Gordon. 'Attachment brings suffering. Anyway, where was I?'

'You told them to stick their job, man,' said Larry. 'You showed 'em.' Was that sarcasm in his voice? Gordon found it was difficult to tell with Larry. They had bumped into each other first in Kathmandu, at a café which described itself as 'Where the Jet meets the Beat' – a phrase they both relished, asking each other occasionally if they felt 'more jet than beat today' – and then again at Mr Jain's in Delhi and now in Calcutta.

'I don't think I showed anybody anything,' said Gordon, the benign blur of the dope bleeding away. Should he fire up another chillum? He was wary now of overdoing it since his blackout in Delhi after Larry had given him some of his Peshawar morphine. A whole day lost.

'So, Freddie, who are our new Australian neighbours at the Lux?' said Larry. 'Nice to have a woman in the room, no? Or have you reached a plane beyond carnal desires? I don't think Gordon has – I saw the way you looked at her, man.'

Had it been that obvious? When Karen and Kieran moved in to the dormitory and shoved their beds together, Gordon's heart sank. There would be all those muffled cries of passion, the rhythmic bedsprings in the night. The previous week, in the same two beds, there had been a young Dutch woman and her young son, ill with earache, who often wept during the night. Why was the sound of two people in rapture so much more disturbing than the sound of a child in pain? Jealousy, he knew. He had never managed to banish that. When Grace had told him that she had slept with Jeb, who lived in the basement of their Clapham squat, while Gordon had been in Cannes to get the Silver Lion for his Homme Sauvage aftershave commercial, he had been hurt. And this despite the many times he had told Grace that they had to be open, and the occasions when he had come back from a fling with, say, someone he had met at the Flamingo or the Arts Lab and shared, as he felt he should, the previous night's love-making with her.

'And who's the new guy in the robe? I saw him in the bathroom shaving his skull. Weird dude.'

'Mudd,' said Freddie.

'Mud?'

'The name he wrote in the book,' said Freddie.

'Why is that familiar?' asked Gordon.

'Think about it,' said Larry. 'Where shall we go? Maidan? Museum? Cemetery?'

The Park Street cemetery, a ten-minute stroll from the Star, was of classic eighteenth-century design, straight paths between towering stone tombs. Remy had introduced them to it. There were few visitors. It was a good place for an undisturbed, open-air chillum.

A rangy, street-fighting, marmalade cat scampered away as they entered, throwing a dismissive glance at them over its shoulder. The names on the tombs were mostly British. This had been the graveyard for the empire, the final resting place for the poorly wives and sickly young colonial civil servants and subalterns, 'called home' or 'promoted to glory' by mishap or malaria. They paused in front of a solid, unflashy mausoleum. Gordon read the words chiselled in memory of a Lewis Grant who had died aged thirty-eight in 1813. He recited:

His early death involves in grief severe,
A loving partner and five infants dear.
The former, while she mourns her widowed state,
Beholds the latter and laments their fate.
Too soon, alas, deprived of their best guide,
They're left to traverse life's inconstant tide.
But though with peril their condition's fraught
To rest on God their little hearts are taught . . .

'Oh, to be able to traverse life's inconstant tide,' said Larry.

'This is an amazing place,' said Gordon. 'If you look at all the inscriptions, you realise what were considered the greatest virtues then. Here, look at this: Margaret Mercer, died, aged twenty-seven, in 1804, "a tender mother, an affectionate wife and a dutiful daughter". Isn't that touching?'

'Oh, to be tender and dutiful,' said Larry, looking round. 'We lost Freddie. Where did he go?' A siren sounded in the distance.

They strolled together down the path. Larry patted his pockets.

'Just getting my paraphernalia out, droog. I think it's time for my medicine.' They sat down on the edge of a moss-covered grave as Larry fired up his chillum. He handed it to Gordon and excused himself 'to make an offering to the gods of the voided bowel'. Twenty minutes later, he returned.

'Hey, you haven't finished that, have you?' he said, examining the chillum. He was sweating.

81

'You're lucky I'm still here,' said Gordon. 'I find this place a bit creepy.' They stood up together and started walking down a circular path towards the entrance. 'It's like a place in a Dracula film. You expect to see a hearse pulled by four horses with black plumes coming round the corner – hey, look, that's Remy over there, isn't it?'

Fifty yards off, sitting with his back to a musty gravestone, Remy was gazing in front of him. He seemed tranquil.

'Hey, Remy, man,' said Larry.

There was no answer.

'Out of his fucking head again.'

'Remy?' said Gordon as they reached him.

Larry looked down at Remy, narrowed his eyes and then knelt beside him. He placed a hand on Remy's forehead.

'Do you think he's ODed?' asked Gordon.

'Why? You got a handy ice cube to shove up his anus?' Larry bent closer over Remy. 'Remy, man?'

He looked up at Gordon and pointed at Remy's neck.

His throat had been cut with the neatest of incisions. Pinned to his kurta was a scrap of lined paper on which was scribbled the yin and yang sign with a line through it.

Chapter Eight

THE BLACKOUT WAS at its blackest when Britt stumbled out of bed and into a shower after her 4 a.m. wake-up call. There was a packed lunch waiting for her at reception: chicken sandwich, boiled egg, twist of salt in greaseproof paper, apple, fruit cake, bottle of Schweppes tonic water.

There were four army vans in the convoy, each one with room for five passengers. A military press officer was directing journalists into them as they stumbled out of the Oberoi Grand.

She recognised a couple of figures from the bar the night before and from the accreditation office: Bob, the Australian; the nice Englishman called Nick; a fair-haired woman, another photographer, who could have been English or Australian, called Penny or Jenny. They had their little grey press cards, which they clutched, she thought, with the same air of entitlement that she had seen on the faces of the people carrying tickets on their way to the George Harrison concert for Bangladesh in Madison Square Gardens in the summer.

That had been her introduction to all this. She and Josh

had been spending a week with Josh's brother in New York when they heard about it. Ravi Shankar had asked George Harrison to help raise money for the refugees and together they had arranged this concert. Josh had ended up paying a scalper $40 for two tickets but, wow, it was worth it.

George in his white suit and marigold shirt and Billy Preston in leather trousers and a lilac knitted hat, playing 'That's the Way God Planned It'. Ringo on tambourine. She smiled as she remembered it. Some British band called Badfinger had come on and, oh yes, Leon Russell, in a tank top. Ravi Shankar had played something quite free-form and short and everyone had applauded loudly.

George said, 'I'd like to bring on a friend of us all,' and there was Dylan. Dylan! There was a ripple of self-satisfaction – an unspoken, 'We're here when history is being made, man, Bob Dylan is playing with the Beatles for the first time' – running through the crowd. She and Josh sang along with 'Just Like a Woman' and 'Here Comes the Sun' and tried to hear the words to the song George had specially written, called 'Bangladesh', about a friend coming to him with 'sadness in his eyes'. People had been in tears.

They had been suitably solemn for a while and then swapped gossip with their neighbours in the audience: how John Lennon had wanted to be there but was helping Yoko with legal hassles in London; how Mick Jagger had tried to come but the US Embassy in London – bastards! – wouldn't give him a visa in time; how Bob hadn't wanted to sing 'Blowin' In the Wind', which George had suggested, and had even asked George how he would feel about having to sing 'I Wanna Hold Your Hand' and how George had said that that was different.

She and Josh – was this a hint of problems to come? – had had a minor row when she asked where the women singers were and he had snapped back at her, 'Janis is dead. Can you think of any others?' Then they had another row about what Germaine Greer had said about Dylan, that his women were either sad-eyed ladies and girls from the north country or else contemptible, and Josh said she had missed the point, that not everything in a song was literal.

She kept in her scrapbook the *Rolling Stone* report, complete with its Annie Leibovitz photographs, in which the concert was described as 'a brief incandescent revival of all that was best about the sixties'. As they had filed slowly out, a cheerful roadie in a denim vest asked her if she wanted to come to the after-show party and she had smiled back at him. Josh had grabbed her arm and pulled her towards the exit. 'What would you have done if I'd gone off with him?' she asked. 'Offed him, of course,' Josh had replied without even the hint of a smile.

Now the press officer ushered Britt into the third van in the convoy bound for the border. Already inside was a Frenchman in a sky-blue polo shirt with a silk scarf tied casually at the neck, a lugubrious Kenyan photographer and a bespectacled Indian reporter who gave her a wan smile that made her feel that he would be a good travelling companion for the day ahead.

Sitting against the door, Britt glanced guiltily at the packed lunch on her knees as a cloud of beggars, spotting the lights from the foyer, drifted towards the entrance of the hotel.

'Room for one more in here,' the press officer said as he held open the door.

Britt shifted her bottom into the middle of the back seat and checked for the eleventh time that she had her camera, her light meter, her accreditation card. As she did so she caught a whiff of sweat, alcohol and cheap cologne as another body squeezed itself in beside her. I know that smell, she thought.

'Well, what do you know?' said Hugh. 'Here we are again. Pretty good lunches in the circs, don't you think?' A beggar tapped on the van window. 'Sorry, old boy,' said Hugh, adding, to his fellow passengers, 'Apparently, they're all bussed in every day by some crime syndicate – they even cut their hands off to make them more marketable.'

She did not believe him but was too tired to start an argument. She moved slightly so that their thighs did not touch. The vans shot through the early morning, shrouded headlights picking up the earliest movements of the city, bodies sleeping on the sidewalks stirring themselves, going about their ablutions with a balletic grace, lame stray dogs scuffling through scraps in the gutter. The drone of aircraft in the skies.

Hugh was busy introducing himself to the rest of the car: the Frenchman, Jean-Pierre, who turned out to be a photographer from a news magazine; the amiable Indian reporter, Jawid, from Bangalore, whose expression suggested a gentle cynicism; the Kenyan photographer, John, who wanted to chat about light meters when she wanted to doze. The English have become a caricature of themselves, she thought. All this politeness and hand-shaking, this necessity to charm. Why was 'charming' seen as complimentary? Surely it meant a form of deceit, a game played by someone who had realised that a smile, a feigned deference, opened doors to homes and bedrooms.

Confusion on the road. Some refugees were still heading south for Calcutta while others, encouraged by the news of the Indian army's intervention and the flood of troops towards the border, were starting to return north, on scooters, on bicycles, on foot, carrying improbable quantities of luggage, battered cardboard suitcases, old kitbags. Here we are, thought Britt, foreigners and outsiders, being chauffeured in, while the people whose homes have been abandoned are making it back by foot. A sign caught her eye. 'FREE TEA FOR OUR GLORIOUS JAWANS COURTESY OF BROOKE BOND.' She made a vague attempt to ask the driver if he would pull in so she could take a photo of it but there was no way he was going to dip out of the convoy.

'You should get some good material today, lots of burning tanks,' said Hugh as he plucked open his lunch box and cracked the shell of his boiled egg on a khaki knee. ' 'Scuse me eating but I missed breakfast.'

Britt lit a Salem. Only two left in the packet now.

'We are having to take the long route because the Pakistanis have blown up so many bridges,' said the press officer over the roar of the van's engine. 'We can only cross the river by one of our own pontoon bridges but we will shortly be with the troops.'

'Any chance of chatting to some of the glorious jawans when we get there?' asked Hugh.

The press officer gave him a withering look. Hugh seemed oblivious. There was a jam of cars in front of the convoy.

'Army vehicles?' asked Hugh.

'Tourists,' said the press officer. 'Tourists going to see the aftermath of war.'

'Good God!' said Hugh with what sounded like disapproval. 'Already? But it's hardly started.'

'Pakistani tanks. Nice photo,' said the press officer. Britt could not tell if he was being ironic or not.

'God,' said Hugh again.

'Old British tradition,' said the Indian reporter, Jawid. 'The wives of senior officers often used to stroll on to the battlefield in the Crimea after the killing had taken place.'

'Are you sure?' said Hugh.

'Oh, yes,' said the reporter.

'I don't think we got that in our history lessons at school,' said Hugh.

'I'm sure you didn't.'

Britt gazed out of the window. The convoy was halted briefly behind a train of bullock carts. She was struck by the delicacy of the bones in the bullocks' flanks, like the gracefully protruding hip bones of a slim teenage girl on a beach.

The convoy arrived in Jessore. They spilled out into the hot streets, buildings pockmarked by bullet holes, curious pedestrians, many on makeshift crutches.

'For those of you who wanted to interview members of

the Mukti Bahini,' said the press officer as his party unfolded themselves from the van, 'here are two gentlemen who can help you.'

Britt looked at the two figures. They were like children, whippet-thin with smooth, flat stomachs showing above their lungis and beneath their flapping, tattered cotton check shirts. One was barefoot, the other in cheap pink plastic sandals. Old guns dangled over their shoulders and each had a small posse of admirers nearby, gazing at the young men who must have learned how to load a rifle before they had learned how to shave.

'OK if I take your picture?'

Both young warriors smiled, waggled their heads in assent and struck poses. She manoeuvred them round so that their eyes were not scrunched up against the sun and shooed away some children who were plucking at their heroes' torn sleeves. The shots seemed stilted. She tried to persuade the children back into the shot so that she could capture the adoration in their eyes. This confused them. By the time they had reassembled, their expressions had changed and they had become solemn souls posing for the camera, arms rigidly at their sides. The two Mukti Bahini carefully spelled out their names for her with the help of the press attaché. Get the names right, Mok had told her, rule number one, get the names right. (It was one of Mok's many 'rule number ones', along with 'get in close' and 'always shoot one more for luck'.)

Another young man, slightly older than the two Mukti Bahini and better dressed, approached her, introducing himself and politely asking in precise English where she was from. 'These are historic days,' he told her. 'We are building a new world here, a secular state where everyone will be able to say what they want without fear.'

'That's . . . great,' said Britt, uncertain how to respond.

'We will be free at last,' he said with a beaming smile. 'The government in West Pakistan has been no use for people here. Like Sheikh Mujib said, we just exchanged a white sahib for a brown one. Now it will be different.' He nodded, shook her hand and smiled his farewell.

Half an hour out of Jessore, the convoy halted again. 'Picnic time,' they were told. They were in the countryside. As they left the vans, they were hit with the heavy whiff of rotting flesh. On the lip of a ditch were the bodies of half a dozen Pakistani soldiers. Their uniforms had been ripped from them or else they had torn them off as they tried to flee. They were decomposing in their torn underwear. A flock of vultures picked frantically, attacking the heads rather than the bodies. The bare legs were almost untouched. One body was completely naked, a little shrivelled cock lending it an awful vulnerability. Britt recalled the photos from the concentration camps, that haunting shot she had studied in film school of a Nazi firing squad with five naked victims – Jews? Gypsies? Communists? – standing beside an open grave waiting to be shot. The Nazis in the photo had looked as though they were on a picnic, too, a hunting afternoon perhaps, and the naked figures seemed to mean no more to them than would a couple of rabbits or a wild boar. She crouched down and starting shooting.

'Shot!' said an English voice behind her. She turned to see Hugh, sandwich in hand. 'Not so hot for us,' he said. 'No one to interview.'

The French photographer had wrapped his scarf round his nose and was suggesting to the press officer that they could easily stop a couple of hundred yards down the road where there would not necessarily be so many rotting bodies to share their lunch. The press officer listened with an expressionless face.

One body was alone, about fifty yards from the others, lying half on its front as though its owner had made an almost successful bid for freedom. The eyes had been picked from the head which was turned to one side. Britt shot a close-up of the face, the dried black blood on the eyebrow, the lips pulled back from the teeth like a dead cat, run over in the street, flies tunnelling into the nostrils. She took a step back on the hard earth and shot the whole body, the buttocks exposed, barely covered by the tail of a khaki army shirt.

There was a sudden crackle. Bang, bang, bang, bang, bang. Five shots. Gunfire? The retreating Pakistani troops? 'Mopping-up', the blandly domestic euphemism for killing stragglers? She was already mentally using the jargon, she realised. She was briefly gratified to feel that curiosity rather than fear had been her first emotion.

'Uh-oh,' said Hugh and she saw him hunch his shoulders and stalk back towards the shelter of the van. He nodded at her knowingly.

'You hear what I hear?' he said. 'That sounded like an AK-45, if I'm not much mistaken.'

'Is that the same as an AK-47?' She noted a flicker of uncertainty in his eyes.

'Er . . . similar,' he said.

The press liaison officer smiled at them with what might have been the tiniest hint of condescension.

'Fireworks,' he said. 'People celebrate.'

She looked again at Hugh, great pools of sweat soaking his jacket. He was narrowing his eyes and pretending to concentrate on something in the far distance.

The Kenyan photographer, John, had joined her now. They nodded to each other as they worked, the clicks of their cameras briefly obliterating the sound of the flies. When she rejoined the picnickers, the press attaché was dictating to Hugh, who was scrawling the words into his little black spiral notebook.

'Mukti Bahini means "free forces", not to be confused with the Gana Bahini, who are the irregulars, or the Niyanita, who are soldiers who used to be with the East Pakistan Rifles or the East Bengal Regiment . . . How many Mukti Bahini in total? Difficult to say. I have heard seventy thousand but there is no official figure.'

John sat beside Britt. She offered him her club sandwich. She realised that she had not thought of Josh all day.

Chapter Nine

'HUGH DUNN IN JESSORE.'

He looked at his dateline with satisfaction. There, everyone would know where he was when they picked up the paper tomorrow. He mouthed the words slowly to himself as he re-read them on the typewriter. 'Hughhh Dunnnn in Jessorrrre.' He wrinkled his fingers over the typewriter keys like a pianist preparing himself for a concert before a deferential provincial audience.

'As the sun set over what its xx million (SUBS PLEASE CHECK) inhabitants believe . . .' he typed over 'believe' with a line of xxxxxxs and replaced it with 'pray' '. . . will soon be the independent country of Bangladesh, vultures hovered low over the bodies of the dead . . .'

No, he thought, if they are bodies, they must be dead. Hmm, not necessarily. If someone has a great body, they are very much still alive. For a few seconds he daydreamed about Britt's body, imagining her coming into his room wearing, perhaps, just a towel, to ask for help in captioning her photos. The towel would slip, she would smile at him, he would glance down, she would give him a mischievous grin, he would . . . He forced himself back to the type-writer. '. . . bodies of the dead retreating Pakistani troops.' But if they were dead, could they be retreating? Surely people would know what he meant. That was one for the subs to sort out. He felt suddenly hot, which was puzzling as the fan in his hotel room was going full throttle, so fast, in fact, that he had moved his desk from beneath it in case it should fly off its base and crack the top of his skull.

'Flies hummed . . .' Was there a better word than 'hummed'? It sounded a bit idyllic, like bees in the Sussex garden of his youth, when his father was still alive and they were all sitting en famille on a tartan rug in the grass . . . 'Flies buzzed'? Not really. 'Swarmed'? That was the thing about being out in the field, there was no longer that handy human thesaurus that was the newsroom, where you could throw out a word and a colleague would instantly lob back a synonym. 'Flies crawled across the eyes of the dead.' That was better. Or was that a cliché? Oh, fuck it, never mind.

'In the background came the unmistakable sound of . . .' Well, this was a tricky bit. '. . . sound of explosions.' Could he leave it at that? That was the truth, after all, fireworks do explode, but the sound of them had been, hmm, mistakable. So was it misleading? After all, if one were to read that at one's breakfast table, what type of explosion would it conjure up? A mine, probably, or a mortar attack, rather than a banger or a Catherine wheel. The press officer had said the bangs were all celebratory fireworks but wasn't it possible that he was mistaken? Hugh decided that he would stick with 'the unmistakable sound of explosions.'

The dead bodies, at least, were indisputable. Britt – was she becoming friendlier or less friendly? It was hard to tell – had taken lots of photos of those bodies. Perhaps he could mention this to the picture desk, tell them to check out the agencies, and maybe the paper would run one of hers with her by-line added.

The telex was still down so he filed his copy again by phone to a new copy-taker, also Welsh, but a woman and friendly and unjudgemental, unlike Ifor. When he was put through to the foreign desk, he discovered that most of them were out for their Christmas lunch. Already? he thought. Not halfway through December. He realised that he would be missing the office parties which must now be starting. Perhaps just as well, if this thing with Linda was going to get any more serious. What had Max meant when he said 'Hughie'? Had she already been talking about that night? God. He should really phone Jackie. My wife, he thought, although she objected now when he introduced her like that at parties. He looked at his diver's watch. Nearly midnight. And they had to rise the next morning at 4.30 a.m. again.

He went on a hopeful sortie to the bar but found only a barman and the rather effete French photographer with the cravat. He had a beer, retreated to his room, flopped on the bed with his le Carré and awoke without having read a full page, in his clothes and to the sound of, 'Early morning call, sir, four-fifteen, sir,' on the room telephone.

He slept through the border crossing into what was still East Pakistan but would, he presumed, soon be officially Bangladesh, and almost all the way to Khulna, jammed between the Frenchman and Bob, the Australian. Britt was in front beside the driver.

'We are here now in Khulna,' said the press officer when they finally stopped. 'Please be back here within half an hour.'

Hugh strolled away from the van and round a street corner to an alleyway where he saw a small crowd gathered, their attention caught by something in the ditch by the side of the road. Small boys in the crowd were animated and shouting, as though watching a game or a boxing match, shouting and cheering and urging each other on, straining their heads to see what was happening. He recalled a similar scene when he had been covering a fox hunt once, a colour piece for the features department, the excitement at a kill. Taller than most in the crowd of thirty or so, Hugh was able to see over their shoulders at the object of their curiosity.

Lying in the trench, in an inch or so of muddy water, was a middle-aged man. He was barely alive. The face was a bloody pulp, one ear almost detached, it seemed, from the side of his head. His clothes, a singlet and a lungi, were soaked in blood or mud. As he took in the scene, Hugh realised that two of the older boys were dropping paving stones on the man's head. For some reason, it reminded him of boyhood holidays on the Yorkshire coast, in Filey, dropping stones from a height on to translucent, passive jellyfish.

'Bihari! Bihari!' the boys chanted. 'Bihari! Bihari!'

The cries attracted a larger crowd, who brought with them the ominous, intangible whiff of the mob. Hugh turned back to the man – surely dead now after the last barrage of bricks to the skull? He saw the chest rise beneath the vest and there was a sigh of immense weariness. Hugh turned to see if there were any Indian troops around who would intervene.

The chants grew louder and the crowd parted for two boys, neither of whom could have been much more than twelve years old, clutching a paving stone almost as big as them. The others made a passage for them so that they could stand almost directly above the man's head at the edge of the ditch. They dropped the stone to yells and cheers. A final heave from the chest below, then stillness. The crowd started to move off, laughing, eyes bright, like the people in photos Hugh had seen of lynchings in America's deep southern states when the spectators seemed caught up in a carnival atmosphere.

He turned again to see if there were any army personnel on hand and noticed first a camera and then a face behind it. Britt.

She must have been taking photos. She was crouched down so he had not seen her at first. She paused for what seemed like almost a whole minute before taking a final shot. She pushed the hair out of her face and wiped her mouth and forehead with the blue spotted bandanna round her neck.

Their eyes met. She looked down at her camera, clicked a couple more shots into the palm of her hand, wound on the film to its end and shuttled it out of the camera and into one of the pockets of her check cowboy shirt.

Hugh tried feebly to ask one of the departing spectators

what had prompted the attack on the body lying beneath them.

'Bihari!' shouted a teenager at him impatiently, as though that was explanation enough. 'Bihari.'

A young man who had overheard his inquiries joined in. 'Bihari informer, sir. Informer.'

Hugh nodded and they both looked again at the abandoned body, now the subject of attention from two small dogs that had scuttled their way across the road. Hugh kicked them away with his desert boots. He felt a tug at his sleeve and turned to see an old man, bent over and walking with an elegant walking stick.

'You are from a newspaper?' said the old man. 'Which one, I am asking.'

When Hugh told him, the man stared at him knowingly. 'Can I tell you a history, sir?' The old man trembled as he spoke. 'They put me in front of my house, sir—'

'The Pakistani army?'

The old man nodded abruptly. 'They put me in front of my house. They take my son and they place their guns against him. They tell him they will shoot if he will not watch them violate his sister, sir. They are pointing their guns with their bayonets.' He said the word as if it had three precise syllables: bay-on-ets. 'When he will not watch them, sir,' the old man trembled more as though the words once uttered might crack his fragile frame, 'they stab him in the eyes with their . . .' He choked on the words before they could come out.

As the old man spoke, others gathered. Soon there were around fifty people. In the background, Hugh could see

Britt. She was taking more shots of the body which was now being examined by three little girls, who were holding hands and peering over the edge of the ditch with an innocent curiosity. Three little maids from school are we . . . Life is a joke that's just begun . . .

Another voice demanded his attention. 'They made us give blood for their wounded soldiers. They said we each had to give a pint of blood. And one boy –' here other voices joined in, clearly knowing the story and anxious to be a part of it – 'one boy they took, sir, he was only twelve years old—' Voices interrupted, attesting that the boy had been thirteen or fourteen or ten. The original voice persisted. 'This boy, sir, they drained him of all his blood.' Hugh scribbled frantically, suppressing an urge to start giggling madly as the memory of Tony Hancock and the blood donor sketch flashed through his head: 'A pint – that's very nearly an armful! It may be just a smear to you but it's life and death to some poor wretch . . .' He felt a troubling disturbance in his stomach. He should not have eaten that samosa that he had picked up at a stall at their border stop.

There was no shortage of material. Stories of executions with the victims ordered to stand very still because the Pakistani soldiers did not have fast enough film in their cameras to record the event if it had too much movement in it. Round-ups and slayings of the town's teachers because they were in a union and thus must be subversive. Stories of Pakistani troops fleeing, tearing off their uniforms and grabbing drying laundry from the riverside to try to obscure their identity.

The press officer was gathering up the journalists now. Hugh felt another churning in his stomach. Oh, God. He didn't even have his diarrhoea pills with him. Could he ask Britt if she had any? Not a very seductive query.

'Are we all here?' asked the press officer.

Oh, God! Hugh felt a hot jet of shit squirting down his trouser leg. He tried desperately to halt the flow but knew it was hopeless. And he was wearing his light khaki trousers! Why hadn't he thought to put on his dark grey flannels? Because he thought he looked more dashing in khaki? Another evacuation, this time more solid, slid down the inside of the left leg of his trouser. Was it his imagination or did the press officer wrinkle his nose?

'Everyone in the vehicles, please,' said the press officer.

Hugh waited until everyone was in the van before he hoisted himself stiff-legged into the back. He felt the shit caking his left calf. Britt was in the front seat as far removed from him as she could be. Could she tell? As the convoy pulled away, the press officer slammed his window open. Hugh sighed.

'Stepped in some bloody bullock dung,' he muttered to his fellow passengers. No one responded.

File straight from the notebook. He remembered the instructions from his first news editor in Chester when they were up against a deadline. He scribbled his intro as the convoy bumped back through the now dark streets of Calcutta and as Britt dozed in the front seat. Her head bounced forward as she slept. How he would have liked to have kissed that long, pale, downy neck. For a moment, he forgot his shit-encrusted trouser leg and the spiteful coffee-grinder where his stomach had once been. Fortunately, it was dark when they reached the Oberoi Grand and he was able to hirple out of the car, shielding his two-tone trouser leg from the rest of the party and crying, 'Must hurry and file!' as he stiff-legged it upstairs to the sanctuary of his room. He stuffed the offending trousers and Y-fronts into the gingham laundry bag and showered gratefully.

The wires carried news of Pakistani air strikes in Haryana, Punjab and Kashmir and of a thrust by Indian infantry divisions. The Indian navy was blockading East Pakistan – or Bangladesh, as people increasingly seemed to be calling it.

Hugh phoned the newsdesk, a Kingfisher beer from room service at his elbow. He could hear the hum of activity in the background in the office in a chill December London, a reminder that his would be one of a dozen foreign stories competing for column inches that night. Were they already tiring of the war, after barely a week? How many bodies had to come out of Bangladesh to equal a British body? He remembered Henry explaining that, in news terms, one British dead person equalled ten Americans, equalled twenty Europeans, equalled a thousand Asians or Africans.

'Sounds great,' said Max. 'Can you make it about twelve hundred? We're adding in a bit at this end from parliament – Alec Douglas-Home is calling it the "calamity of war". How's things here? You're well out of it, mate. Linda – yeah, that Linda – her boyfriend showed up in reception today. I dunno what it was all about. Ex-army, I think. The security guys had to sling him out. Must dash. I'll put you through to copy.'

He heard himself recounting the story in the same deadpan tones with which he had once phoned in football reports. Oh, God, he realised as he started his third paragraph, it was Ifor again.

' "They are putting out his eyes",' intoned Hugh.

'The present tense?' asked Ifor.

'That's what he said. It's verbatim.'

'It's what?'

'Verbatim!'

'I know what verbatim is . . . Yes?' said Ifor, prompting him to carry on.

'How many words is that?' asked Hugh ten minutes later. The Kingfisher was drained beside him.

'Er, eleven hundred.'

Hugh paused for a moment but this time Ifor did not ask if there was much more of this.

'Thank you very much,' said Hugh as he concluded.

'Not at all,' said Ifor. A Christmas truce.

Hugh flopped on to the bed, suddenly exhausted. In a half-sleep, half-daydream, he saw himself recounting to an admiring audience the details of his first war: 'Hugh Dunn, the award-winning war correspondent and author of the bestselling memoir . . . joining us now on the line is Hugh Dunn, the distinguished war correspondent—'

He was interrupted by a telephone call. His heart sank but the message was a pleasant one. He went down to the bar, suffused with the satisfaction that came from a news editor saying 'great stuff' and a sub-editor saying that it was on the front page and could he just check one tiny detail.

Hugh was a quick filer, he knew that, so he was not surprised to see there were few other reporters at the bar, mainly blokes from the Sundays and the alarmingly self-confident and urbane men from American news magazines whose deadlines came but once a week.

He helped himself to a handful of cashew nuts, turned to look at the early evening cabaret, which consisted of a Westernised young Indian woman in a cocktail dress, accompanied by a pianist and a drummer, singing 'Begin the Beguine'. He ordered a whisky. A double. His glass was empty before 'Begin the Beguine' had finished. Another drink. He gazed benignly round, even including in his beneficence the French photographer who had changed into a white linen suit and a pair of what Hugh's late father would have called co-respondent's shoes. He caught his own reflection in the gilt mirror behind the bar, looking unshaven and, he had to admit, quite rugged. Then – was this a dream? – he saw standing beside him a long-haired stranger. But was it a stranger? He turned to face the phantom.

'Dunn?' said the voice. 'Bogbrush?'

Chapter Ten

BRITT SAT ON THE edge of her bed and stared at the roll of film in her hand. She tried to call her father (out), her brother, Brad, now on the run in Vancouver (engaged), her oldest friend, Patti (constantly engaged), Josh (out).

Here I have the undeveloped film of a man being killed in front of me, she thought. Could she – should she – have done anything to stop his death? She had had no time to think. But was it right to record someone's death like that? He was going to be killed anyway. Did the film show her complicity in a person's death? No, it was a testament to what had happened.

She changed into a clean grey sweatshirt, slipped the film into the top pocket of her cowboy shirt and headed for the hotel bar.

The one advantage, she thought, as she waited for the elevator to arrive, of having a dilemma was that it threw everything else into perspective. Like Josh. Interesting that he had been the fourth person on her list to call, not the first. Marriage seemed increasingly unappealing. But how could she tell him? He would be livid.

I like being here, she thought. This is what I want to do. I don't want to take pictures of houses in Tiburon or Pacific Heights for design magazines. I don't want to spend evenings watching re-runs of Groucho on *You Bet Your Life* with Josh, even if he was sexier than most of the men she had been with. Not that, compared with her friends, she had had many partners. She hated the word 'partner'. It made love and sex sound like business.

There had been a couple of lovers at high school where she had discovered why the words premature and ejaculation were so often used in conjunction. At film school, in New York, there had been a steady, a Puerto Rican, Rafael, long since married back in San Juan. Then Josh. It had been fine, at first, but when they were sharing an apartment with Josh's friends, another Bay Area couple, there had been that 'bust monogamy' time and she had ended up in the hot tub with Josh's friend, Andy. Josh was furious, although he had been cheerfully fucking Andy's old lady, Louisa. Then the two guys had got off on her and Louisa being in the hot tub together, which had, now she thought about it, been kind of fun. Her friend, Patti, by contrast, could claim scores of different sexual partners. She could not say exactly how many – counting 'conquests' seemed to be something men did – but there were plenty. She would point them out sometimes when they cruised through the Haight together or drove into Marin for a day on Limantour beach. They would giggle as Patti identified them: middle-aged married guys with sensible haircuts, skinny musicians with pigtails, Vietnam vets with tattoos and faraway eyes.

Sex with Josh was predictable. She had watched him starting his Harley a few times when the engine was sluggish and his expressions of intense concentration followed by quiet satisfaction seemed identical. He had his pre-fucking routines: check the temperature on the waterbed, put on 'moody' music (currently the Chambers Brothers and Blood, Sweat and Tears, although she knew he secretly preferred Melanie and the Lovin' Spoonful), throw a T-shirt over the lampshade as a dimmer.

When Patti gave her Germaine Greer's book and she started reading extracts to him, he became increasingly defensive. He was furious when she started reading the chapter entitled 'Loathing and Disgust', which began, 'Women have very little idea of how much men hate them.'

She never had an orgasm with him. How could she tell him? How could she explain that she would like a break, that this assignment was as much about getting away from him as it was about covering a story? The way he looked at her with such intensity, the way he had taken to half humming, half singing that line from 'Reason to Believe' about someone making it hard to live without somebody else, which she never quite understood. If she said that she didn't want to marry – and she knew in the darkness of the Calcutta blackout that she definitely did not – would he immediately head off in pursuit of another 'old lady'? Would she mind?

Which brought her back to the new big dilemma. 'Get in close,' Mok had said. She remembered the story he told her about the English war photographer, Don McSomething, whose work was so admired by the other photographers in Vietnam that, whenever they saw him pausing for a shot, they would rush over and try to take the same image themselves. Get in close. She'd got in close and what she had seen she was still digesting. What was harder to digest was that she felt so little. She had shot at 1/25th of a second. Bam, bam, bam. He had been breathing when she started shooting and had not been breathing when she took her final pictures of the three little girls gazing at his body.

The pictures would be great. Late-afternoon winter light, slanting between the buildings and illuminating his bloodied head. The expressions of disdain on the faces of his attackers, like the fury of the women spitting at shaven-headed collaborators in post-liberation France. She could see the pictures as a quartet: the crowd; the boys holding their paving stone aloft in triumph; the hopeless look of despair as the man prepared for death; and the three little girls holding hands and staring at what had been wrought.

Instinctively, she had finished the reel so that she could whip the film out of the camera before anyone could confiscate it. She had felt the need to hoard her treasure. These were photographs that people remembered. The kinds of shots that Larry Burrows and Don McSomething – McCullers? McCullin! – had taken in Vietnam that defined a war. Americans should see what was happening, that outside Vietnam people were dying hellish deaths unremarked. She pictured herself trying to justify to her mother why she had taken the pictures rather than trying to save the man's life; her dad would never question her decision. She saw the pictures across two pages of a magazine, of *Life*, of *Rolling Stone*. But she needed her mum, or Patti or Josh, even, to say that this was right, that this was not a trespass, that there was nothing she could have done, that the English journalist had been there too, and had done nothing, burying his head in his notebook.

She heard the phone ring in her room as she waited for the elevator.

It was Josh. He asked what she was wearing. Creepy. Does he get off on that? It was a side of Josh she had not seen before. She was short with him, did not tell him what was on her mind. She could sense the hurt in his voice when she said she had to run. She rang her dad again. He was home but stoned.

'Hi, sweetpea,' he said. 'When you coming home?' With relief, she told him what had happened. Her conflicted emotions. Her horror at her first sight of someone being killed, almost for her benefit. How, after all the movie and television killings she had seen, this real one had seemed so banal, so ordinary. About how she had reacted instinctively and shot and shot and shot. Click, whirr, click, whirr, click, whirr. She paused to let him digest this, to tell her it was the right thing to do. To tell her to get printing, to get on to her agency and get the pictures through. She waited.

'Dad? What do you reckon? Daaaad, you understand, don't you?'

She heard the faint hum of his snore, the familiar sound of her father after 10 p.m., a bit stoned, whacked out in front of *Laugh-in*, always easy to wake with a nudge to the elbow. 'Oh, Dad, wake up, you've missed the best bit . . .'

'What was that, honey? I missed that bit . . . When did you say you were coming home?'

'Not sure,' she said abruptly. 'Gotta go. Bye.' She put down the receiver, wondering if he was too stoned to have noticed the disappointment in her voice or whether he was already turning over to nuzzle some bubble-haired model who had stayed over for a joint and a flagon of Mad Dog.

Downstairs, in the hotel's main lounge, a funny little trio was playing bad standards on the stage, ignored by the guests. There was the Frenchman who looked rather sexy in a suit now. Maybe it was the light. He gave her a look which needed no translation. At the bar, slightly flushed, was Hugh, the Englishman, his hair almost neatly combed, his attention directed, uneasily, at what appeared to be another young Brit – that pale skin, the gappy teeth – but long-haired and tie-dyed and happily babbling away.

She took a bar stool beside Hugh and ordered a double Bloody Mary. Hugh was staring straight ahead. She could see his reflection in the bar's mirror. He was nodding, occasionally responding monosyllabically to a series of questions. She peered round him to see who was making him so uneasy. As she did so, the long-haired stranger did the same.

'Hi,' he said. He seemed jumpy, a bit hyper. Stoned, probably. 'You a colleague of Hugh's? Sorry to intrude. I'm Gordon. We were at school together.'

'Really?' she heard herself say. 'Were you friends?'

Gordon laughed uneasily and Hugh gave a resigned shrug. They were difficult to decode, the English. So uptight. She looked at Gordon. Nice face, she thought: sleepy eyes, full mouth.

'I think you could say we were in different tribes,' said Gordon.

'Which tribe were you in?'

'Oh, you know, the pretentious tribe. Mohair sweaters and winkle-picker shoes. We sang Tom Lehrer songs on the back of the bus – "Bright College Days".'

'Soon we'll be sliding down the razor blade of life,' she offered, smiling.

'You know it?'

'My dad knows them all by heart: "Poisoning Pigeons in the Park" and "The Old—" '

'Dope Peddler.'

'That's right. "The old dope peddler . . ." So what else did your tribe do apart from singing Tom Lehrer? Can I get you a beer? You look a bit empty there.'

'I'd love a beer – but I can't buy you one back because I'm almost out of money until the war is over,' he said with another smile and shrug. 'I asked my bank to send me a money order but nothing seems to be getting here.'

'What bad luck,' said Hugh, still staring ahead.

'And what tribe was Hugh in? Are you guys the same age?' Hugh seemed almost middle-aged, the long-haired one a boy in comparison. The long-haired one – had he said his name was Gordon? – deferred to Hugh with a smile.

'Oh, my tribe,' said Hugh, clearly irritated. 'We were the boring farts, weren't we, McGrady? The ones who did the tedious things like editing the school magazine, passing our boring exams and being boringly unable to understand the sub-text of Beckett, hmm?'

Some unresolved shit here, as her father would say. The beer arrived. She ordered herself another Bloody Mary.

'Was there enough Worcester sauce in the last one?' asked the barman.

So that was how you pronounced it. 'Wooster.' She nodded.

'I didn't catch your name,' said Gordon.

'I didn't throw it,' said Britt. Am I flirting?

'Oh, should have introduced you. Britt ... er ... Pedersen and Gordon McGrady,' said Hugh.

'Are you here to cover the war too?' she asked. He did not look like any of the other reporters but you could never tell these days. Corporate lawyers in San Francisco now wore Nehru jackets and flares and had hair like tumbleweed balls.

He laughed. 'No, I'm sort of travelling . . .'

'Hippy trail,' interjected Hugh with some tartness.

'Just happened to be in Calcutta when the war broke out. Been down in Goa, Delhi, Bombay and was heading east to get somewhere I could make some money before it all ran out. I thought I saw Hugh arriving the other day and I knew he was working for a paper and they said all the reporters were staying here. So, are you a reporter or a photographer?'

'I'm a photographer. Are you staying in this hotel too?'

Gordon laughed. 'No. You should see our hotel, it's a little more modest. Six to a room. Or was – one of the other guys in the hotel got killed.'

'No kidding. What happened?'

'Well,' he said, suddenly serious. 'We found him in a cemetery near here.'

Hugh tried to catch her eye, then turned his attention to Gordon.

'Probably an overdose,' he said dismissively.

'His throat was cut,' said Gordon, looking Hugh in the eye. Hugh looked unconvinced.

'Well, good to catch up with you, McGrady, but I'm afraid we –' was he including her? – 'have to grab a bite, swap notes and get ready for another early start. No doubt I'll see you at an OSG reunion one day.' Hugh started lowering himself off the bar stool.

'I kind of doubt it, Bogbrush – I'm sorry, Dunn . . . Hugh.'

'What did you call him?'

'Bogbrush. Silly school nickname. Did you have one?'

Pretty Britty. That's what the boys called her at high school. She was not sure she wanted to share that. She smiled. The second Bloody Mary was taking effect.

'Mine wasn't that imaginative.'

The receptionist had left his post and was looking urgently round the bar. He spotted Hugh and nodded.

'Ah, Mr Dunn. A Mr Max is on the telephone. You can use the bar extension if you wish.' The barman shoved the cream Bakelite receiver towards him. Britt heard Hugh's end of the conversation. He was obviously irritated.

'What? No one suggested that earlier. What? Can't someone do that from your end? . . . Mmm . . . How much? Another six hundred words? You must be joking . . . OK,

OK . . . Yes, I suppose so.' His shoulders slumped. 'Bloody newsdesk,' he said as he replaced the receiver. 'Bloody fucking newsdesk.' Then, between his teeth, 'See you later.' He jerked his head in farewell. She and Gordon looked at each other.

'Well, I guess he's not going to make dinner tonight,' she said. 'I'm starving. You're welcome to join me. I can get it on expenses, I think.'

'I couldn't. Why don't you come to Nizam's with me?' There was something urgent in his tone. 'It's great food. See a bit of Calcutta. I'll get you back here safe and sound, I promise.'

She scanned the bar. Bob, the tanned Aussie, was holding forth to some young reporters. She heard his nasal drone and the words, 'Yes, I was on the first helicopter in there as it happens . . . yeah.' She realised that she had seen nothing of Calcutta.

'OK. Let me go up to my room and get my camera and a shirt.'

Gordon was waiting for her in the lobby when she came down five minutes later.

'You smell nice,' he said. 'What is that?'

'Oh, just rose water.'

It was pitch black outside but a trio of boys picked them out and followed. Gordon handed them each some change.

'Hippy! Hippy!' said one.

'It's wrong to stereotype people,' said Gordon, deadpan, to the smallest of the boys who looked at him with amazement but soon realised that they were in a game and responded with a smile slow enough and wide enough to have got him a screen test. Britt unslung her camera from her shoulder and shot the boy before the smile disappeared. The boy's expression altered and he frowned. 'No mummy, no daddy.'

'OK, OK,' she said, digging a ten rupee note from her jeans and handing it over. She became a sudden magnet to the rest of the children on the street.

'You've been too generous,' said Gordon, closing his hands in a 'namaste' gesture to denote 'no money' to the swarm that encircled them as they strode along. 'But that's better than the opposite, isn't it?' The swarm grew as word spread. He steered her round the corner. 'Nietzsche used to say that beggars should be executed – if you gave to them, you felt a fool; if you didn't, you felt guilty.'

A slit of light at the end of the next street was the sign that they had arrived. Nizam's was warm and glowing inside, lit by a battery of candles.

'Great smell, isn't it?' said Gordon.

'Mmm, what is it?'

'Cardamom, I think,' he said. Josh would not have known.

They sat down at a long table with benches on each side.

'Why don't you go ahead and order?' she said. 'They do vegetarian, right?'

'The best,' said Gordon.

'What was that name you called your old schoolmate?' she said.

'Bogbrush. It was his nickname at school. He used to have this hair – still does a bit! – that looks like a lavatory brush. Childish, isn't it? A lot of the nicknames were pretty unkind. There was a guy who had had polio who was called Spaz, as in spastic. "Crater" had terrible acne and so did his little brother. So they were Greater Crater and Lesser Crater. And "VD" – some poor sod who started the Scripture Union at school so we chose him the name he would find most upsetting. Why were we so cruel?'

'Yes,' said Britt, 'I got a little hint of that earlier. It seems we've both met up with the dead recently . . .'

'I still can't believe it,' said Gordon. 'It was this French guy, Remy. He was a junkie and if he had ODed, I guess it would have had no effect on me, but it looks like he was killed by someone who's bumping off travellers. He cuts their throats and leaves a little yin and yang sign on the body. I love India but it seems like it's time to get out, but there's no way to do that. I'm sorry, you've just been seeing the bloody war. I guess it's much worse than one dead bloke in a cemetery but – are you OK? I'm sorry, is something the matter?'

And she told him, from the moment she had heard the cries of the boys, how she had been beckoned over, tugged by the sleeve as if to a treat, the sudden realisation that there was a living human being in the ditch, not a trapped wild animal, the paving stones, the sound of cement on bone, the sigh – the sigh! – the faces of the small boys, the one who could not have been more than four or five who had spat on the body, the stories they had heard afterwards of how the informers had led the troops to the Mukti Bahini, details she knew she was adding to soften whatever disapproval this man might be feeling at the idea of chronicling the death of a fellow human being rather than intervening.

She heard him say, 'Two salt lassis, please, Ashok, aloo matur, sag, brinjal bhaji.' She saw pickles and onions appear in front of them and realised that he was holding her hand.

'Look, you did exactly the right thing. They were obviously going to kill him anyway, poor bastard, but people should see what is happening. We hear about Vietnam but nothing about all this and many more people are dying here. Have you developed the photos?'

'I've got the film here.' She gestured at her shirt which she had slung over the seat behind her and, as she did so, noticed his gaze shift from her to the entrance.

'Well, hi, guys.'

The door had opened and out of the darkness tumbled a strange array of humanity. A man with a shaven head and large beard, whose self-confident bearing suggested he was American, nodded at her and pulled a large joint from his wallet as he sat down. A young man with fair curly hair, introduced as Freddie, joined him. A very thin couple – Australians? New Zealanders? – completed a circle round them.

'You're not Sagittarius with Virgo rising, are you by any chance?' asked the bushy beard.

'Er, no . . .'

'Just ignore Larry,' said Gordon. 'He's taking the mick.'

She saw Larry wink at Gordon who shook his head back at him, as if telling him off for teasing her.

The joint was strong, much stronger than the grass she was used to in San Francisco.

'Thai stick,' said Larry, the bushy beard. Draft dodger? Deserter? He put the joint out by crushing the burning end between his wetted finger and thumb. 'They don't like you smoking here,' he explained. The thin couple turned out to be Australians called Karen and Kieran. They seemed strung out. On smack?

'Anything new on Remy?' asked Gordon of the group.

'Mr Bose has been to the French Consul,' said Larry. 'The police want to take a statement off you. They asked if it might be a suicide.'

'You're kidding. Where was the knife or whatever he did it with?'

They ordered a spinach and potato curry and some sweet orange soda.

'Yeah,' said Larry. 'I explained that the blood was already drying when we found him.'

'And who put the sign on him, man? Don't they realise what's happening?'

'I guess they have other things on their plate,' said Larry.

'And has anyone seen – what's his name? The skinny monk?'

'Mudd,' said Larry. 'He's in a non-speaking order apparently so the police haven't been able to interview him. They want to ship Remy home because it's standing room only at the morgue. I suggested that they—'

'Can we please talk about something else?' said the Australian woman, Karen.

So they did. Monty Python came up, that English television series that Britt watched with her dad. She and Gordon liked the same sketch about philosophers playing soccer. She asked Ashok, the waiter, if she could take pictures in the kitchen and was invited back to wonder at the barrels of ghee, the turmeric and aubergines in the skillet being expertly twirled above the flame, the neatly rolled frisbees of dough waiting to be plunged into the boiling fat.

Back at the table, she took pictures of the assembled company, finished off a roll and asked Freddie where he was from. 'Atlantis,' he told her. He seemed unhappy about having his photo taken and half hid his face, saying something about his 'essence'. Larry and Gordon both rolled their eyes at each other and included her in their collective shrug at Freddie's strangeness. She interrogated them all, teasing them about what they were doing in Calcutta.

'Ask no questions, be told no lies,' said Larry when she cocked one eyebrow at him to ask what his story might be.

'Well, I've got a little brother who is going to spend the rest of the war in Vancouver, I guess, and a cousin who's just signed on for a second tour of duty with the 82nd Airborne so I'm used to hearing both sides of the story,' said Britt. She was feeling tired but good. 'What do they think of it all in Britain, Gordon?'

'Well, Harold Wilson refused to send any troops when LBJ asked him and I think Heath has the same idea. I was on that Grosvenor Square demo, the big one – did you read about it?'

'Er, I don't think so, no,' said Britt. Was he trying to impress her? Probably.

'Most people are opposed to it in Britain, I would say. I'm

119

sure if I was American, I would be like your wee brother.'
My 'wee' brother, she thought. 'But I thought you could get
out of the draft quite easily.'

'It used to be easy,' said Britt. 'All my friends at film
school swung something. One put on lipstick and carried a
purse – he would have made a beautiful girl, as it happens –
and said he lonnnnnged to be in the US navy so they
exempted him right away. Another one ran up and down
the stairs in our apartment about ten times before his
medical so his heart rate was phenomenal. But they got
wise to the dodges, didn't they?' She threw the question at
Larry.

'So I heard.'

'What were you doing, Larry?' she asked.

'Ah, that is what Freddie would describe as the half-
remarkable question.'

'What's a half-remarkable question?'

'That is,' said Gordon. 'I'm sorry, a half-remarkable
question is a song by a group called the Incredible String
Band. You won't have heard of them in America, I don't
think.'

'Look, kid,' she said narrowing her eyes and drawing in
her cheeks in a caricature of cool, 'I saw the Grateful Dead
when they were still the Warlocks and Jefferson Airplane
when they were the Great Society. How cool is that? I know
the Incredibles. They played Woodstock.'

'Dreadful British warbly fairy medieval nonsense,' said
Larry. ' "Cousin Caterpillar"! Give us a break.'

'Come off it,' said Gordon. 'I heard you humming "Air"
the other day.'

'Don't criticise what you can't understand,' said Freddie. She caught his sudden intense gaze and returned it.

Larry spotted the look and leaned in her direction. 'Don't get too close to Freddie,' he said conspiratorially. 'Don't stare into the vacuum of his eyes.'

'Why not?'

'He has crabs in his eyebrows. The Incredible String Band are incredible because it's incredible that anyone would listen to them.'

'As opposed to whom?' said Gordon amiably.

'Velvet Underground.'

'The Incredibles represent optimism and life to the Velvet Underground's pessimism and nihilism,' said Gordon. 'I am sure Gandhi would have preferred the Incredible String Band.'

'Don't bet on it,' said Larry. 'He was a cool dude. He certainly whupped your British ass.'

'Did anyone see the film about him?' asked Karen, unexpectedly engaging in the conversation.

'Which one?' asked Gordon.

'Five Hours to Something, I think,' said Karen.

'*Ten Miles to Midnight*,' said Larry.

'No, no,' said Gordon. 'It was *Five Hours to Rama* – it was pretty dire. It had Robert Morley playing an Indian guy.'

'I think it was Seven Hours but what does it matter?' said Kieran.

'Twenty-Four Hours to Tulsa,' said Freddie.

'I knew someone was going to say that,' said Gordon. A moth flew straight at the candle in the centre of the table and burned.

'Do they feel pain?' he asked.

'Of course they do,' said Larry. 'And do you know why they are always drawn to the flame?'

'You're going to tell us,' said Britt.

'I am,' said Larry. 'Because moonlight is the moth's radar and every time they see a light, they think it might be the moon.'

'Cool piece of knowledge,' said Kieran. There was an odd tone to his voice, thought Britt. Or is it because he's Australian?

'I want to read a poem,' said Karen, suddenly assertive. Britt caught her eye and Karen half nodded at her. She had beautiful, sad eyes. They were the only women in the group. Britt noticed that Karen's hands were shaking and wondered whether the poem would be embarrassing. Patti had had a poetry-reading phase – seagulls and dragonflies and ocean beds featured a lot – and it had made her cringe. Karen opened a notebook with a golden starburst on its cover and read, in a soft Australian accent, a poem about everyone suddenly bursting out singing and birds winging their way over dark-green fields. It ended with the words 'on, on and out of sight'. Britt was impressed.

'Outtasight,' said Larry.

'That's lovely,' said Britt, although she thought that the last two lines were slightly clunky. 'Did you write that?'

Karen smiled and seemed, for a moment, about to claim authorship. Then she shook her head with a sweet smile. 'Siegfried Sassoon wrote it.'

'D'you think that's where the expression "out of sight" came from?' asked Kieran.

'No,' said Larry.

There was a pause. Britt suddenly remembered that she had to rise early. She waved at a waiter. The check for the entire meal, which she insisted on paying, despite Larry's protestations – 'Better six wounded than one dead' – came to about the same as a single cocktail at the Oberoi Grand's bar.

'What do all your families think about you being here?' Did that sound patronising? she wondered.

'I send them postcards from everywhere saying what a healthy time I'm having,' said Gordon. 'Here is Kabul. Here is a picture of the Khyber Pass. That sort of thing. My father tells his friends that I'm climbing in the Himalayas. Nepal. That's where you should go while you're over here. Hire a sherpa. Go trekking. See God. You would love it.'

'How do you know?' she asked. 'What's Afghanistan like?'

'Beautiful countryside, friendly people, terrible food – all bone with tiny bits of goat attached. Except for Siggi's place, where everyone hangs out. We stayed off Chicken Street – Christ, I can't even remember the name of the place. What was it called, Larry? We had to overstay because they couldn't get a new fan belt for the bus. It's great, very relaxed, you see these glorious caravans of camels going across the desert on the road. Like paradise. But it's changing already, all those hustlers buying up Afghan coats and hats. In a few years' time, it'll be full of tourists and Club Meds like Greece and Morocco.'

'Bit fiercer than there, man. Didn't you hear about what

happened to that Danish kid outside Kandahar?' said Kieran.

'What was that?' asked Britt.

'Danish family, couple, freaks, three or four kids, in a Volkswagen van last summer, driving down a mountain road, little Afghan kid runs into the street. They can't stop in time. Whack. Dead kid. They stop the van. They're horrified, obviously. The kid's family show up. No one speaks English. The Danes are full of apologies, it's all tears, offers of money. Then the patriarch shows up. Big guy, turban. Looks at the Danes, grabs their smallest kid. Pulls out a machete. Whish! Beheads the Danish kid. Turns round and drives off.'

'Wow,' said Britt.

'I heard it was a Dutch family, man,' said Gordon. 'And it was years ago. Anyway, since we're all talking about death, what is really happening about Remy?'

Britt sensed an immediate unease at the table. Karen scuttled to the toilet. Kieran busied himself counting a roll of rupees. Freddie closed his eyes.

'Look,' said Larry. 'Don't panic. Whoever is doing this is not going to come into a hotel room with six people in it.'

'It's not six any more,' said Gordon. 'Remy's dead.'

'They've put the silent monk in there,' said Kieran. 'What's his name meant to be – Mudd?'

'I don't like talking about this,' said Karen, rejoining them. 'Not at night.' They all started to get to their feet.

Gordon nodded at Britt. 'Finish the bhajis. They're better than that ersatz stuff you get in hotels.'

'Ersatz, my droog,' said bushy beard. 'Assuredly, you

speak in the tongue of the enlightened one. These are fine words. Does the enlightened one seek to impress?'

'You're not impressed by someone using the word "ersatz", are you?' Gordon looked straight into her eyes. She held his gaze. He is flirting with me, she thought.

'I'm quite easily impressed.'

'Me, too,' said Gordon.

'We are now closing, please,' said the owner, thanking her for what her friend, Patti, would have described as a righteous tip.

She turned round to put on her cowboy shirt and feel the reassuring presence of the roll of film which she must now develop and process. But the pocket, where she was so sure she had placed the precious film in its canister, was empty. It could not be. She had barely been away from the table, a few moments in the bathroom and perhaps five minutes taking pictures in the kitchen. She searched the pockets again and then for a third time, panic mounting.

The roll of film, the film that would have made Mok kiss her feet when she returned, that would have opened a thousand doors, had vanished.

Chapter Eleven

'ARE YOU SURE it was there when you left the hotel?' asked Gordon. I am being Mr Calm, he thought, a part he had had to play sometimes in the squat when someone was freaking out – sudden explosion of jealousy, row over the share of the telephone bill, bum acid trip, that sort of thing.

'I'm positive,' said Britt, feeling the pockets of her shirt for the umpteenth time. He recognised despair. 'Fuck. Fuck. Fuck. Fuck. Sorry, but there's no other word for it.'

'Don't apologise,' said Gordon. He knelt on the ground and scanned the floor beneath the table.

The staff at Nizam's were concerned, anxious that no one should imagine that this was the kind of place where thievery could take place. There was much waving of arms. Everyone seemed to be searching although no one was quite sure for what.

'Where was this camera?'

'No, no,' said Britt, on the edge of weary tears. 'No, not a camera, a film, a roll of film. In a . . .' She searched for the word. 'In its little container, canister – you know.'

Larry looked blankly at her.

'You know,' Gordon told him. 'The little thing you keep dope in.'

'Oh, yeah,' said Larry, dropping down on the floor on all fours.

'Don't start doing downward facing dog now, for heaven's sake,' said Gordon under his breath and immediately regretted it as he could tell that Britt did not think it was funny. Kieran and Karen joined the search lethargically. Karen seemed more animated after her poetry reading although there was a wild, erratic air to her. Freddie beamed beatifically, untouched by the concern around him. Has Freddie found the secret I am looking for, untroubled by temporal matters? wondered Gordon.

'Don't worry,' he said, his hand on Britt's shoulder. 'We'll find it. It may have dropped out of your pocket on the way here. We can retrace our steps. You're absolutely sure it's not still at the hotel?'

'YES. I'M SURE!'

'Sorry, sorry.' Gordon resumed his search.

'She knows too much to argue or to judge,' said Freddie, sotto voce.

'I'm sorry,' said Britt, apologising for the fierceness of her response. 'It's just that I know I put it in that pocket. Oh, God . . .'

'Look, it's a drag,' said Larry. 'But, you've lost a film. Over there in Bangladesh, people are losing their lives. Hell, Remy, malodorous Gaul that he was, has just lost his life.'

'I know, I know, I'm sorry,' said Britt unhappily.

It was soon clear that all the obvious places where the film might have rolled had been diligently searched. It was missing. Nizam's was closing. The owner was apologetic but clearly felt that he had done all that he could. He was, after all, not unused to these long-haired customers suddenly embroiling themselves in some crisis or catastrophe, real or imagined. He and Gordon exchanged understanding shrugs over the bent bodies of the searchers.

'I'm really sorry,' said Gordon to Britt. She seemed beyond comfort.

'I can't believe I was so stupid,' she was saying to herself. 'How could I . . .'

The opening of Nizam's door threw a sudden beam across the street, illuminating a nightwatchman engulfed in an ancient khaki greatcoat. He stirred from his slumbers, grasping his stick, saw the motley crew, processed them mentally as harmless and slumped back into his doze. A feral dog, all ribs and bent ears, scampered across the almost deserted street.

'We'll retrace every step,' said Gordon. Concentrate, he thought, lose attachment. Banish the thought that the main reason you want to find the film is so that Britt will want to show her gratitude in, well, who knows what way.

'I know it's gone,' said Britt flatly. She took his arm as they stepped between the sleeping bodies on the pavement. Gordon scoured the gutters in the half-light, occasionally turning items over with the toe of his moccasin; a reel of thread, the empty tin of a bicycle repair kit. He glanced at her and wondered whether to tell her what this reminded him of – John Bull's bicycle repair kit, punctures, end of empire – when he caught her troubled, faraway look.

'I'm so sorry,' he said. 'I wish I could magically make it reappear.'

'I know,' she said. She squeezed his arm.

They were near the Oberoi Grand. Another slash of light split the courtyard outside the hotel.

'I still think we – you –' he did not want to be presumptuous, she looked even more desirable in the near-darkness – 'should have a real look in your room. You never know . . .'

'Oh, I suppose so, but I'm sure it's not.' The despair was back in her voice. 'But come up and help me look anyway.'

'OK.'

The commissionaire looked over the tops of their heads as they entered. Britt had problems with getting the key in the door of her room. Gordon took it from her and undid the lock.

'Perhaps you can tell me,' he said. 'You know that Melanie song – what does she mean, "I've got a brand new pair of roller skates, you've got a brand new key"?'

'You really don't know?' said Britt, unexpectedly smiling once they were inside the room. He felt suddenly nervous. Was this going to lead to bed? Was his radar still working? He had never been to bed with an American woman, he thought. She was almost as tall as him. He had never been to bed with anyone taller than him. A secret ambition. He looked at the rolls of film on the top of the chest of drawers. She caught his glance and shook her head.

'It's not there. It's gone.' A big, deep sigh.

'But shouldn't we look, just in case?'

They were standing very close to each other. Her hand went to his belt, the big-buckled Mexican belt Grace had given him the Christmas before last. They encircled each other with their arms, kissing, fondling. They rubbed cheeks and noses.

'You don't have any . . . er . . . diseases I should know about?' she asked.

'Fat chance,' said Gordon. 'I've been like a monk since I left England.' A moment's panic. That itchy rash round his groin. Crotch rot? Damp mattresses? When he had inspected the area in the faint, cold drizzle of the shower that morning there had been no sign of it. Had the ointment from the chemist's at the end of Sudder Street actually worked?

'Isn't that why you came? To be like a monk?'

'That was the one part of being a monk I hadn't reckoned on.' For a second he thought of the thin silent monk. Mudd. Mudd had a razor blade. The closeness of her breasts banished the thought. He unbuttoned her shirt and slipped it off her shoulders. She tugged his flares down from his waist. 'I didn't realise that most of the people on the road would be other blokes or couples or . . .'

'Or?'

Duncan Campbell

'Well, there's a lot of hepatitis around, which is not exactly an aphrodisiac. And junkies are not interested in sex.'

'You don't say?' she said, imitating his accent. They stood naked in front of each other. He took her hands in his. She flashed him a big, wide smile as she pretended to wrestle with him and nipped his earlobe with her teeth. They flopped together on to the immaculately made bed. She rolled on top of him and straddled him, bending down to gaze into his eyes with what seemed like a frown on her face. She took him inside her and half closed her eyes, rocking slowly backwards and forwards, biting her lips.

I must not come too soon, he thought. He tried the meditative technique he had studied in Kathmandu. He came too soon. Why did that have to happen?

'Sorrrrry,' he said. 'It was just such a glorious feeling being inside you.'

'Don't worry,' she said. 'The convoy doesn't leave for a few hours.' She slid her hand down between his legs. 'I'm sure we'll be able to do something about it.' Her head slipped down his chest with light kisses, her tongue tickled his belly button. He looked down at the tousled blonde head, the brown shoulders, the paler snakes of skin around her breasts and loins that must have been hidden from the Californian sun by the tiniest of bikinis. They lay silently together. Britt stretched over a long, bangled arm and switched off the ornate bedside lamp.

'What . . .' He paused.

'Go on, ask it.'

'Ask what?'

'You were going to ask me some personal question and then, being a sensitive guy, you thought better of it.'

'Well, OK, then. What are you doing when the war ends? Are you on the next flight back to San Francisco?'

'Haven't thought about it. I guess so. Mok, the guy who runs the agency, said I should be looking to see if there are any other stories here . . . Oh, God, that fucking film I lost!' She seemed suddenly bereft. A deep sigh, then, 'Perhaps I could do a story about all you guys, the hippy trail, those murders . . .'

'Oh, I see, this is why you went to bed with me, just to get a story.'

She rolled over on top of him and pinned his shoulders to the bed. 'That's right.' She raised herself above him slightly and swayed slowly so that her breasts brushed lightly against his chest. 'Now you vill tell me all ze secrets of ze hippy trail. I vant to know everyzing – EVERYZING!'

'Ahhh, I did not expect an inquisition.' He pulled her tighter.

'No one expects the Spanish inquisition!'

He rolled her suddenly over on to her back and pinned her to the sheets. He paused dramatically.

'Oh, no!' he said, staring at her left shoulder.

'What?'

'Not a butterfly. Please, not a butterfly.'

'Look, I was only sixteen. What did you want me to get? A skull and crossbones?'

'That would have been funkier.'

'I bet you were too sissy to get a tattoo at all.' She wrestled him over on to his back again and leaned on his shoulders with her elbows.

She was right. He had considered it when hitch-hiking through France on the last holiday before he was thrown out of Sussex University. There had been a tattoo parlour in Marseille, a chance of a rose-and-dagger on his forearm. At the last moment, he had thought of his parents, his father's inevitable, 'For heaven's sake, do you want to look like a navvy?' or his mother's, 'Oh, darling, it looks awful, you'll get some disease.' His hitch-hiking companion had paid ten francs for a badly drawn dragon.

'Remind me tomorrow and I'll get one with your name and a heart on my right bicep,' he said.

She examined his bicep in the pre-dawn light. As she did so, Gordon shot a sidelong glance at his groin. Phew. No rash. Either the meditation or the medication was working.

'I don't think there'd be enough room there for my name.' She squeezed his bicep, with a smiling disdain. 'You Brits are such pussies, aren't you?'

He fought back and they wrestled beneath the sheets until their lips met and they explored each other, licking and stroking. They made love again and lay in the half-light. He traced a thin scar on her hip.

'How did you get that?'

'Josh – guy I know – he threw a coffee cup at me once. I don't think he meant to hit me but he lost his temper and it caught me right on the bone.' She examined a scar of his on his shoulder. 'What's that?'

'Dislocated shoulder, fell out of a tree, doctors pinned it. Well, at least we'll be able to identify each other's bodies in a morgue.'

'God, what a weird thing to say.' They kissed again. 'Weirdo.'

'Who are you calling a weirdo?'

They tussled so strenuously that they fell out of bed and landed heavily on the carpet. There was a knocking on the wall.

'Shhhhh!' they both said to each other, giggling loudly.

'God, this is like my hotel. Someone is always telling you to be quiet at night. The other night we were having this discussion about whether the darkest hour is really just before dawn and—'

'That's the kind of thing you discuss, is it? I thought you'd all be trying to discover something a bit deeper. I thought you were more Maharishi and less . . . Furry Freaks.'

'Oh, we had a discussion the other day about whether cockroaches experience fear.'

'And?'

'We decided that fear only comes later down the chain and that when they run away they are reacting instinctively, not fearfully.'

'Jesus, that's deep.'

'Then we discussed whether only humans feel guilt.' Gordon kissed her ear. 'Karen was talking about being bitten by a monkey up at Swyambhu, the Buddhist temple in Kathmandu, and she said that the monkey looked guilty afterwards. Larry said that guilt is a post-Christian emotion.'

'No kidding?' She traced the flatness of his stomach with her thumb. 'What's this scar?'

'Knife fight in Naples.'

'Liar.'

'Came off my bicycle on holiday in Crail when I was seven.'

She imitated his accent again, deepening her voice. 'Came off ma bishicle on holiday in Crail when I wash sheven.'

'Are you trying to imitate Sean Connery?'

'Oh, you think you're like Sean Connery now, do you? Get one drunk American chick in the sack and you think you're James Bond?'

'I heard him being interviewed on the radio just before I left London,' said Gordon, cupping her left breast in his hand and stroking it absent-mindedly. God, you're beautiful, he thought. 'He was being asked by some pushy interviewer if he minded going bald and he said –' he slipped into Sean Connery's voice – ' "Well, it'sh not great but who do you complain to?" ' He kissed her below the ear. She stared at him.

'Are all men sad after fucking?'

'*Post coitum, omnes homines tristes sunt,*' he said, pushing her hair away from her eyes. 'After intercourse, all men are sad. It's almost the only Latin I remember.'

'Never mind the Latin, is it true?'

'Do I look sad?'

She shook her head and laid it on his shoulder. She closed her eyes.

'How tall are you?' he asked.

'Five foot eleven.'

'Pity.'

'Why?'

'I've always wanted to go to bed with someone taller than me.'

'How tall are you?'

'Five foot eleven and a half.'

'I'm still growing.'

'And you have beautiful, long toes – I don't think I've ever said that to anyone before. You could play the piano with them. Look at them!'

They both examined her feet for a moment or two. She kissed him hard on the lips and rolled over towards the wall. A few moments later she was in the deepest of sleeps. He heard her long, calm breaths like waves on a shore. He gazed at her. Her head upon the pillow like a sleepy, golden storm. Is there no way of looking at something without a line from a song coming to mind? he wondered. He kissed her very delicately on the cheek and wondered if her tiny half-smile was in response to that or some cat-like dream into which she had already slipped.

Gordon awoke to a banging on the door. He sprang from the bed and hurried naked and unthinking to open it before he remembered where he was. He looked over his shoulder. Britt was still asleep, her hair across her face, one long arm with its turquoise bracelet stretched out and almost touching the ground. She was half covered by the top sheet, one shoulder and one breast exposed so that the overall effect was of the jacket of a fifties pulp novel about dope and dames. He pulled the sheet across her and gently pushed the hair from her face but she did not wake. More banging at the door. Wrapping a towel round his middle, he hurried to open it and flung it open rather more theatrically than he intended.

Standing there, notebook in hand, looking a bit like the private eye from the cover of that same pulp novel, was Bogbrush – Hugh Dunn.

'Hi,' said Gordon.

Hugh Dunn did not respond, his eye coolly taking in the wanton jumble of clothes on the floor and the sleeping form of Britt. Then, forcing his gaze back to Gordon, 'Press convoy's leaving. She's got about five minutes to get on it.' He turned on his heel.

Gordon was impressed at the speed with which Britt dressed. He remembered a passage in *Saturday Night and Sunday Morning*, which had passed from hand to excited hand at school, in which the main character, Arthur Seaton, had watched as – was it Brenda? – had dressed and how puzzlingly erotic this had seemed, how much sexier than undressing. Now, as he watched Britt getting into her clothes, gracefully fastening her white bra, swaying into her jeans, pulling on her cowboy boots, he understood. He wanted to drag her back to bed. He stood to kiss her goodbye. His saffron scarf that she had admired lay on top of the pile of his discarded clothes. He slung it round her neck. 'You liked it – it's yours.' She pressed her groin mischievously hard against him, stuck her tongue down his throat and then, moments later, cameras over shoulder, she was gone.

Blimey, he thought, I'm in love.

Chapter Twelve

ANAND HAD ACQUIRED the habit of the morning newspaper from his late father, for whom a day had to begin with the simultaneous consumption of sweet tea and *The Times of India*. The habit had persisted through his years in England when *The Times* of London had accompanied his toast and instant coffee. This pattern, with the substitution of sweet chai for the anodyne Maxwell House instant coffee which the English drank and *The Times of India* again, continued now that he was back in Calcutta. The front page, followed by the sports pages for the cricket. That was his routine, unless he was feeling under the weather and could persuade Baba to bring him bed-tea.

This morning the front page and the sports pages seemed to have elided. On page one was a scorecard, not unlike that in a Test match.

	India	Pakistan
Planes lost	31	73
Tanks lost	49	124
Warships lost	0	3
Gunships lost	0	9
Submarines lost	0	2

All that seems to be missing, thought Anand, as Baba brought his second cup of tea, is the bowling averages.

'How goes it with the guests?' Anand inquired. Baba was his source of information about the clientele: who was ill and would necessitate a trip to Bay's Medical Stores; who had not paid. He realised that he knew nothing about Baba's background. He had been working at the hotel for twelve years before Anand took it over and it seemed impolite to ask him about his personal life. How educated was he? What were his politics?

'Police are coming again to talk about Mr Remy,' said Baba. 'Mr Mudd has not paid. Gordon was not being here last night. But his effects are here so I am sure he will return. Maybe he was with a lady friend!'

Anand ignored the invitation to speculate.

'The gentleman from Australia is very anxious to leave and does not believe that there are no flights out of Calcutta,' continued Baba.

'Does he know there's a war on?'

'Sometimes I am not sure, they are all stoned out of their skulls,' said Baba, who now often talked in much the same way as his charges, relishing the use of new phrases he acquired. 'Stoned out of their skulls. Freddie is still bloody nuisance. I saw him looking in other people's personal things – he said someone had stolen his nail clippers! I saw him near the bed of the Australian woman. I wonder if he is also not something of an eve-teaser.'

'Ah, Freddie. I fear he has lost more than his nail clippers. Do you happen to know what became of my cricket flannels, Baba? I left them out to be cleaned.'

'They are with the cleaning woman, I will tell her to bring them over.'

'And the shirt. I've got a game this afternoon. Oh, and can you take the names of all the foreigners to the registry – I forgot to do it yesterday. I'll bring the book down with me when I come.'

Baba showed no interest in or, indeed, disapproval of the idea of Anand playing cricket while the brave jawans fought a war of liberation not so far to the north. Anand had not played for more than a year since his last game with a scratch side of fellow Indians and friends from the London School of Economics, who arranged odd fixtures on council playing fields in the London suburbs, slightly depressing islands of worn-out grass, dotted with wire litter bins and the occasional unfeasibly large dog turd. In his last two years in England, the team had gone on a week's tour in Somerset, playing village sides. He remembered sitting, waiting to go in to bat and wondering: is it possible to feel nostalgic about something before it has happened? It had seemed so perfect: Bunny and Randeep opening the batting; Nii, who had learned his cricket at boarding school in England, warming up in the nets; Vanessa, long red hair, flowing skirt, bare white legs, clapping embarrassingly loudly as he walked out to the wicket; the cheers from the team when his half-century came up; pints of shandy in pubs with low-timbered beams in villages with improbable names like Stogumber and Nether Stowey; strolls down moonlit lanes to their bed-and-breakfast abodes after the pubs had closed.

He brushed away the one shadow from this idyllic

picture. It had happened on the last night of the last tour. Vanessa had broken up with a brief boyfriend and he heard her in the pub telling Nii's girlfriend about how nice it was to be 'fancy-free'. For nearly four years he and Vanessa had had a friendship that people would have called platonic, which Anand had discovered was the English euphemism for asexual. He comforted her when she was dumped by some new toff, making jokes about him and imitating his accent – 'Vanessaaah!' – until she wept with laughter. And she reassuringly held his hand when he was left by the Jordanian student with whom he had become infatuated – 'Oh, Anand, she is just too gorgeous for words but I don't think it was meant to be.' He comforted her again when her mother died and she had wept great racking sobs on his shoulder in the student canteen before departing for the funeral at the family estate. And she surreptitiously paid his overdue rent after a cheque had bounced. That last night on the cricket tour, they were both a little tipsy. There was no port and the local scrumpy had been stronger than the fizzy bottled stuff he was used to. Vanessa had been knocking back the G and Ts. They were both in the same bed-and-breakfast. They stopped at the top of the stairs. Was it his imagination or did she open her mouth as if to be kissed? And then Bunny – or was it Randeep? – emerged from the bathroom on the landing and Vanessa had laughed, pecked him on the cheek and scuttled to her room. What if . . . what if . . . ?

His reverie was interrupted by the sound of singing from below. Someone, either Larry the American or

McGrady, was playing the guitar again. The tune was very familiar but the words, the words – Anand strained to listen.

> A third-class ticket all the way to Delhi,
> A rolled-up tube of contraceptive jelly,
> And now my nose has rings –
> These foolish things
> Remind me of you.
>
> A saffron prayer-wheel that just keeps on spinning,
> A junkie's story that has no beginning,
> Ah, how my kaftan clings –
> These foolish things
> Remind me of you . . .

There was laughter after the song. Anand detected Larry's chuckle and that of McGrady, too. He rummaged around in his chest of drawers for his white socks. He had not worn his cricket boots since Somerset and there were still signs of that bright, crayon-green English grass on the toecaps.

Cousin Vivek was coming round to pick him up to drive to the ground. Vivek was a serious young man and Anand was quite surprised that he had not dropped out of the game at this time of national drama. He went through the hotel register as he waited, looking at the strange scrawls and the obscure home towns of all the young men and women who had wound up at the Lux. One of the chores of the hotel was to take a daily docket of the names of all foreign visitors to the government registry where they were solemnly entered into a ledger. Who knew why. Sometimes Anand had to help the clerk decipher the names that had been scrawled by his guests, some of which he knew, or guessed, were bogus. 'Major Major' was one current entry. And who had signed in as Henry Chinaski? In the 'arriving from' column, one guest had written 'Doggy Biscuit'. He looked at the other recent names. Gordon McGrady. Larry – he could not make out the surname – shouldn't it be Anunziato? Frank Mills. Who was Frank Mills? And Bobby McGee? And S. Paradiso? The two Australians, Kieran and Karen, had failed to write down their passport numbers. Mudd had signed in but had still added no further details. Ah, there was Remy's name. When Gordon and Larry had told him of his death, he had been uncertain what to do. He rang the police first and then the French Consulate, who seemed irritated. The body was apparently already at the morgue. Did Remy have people who loved him somewhere, who would wonder when they did not hear from him? Or had he cut all ties?

There was a light tap on his door. It was Vivek with a rather lovely young woman on whose lips was the trace of a smile, as if at a secret joke.

'This is Cousin Anand,' said Vivek to the young woman. 'Did you ever meet him? We have great hopes for him becoming the first successful capitalist in the family.'

'Yes, as you can see,' said Anand, rising and offering his seat to the young woman in the turquoise and pink sari. 'This is the foundation of a chain which will one day rival the Hiltons. Would you care to see one of the penthouse suites? Let me find out if the maharajah has vacated his quarters yet. Coffee or tea? We could have it on the balcony off the ballroom as the weather is so splendid.'

The young woman, Deviani, as Vivek off-handedly introduced her, laughed. 'Coffee in the ballroom sounds grand. Table near the orchestra perhaps?'

'Do we have a full team?' asked Vivek, stroking his short and dashing beard. 'Did Duleep explain he was not playing?'

'No. Why not?'

'He said something about not wanting to be taking leg guard while thousands of people were being killed in a war of liberation and the US fleet is in the Bay of Bengal.'

'Well, that means we are two short. Is the US fleet really there?'

'Oh, yes. Mr Nixon wants to scare us but I don't think they have the balls to enter another war. Anyway, we've just sunk one of Pakistan's destroyers, it said on the wireless. What about asking some of your guests? I saw one very muscular fellow in the courtyard with a bald head and a bushy beard who looked like he should be a fast bowler.'

'I'm afraid he's American. I don't think there are too many cricketers among the rest of them. I don't know if the chap in the robes is from a cricket-playing country. What would you think? French, Danish, American? You don't play, do you, Deviani?'

She flashed him a smile.

'I thought you had lots of English and Australians here,' said Vivek.

'That's true. I can go and see if there are any volunteers

but I kind of imagine they were not the sporty type at school.'

'Oh, come, come, Anand, nor was I. Cricket is not for sporty types anyway, is it?'

'You are going to quote C. L. R. James at me now.'

'I'm not – she might. She's a Naxalite, you know.'

'No, I'm not!' She laughed again.

'I thought the Naxalites were a spent force – "the Naxalites are going out all over India". I thought the days when every student worth his salt wanted to be a Naxalite had passed. But I have been away . . .'

'The reasons they exist are not spent forces,' said Deviani, looking him in the eye. 'I'm glad someone has the guts to challenge what is happening here.'

There was another knock on the door. Two of the long-haired Britons, Gordon and Freddie, appeared. Both looked ecstatic. This was normal for Freddie but Gordon usually looked a little ill-at-ease. Now he was beaming. Probably very, very stoned, thought Anand.

'Hi, sorry to bother you, but there's no water at the moment.'

'I will ask Baba now. Oh, by the way, neither of you two gentlemen play cricket, do you?'

'Wow, funny you should ask that,' said Gordon. 'I just had a dream about playing at school. Yeah. Why do you ask?'

'We are two men short for a game. Just a friendly.'

'I don't have any whites or cricket boots,' said Gordon.

'I rather imagined that that might be the case. I think I have some plimsolls and an old pair of white flannels. That top –' he gestured at Gordon's off-white embroidered kurta – 'would be fine. And Freddie, how about you? I kind of imagine a left-arm spinner.'

'For the masters make the rules for the wise men and the foooooools,' said Freddie, letting the last word answer for him before he graced them all with his beatific smile, a peace sign and a retreat down the stairs with his hair streaming behind him. Gordon remained, effusing over the chance to play cricket, saying he was a bit out of practice, did not mind where he batted in the order and, yes, he did happen to bowl a bit of off-spin but it would be very rusty. He departed to try on some of Anand's old plimsolls and trousers, clearly thrilled to have been asked to play.

'These immigrants are ruining this country, wouldn't you say?' said Vivek after Gordon had gone. 'They come here, they take advantage of our hospitality, make no effort to integrate or speak the language, have all these dirty habits . . .'

'Don't bother to work,' continued Anand, joining in, 'have unpleasant, unhygienic customs.'

'Dreadful food,' said Vivek.

'Oh, it smells, doesn't it?' said Anand. 'All the vinegar on their fish and chips. And their revolting sweets – those pink wafers and, what was it called? Instant Whip. And those biscuits,' he recalled Vanessa's description of them as 'fly cemeteries', 'Garibaldis, is it?'

Deviani shook her head at them, smiling. 'Do they manage to pay their rent? They all look so disorganised.'

'Oh, yes, they are mostly pretty good at that,' said

Anand. 'At seven rupees a night, they don't exactly have to break the bank. Sadly, we lost one of them the other day. They found his body in the Park Street cemetery.'

'What happened?'

'That's what the police are trying to find out. There does seem to be someone bumping off hippies. There were two of them killed in Bombay in the same sort of way. There are all kinds of rumours.'

'What are they like?' asked Deviani. 'Do you mind if I smoke?'

Anand waved his assent. 'A mixture. Some arrogant creatures who treat everyone here as though they were their servants, not to be addressed as fellow members of the human species. Some seem to be in such a daze that it is hard to tell what they are like. Remy, the poor chap who died, was a junkie. Some are sweet, innocent creatures like Fotherington-Thomas—'

She frowned at him.

'Fotherington-Thomas – a frame of reference from a different era. He is a character in a funny English book called *Down with Skool*. He had curly fair hair and was very sweet and fragile and would say things like, "Hello, clouds, hello, sky," and all the rough boys laughed at him and mocked him. There are a few like him. They gaze at the stars at night – now that there is a blackout on and you can see them – and they are very respectful, too respectful, perhaps, of everything here. They keep telling me that India has the answer and the West has lost its way. They are impressed that we have a woman prime minister here.'

'Ah, but they have their Queen,' said Deviani.

'Not really Empress material, is she?' said Vivek.

Baba arrived with a tray of teas.

'What do you hear of the war?' asked Anand.

'Over soon, I understand,' said Vivek. 'I just hope that Sheikh Mujib is not another chimera, another charismatic figurehead who lets everyone down.'

'Is there any other kind of charismatic figure?' asked Deviani.

'I am optimistic,' said Anand. 'This is a justified war. It will be over soon.'

'Unlike Vietnam which will take years before it is finished because the North will never surrender,' said Deviani. She reminded Anand of the didactic Trots at the LSE who felt that, by stating the obvious, they were somehow advancing the discussion and the revolution simultaneously. But he warmed towards her. Vanessa would have said she had 'spunk'. Was Vivek serious about her? he wondered.

A tap on the door.

Outside stood Gordon, wearing a pair of white flannel trousers at least two sizes too big for him, held up with what had been his headband, black plimsolls with rubber toecaps, his kurta tucked neatly into his trousers and a bright smile on his face beneath his wet hair.

'Good God,' said Vivek. 'It's Ray Illingworth. We'll be down in a moment.'

'Who is Ray Illingworth?' asked Deviani, blowing an elegant smoke circle into the centre of the room as Gordon hopped down the stairs.

'An English cricketer,' Anand told her. 'Not as good as

Chandrasekhar or Bedi but not bad for an Englishman. I'll get the kit and then it's off to war we go.'

He collected his battered leather cricket bag and led the way downstairs. As they approached the open door of the hotel's largest bedroom, he heard Larry strumming on his guitar. At first it sounded as though he and McGrady were singing the Hallelujah chorus. Then Anand realised that they were substituting the word 'Hepatitis!' for 'Hallelujah!' He exchanged raised eyebrows and shrugs with Vivek and waved to Gordon to catch his attention.

'Hepatitis! Hepatitis!' sang Larry as they departed. 'And we'll be ill for ever and ever . . .'

Chapter Thirteen

BRITT SKIPPED DOWN the stairs at the Oberoi Grand, not bothering to wait for the elevator, Nikon, Leica and new saffron scarf draped round her neck, camera bag slung over her shoulder with a dozen films inside it as a baleful reminder of what she had lost. One of the waiters pursued her with a packed lunch as she hurried into the last of the army vans, its back door hanging censoriously open for the final member of the party.

The French photographer, Jean-Pierre, gave her what her mother would have described as a winning smile – what is a 'losing smile'? she had once asked – and both Jawid, the Bangalore reporter, and John, the Kenyan photographer, greeted her amiably. She glanced sideways at Hugh who was very deliberately reading a newspaper, acknowledging her presence with a slight grunt only once the convoy had lurched off towards the border. She smiled anyway. I am tingling all over, she thought. How strange.

She looked out of the window as dawn came up. Small groups of what she presumed were Bangladeshi refugees, some on foot, some on bicycles laden with pots and battered cardboard suitcases, were travelling in the same direction. Some camped at the side of the road, crouching over a small fire, women nursing babies, old men clutching a walking stick in one hand and a small, bow-legged child in the other. She thought back to the night that had barely passed, smelled the saffron scarf round her neck and had to stifle a laugh.

'You are cheerful today,' said Jawid.

Do I smell of fucking? she wondered. Hugh gave her a sidelong glance, laden, she felt, with disapproval.

'No . . . it was just . . . I was just looking at all these people heading home with hardly any belongings and thinking . . .'

'You have an easy life in the West?' he said without disapproval or judgement.

'Exactly.'

In Khulna, just inside Bangladesh, the mood was euphoric. Small boys swarmed over Indian tanks. Garlands of marigolds were draped over the gun barrels. The tank commanders had that blissful look of restrained self-satisfaction which Britt had seen on the faces of tennis champions whose portraits she had taken after tournaments in Palm Springs. Palm Springs! So far from here.

Each Indian army vehicle was cheered. Troops mingled on the streets, an army of liberation, enjoying all the traditional favours. Food was pressed into their hands, children grabbed at their sleeves, young women waved shyly from the roadside.

This time there were many more Mukti Bahini on the street, most of them even younger than the Americans now being drafted to go off to Vietnam, she thought. They were happy to pose, shouldering arms or sitting cross-legged for a group portrait, pushing each other, like schoolboys, to get the best position, flirting with her, giggling and joshing and giving her their best 'cool guy' imitations, all hooded eyes and sucked-in cheeks. They displayed their makeshift weapons – machetes and pistols, even pieces of piping. They gave her their addresses so she could send them copies of the photos; they wanted to know what newspaper or magazine they would appear in. A slightly older man joined the group and said something quietly into the ear of one of the Mukti Bahini. He pointed at a pick-up truck and soon all the young men were piling aboard it.

'Where are you going?' asked Britt.

'Pakistanis – we look for Pakistani soldiers!'

A posse of around a dozen clambered aboard and drove off, waving like football fans on their way to a match they knew their team would win.

She had to force herself not to ask if she could join them. The journalists had been told that they were being taken to a place where prisoners-of-war were being held. She could not abandon the convoy.

She felt a tug at her sleeve and saw a small boy who pointed across the street. There were four girls, who could not have been much more than fourteen or fifteen, dressed in bright and clashing clothes and wretched little plastic slippers. One had lost the heel of one shoe which gave her a lopsided gait. They were being shepherded down the street by a stern middle-aged man in a grey cardigan.

'Who are they?' she asked the little boy.

'Bad girls.'

'What have they done?'

'They go with the Pakistani soldiers.'

'Perhaps they didn't have much choice about it,' she said almost to herself. There had been many reports of rape, of women rounded up and held in army camps, gang-raped by Pakistani soldiers who were shown porn films in their camps to inflame them. The girls were so slight, they could not have weighed much more than eighty pounds each. Incongruously, two of them giggled when they spotted her, nudging each other. She started to take their photographs but their captor gestured the girls on and shook his stick at her. Another tug at her sleeve. A smiling young man with an ancient rifle over his shoulder.

'You're Mukti Bahini?' she asked him.

'Yes. I kill many Pakistani soldiers.'

'What will you do when the war ends? Are you going to be in the army?'

'Army no good. I go to university.'

'How old are you?'

'Seventeen.'

He asked her if she knew the British MP, John Stonehouse. The name meant nothing to Britt, which caused mild puzzlement. 'Good man,' said the teenager. 'Do you know George Harrison?'

'I don't know him but I saw him play in New York, at Madison Square Gardens, in a concert for Bangladesh. With Ravi Shankar.'

This elicited some interest. The word that this strange, tall woman had seen Ravi Shankar play provoked smiles.

She told them about the concert, of how people had shouted 'Jai Bangla!' at the end.

'Jai Bangla!' shouted some of the little children on the periphery of the crowd. 'Jai Bangla! Beatles, Beatles!'

An old man presented her with a flower and bowed at her and she tucked it behind her ear and shook hands with him. Everyone full of goodwill. I am full of goodwill, too, she thought, trying to let the joys of the past night blur her nagging fury with herself for being so careless with her film. The Kenyan photographer beckoned to her that the van was moving on. Two little girls pressed their faces against the van window as it departed.

The heat was intense and Britt felt her head nodding, banging against the window as the convoy drove down the dustier roads outside the city. Bullock wagons, loaded with sacks of rice, were overtaken by speeding armoured cars.

As she dozed, she thought about Gordon. How nice to fuck someone who did not gaze earnestly into her eyes afterwards, wanting her to say she loved him, begging for commitment. Josh had recently become more desperate somehow in his love-making, thrusting his fingers inside her as though trying to locate a key hidden on the other side of a letter box. He had also recently taken to shoving his tongue as far down her throat as it would go, which made her nearly gag. Did he think that was sexy? She and Patti had a phase a couple of years ago when they classified men: 'FBB' meant 'fuckable but boring' and 'FBF' was 'fuckable but fickle'. Josh, she realised with a sinking feeling, was now 'FBB' and she was increasingly unsure about whether he still merited the 'F'.

Would she see Gordon tonight? She did not know the name of his hotel. Would he be at the same restaurant? What was it called? Would she find her way there? Would he come and look for her at the Oberoi Grand? Was he telling the truth when he said she was the first woman he had been to bed with for months? Why would he lie? I am free, free of Josh, she thought.

She knew it would play well with the agency if she came up with a feature story on the hippy trail and these weird murders. Mok had left a message congratulating her on the shots of children looking at the dead Pakistani soldiers. They would like the ones of the Mukti Bahini, young men prepared for combat. They had plenty of shots of young Americans, black, white, brown, with their dog tags and their helmets, their open smiles, Lucky Strikes dangling from their lips, in Da Nang or the Mekong Delta, and all those other places made famous only because of battles and bloodshed, yet there was still an appetite for photos of handsome young dogs of war.

Hugh gruffly asked her if she had got 'any decent shots'. He was clearly trying to step over the embarrassing threshold of the morning, a threshold crowded with her unmade bed, the detritus of underwear displayed across the floor. It must be hard for him to deal with the fact that his feckless schoolmate, who had used his old unflattering nickname in front of her, had ended up in bed with her. Too bad.

She decided not to tell him about the lost film. They had not even mentioned to each other the man killed before their eyes. Had he thought to intervene? There seemed to be a tacit understanding that they would not discuss it. How lucky he was to be a reporter and not a photographer. If you were a reporter, you did not have to worry about losing film, about the right exposure, about whether your equipment was safe, about dropping your camera. All you needed, it seemed, was a notepad, a ballpoint pen and an attitude.

'Got some good ones of the Mukti Bahini this morning,' she said, 'and, I hope, a couple of some of the girls who were accused of going with the Pakistani soldiers.'

'Oh, I didn't see that. What was happening to them?'

'Didn't you see them? The girls in bright clothes. They were being taken off by some very disapproving-looking guy,' she said. 'They seemed so young and I'm sure they had no choice.'

'Had they had their heads shaved?'

'No . . . it think that's a European thing.'

'Perhaps it is.' Hugh had decided to change the subject. 'Funny thing, hair. Our paper had a piece about it the other day, about how even policemen are starting to wear their hair over their collars in London and how it signified a final capitulation to fashion and so on. End of the short-back-and-sides era. On the next page, there was a feature about how the Sikhs were a key part of the Indian army and how brave and admirable they were. We love the Sikhs in Britain. No mention of their long hair . . . Do you want my boiled egg?'

So the threshold had been quietly crossed. She almost felt sorry for him, sweating in his odd clothes, scribbling surreptitiously into his notepad. She thought again of

Gordon and the threshold she had crossed there. How would she tell Josh? Men couldn't bear it when you told them to their faces that you had fucked someone else. Often it was a simple way to end a relationship: 'Sorry I didn't ring last night but I hooked up with this old boyfriend from high school and we smoked too much weed and ended up fucking. You don't mind, do you? Hello? . . . Hello?' Easy to be hard.

'We are now approaching the camp where the prisoners-of-war are being held,' said the press officer, leaning over from the front seat of the van as it lurched past a burned-out tank and another gathering of vultures snacking fastidiously at the side of the road. 'Please observe all protocol.'

Chapter Fourteen

'MRS GANDHI CALLS For Peace,' Anand read aloud from the newspaper as Vivek nudged his battered caramel Ambassador through the traffic in Tollygunge. 'America Considering Sale of Arms to Pakistan.'

'Bastards,' said Deviani.

Anand was mildly shocked. She must have sensed his reaction from her place in the front passenger seat.

'I'm sorry,' she said. 'But they are. They are taking Pakistan's side merely because Russia has been helping us to help Bangladesh. There is no principle in it at all. The two superpowers see us as little pawns they can move around their chessboard and who cares if a million people die here? They think that, if Pakistan wins, then Russia will have lost face on the subcontinent and will have less influence. They would rather have anything than communists.'

'See, Deviani has become a Soviet-style communist,' said Vivek, negotiating a trio of daredevil scooter drivers. 'That's what happens when they go to university in Hyderabad. She will be going to Moscow to learn how to be our new commissar.'

'It just makes me mad when I see Mr Nixon on television talking about peace and international understanding while he gives arms to Pakistan and bombs Cambodia,' said Deviani. 'I don't want to go to Moscow but who else is helping people in liberation struggles? Mr Edward Heath?'

'What about the liberation struggle here?' said Vivek. 'Lenin said that the road to world revolution lies through Peking, Shanghai and Calcutta. Remember when our parents used to take us to the House of Soviet Culture, Anand?'

'Ah, so you are still a communist?' said Anand, hunched beside Gordon and the cricket kit in the back seat.

'Well, communist with a small c,' said Vivek.

'And getting smaller all the time,' said Deviani, sotto voce. Anand giggled.

'I think she must be a Trotskyist,' he said. He was enjoying this mild, sideways flirtation with his cousin's girlfriend. 'Neither Washington nor Moscow, isn't it?' The car slowed as it approached the end of a march of a few thousand people, probably refugees, carrying pictures of Sheikh Mujib and chanting 'Jai Bangla!' Vivek tooted the horn in time with the chants and waved. Gordon gave the marchers a peace sign.

'I am not an anything that ends in an "ist",' said Deviani. 'I can't stand all this labelling and naming – Marxist, communist, Trotskyist, fascist, situationist, anarchist, feminist. When people tell me they are a Marxist or an anarchist or whatever, I ask them, so what do you do? What does it mean? If you are a Marxist, can you have servants and stocks and shares? If you are an anarchist, can you pay taxes that go to the ministry of defence? If you are a communist, how much of your salary do you give to the untouchables? Or, when people say they are Christians or Buddhists or Hindus or Muslims, what does that mean? All these missionaries here at the moment – the Baptists and the Mormons, they are like Coca-Cola and Pepsi, trying to get their franchises established. You quote the bible at them and they give you a blank look. "Thou shalt not kill"? So do you come from a country with the death penalty and what are you doing about it, please? All that stuff about the rich man and the kingdom of heaven and the camel and the . . . the . . .'

'Eye of the needle,' said Gordon from the back seat where he was almost hidden beneath a battered cricket bag stuffed with pads, wicketkeeper's gloves, unsavoury protective boxes, stumps and bails. Deviani flashed him a smile.

'That's right,' said Deviani. 'Look at all these wealthy chaps who say they are Christians and who know people live in hunger and poverty and—'

'Spoken like a good Hindu,' said Vivek.

'Not at all,' said Deviani. 'You know what I think about that. That's one of our problems here. All the Christian countries and all the Muslim countries are used to going to worship together, that's why they are all so well organised. Here we don't have Sunday morning services or Friday prayer, it's everyone for himself. Perfect breeding ground for capitalism.'

'I think she must be a Naxalite after all,' said Anand. He

did not want to present himself as the old fogey but he felt that she would respond to a bit of ribbing. He liked her company.

'Er . . . what is a Naxalite?' piped up Gordon. Anand had almost forgotten about him.

'They are militants, a breakaway from our official Communist Party,' said Deviani. 'They want to bring about revolutionary change, by armed struggle, if necessary. It started in a little place called Naxalbari in West Bengal about four years ago, that's how it got the name. It started as a land issue, didn't it, Vivek? But it has grown now into other things. A lot of students are joining them.'

'Yes, you'd better watch it, Anand,' said Vivek. 'They don't like the landlord class.'

'Well, this country needs something like that to shake it out of its sloth and its corruption,' said Deviani. 'This war is just going to be a chance for us to forget all about that for the next year or two while we thank our glorious jawans and our glorious Mrs G and feel proud because we have defeated a nasty little army. For what? Next thing will be that the Pakistanis get the Americans to give them a nuclear bomb and then who knows what will happen.'

'Argue with her, Anand,' said Vivek. 'You used to be such a good debater when you were at school.'

'I can't argue with you, Deviani,' said Anand. 'I have been softened by four years in the belly of the beast – or the belly of one of the beasts. The view is never so clear from close up. The more one sees of the Soviet Union or Mao's China, the less attractive it seems. Any country where it is hard to leave freely and where you can't write what you like seems unattractive to me.' For the first time since Vanessa, he felt close to a woman.

'But look what the Soviet Union has accomplished,' said Deviani. 'They are the only people helping the liberation struggles – in Vietnam, in Cuba, in South Africa. Their system may not be perfect but the alternative is what? Fascist dictators and military governments? Look at Mother England and all the racists there, calling you Paki and telling you to go home.'

'There is just as much racism here,' said Anand. 'Look at the way they treat African students in Delhi. And all those advertisements for brides in the paper – they all boast about their light-skinned daughters, don't they?' He gestured out of the car window at the advertising hoardings of models bidding people to buy televisions and take flights. 'Look at all those – all light-skinned people, some of them are almost white. What does that say? At least in Britain these days you don't have to stay cleaning streets all your life just because you have been born into a caste.' He shot a sidelong glance at Deviani.

'Things have been changing since you've been away,' said Deviani, trying to light a cigarette against the wind blowing in from Vivek's window. A tiny piece of ash caught Anand in the eye. 'Anyway, what does our representative of Her Majesty think?'

'About what?' asked Gordon, who had been gazing at the criss-crossing of the cars on the road, clearly awestruck by the ability of pedestrians to avoid being hit as they navigated a passage to the other side.

'About everything,' said Deviani sharply. 'After all, if the

British hadn't made such a mess of partition we would not be in the middle of this war. I don't suppose you learned any of that in your history lessons, did you? About the million who died in communal riots because you messed up the handover? About the two million who died from famine in the Second World War because Britain wanted the food for itself? I bet it was all the heroics of Clive and the Black Hole of Calcutta and how you stopped the nasty practice of burning wives. And how Mountbatten was a hero.'

'Well . . . er . . . yes, Mountbatten is certainly still pretty popular in Britain . . . What do people think of him here?'

Deviani snorted. 'What's going on now is all his fault. He was bored here so he rushed to partition. No one was ready for it. He could easily have waited but he was too arrogant, too vain. He thought – like all the colonisers – that they can just draw a line here and pronounce that this is this country and that is that country. Look at what you've done everywhere – Rhodesia, Palestine, Ireland. Here Mountbatten got bullied by Jinnah. Never thought it through. He wanted to go home to England. So, twenty-five years later, we have to clear up the mess – or the Bangladeshis do.'

Anand was impressed. Both his parents had been strongly opposed to partition, had believed that India's best chance was as a united country. He only vaguely remembered the late-night family discussions on the subject when he was still at school and wished they had both not died so young. He missed them. He noticed Gordon's prominent Adam's apple as he swallowed. Poor chap, he looked out of his depth against Deviani in full anti-colonial combat mode.

'Well, obviously,' said Gordon, swallowing again, 'I want India to win this war and Bangladesh to be free but as for . . . I went to the Soviet Union on a holiday three years ago, one of those bus trips. There was an Anglican vicar on it and an Australian trade unionist. We came into the outskirts of Moscow and there was a bunch of women working on the roads. The vicar said, "Oh, look, isn't that awful, the women have to work on the roads," and the Aussie trade unionist said, "Oh, look, isn't that great, women have real equality here." So I suppose you see what you want to see . . .' He petered out. Deviani gave a silent snort.

'How very much the British diplomat,' said Anand, glancing round at Gordon. They did not have much in the way of politics, these wanderers, he thought.

Vivek seemed preoccupied. Perhaps he was starting to wonder if it was right to be playing cricket on such a day. There was no sign of any other game as they approached the ground. The playing fields seemed deserted.

' "No Lords this year",' Anand recited, recalling suddenly Kipling's poem about the Eton and Harrow match being cancelled during the First World War because the young players would be taking guard on the battlefields of France.

'Where's that from?' asked Gordon.

'Kipling. Don't you know your Kipling?'

'Only "If " . . . and . . . er . . . some of the Jungle stories, I'm afraid.'

Anand sighed. 'Oh, turn right here, Vivek, there's the pitch over there.'

Some of the other team had arrived and were going through the preparatory rituals of stretching and catching practice. Vivek shook hands with the opposing captain and introduced him to Anand and Gordon. Deviani lay down with the morning's papers on the rug that Vivek spread out for her over the dusty brown grass.

'Ah, you have brought in a ringer from the MCC, have you?' said the other captain.

'That's right,' said Anand. 'This is Ken Barrington in a wig. We hoped you wouldn't realise. Any news, by the way?'

'The war? Looks like it's going to be an innings victory for us. I heard on the wireless that the Pakistanis are stampeding to surrender. If this was a game of cricket, I think the Indian army would have declared by now.'

'Don't be too sure,' said Vivek. 'I heard the Americans are sending more arms to Pakistan.'

'Too late, I say, too late,' said the captain. 'Shall we toss up?'

Gordon crouched down between Deviani and Anand on the boundary. Anand noted that Gordon was taking care to see that the flies of the borrowed cricket flannels, which were missing a couple of buttons, did not flop open.

'D'you like cricket?' Gordon asked Deviani.

'I like watching Vivek behaving out of character, shouting at the umpire and so on,' she said. 'I like the sound of the bat and the ball . . .'

'Leather on willow,' Anand offered.

'Leather on willow,' she repeated. 'I like that sound. It's comforting. It reminds me of my childhood.'

'Your childhood?' Anand smiled at her. It seemed strange to hear someone who could not have been much more than twenty talking about their childhood as though it was a far-off land.

'My father used to play,' she said. 'There were games with the British who had "stayed on" after '47. Maybe it was because I was a child or maybe it was because it was such a hopeful time. We were a new country, the world's biggest democracy, all that stuff, you know, perhaps all of that percolated down. Care for a cigarette, Gordon?'

He reached for his bidis and showed them to her.

'I don't know how you can smoke them, I think they're disgusting,' she said. 'Don't you want a real cigarette?' She offered him a Scissors.

'We've won the toss and we're batting because the pitch looks like it might start to break up later,' said Vivek as he returned from the middle. 'Gordon, I'm putting you in at number six on the grounds that you may be understating your abilities.'

'I promise you I'm not, I haven't played since school,' said Gordon, stubbing out his cigarette and rising to his feet.

'Well, he should be nice and fresh,' said Anand.

'Get your pads on, Anand,' said Vivek. 'And let's win this one for our glorious jawans.'

Anand padded up and twirled his bat a few times. Gordon offered to bowl to him in the makeshift net, watched by the crowd of small boys who ooooed when the ball went wide and aaaahhhed when Anand clumped it over Gordon's head. Cricket had been Anand's comforter from an early age, when he had discovered as a schoolboy that he could bowl a ball to hit the playing card that his cricket master had laid down on the pitch as a test of accuracy. Apart from nights of jazz at Ronnie's or the Three Bells, cricket had been his main escape from the chill of London, the condescension of some of his lecturers and professors who never even bothered to learn his name properly.

'Are you going to score a century, Anand?' asked Deviani as he prepared to walk out with his opening partner, a pockmarked young man who, Vivek said, captained his school team the previous year. 'Is that what you do?'

Anand smiled at her. How serious was Vivek about her? He seemed to have a new girlfriend every time he saw him. He tried to banish all non-cricketing thoughts from his mind as he took middle-and-leg guard. Banished the death of Remy, the broken water cistern and his unanswered letters to Nii and Vanessa, banished the war and whether he could have been doing more for the refugees, banished that strange note, 'PLEASE TREAT MY DEATH AS SUSPICIOUS', slipped under his door – could that have been a fearful Remy? – banished Baba's incongruous appearance in a suit on the street.

He flashed at the first ball which shot past his off stump. He was rusty. Must concentrate. He tapped his bat into the crease and tucked his ruby red cap down over his eyes.

A maiden over. He consulted briefly with his opening partner in between the overs and sighed as the young man flashed twice, missed twice and connected with his third ball to give an easy catch to first slip. The other side cheered and gathered in a self-congratulatory huddle as he trudged off with his duck and his ragged complexion. Cricket is such a cruel game, thought Anand.

Vivek joined him in the middle and by the next over Anand was back in his dreamland. The balls came magically to the middle of his bat. He cracked two boundaries through mid-wicket that were drawn like heat-seeking missiles to the side of Deviani. She stretched out an elegantly bangled hand to field one although, he had to admit, she threw it back like a girl, arm bending at the elbow.

By the time the drinks tray arrived, he and Vivek had put on 64. The opposition were starting to look dishevelled. They brought on their spin bowlers, one of them a young chap who could not have been more than thirteen, but to no avail. The sun shone. Vivek was clean bowled taking a swipe and the number four went for a golden duck but Anand was still cracking the ball wherever he wished. He was 72 not out and the team were at a comfortable 133 for three as he doffed his cap and strode in for lunch.

'Excellent stuff,' said Gordon. 'A pleasure to watch.'

'So you are following my instructions and scoring a century,' said Deviani, still in her mock-posh voice.

'Of course, memsahib,' said Anand, disappearing discreetly behind the sightscreen before emerging with his box in his hand.

'Why do you all have such big protector things?' asked Deviani. 'Do you think we are all fooled by them?'

'I think you have been reading too much Nabokov and not enough Wisden,' said Anand. 'Where are the cucumber sandwiches?' He mock-foraged through the tiffin carriers.

'Wrong country,' said Deviani. 'Ah,' she said, looking at Gordon, 'you can tell me, as an Englishman—'

'Scotsman.'

'I apologise. But you can still tell me. Where does the expression "cool as a cucumber" come from? What is cool about a cucumber?' She stretched out the word 'cool' deliciously.

'It is the shape, of course,' said Vivek, opening a bottle of Kingfisher.

'Now, now,' said Anand.

A jet roar filled the sky and he looked upwards. Six planes from the Indian air force were flying overhead in sweet formation, bound for Bangladesh and glory.

Chapter Fifteen

HUGH WONDERED VAGUELY what 'protocols' they were meant to be observing at the PoW camp. They were greeted by an Indian air force officer who gestured at the vast pile of trophies arranged neatly, like a bring-and-buy sale, at the entrance to the makeshift prison.

Boxes of ammunition with labels on them showing two hands joined in front of the American flag and the words 'In Friendship' written below. Gas masks, berets, helmets, boots, hand grenades and shells. How Laurence Corner, the shop in Chalk Farm, which sold army surplus goods and where he had bought an RAF greatcoat when a student at East Anglia, would have loved it all, thought Hugh. There were also bundles of notebooks and buff envelopes on a low trestle table. He picked up a notebook from the pile.

'Individual Training Record Book,' it said in English. 'Army Press, Karachi. 1282625, Bashir Hussain Sha DMT. F-21. 2 Troop 6MT TRG BTY.' He could not read the rest, except for the page at the back which said 'football – full back'. He wondered idly for a moment why the Pakistanis, so good at cricket and hockey, were not a force at football.

There were identity cards, too, presumably of dead soldiers, tucked neatly into envelopes.

He saw the French photographer grab a helmet and slip it under his jacket with a slightly shamefaced grin. Hugh pocketed a few regimental badges as souvenirs. He would give one to Henry.

Inside the compound, the mood was restrained. Half a dozen Pakistani soldiers were having what looked like mutton with dhal and rice. Outside the compound, a group of locals had gathered, gazing on as the captured troops, their tormentors, ate.

The Pakistani prisoners-of-war were neatly dressed and fit-looking, the opposite of the traditional images of the PoW with which Gordon had grown up through films: the starving figures from *Bridge Over the River Kwai*; the jolly, truculent Brits from *The Colditz Story*; or the glossy, well-fed film stars of *The Great Escape*. The Colonel Bogey tune from *Bridge Over the River Kwai* flashed through his head: 'Hitler has only got one ball/ Goering has two but they are very small/ Himmler/ Has something sim'lar/ But poor old Goebbels/ Has no balls at all . . .' Did the Bangladeshis have their own war songs, he wondered, that mocked Pakistan's leader, Yahya Khan, and their general, Tiger Niazi?

A group of prisoners approached them, gesturing at Britt not to take their pictures.

'No photos, I'm afraid,' said the press officer. 'Geneva Convention. Protocol.'

'Can we interview them?' asked Hugh.

'If they are agreeable, yes,' said the press officer.

They were agreeable and quite cocky for a defeated army facing allegations of genocide, thought Hugh. They were not prepared to give their names but seemed to feel they had been let down by their commanders. More than one pointed out that they were heavily outnumbered by the Indian armed forces. 'There are one million, two hundred thousand of them and only four hundred thousand of us,' said one plaintively, like a small boy complaining of an unbalanced football match. 'We can fight again,' said one with a small moustache.

Were they being well treated? Hugh asked. His latest hangover was a bother in the heat. He wished he had packed more bottled water. A breeze had dried the sweat. His shirt, freshly washed by the hotel's efficient laundry service, already felt sticky.

'Oh, yes, we are being very well looked after – although the rice is overdone,' twinkled one of the officers. 'Where are you from? Oh, yes, London, very good. I know Bayswater well. How is Bayswater?'

'Oh, I think Bayswater is . . . much as it was,' said Hugh. 'What happens to you now, do you know?'

'We are going for a little holiday in India,' said the officer.

Outside the compound, the crowd of indignant locals, some carrying empty pots and plates, had grown. There were sounds of spasmodic gunfire nearby. 'Mopping up,' said the press officer to the unasked question.

The Indian air force officer in charge of the encampment spoke genially but without the specifics that Hugh wanted about what was happening elsewhere in what now seemed to be an inevitable Indian victory. They were shown the medical facility, as if to prove that the wounded prisoners were being well looked after. Hugh and the reporter from Bangalore tried a few perfunctory questions but the wounded PoWs were reluctant to talk. They looked bored and embarrassed.

Hugh watched Britt climb into the van; he could hear Henry's distant voice saying, 'Halll-ooo!'

How on earth could she have ended up in bed with Gordon McGrady? Wasn't she worried about catching something from him? God, McGrady didn't look as if he'd had a bath since he left Britain. He had always been a smart alec at school, one of the 'awkward squad', as the headmaster called them, the bolshies who thought it was clever to smoke Gauloises behind the fives court and wear mohair sweaters.

Hugh wondered how well McGrady remembered what happened that day in the showers. He knew McGrady had been there when Farquar-Fox had been held under the water in the bath. Not that Hugh had initiated it. All that he had done was tell F-F, as they called him, to stop blubbing. Then Farquar-Fox had gone to the gym after lights out one night, put a rope round his neck, looped it over a beam, stood on a rugby ball and kicked the ball away. Topped himself.

He remembered the sight of Mrs Farquar-Fox – divorcee, wasn't she? – arriving at the school, handkerchief clutched to her pinched face, with the headmaster awkwardly taking her arm. And he remembered being summoned to the headmaster's study, to answer questions about whether he knew that Farquar-Fox was being bullied. Well, everyone knew, didn't they? Was he one of the people who had held him under water? the headmaster asked him. He had been able to say, in all honesty, no. Then someone had pinned up a notice on the school noticeboard with a list of the boys who had bullied Farquar-Fox and his name had been on it. It had been signed 'Farquar-Fox's Avengers' with a little bowler hat symbol drawn on it. Was McGrady one of those avengers? But that was all – what? – ten years ago now.

He knew McGrady had gone into advertising after being kicked out of Sussex University for doing bugger all and had been writing jingles and stuff. There had been a vague rumour at an OSG reunion that he was living in some commune or squat where everyone slept with everyone else. He wondered what McGrady's parents, who must have spent a good few quid on educating him, felt about it: their son a fully paid-up hippy, complete with beads and bell-bottoms. It was OK to do that kind of thing when you were a student. Hugh himself had tried a joint with Jackie in his last year at East Anglia but, by now – well, their meeting said it all, really. Here he was, a Fleet Street war correspondent, and there was McGrady – Low Grady – wandering around like one of the Lost Boys in *Peter Pan*. He doubted that McGrady's name would be appearing in the Old Boys' Notes section of the school magazine along with the people who had actually achieved something, former pupils who had been chosen for the British Lions tour of New Zealand or had become junior cabinet ministers or big cheeses in ICI.

Britt was obviously not quite as bright as she had appeared, clearly a couple of sandwiches short of a picnic, as Henry would say. Just as well he hadn't made an effort there, she probably had some sexually transmitted disease up her sleeve. But he had to admit that, as she dozed now in tight jeans, her long legs splayed apart and her head against the van's window, she did look rather fanciable.

To distract himself, he started formulating his story. 'The men of (CHECK REGIMENT) of the Pakistani army are going, they said, for "a little holiday" in India. They are amongst the tens of thousands of Pakistani troops who have now surrendered to the Indian army, which appears to be on the eve of victory in the war for the independence of Bangladesh . . .'

'Yes?' came that familiar Welsh voice as Hugh read the paragraph through five hours later from the phone in his hotel room with a towel round his waist and a glass of cold Kingfisher in his hand. Why was the telex machine still not working? Why did he always have to get Ifor when he phoned through his copy? Where were all the other copy-takers? 'Yes?'

'Just a mo . . . can't read my writing.' Hugh could hear the sigh coming down the line from the poky little basement room where the copy-takers were entombed. 'Ah, yes . . . here's where I was . . . In the streets of Khulna, that's K for Kilo, H for Hero, U for Unicorn, L for Lima, N for Noddy . . . NODDY . . . You know, Noddy and Big Ears . . . I'm sorry, I didn't realise you'd got it already . . . the price for collaboration was already being paid stop. A small group of young girls comma aged as young as thirteen and fourteen comma was being rounded up by angry vigilantes stop. Their offence colon associating with the Pakistani invading forces . . . I'm sorry, it's a bad line . . . Where had we got to? Their pitiful costumes of brightly coloured dresses acted as a jarring counterpoint to the sight of Indian tanks majestically driving through the streets stop. New par.

'Garlands of sunflowers . . . Sunflowers . . . Yes, I know what a sunflower looks like . . . Well, if they aren't indigenous to Bangladesh, maybe they were imported. They looked like sunflowers to me . . . You say they would have been marigolds? Well, I was there . . . Well, orange flowers if you want . . . I've lost my place now.'

Hugh's towel had slipped and he noted with minor anguish the swelling belly that Linda had remarked on and that Jackie was continually drawing his attention to, suggesting exercise: squash, perhaps. As though he had time for that. Why was she bothered anyway? They hardly had sex any more. Despite all the effort he had made with foreplay and all the stuff you had to do nowadays. The last straw had been when he had been diligently massaging her clitoris for at least ten minutes and she had told him not to bother because an orgasm was just a 'vaginal sneeze' anyway. A vaginal sneeze! God, what next? At least Linda had no complaints. His beer was finished and another bottle was cooling in the basin just out of arm's reach. He eyed it.

'Hang on a sec,' he said. 'Someone at the door with a press release. I'll be right back.' He scuttled naked across the room, picked up the bottle, opened it neatly with his

Swiss Army knife bottle opener and started pouring. He knew from Ifor's abrupt 'Yes?' that he must have heard the fizz of the beer as the top came off.

'Garlands of orange flowers were slung across the gun barrels of the Indian army tanks as they snaked across the city to cheers of open single quotes cap J Jai – that's J-A-I – cap B for Bravo Bangla exclamation mark. Jai Bangla exclamation mark Jai Bangla exclamation mark . . . Yes, three Jai Banglas. All with an exclamation mark. Yes, THREE . . . Well, in fact, there were many more. To be strictly accurate, we should have about three or four hundred but I somehow don't think the foreign desk would be terribly happy if – OK, OK. Leave it at two, then, that's fine. I've forgotten where I was again.' He drained the last of the Kingfisher, stifled a belch and was admiring the logo on the bottle when he heard the dreaded words.

'Is there much more of this?'

There was not. Indian troops advancing in the west, sinking of Pakistani destroyer, some Pakistani troops supposedly fleeing to Burma. He signed off after checking the word count. Ifor told him that the foreign desk wanted a word and transferred him.

'Hello, mate,' said Max. 'Good stuff. How's it going? When do you think it's going to end? Going to be back for the Christmas party? Someone here is anxious to know . . . Hughie.'

Oh, God.

'You still there?' Max had lowered his voice to an ominous conspiratorial whisper. 'Yes, Linda asked me to let you know she was asking after you. You haven't been "freelancing", have you? Just joking. Anyway, I'm just passing that on since her boyfriend's a trained killer . . . Hey, calm down, only joking . . . Keep up the good work. Speak to you same time tomorrow.'

Hugh lay back naked on the bed. 'Christ on crutches,' he muttered under his breath. His nose had gone quite red in the sun and there was a V of raw red flesh below his neck. He rang Jackie. No answer again. Where on earth was she? She should have been home from school. He looked at his chest and saw a blue stain below the heart. The bloody ink had run in his pocket again.

Chapter Sixteen

A S THE CRICKET CONTINUED at a dreamy, comforting pace, Gordon felt the effects of the almost sleepless night, his mind wandering to the long kisses from Britt. Phew. He felt dizzy, breathless with – what was it? Desire? Infatuation? Love? Would he see her tonight? Was this a one-nighter? Surely not. It was too perfect. She was too perfect. She was so beautiful, so lively. He pictured her naked again, the dusting of freckles over her breasts, the long legs draped languidly over the side of the bed. Maybe she would come to Thailand with him. They could go to Phuket together, lie on the beaches at night. She could take pictures and they would visit the temples in Chiang Mai. Then maybe Rangoon? The Burmese Embassy was not far away and visas for a week's visit were easy to get. For a moment, the image of Remy and that neat necklace of blood cast a shadow. Love and death. Was this all a teaching? Death and love.

Gordon wandered behind the pavilion, or rather the groundsman's hut that was doubling as a pavilion, and took two brief hits from the joint with which Larry had greeted him that morning. Wooooh, strong stuff. Bit too strong.

He strolled back to join Deviani at the boundary, with a purposeful 'I-am-not-stoned' gait.

To try to centre himself, he flicked through the newspapers beside her on the rug. Whole-page advertisements punctuated the war reports in *The Standard*.

SHED A LITTLE BLOOD FOR YOUR COUNTRY!
Our jawans need it now. Donate blood.

(Issued by Coca-Cola)

'Coca-Cola are asking us to donate blood,' he said. He glanced up at the cricket: 'Oh, lovely shot!'

'Coca-Cola,' said Deviani, 'are terrified that they will lose sales because the American government is supporting Pakistan.'

'This is better,' said Gordon. He read out aloud: ' "SWITCH OFF THOSE HEADLIGHTS – you're on GEC Street . . . Give what you can to our boys at the front: cigarettes, matches, ballpoint pens, shampoos, hair pomade, combs, toilet soap." ' He looked up from the newspaper at Deviani. 'It's interesting what they reckon soldiers need most, isn't it? Hair pomade? I dunno. My granny said that, in the First World War, you could get Fortnum and Mason to send hampers to a young man at the front and they would include drugs, morphine – "fear banishers" I think they were called. All legal in those days. I think that's what I would want at the front rather than hair pomade. How about you?'

Deviani gave him the hint of a smile. He found another

page and flattened the paper out so that he could read it properly. An ant crawled over his wrist.

FATHER SAW THE GLIMPSES
DAUGHTER MAKES THE HISTORY

(CI Brewery)

'And how about this one?

ARMY BOTTLES IN THE EAST
THROTTLES IN THE WEST

(MHB Ltd. HO Solom Brewery)

'Which glimpses did Father see?' he asked Deviani.

'Ah, Nehru saw the glimpse of a great free nation, our tryst with destiny – "May that star never set and that hope never be betrayed" – an example to all the other colonies,' she said. 'He also saw the glimpse of Lady Mountbatten's suspender belt, I think. How long are you staying in our country?'

'Well, I've been here for nearly four months. I love it but I suppose at some stage I will have to move on. I have to get to Hong Kong and earn some money.'

'Can't you earn money here?'

'I'm not sure there's a great demand for unemployed advertising copywriters,' said Gordon. 'I don't think I could compete with "Bottles in the west, Throttles in the east" anyway.'

'So you're an advertising copywriter,' she said.

He could spot the note of mild disdain in her voice.

'I'm a recovering advertising copywriter.'

'So now you travel the world seeking enlightenment from the ancient civilisations, reading the *Bhagavad Gita* for inspiration and ending up on a holy mountain somewhere.'

'Something like that. Oh, nice shot, Anand.'

Deviani had a cigarette in her mouth. Gordon stretched across and lit it with what he realised was Larry's precious lighter. He must have popped it into his pocket without thinking. She cupped his hand to shield the flame from the slight breeze. They switched their attention to the game. Anand skipped down the pitch and dispatched a ball for six, to the delight of the growing swarm of small boys who fought one another for the honour of throwing it back. The next over, Anand's partner was clean bowled.

'You're in, old man,' said Vivek, giving Gordon a close look. 'You OK?'

'Acha,' said Gordon. He strode to the wicket. Anand came from his crease to greet him and patted him amiably on the arm. Gordon found it hard to reconcile this agile sportsman with the slightly crumpled and world-weary landlord who took his rent.

Anand was on 82. Gordon remembered enough from his last game at school, eight years earlier, to know that all he had to do was let Anand have the bowling. He poked and prodded and caught one ball painfully in the stomach. Another one rattled his box and what Mr Blackwood, his cricket master, used to refer to heartily as the 'crown jewels'. He limped down the pitch and received a sympathetic pat from Anand. Strange and wonderful, he thought, playing cricket in Calcutta, the warm sun at your back, the breeze billowing your shirt, the memory of Britt, slim and naked, as she pulled on her clothes and grinned at him. Remy's shadow again. The bounce of the ball seemed about twice as high and hard as it had been on all those damp, green Scottish pitches of his schooldays. Concentrate.

Anand was now on 98. He strolled down the pitch towards Gordon.

'You OK?'

'Sure,' said Gordon. Didn't he look OK? That grass had been strong but if he really, REALLY concentrated, it all seemed clear enough. He had scored four, admittedly all off the edge of the bat but they counted the same in the scorebook, as Mr Blackwood had said. He thought about Britt, how grand it would be if she was on the boundary now, how he could have explained the rules of cricket to her. Life was good. He watched as the bowler came in to bowl at Anand and then spotted far, far in the distance six more fighter planes, presumably of the Indian air force, in perfect formation, jet streams threading through the sky behind them, sun gleaming on their wings and flashing off their cockpits. What a sight. What must it be like to be one of those young pilots, flying off to war? He remembered when he first started growing his hair long as a student and his father had asked disdainfully if he minded looking like a 'nancy boy' and his mother had defended him by saying that all the Battle of Britain pilots had long hair and wore silk scarves. He barely heard the shouts around him.

'Yes! Yes! Two runs there!' seemed to be coming from the far end.

'Run, for God's sake, run!' was coming from the boundary, as if in stereo. And there were the shrieks of the small boys. What was—

Oh, God, he suddenly saw Anand standing inches from him and realised what was happening. He started to run to the other end but his feet would barely move, as happened sometimes in his nightmares when he would be fleeing some horror and waking to find his legs entangled in the sheets. He skidded and saw Anand himself double back but too late to get to the crease before a delighted wicket-keeper had whipped off the bails. Anand shook his head, apparently not hearing Gordon's pained, 'Sorry, realllllly sorry,' as he retreated. Oh, God. All the euphoria of the day and previous night evaporated. He had cost his landlord the chance of a century, thrown away their best batsman's wicket, made a fool of himself. He could barely exchange a word with the new batsman, a thin fellow with sunken cheeks who did not look as if he would be able to hit the ball far but proceeded to smash his first two deliveries for boundaries.

Partly so that he did not have to confront Anand too swiftly and partly out of contrition, Gordon concentrated harder than ever now, although his forehead was pounding and the lack of sleep was starting to tell. The bowlers were weary and he was able to tuck away some balls down the leg, even hook a full toss to the boundary and generally assist his new partner to take the total over 200 before he was defeated by a shooter. He made his way back to the boundary and humiliation.

'I am so so SO sorry,' he said to Anand, who was having a cup of tea with Deviani and Vivek.

'Not to worry,' said Anand briskly. 'These things happen.'

'That's not what he said when he came back twenty minutes ago,' said Deviani mischievously.

'Now, now,' said Vivek. 'We're doing fine. The wicket is crumbling and we have a devastating spin attack that will rout them like the retreating Pakistani army. I am going to declare in another couple of overs anyway. It is good for Anand's karma – it will keep him humble.'

Deviani pressed a cigarette into Gordon's hand. It was the tea break. He savoured the tobacco and decided to change his brand once more. One of his aims when he left England had been to give up smoking but he had found it hard to resist the temptation when cigarettes were sold in ones or twos rather than just in packets of twenty. Many of the brands carried the whiff of empire in their names: Windsor, Regent, No. 10, Gaylord, Envoy. He deviated between Charminar, because of its gaudy yellow pack, and bidis at a paisa each.

Two boys who had been watching the cricket drifted past, eyeing the picnic. They paused and looked at Gordon.

'What country are you coming from?' asked the smaller of the two. 'And what is your good name?'

'Scotland. And Gordon.'

'And what is your purpose?' asked the older of the pair.

189

'Good question,' answered Gordon. The boy gave him an odd look.

'So what is your purpose?' asked Deviani as the boys wandered away. 'What brings you all here?'

'I travel for travel's sake,' said Gordon. 'The great affair is to move.'

'That sounds like something someone else said,' said Deviani.

'Yup, Robert Louis Stevenson. But there is something seductive about getting on a bus or a train in the morning and not knowing where you are going to end up sleeping at the end of the day. To be freed of your own . . . er . . . controls, I suppose.'

'But what exactly do you fellows do all day?' she asked.

'Us fellows?'

'You hippies.'

'Well, you spend a lot of time planning your next move.'

'Like chess?'

'Like chess but slower.'

She smiled at him. Was it the grass or did every woman now seem beguiling? He realised that he had not thought about Britt for more than ten minutes.

'And?' she asked.

'Well, there's a bit of sitting around and discussing where to stay in Benares – which ghat to go to, the Dashash . . . Dashashed . . .'

'Good try – it's Dashaswamedha,' said Deviani.

'. . . where to stay in Goa. There's a French junkie beach – Anjuna – and a beach where women can make ten rupees by posing with tourists – twenty rupees if they take their tops off. Where to get toddy there, just as the sun comes up. Then there's finding out where the best black-market rate is—'

'Is there much sex?'

Gosh, she's frank, thought Gordon.

'Hmmm. Well, men outnumber women by about five to one, I would say, and then there's quite a bit of hepatitis around which is not the greatest aphrodisiac.'

'Why do so many of you British boys come out here?'

'I dunno . . . because we can. We're the first generation for ages that didn't have to go off to war or do national service. I think maybe we feel that—'

'You have to have a little adventure, go zigzagging across the world.'

'Zigzagging, hmm. I think people are curious about the East, that it has something that the West lost. Or never had.'

'Isn't that a bit patronising?' She said it with a smile.

'Is it?'

'And do you all find enlightenment?'

'Some people find a sadhu—'

'Oh, they are such rogues.'

'Well, some people find a sadhu that suits them. I heard that some even go with their sadhus and have sex with dead bodies in Benares as a spiritual exercise but maybe that's just one of those apocryphal tales. You learn about your body, about breathing, how to see your throat like a swinging door so you learn how to breathe properly. Some go to Nepal and learn about Buddhism, some find a guru.'

'So it's Buddhism and gurus, is it? Hinduism a bit too

exotic for you, is it? All those monkey gods and elephant gods and women with lots of arms?'

'A bit too exotic for me, too,' said Anand who was rummaging around in the cricket bag, looking for old balls. 'Not that the British don't worship animals. Only different ones – they'd be Hindus if Ganesh was a labrador or a golden retriever.'

Deviani was not to be diverted. 'Your guest has been telling me that he has learned how to breathe since he came here.'

'Oh, that must be handy,' said Anand, distracted. 'Where have all the balls gone?'

'So what else have you found?' asked Deviani.

'I'm still looking. You know, we are all just souls seeking escape from illusion, aren't we?'

'So what have you learned?'

'Never assume.'

'And?'

'Don't water the seeds of your wrath.'

'And?'

'Don't grasp. Lose attachment. Attachment and unfulfilled desire are what lead to unhappiness. Try not to be judgemental.'

Lose attachment? All those weeks trying to lose attachment and now here he was longing – longing – for nothing more than to be attached to Britt. How did he explain that?

'And?'

'Isn't that enough for one day?' Gordon's mind flashed back to Edinburgh and his father, who had a homily for every occasion. 'The little more how much it is, the little less what miles away,' when they were weeding the garden together. 'Laugh and the world laughs with you, weep and you weep alone.' Were they any less profound?

'Why do you need to go to a holy man or study religion for that? That's just common sense. Be kind. Be just. Isn't that all there is to it? Organised religion is just about fear and guilt, you know, and trying to rationalise our terror of dying. Or our natural desire to belong to a pack. Do you all take drugs all the time?'

'Oh, well, there's a bit of that, mainly hash, Thai grass, a bit of peyote, psylocybin, magic mushrooms – the flesh of the gods – Mandies – Mandrax – morphine, but cocaine, too, people smuggle it around in the backs of their hairbrushes, in tubes of toothpaste . . .'

Deviani laughed at the idea of the hairbrush as a tool of the smuggler.

'What are Mandies?'

'They're like Quaaludes.'

'What are – Kway-loods?'

'They're like tranquillisers. They make you flop around and bump into walls.'

'Is that fun?'

'Not really my bag.' Gordon felt defensive but it was a relief to have a conversation that did not disappear into a hazy cul-de-sac. 'And there's heroin . . . Opium, there's quite a nice den here in Calcutta. A Chinese guy runs it.'

'Just like those old black-and-white American movies.'

'Yeah, the front of the house is like a tailor's, lots of women doing seamstress stuff and so on and then in a room at the back is the opium. They fire you up a pipe, give you a little mat with a wooden headrest and leave you to it.'

Deviani smiled. 'What is the great attraction of –' she searched for the right word – 'dope?'

'I don't know. I suppose it's like taking a little holiday from life, going into a magic garden. Seeing things with a different pair of eyes. It takes the edge off things. You laugh a lot. You're in the present, you know – "be here now". Moving from a black-and-white world to a technicolour one. First time I got stoned, I was listening to an LP and suddenly all the words made sense, they were the most brilliant, imaginative ideas in the world and I looked at the people I was smoking with and they were smiling back as though they knew exactly why I was smiling – it was like being welcomed into a fabulous club. Yes, I know, I know damage can happen . . .' The blackout, he thought, two now. Had that been the Peshawar morphine or just some too powerful Thai grass? What had happened in the missing hours between passing out and waking up?

Deviani frowned. 'Escaping into a magic garden.'

'If you like. It's hard to explain it unless you try it, it's like describing what chocolate or champagne is like to someone.'

She frowned again. 'Now Anand was telling me about that French fellow from the hotel who was killed in the cemetery.'

'Remy. Yes, it's pretty grim.'

'And someone left a little sign on his body. Isn't that frightening to you all?'

'Yeah, but no one can get out while the war's on.'

'Who do you think it is?'

'There are all kinds of rumours, that it was an Indian guy who wanted to drive out all the travellers. Or some psycho Vietnam vet, a sort of Charles Manson thing. There are some pretty odd guys on the road.'

'Aren't you worried?'

'I think walking across Chowringhee at night in the blackout is more risky.'

'So you are scared. Now, what do you all do for money?'

'It's pretty cheap to live. For a couple of hundred quid, three or four hundred dollars, you can live here for five or six months. Some people send dope home, or rugs, perhaps. Some of them get caught and have to pay lawyers to bribe magistrates to get 'em out. There are a few in jail who didn't have the money. In fact, quite a few end up locked up or deported. Or you can sell your watch or send back matchbox models of people making love in strange positions from the Khajuraho temples. I think they sell for a fiver in London now. Some people's families send them money, the new remittance men.' He watched Anand and Vivek traversing the boundary, Anand glancing at his wristwatch.

'When I came down from Nepal, there was a guy who had burned his passport as a symbol of his liberation from samsaric values and he was stuck in no-man's-land at the border. The Indian immigration people wouldn't let him in and the Nepalese wouldn't let him cross back into Nepal. He's probably still there now.'

'And what about the politics?'

'Not a lot. There are Americans who either were in

Vietnam and want to forget it or have been drafted and are on the run.'

'What about this war?'

'Oh, everyone wants India to win, I'm sure.'

'Have you met any of the refugees from Bangladesh?'

'I haven't.'

'You can come with me and meet some if you like,' said Deviani. 'I'm going to be working in the dispensary at one of the camps tomorrow. D'you want to come to Gobindapur with me?'

'Come along now,' said Vivek, looming up behind them. 'The umpires are going out. You shouldn't be so hard on him, Deviani. All these hippies are rescuing Eastern culture from the condescension of imperialism which thought that nothing east of Athens was worth a fig. Anyway, let's go and get these chaps out.' Deviani and Gordon exchanged glances.

The skies were darkening as they took the field. The other side were chasing a total of 222 and, despite Vivek's confidence, they soon seemed well on the way to reaching it, hurrying, lest rain fall, to 180 for four. Vivek beckoned Gordon over.

'Take the next over, would you?'

'Oh, I'd rather not, after what happened. I haven't bowled for ages.'

'Well, try one over. Badeshi thinks he's pulled a muscle and can't bowl any more.'

Gordon felt the dark clouds of dread descend again. Since God had let him down badly with his A-level exams when he was seventeen and he had barely scraped into

Sussex, he had never prayed for anything else. Was there some guidance in what he had learned in India and Nepal about the way the mind can command? He thought of what Deviani had asked about enlightenment. As he rubbed the ball feebly on his flannels and saw the looks of vague apprehension on the fielders' faces, he summoned up the Buddhist teachings from that first week in Kathmandu. Lose attachment, he told himself, do not grasp. Attachment is the cause of suffering. He let the ball escape freely from his hand.

'Wide!' said the umpire rather unnecessarily loudly, throwing his arms out to the side like a startled penguin.

Do not grasp, Gordon told himself again as he tried to alter his run-in.

'Wide!' came the shout. Deviani was staring out from the boundary with her hand over her eyes. Was she shielding them from the sun? Or was she covering her face to hide her laughter?

'Don't worry,' said Vivek, polishing the ball energetically on his sleeve. 'Just take it easy. Give it a bit of air.'

Gordon drew a deep breath. Water, if you do not stir it, becomes still, he remembered from his teachings. The mind left unaltered will find peace. He tried to empty his mind. There. That seemed empty now. He ran in and bowled again, lofting the ball high into the air. Almost immediately he could hear the derisive cries of the little boys even before the opposing batsman had dispatched the ball, one bounce, for four. Oh, God, was he going to deliver victory to the other team before the end of the over? He longed for an intervention, a Pakistani air raid would be perfect.

He threw the ball up again and the batsman took a nonchalant swing at it, gazing towards the boundary and the ball's intended destination. Too nonchalant. The ball clipped the top of his bat and soared directly upwards.

'Mine!' shouted the wicketkeeper. He pouched the catch and Vivek slapped Gordon on the back.

'There you are. Easy, eh?'

Gordon remained filled with dread. He still had to bowl four more balls. The batsmen had crossed so he was faced with another man with his eye in and 42 already to his name. Oh, Ganesh, God of obstacles, assist me, he muttered inwardly, and I will do something to repay you. Why does it matter? Why does this upset me more than Remy's death? he asked himself. He skipped in again, once more getting the run-in wrong and ending up throwing a dolly ball into the air. Again came the contemptuous swipe and the ball headed for the boundary, for six.

But some deity had heard Gordon's pleas. The batsman had not quite middled the ball and it hovered a few yards inside the boundary as Anand sprinted towards it and took a masterly catch five or six feet short of an indistinctly marked white line. More backslaps, more cheers, although Gordon was not so elated that he did not detect an ounce or two of mockery in the hurrahs of the small boys.

'Hat-trick ball!' called Vivek, clapping his hands and putting his side on alert.

The new batsman, immaculately turned out, could not have been more than eighteen. He took middle stump guard and surveyed the field placings like an ancient general checking the battle formation of his lancers. Gordon, guided for a moment by at least one of the gods he had summoned, glided in and bowled an off-spinner which pitched perfectly and spun in about ten inches, clipping the bails before the young man had even had a chance to move his bat from its elegant forward defensive position. Vivek embraced Gordon and Anand ran in from the boundary as the rest of the team gathered round, slapping his back.

Oh, if only that was the end of the over, thought Gordon. The new batsman had arrived, flustered, and was taking guard. The fielders gathered round, turkey vultures who had spied the carrion of a collapsing batting side. Gordon bowled again, over-pitched this time, but the batsman was so nervous that he prodded it forward and in the air. Gordon saw the ball come towards him as if in slow motion, felt it strike his chest, felt it in his hands and his fingers round it as it bounced forward from his breastbone. Then suddenly he was on his back holding the ball triumphantly in the air.

The rest of the over, two more wides, a full toss that went for two, passed in a daze. He did not have to ask Vivek to take him off.

'Fabulous stuff,' said Anand when they passed in the field. 'And I use the word advisedly.'

One of the opening bowlers wrapped up the tail for another two runs. It was time for handshakes, putting all the gear in canvas cricket bags and heading back through the evening streets of Calcutta.

'So you are the hero of the day,' said Deviani as they drove back. 'The hippy hero.'

'Except I ran out our star batsman two runs short of his century,' said Gordon.

'All is forgiven,' said Anand, as they passed the Maidan, the vast park in the city's centre, en route to the hotel. 'That final catch will live in the memory. See the Maidan on the left there? That's where the first ever game of cricket was played in Calcutta. The first ever century was scored there, too. The Old Etonians played against Calcutta which, I think, in those days, consisted of swells from the East India Company.'

'Like my great-great-grandfather,' said Gordon.

'A little before even his time, I think,' said Anand. 'The game was in 1804, I think. They didn't allow us to play for a while.'

'But I think we were allowed to serve them gin and tonics afterwards, weren't we?' said Vivek.

'And carry the sofas into the marquee,' said Anand.

Vivek and Deviani dropped them off at the Lux. Anand patted him on the back as he went off to his own quarters. A shower, if the water was on again, a change and then . . . well, down to the Oberoi Grand. Would Britt be back yet with the convoy?

Larry, Freddie, Karen and Kieran were all gathered in the room. Remy's belongings had been packed into a battered kitbag and placed by the door. Somehow that was a sadder sight than Remy dead. Mudd the monk was already stretched out on Remy's bed, apparently asleep.

Nodding at Gordon, Larry picked up his guitar and sat

on his bed. He started singing, to the tune of the song 'Chicago': 'Benares is my kind of town, Benares is . . .'

'The burning-ghat,' suggested Gordon, singing along. 'That's where it's at . . .'

'In old Benares,' sang Larry and Gordon together.

'You can drink a lassi,' sang Gordon, the words suddenly coming to him, 'right here in Varanasi . . .'

Karen burst into tears and ran from the room. Kieran shot them a look which said, 'Have you guys got no fucking compassion?' and strode after her.

'Bad taste?' asked Larry.

'I guess,' said Gordon. 'But Remy would not have expected anything better from us. I'm going for a shower.'

'No water,' said Larry.

Gordon walked across the courtyard and coaxed a pencil-thin jet from the showerhead. He reached into the tiny alcove beside the shower and saw, balanced on the collected slivers of soap, a glistening razor. Mudd's? Should he leave it there? What if Mudd was mad? Hard to tell when you couldn't engage him in conversation. He seemed pretty serene but that was what people said about Dr Crippen.

Gordon washed his hair and under his arms. The crotch rot seemed to have abated. He returned to the room to dry himself with an increasingly threadbare towel.

'Hot date?' asked Larry.

'Don't be jealous, it's not a pretty emotion,' said Gordon, selecting his clean white kurta which Baba had just retrieved for him from the laundry. There was a tap at the door and a young Indian man in a shiny suit walked in

Duncan Campbell

with a badly wrapped parcel under his arm. He nodded at Larry.

Larry nodded back. 'Let's go into the courtyard for a moment and settle up, amigo. See you later, O enlightened one. Treat her right.'

Gordon half walked, half ran down Chowringhee. Spiderman was in pursuit. Feeling cheered by the cricket, the impending end of the war, the victory over crotch rot and, most crucially, the prospect of taking Britt in his arms again, Gordon handed him five rupees. Was that the hint of a smile on Spiderman's normally unforgiving face?

Within seconds, it seemed, he was at the reception of the Oberoi Grand. He smiled at the receptionist. Everyone was his friend today.

'Hi, I wonder if you could ring Ms Britt Pedersen's room?'

He heard a cough at his side and smelled a faintly familiar whiff of beery breath.

'She's gone,' said Hugh Dunn. 'She's gone to Dhaka to cover the victory celebrations. I doubt she'll be back.'

Chapter Seventeen

WHEN HIS GUESTS were out, Anand liked to wander through their rooms. They were strange creatures, both knowing and naive, organised enough to cross continents on tiny sums of money, yet almost childlike in their tastes and habits.

The main dormitory room was empty, its inhabitants scattered across Calcutta, hunting down their travel agents to try to secure their exit routes. Some, he suspected, just kept moving because the journey had become an end in itself, a chance to put off all the difficult choices spread in front of the educated Western young. As long as they were on the road, they could imagine that they were Jack Kerouac or Siddhartha.

He was always keen to see what they were reading. Vanessa had once told him that you could learn all you needed to know about people from their bookshelves and their bathrooms, both of which were mirrors of the person's perception of themselves. By the beds in the dormitory, there were all the usual suspects: Hesse and Tolkien, Burroughs and Henry Miller, Gibran's *The Prophet*, *Catch-22*, of course, and the standard paperback *Bhagavad Gita*.

Who was reading Genet's *Our Lady of the Flowers*? he wondered. Richard Neville's *Play Power* was there, part of the hippy canon, he supposed. Richard Brautigan's *Trout Fishing in America*, another book that many of the young travellers seemed to carry. On the cover was a picture of the author and a woman, dressed much like many of his guests: old pinstriped waistcoat, beads, floral shirt, stovepipe hat, droopy moustache, rimless glasses for him; headband, boots, long skirt for her. 'Gone now the old fart' was how one chapter started. He skimmed through it, imagining that it was probably a good book to read if your attention span was limited. The chapters were short. One, entitled 'The Kool-Aid Wino', was barely two pages long.

There was a battered Penguin paperback of V. S. Naipaul's *An Area of Darkness*. Anand remembered the fuss in India when the book came out a few years earlier, the accusations that the country had been unfairly portrayed as a place where men evacuated their bowels by railway lines. Whoever was reading it – or possibly a previous owner – had turned down pages and underlined passages.

One underlined section was about Naipaul's encounter with a young American woman, one of a breed 'slumming' and 'scrounging' their way around the world. Towards the end of the book, underlined twice, was his conclusion that Calcutta was dead, having lost half its hinterland through partition and having also suffered a death 'of the heart'.

Naipaul's book had been the subject of much heated discussion between his parents about whether Bengal's greatest days, when it had led the country politically and intellectually, were now in the past. His father had contested the view that even to Indians, Calcutta now represented, as Naipaul suggested, 'crowds, cholera and corruption'. His mother had backed Naipaul.

He heard someone approaching along the corridor and replaced the book. Was this the police coming back to talk about Remy? They had indicated that, with the war on, the death of one foreign junkie was hardly a priority. Perhaps it was the French Consul.

Anand found most foreign consular staff unhelpful. A few weeks ago, he had had to take a young American called Curtis to the US Consulate to have him sent home after he had burned his passport and thrown away all of his clothes, apart from a pair of shorts. The consulate official had queried whether Curtis was genuinely American and had asked him, as a test, to 'tell me the name of the vice president of the United States'. Curtis turned to Anand and said, 'Hey, this guy is a fucking impostor – he doesn't even know the fucking vice president's name.' Which had made Anand wonder if maybe Curtis was not so mad.

He sniffed. The air was heavy with hash smoke. He himself had given up all smoking after Vanessa told him that the Wills's Whiffs he enjoyed were 'fantastically petit-bourgeois, only travelling salesmen and football managers in sheepskin coats smoke them, dear'.

Baba bustled in. Anand picked up the Naipaul book again and turned to the last passage that had been underlined.

'Do you think that Calcutta conveys crowds, cholera and corruption?'

Baba considered the idea. 'Crowds, yes. Cholera . . . hmmm. Corruption, yes.'

Anand picked up a copy of *Life* magazine. He glanced at its date. Only a few months old. A special issue on how young Americans felt – 'The New Shape of America', it was called. He flipped through it. There was a survey of the people most admired and most hated by American students. He skimmed it.

'Who would you think that young Americans admire most and hate most?' he asked Baba.

'Like Beatles and Elvis, hate Mr Nixon,' said Baba.

'How wrong you are,' said Anand, reading the magazine. 'Their heroes are John Wayne, Robert Kennedy and someone called Bill Cosby and they hate Fidel Castro and Ho Chi Minh.'

Baba seemed uninterested in the information. He shrugged and left.

Anand shook his head and resumed his anthropological literary dig. Was the feckless, cricket-playing Scot reading Naipaul? Or maybe it had just lain there, like the old copies of *Life* and *Oz* and *Rolling Stone*, to be pecked at in passing. He smiled as he recalled the dozy batting and the preposterous bowling of the previous day's cricket match. Or was it what the enigmatic American, Larry, was reading? Larry was one of the growing number of Americans funnelled to India because of the Vietnam war, either fleeing it or recovering from it. Would any of them make homes here? He doubted it. No, as he had travelled in Europe as a passer-by, so they travelled here. But why did they choose such strange role models, those holy men? It was as if he had gone to England and chosen to imitate an eccentric country vicar.

Who was reading Zola? Could Freddie Braintree be digesting *Germinal*, finding relevance in Zola's depiction of the 'grim struggle between capital and labour in a coalfield in northern France', as the blurb had it? Did they read these books or were they just accessories, something you carried with you like a saffron scarf or a Ganesh pendant, to make you mildly more exotic?

Beneath the Zola, he was touched to see Rabindranath Tagore's *The Religion of Man*, a series of lectures he had given in Oxford in the thirties. Again, the pages were turned down and again there were underlinings. One passage had been scored and exclamation marks placed in the margin.

Tagore had been talking about Western literature's emphasis on the malignant aspect of nature and how people of the West liked to spread their coat-tails on other people's thoroughfares and enjoyed 'the thrilling risk' even if it meant hurting other inoffensive people. Who had placed the exclamation marks there, beside 'the thrilling risk', and scrawled the words 'a risky thrill'?

At least someone was reading the literature of Bengal. Anand remembered his astonishment when he arrived in London to discover how ignorant the British were about Bengal, how few people had heard of Tagore, knew that he had returned his knighthood because of the Amritsar massacre – or knew of the massacre at all. While it was assumed that he himself would be familiar with Shakespeare and Wordsworth, Dickens and Austen, hardly anyone had read Tagore or Prem Chand. Of course, they had never heard of Shamsur Rahman and their eyes clouded over when he tried to describe what Rahman's poem, 'Alphabet, My Sorrowful Alphabet', was about. He knew more Kipling than they did. People would talk of 'the classics' but shake their heads when he asked them if they had read any of the *Mahabharata*, which was ten times the length of the *Iliad* and *Odyssey* combined. Even some of his film-loving friends were unfamiliar with Satyahit Ray and Mrinal Sen, let alone earlier directors like Barua and Bimal Roy, while it was taken as given that he would know the work of Godard, Pontecorvo, Fellini.

There were a couple of tapes of Ravi Shankar. He smiled. When they held that fund-raising concert for Bangladesh in New York in August, he had read in *The Times of India* how Ravi Shankar and his musicians had taken a long time to tune up because the lights were so fierce that it affected the strings of their instruments and the American audience had politely applauded the tuning up because they thought it was a musical number.

There was Turkish, Afghan, Iranian and Kashmiri music, presumably bought en route, with scrawled handwritten sleeve notes tucked into the cracked tape containers, mixed up with – what was this? 'Hello/Goodbye' sung by someone called Tim Buckley, who appeared to have a glass eye, Janis Joplin, Isaac Hayes, Jethro Tull, Country Joe and the Fish. Something called 'Weasles Ripped My Flesh'. The titles of some of the tapes had a sort of poetic quality to them although he was not quite sure what 'The Low Spark of High-heeled Boys' actually meant. If anything. No jazz, he noted, jazz lovers being too smart to end up in a hotel room five thousand miles from home, sleeping two feet away from someone with the same tastes as them in music, books, drugs and fashion.

He travelled back for a moment to the nights at Ronnie Scott's with Nii and Vanessa, with Ronnie on stage delivering his deadpan one-liners in between numbers: 'That was by Cole Porter – not *the* Cole Porter but a coal porter . . . We have in the band the finest bass player in the world – sadly, he's not with us tonight . . .' Anand loved the music there, remembered seeing a clarinettist called Monty Sunshine and wishing that he had such an easily memorable name. English people didn't seem able to handle 'Anand Bose'; they would call him 'Alan' or 'Annan' and pronounce his last name 'Bosey'. Other friends at LSE had taken him, just before he returned to India, to see a concert by a group – a 'supergroup', whatever that was – called Cream, which they said he would like because it was closer to jazz than pop. It had been a grim evening, music played far too loud by three strange-looking characters, one with red hair and an emaciated face, singing impenetrable words.

The guests' haversacks were neatly stacked. Here was a patchwork waistcoat, embroidered with love by some distant girlfriend, no doubt. What was that meant to evoke? A jester? Did they see themselves as jesters and tumblers?

Ah, the *I Ching*, of course. He had watched them sometimes, in the evenings, plotting their next moves by asking the *I Ching* to make up their minds for them. Throwing the coins and then turning to the book for the responses that they could interpret as they wanted. The book fell open at a page with a downturned corner. 'When decay has reached its climax, recovery will begin to take place,' said the message at the top of the page. Had someone found that helpful? For people from such a secular culture, they were strangely superstitious, asking each other what their signs were and nodding knowingly, as if being a Leo or a Capricorn carried some special cachet.

Baba returned with the morning newspapers. The bodies of twenty of Bangladesh's leading intellectuals had been found. Anand felt a stab of anger at the vindictive spite of it all. The retreating Pakistani army was already blowing up power stations and printing presses, destroying the infrastructure. Now they were wiping out the country's intellectual core, killing the people who could help Bangladesh fulfil her dreams. He remembered Nii telling him how the Belgians, when they abandoned their colonies in Africa, had smashed all the machinery as they left, throwing even typewriters out of windows, scuppering the old imperial vessel in the hope that those left on board would drown.

The sports pages had news of a charity cricket match to be held at Eden Gardens to raise money for the refugees, who would soon start travelling back to their homes in the new nation. The Nawab of Pataudi, Bedi and Wadekar were due to play. He would see if Vivek wanted to come to the game with him. That would give him a chance to inquire, ever so gently, about Deviani. Were she and Vivek a serious couple?

Two men, both in suits and ties, were at the door. Travel agents, no doubt, looking to finalise the post-war escape routes of his guests. But no, each politely produced his police identity card.

'Ah,' said Anand. 'You have come about poor Remy . . . Remy Duval.'

'Yes,' said the older of the two. 'Did he leave anything here? A suitcase? Could we see it?'

All of Remy's worldly goods were contained in the battered, khaki army kitbag, his name scrawled in Biro on the side. The older of the two officers unfastened it and pulled out a pair of what looked like pyjama trousers, a grey T-shirt, a scrumpled kurta. From a side pocket, they removed some rolling papers, familiar now to Anand by their Zig Zag logo, and three black-and-white photos of a young woman. His girlfriend? Who knew? The officer pocketed the photos and ignored the rest of the kitbag's contents.

'Under what name was he staying?'

Anand called Baba in and together they showed the policemen the registration book. One officer pointed out the name 'Major Major' to the other, who shook his head.

'Is there not a Mr King staying here?' he asked. Anand skimmed the names but found no King. He was trying to be as helpful as possible. The police carried out periodic drug raids on the hotels in Sudder Street. There had been two at the Lux since Anand took it over; the first had led to a couple of arrests, two goofy Danes had been picked up

Duncan Campbell

and released after paying a 'fine' of 100 rupees each. The policemen asked politely if they could look through the hotel. Anand shrugged his agreement. He heard their footsteps on the roof.

Soon this room would be empty of its current guests as Calcutta entered a post-war world. In Britain, everyone referred to the Second World War as 'the war' and the period after it as 'post-war', as though there had never been any other conflict in the world. (Except for Vanessa's father; when Anand had stayed at her family home for the New Year, the old man referred to the conflicts as 'the Kaiser's war' and 'Hitler's war'.)

Baba pointed at the Janis Joplin tape beside one of the beds, put his hands over his ears and made a face. 'Oh, Lord, won' you bymee a Merzedybenz?' he sang in baleful imitation.

Chapter Eighteen

L IEUTENANT-GENERAL JAGJIT Singh Aurora, commander of the Indian and Bangladesh forces in the 'eastern theatre', entered the press conference as conquering hero. Hugh noticed that even some of his own colleagues were applauding.

A good-looking, tall, well-built man with an even taller colonel beside him, Aurora greeted the packed Calcutta gathering with a broad smile. The mood was euphoric, the Indian media openly delighted by the news, the Western journalists pleased that the story had tied itself up neatly in time for Christmas. A junior officer shuffled a sheaf of press statements towards the grabbing hands of journalists.

'Instrument of Surrender,' it was headed. 'December 16, 1971.'

> The Pakistan Eastern Command agree to surrender all Pakistan armed forces in Bangladesh to Lieutenant-General JAGJIT SINGH AURORA, GOC-in-C of the Indian and Bangladesh forces in the eastern theatre. This surrender includes all

Pakistan land, air and naval forces and also all para-
military forces and civil armed forces. These forces
will lay down their arms and surrender at the places
where they are currently located to the nearest
regular troops under the command of Lieutenant-
General Jagjit Singh Aurora. Lieutenant-General
Jagjit Singh Aurora gives a solemn assurance that
personnel who surrender shall be treated with
dignity and respect that soldiers are entitled to in
accordance with the provisions of the GENEVA
convention and guarantees the safety and well-being
of all PAKISTAN military and para-military forces
who surrender, ethnic minorities and personnel of
West Pakistan origin, by forces under command of
Lieutenant-General Jagjit Singh Aurora.

It was signed by Aurora and Lieutenant-General Amir
Abdullah Khan Niazi, 'the martial law administrator and
commander of the Pakistan armed forces eastern
command'. Niazi, Hugh was told, handed over an empty
pistol as a symbol of surrender. He wondered if he should
start his story with that. Perhaps give the impression he
had witnessed it. 'General Amir Niazi slowly unbuckled his
pistol from its tanned, leather holster. For a moment, his
hand seemed to pause . . .' Maybe not.

The press conference began. Hugh raised his hand to ask
a question, aware of the fact that newsdesks were now
starting to watch television news bulletins closely to see if
their reporters were at the thick of the action. The questions
rained in from every corner of the room.

'How many troops have surrendered to you, General?'

'Ninety-three thousand,' said Aurora in what Hugh wanted to call a pukka accent – had he been at Sandhurst?

'Did you think there were as many as that?'

'No, I thought about sixty-five thousand,' smiled the general. Hugh wondered what the correct word was for the hairnet that neatly enclosed the general's beard. 'Beard-net' sounded odd and wrong. 'Perhaps we would have not asked for the surrender if we had known there were so many!'

'What did you say to General Niazi?'

'We talked about things that generals talk about. He spoke to me of his family, he is very concerned that they were well. It was all very chummy.'

'Have you taken a lot of arms from the Pakistanis?' asked Bob the Australian who, Hugh noticed, was sitting cross-legged at the front of the press throng.

'No. We are leaving them with their arms because the situation is dangerous for them. They said they were very glad that it was the Indian army that took them, they do think they would not have stood much of a chance with the Mukti Bahini.'

'General, is it safe to leave a large army with their weapons?' asked an Indian voice.

'Oh, this is quite standard practice – we did it in the last war when the civilian population was very hostile to the enemy. Quite standard practice.'

Hugh noticed a lithe female body snaking her way up on her knees to the front of the press conference to get closer to the general. So Britt had not made it on to the plane to

Dhaka after all! How fine it would have been to be spending the night with her, both heading off in different directions afterwards, no commitment, just a friendly roll in the hay. He wondered if McGrady was aware she was still in town, whether he would be pissed off with him for saying she had left. The general spotted her, raised his eyebrows and smiled as she clicked away below him.

'Where will the prisoners be taken to?'

'To India. They would not be safe in Bangladesh, I'm afraid.' He gestured at Hugh, who suddenly realised he had forgotten what he was going to ask.

'Er ... my ... er ... question has been answered already, thank you.'

'Will we be able to see General Niazi?' asked an Indian reporter.

'No, I'm afraid not,' smiled the general.

'Did you think the war would take this long, General?'

'Well, I thought it would have taken a few days longer. My prediction was that it would last about seventeen or eighteen days. Incidentally, one thing General Niazi said was that he was surprised by our decision to move five thousand paratroopers in and this was one reason for his surrender. I think he read a report of it in a Calcutta paper but this was a misprint. In fact, I had said five hundred!'

There was loud laughter all round. Britt turned round to move away from beneath the general and caught Hugh's eye. She winked at him. He nodded to her but her gaze had already shifted.

'What are your plans now, General?'

'I think a game of golf, perhaps.'

'What else did Niazi say to you?'

'Oh, we talked of mutual friends – we were at military academy together, many of us.'

'How much did the Mukti Bahini help you?'

'A great deal, yes, a great deal. They helped shorten the war, certainly, because they were able to keep us informed and to show us short cuts. Niazi said they were a key factor in our victory.'

'What is your opinion of the Pakistani troops?'

Hugh was anxious now that the press conference should end swiftly; his stomach was semaphoring him an urgent message.

'They are good fighters but their strategy was poor and they were badly led.'

'What about their behaviour to the civilian population?'

'Well, I was very surprised, particularly by their treatment of the women in Bangladesh,' said the general, frowning for the first time. 'I was very shocked that soldiers should do such things.'

'What do the people of Bangladesh feel about Niazi?'

'They refer to him as "that animal".'

'That animal?' a reporter repeated. There was a brief pause.

'I wonder if you could strike that out, please. It is not right for us generals to be calling each other names.'

An Italian journalist, who had been straining to have his question answered, finally caught the general's attention. 'I paid my money for the trip to Dhaka with the army earlier and I wasn't allowed on the plane! Can you explain that?'

There was a mild hum of disapproval from the rest of the press at this show of Latin solipsism.

'I'll see that you are on the first plane in our next war!' replied the general with another broad smile and the room roared with laughter. Hugh joined in.

'When will that be?' asked a voice which was subsumed by a wave of further laughter.

Hugh was reminded of a cheerful victory conference held by a Conservative MP on election night the previous year when Ted Heath's government had been surprisingly returned to power. There had been the same air of cheery complicity between the winning MP and much of the press. Hugh had been secretly pleased at Heath's victory as he found Harold Wilson seedy and uninspiring and couldn't stand his flat, Yorkshire accent but he kept his feelings to himself because Jackie had been campaigning for some overweight Labour time-server in their constituency. He made a mental note to get her a present. Maybe a sari? Did saris have sizes? What was her size? He had no idea. He wondered if Linda would expect something too. Oh, God.

The general was winding down, thanking his troops for performing 'wonderfully well', thanking the press for their cooperation. Smiling and waving, he left the room.

By the time Hugh reached the street, it was packed with a cheering crowd, some standing on the roofs of cars. They were roaring their approval, as were some workmen, perched on bamboo scaffolding on the building opposite. Pakistan had been not just defeated but humiliated. He watched two workmen help Britt on to the scaffolding so that she could capture a shot of the general waving and shaking some of the dozens of hands thrust towards him. Hugh stood on the edge of the crowd until the general had disappeared into his jeep.

He saw Britt and the French photographer, Jean-Pierre, putting their cameras away. They all shared a cab back to the hotel. There was anti-climax in the air; the 'Thirteen-Day War' was over. By this time tomorrow, most of the pack would be scattered.

'Entertaining guy,' said Hugh, as the taxi slid its way creatively through thick traffic.

'*Bien sûr*,' said the Frenchman. 'He is a Sikh, yes?'

'The warrior class,' said Hugh. 'So, is everyone heading off today? Tomorrow?'

'I might stay on a few days to do this feature, there seems to be some interest in these murders of hippies here,' said Britt, checking that all her film was safely located.

'Gordon McGrady going to help you?' said Hugh.

Britt looked at him hard. 'Maybe.'

'Has he told you about the commune he was in in London?'

'He didn't say it was a commune exactly. I think he just shared a house with friends.'

'Free love kind of thing, apparently.'

'Mm,' said Britt, looking out of the window.

'Bit of an . . . outsider at school,' Hugh found himself saying. 'He had a leg-over with the headmaster's au pair, so rumour had it.'

'Really.'

'A "leg ova"? What is a "leg ova"?' asked Jean-Pierre.

There was a frenzy at the reception area at the Oberoi Grand as guests tried to check out. In the courtyard, two reporters were haggling with a carpet salesman, trying to bargain him down by shrugging at his prices in an exaggerated way.

In his room, Hugh found two notes on his pillow. The first said that 'Jacky' had rung. The second indicated that Linda had called. He went down to the bar, with its stately billiard table and cabinets full of old compasses, and joined the growing company there for a beer before returning to his trusty Olivetti and hammering out the story of the end of the war. He skimmed through his notes, looking for the general's best quotes. The phone rang. It was Jackie.

'Hi,' he said. The first time they had spoken since he left London. 'Just got in from the field, great to hear you . . . how are things . . . Should be back the day after tomorrow . . . Who rang? Linda? Oh, I think she's the newsdesk secretary . . . I can't think why . . . How're your folks? Good . . . Good . . . yes, as soon as I know what my flight is, I'll let you know . . . Oh, yes, it is good news. Absolutely. People are very pleased here, yes . . . liberation . . . yes, privilege to be here. OK, sweetie . . . must go, someone's at the door with a press release . . . Oh, is there anything you would like from here? A carpet? Well, just a bit bulky . . . There're some lovely mats . . . no, no, that's fine, I'll do my best.'

He had barely replaced the phone in the receiver when it rang again. He immediately recognised Linda's voice.

'Hello, hello? Hello? Can't hear anything,' he said, although he could hear her as if she was sitting on the end of his neatly made bed. 'Hello? Anyone there?' He flicked his finger a few times on the receiver, repeated a couple of 'Hellos?', replaced the phone firmly, grabbed his wallet and bolted from the room before it could ring again.

Chapter Nineteen

THE CROWDS WERE gathering on the streets in celebration as Britt rang the agency. She told Mok about her latest shots of the general and victory.

'The thing is, princess,' said Mok, in his familiar laid-back adenoidal drone, 'we will have all the celebration pictures in the papers tomorrow and in the news magazines on Monday and I just kind of feel – enough celebrating. Hubert Humphrey has just called for the recognition of Bangladesh so that proves it's an old story. I feel the caravan is moving on . . .'

'Where is the caravan going, Mok?'

'Speak up, princess, you know I'm going deaf.'

'Where do you want me to go next? Do you still want that hippy trail stuff?'

'Yes to the hippy trail but, well, you know, budgets are tight. Can you do it in a couple of days? Maybe some shots of freaks on the beach at – where is it – Goa?'

'You want some shots of topless hippy chicks on the beach, is that right, Mok?'

'Ha-ha . . . The other thing is, there's been some more stuff in the papers here again about those two Americans who were murdered in Bombay last summer. Anyway, according to the *Chronicle*, there's more of these murders going on. You think maybe you could combine the two? Get some nice pictures in Goa and maybe a picture of the hotel where these people died?'

'Goa is hundreds of miles away, Mok. And anyway, another of the murders has just taken place here. A French guy. Another junkie. I could get pictures of the hotel where he was staying—'

'Not too much interest in French junkies, Britt . . . Hey, I've someone on the other line. Take care and come home soon and everyone thinks you've done a great job. Those pictures of the Muckitty whatever are fantastic. They look like they should be in the Crips or the Bloods.'

'They're fucking freedom fighters, Mok, for God's sake.'

'I hear you. I leave it up to you. If you want to take another week on the road, OK. Are you OK for bread? Yes? See you soon. Bye!'

She showered and washed her hair. The zit had gone. She brushed her teeth. Had she remembered to take her pill today? The phone rang again. It was Gordon. In reception and on his way up. She opened the door in her towel. They embraced, shyly at first. Then he took her head in both of his hands and kissed her very firmly on the lips. He began to laugh.

'What is it?' she asked.

'Oh, it's just you reminded me of an old joke from the pantomimes. There's this Scottish comedian called Chic Murray, a genius.' She was sitting on his knee now on the bed and he was pushing her hair out of her eyes. 'A bit like

Buster Keaton. Deadpan. Everything is delivered in the same monotone. Anyway, I just remember him telling this joke: woman opens the door in her nightgown – funny place for a door.' He laughed and kissed her neck.

What was funny about that? Britt wondered.

'Say that again.'

He shook his head. 'Here's another one. Man walks into a butcher's shop. Says to the butcher, "Is that Scottish steak?" Butcher says, "Why? Dae ye want tae eat it or talk tae it?" '

Britt got that one. She threw her head back and laughed what her grandmother had called, approvingly, her 'unladylike' laugh. 'Ah, I've peed myself,' she said. 'I have to go to the john.' Then they were rolling over and over on the carpet. They made love slowly. Gordon stared for a long time into her eyes but he was smiling while Josh would have been frowning. Afterwards, they sat together naked on the floor with their backs against the bed, his arm between her thighs.

'Hugh told me you'd already left. I was trying to leave a message for you at reception and they said you were still here,' said Gordon, kissing her behind the ear and stroking the inside of her thigh. He slid down between her legs, blew into her navel and looked up at her. 'He said you'd gone to Dhaka.'

'I should have done,' said Britt, running her hand down his arm. 'I never made the plane. There weren't enough seats on it. Were you upset that I was gone?'

'Heartbroken.'

'How could you be? We hardly know each other.' Did

she feel flattered or threatened? Was he going to be as needy as Josh? Why were men so possessive? He sat beside her, put an arm round her and laid his head across her breasts.

'Let me rest my head on your snowy bosom,' he said.

'Is that the best you can do? Anyway, it's not "snowy" – it's a nice bronze, in case you hadn't noticed. A lot of work went into getting it that colour.' She stroked his head absent-mindedly with one hand and noticed, almost by chance, that she was holding his limp cock with the other.

'Let's go for a swim,' she said.

'Where?' He sat up.

'There's a pool here, dumbo.' She uncurled herself and stood up. She felt his lips on the base of her spine.

'I haven't got any trunks,' he said.

'Any what?'

'Trunks – bathing costume. You know.'

'I'm sure Hugh would lend you his.' She would have liked to have seen Hugh's face when she asked him.

'I don't think so. Wrong waist size anyway.'

'They sell them at the hotel shop.' She pulled on the black, one-piece swimsuit that she had shoved into her luggage as an afterthought. She had decided against the pink gingham bikini. Not in Asia. 'I'll get you one. What size are you?'

He cocked an eye at her.

'Thirty inches,' he said with a leer. 'My waist, that is.'

'God, you're such a frat boy,' she said.

She pulled on white linen shorts over her swimming costume, slipped into a crumpled denim shirt, fastened a couple of buttons, shoved her feet into her sandals and headed for the door.

'Don't you run away now,' she said to him.

He beamed at her. Ten minutes later, he was clad in a pair of Bermuda shorts with parrots and palm trees on them and rubbing suntan lotion into her shoulder blades at the side of the pool. There were a handful of other journalists still there. She saw Bob, the grizzled Aussie, holding his stomach in as he glanced round to see who was watching him dive into the deep end.

Gordon lay back on a lounger and closed his eyes. She looked at him and took a deep breath. How complicated life was. She ran the side of her hand down his cheek and he opened his eyes and bent forward to kiss her. She glanced out of the corner of her eye before kissing him back.

Outside, the noise of fire crackers and the celebrating crowds grew.

'Let's get dressed and go out,' said Britt.

The crowds in the street were carrying marigold garlands and posters of Sheikh Mujib and crying, 'Jai Bangla! Jai Bangla!' They found themselves carried along with the mass of people surging down Chowringhee. They held hands very tightly.

'What's that smell?' he asked.

'Sandalwood incense, surely you know that by now,' she chided him. 'Now, whenever you smell that smell, you will have to think of me. OK? Is that a deal?'

'We'll always have Calcutta,' he said out of the side of his mouth.

'I know you think that we're all turned on by your accents but one thing I will tell you is that I have never heard a British person do a decent American accent.'

'Hey, I'm walkin' here!' Gordon said as they crossed the street and an aged Hillman Minx surged into their path.

'Exactly,' said Britt. 'You try and do Ratso in *Midnight Cowboy* and you never get it right. Or you try John Wayne and it's even worse.'

'Let's eat,' said Gordon. 'I'll take you somewhere new. You try an English accent. Let's hear you do an English accent, if you're so smart.'

'How kind of you to let me come.' She gave him her best from *My Fair Lady* which had been her favourite musical as a child. Granny Pedersen had taken her.

'Try a Beatles accent,' he told her.

' "So Ringo, how do you find America?" ' she said in a brisk American interviewer voice. Then: ' "Y'turn left at the Nurth Pole." '

'Dreadful,' said Gordon. 'You made him sound Chinese. Hey, this way.'

At the Espresso, down at the bottom of an alley next door to a busy barbers, Gordon ordered for them and held her hand across the table. Over his shoulder she saw familiar figures arriving.

'I think we are destined never to eat alone,' she said. 'It's like going out with the Addams family.'

Larry, Freddie and Kieran wandered in. Larry spotted Gordon and Britt and made an elaborate double take. The trio joined them, pulling up seats and crowding round them. Kieran was distracted. 'You haven't seen Karen, have you?' he asked. 'She's missing. I haven't seen her since this morning and she's not in a very good way. That stuff with Remy has freaked her. Freaked me, too.'

'Is she ill?' asked Britt.

'We got busted in Kerala a few weeks back and she was in jail for about two months. She had a pretty hellish time. She's not really been the same since. This stuff with Remy has slung her over the edge. I have to find her.' There was a brief silence at the table. Kieran left them without saying anything further.

'Are you guys not worried about what happened to Remy happening—'

'To us?' asked Larry. 'Well, Remy was alone in the cemetery. We have safety in numbers. Anyway, from tomorrow, I guess we'll all be out of here. All the Danes upstairs are shipping out to Rangoon. And Mr Bose is having a party tonight on the roof to celebrate the end of the war.'

'All your seasick sailors, they are going home,' said Freddie.

'Freddie,' said Larry. 'I'm going to miss you. It's been good having you around because however fucked up my head is, I know that there is always someone more fucked up than me.'

Freddie smiled, bowed and excused himself.

'Perhaps Freddie is not so mad,' said Britt.

'You mean that the only sane response to a mad world is madness?' asked Larry.

'He's been reading R. D. Laing,' said Gordon, scooping

a spoonful of onion pickle on to a bed of chapatti and sliding it into his mouth.

The waiter arrived and Larry insisted on trying out phrases from his Hindi phrasebook.

'*Sabr achchi khalslat hai*, man,' he said to the waiter who looked at him in bewilderment. 'That means "patience is an excellent quality". That's OK. *Kuchh parva nahini*.' This time, the waiter smiled. 'That means "never mind". I'm going to learn that one.'

Britt squeezed Gordon's hand under the table.

'I have to go and collect my film from the processors,' she said, standing up. It reminded her of the lost film and she felt a stab of anger and frustration.

'I'll come with you,' said Gordon.

The crowds had thinned. She slipped her hand under Gordon's elbow. She felt him squeeze his arm tight against his side. Anticipation. Soon they would be making love again. As they entered the Oberoi Grand, Hugh, looking preoccupied, emerged, shooing away a cluster of small boys as he did so.

'Hi, Hugh, you heading home now?' asked Gordon, clearly anxious to be friendly.

'Hmm, yeah, still waiting for my marching orders,' said Hugh. 'My newsdesk hasn't fixed a bloody flight back for me yet. Er, I see you found each other. I thought you were off to Dhaka, Britt.'

'Well, we're having a victory party at our hotel tonight,' said Gordon. 'The manager's holding a celebration and told us to ask anyone. So, come along and see how the other nine-tenths live. It's called the Lux. Second or third street on the left down Chowringhee. Just ask.'

'I'll see if I'm still here. You don't know where they sell cheap carpets round here, do you?'

Gordon shook his head and folded his hands in a 'namaste' gesture. Hugh headed off, trailing a small tail of hopeful barefoot boys.

Inside the reception, a new arrival with what looked like a lot of expensive luggage was leaning over the desk, apparently arguing with the receptionist. The cases, with their fat zips and bulky side pockets, looked strangely familiar to Britt. She paused. Gordon leaned over towards her and kissed her delicately on her neck, just below her ear. She felt the tip of his tongue on her skin. As Gordon kissed her, the new arrival turned round and faced them. Britt stared back. She would remember her immediate reaction for ever. It was a mixture of surprise, disappointment and fury.

'Josh!' she cried.

Chapter Twenty

THERE WERE POTS of glue on the counters at the General Post Office, warnings of the activities of pickpockets and long lines of patient souls awaiting service from the clerks who appeared to be in no hurry and could, every now and then, be seen dispatching someone to start again at the rear of a different, equally long queue. Gordon's heart sank.

When he had been seventeen and had first been dumped by a girlfriend in a brisk letter – 'I am afraid I am very busy with A levels this term so I think we should stop writing to each other, yours, Kitty' – sent to him at St Gregory's, he had taken to playing Ray Charles very loud in the senior common room. 'Born to Lose'. 'I Can't Stop Loving You'. 'You Win Again'. If you could have sold self-pity by the hundredweight, he would have been rich. But that was ten years ago. He should be beyond that now. After all, he had barely met Britt. But she had seemed so perfect. Just seeing her brought on a magical light-headedness, half terrifying, like vertigo.

To make it worse, the mood in the lines waiting to send letters and immaculately wrapped gunny bags was one of high spirits. The besting of Pakistan's armed forces was clearly the topic on people's lips. The line for the Poste Restante counter was mercifully short. A small, entitled American was angrily raising his voice at the man behind the counter who wanted to see his passport as proof of identity and who was not satisfied with the offer of a bogus student card.

There were two letters for Gordon, each in the strangely reassuring form of the airmail lettercard with the Queen's head on the right-hand corner. Once you would have been the Empress of India, he thought, recalling the old photographs from the family album of his great-grandfather at the Durbar in Delhi when Queen Mary had visited the jewel in her crown. The array of maharajahs and colonial civil servants had seemed so self-assured and permanent in the photos, a time when the British empire controlled – what was it they had learned in history O level? – a fifth of the world's land mass and a quarter of its peoples, and now, what was left? Hong Kong, the Falklands, the Solomon Islands.

He sat outside on the GPO's steps, slitting open the lettercards with his penknife, saving the one from Grace till second. He sliced the top of his finger with the blade which he had absent-mindedly entrusted to a roadside knife-sharpener for 50 paise. He sucked the blood away but it continued to run and he staunched it with his red-spotted handkerchief.

His mother's letter was a matter-of-fact bulletin in which international events and what Mr McTaggart next door was doing with his garden – broccoli, that's posh for you! – elided seamlessly. There was some local news. A prominent local councillor, a working-class Tory and self-made businessman, had committed suicide in a pact with his young wife. He had been in debt, facing prosecution for fraud, and clearly preferred the peace of the gas oven to the opprobrium of an affronted Edinburgh. She mentioned a new television serial called *Upstairs, Downstairs* which she thought he would enjoy – 'excellent acting'. She pointedly did not ask his plans, said that his father had finally agreed to retire, that his back was giving him pain and that the weather was mild for the time of year. There was a brief reference to Bangladesh, 'which sounds very sad', and an admonition to take care.

Grace's message was short, not even taking up the whole of the already modest lettercard space. The owner of their squatted house in Clapham wanted to convert it into luxury flats. They could find nowhere big enough for them all. Everyone was looking for new places to live. The shared house was at an end. Joe and Andrea were moving to Wales. Jeb had found another squat with people who worked for the Islington Gutter Press and had been arrested for assaulting a police officer during an eviction of another squat. He would go on trial in February. She, Grace, was going back to university. Manchester had offered her a place on a postgraduate course in social studies. She had read some reports on Bangladesh in the papers and hoped it would not be a long war. She signed 'with love' and added two kisses. He remembered when an entire envelope would have been surrounded by kiss-crosses in the shape of a heart. And he recalled their last weekend together, watching *Carnal Knowledge* at a West End cinema so crowded that they had to sit crick-necked in the front row, holding hands by habit, gazing up at the distorted images of Ann-Margret and Jack Nicholson on the screen.

Gordon stuffed both lettercards into his wallet and digested the bustle around him: to his left, between two men offering a parcel-wrapping service, an elderly, bearded man with a typewriter was composing letters, for a fee, for people who could not write. The man agreed to rent him the typewriter for half an hour for a rupee. Gordon dashed off a page to his parents, full of reassuring news, of plans to move on to Hong Kong (which they would find reassuring, as a cousin was now working there for Jardine Mathesons), of the delight with which Calcutta was greeting the end of the war.

It was hard to write to Grace. The most exciting thing that had happened to him was meeting Britt and he was hardly going to sit on the steps of the Calcutta GPO and tap out a hymn to her beauty and an account of his dismay that she was gone. Josh. That was his name. With all that expensive poncey luggage. Britt had seemed – or was this his imagination? – torn for a moment. Then she had turned to him and said, 'Gordon, I'm sorry. I have to handle this. I'll see you later.' But she had not said where or how as she steered Josh to the lift without a backward glance. Should he write about Remy? It seemed morbid. His fingers hovered over the rented typewriter. A shadow loomed above him.

'How much do you charge for typing out a letter, sir?' asked Larry, a large parcel under his arm.

'Hi, there,' said Gordon. 'You posting that?'

'*Seguramente, chico*,' said Larry. 'Stick around.'

'Have you seen the queues?' asked Gordon. 'I'll see you at the British Council in half an hour.'

'You're so romantic. Hey, that woman. She's something, isn't she? What does she see in you? Would you say that the ghosts of electricity howl in the bones of her face?'

'Forget it.'

'Shit, droog, it's not over already, is it?'

'Would you believe this, her fucking bloke, her boyfriend, arrived from America. Just showed up. How the fuck did he get here? I thought all the planes into India were cancelled. It was just so . . .'

Larry gave him a sympathetic shrug followed by a sympathetic hug. Gordon's eyes alighted on an elderly man squatting on the pavement and having his ears cleaned by a man – a kan mad wallah, was what Baba had called them – using a long wooden scoop.

'Have you had your ears cleaned since you've been here?' asked Gordon.

'Are you trying to make a point?'

'No, just idle curiosity. Kieran had his done and said it was great. Reasonably priced.'

'I wouldn't like someone poking around in my ear.'

'It's a question of trust, isn't it? You would let a Western doctor cut your stomach open and fiddle around with your intestines while you're unconscious but you don't like the idea of an Indian guy fiddling around in your outer ear.'

The kan mad wallah realised that he was being

Duncan Campbell

discussed, smiled and beckoned them over with a nod of his head.

'Go on, O enlightened one, prove your point,' said Larry.

'My ears are clean.'

'Chicken,' said Larry. He paused and looked ahead. 'We could always frag the boyfriend.'

'What?'

'Britt's guy. This is a city in the midst of turmoil. Something could easily happen to him. Look at what happened to Remy. Ask him round to the party tonight and we'll off him in the blackout. We can even pin a little yin and yang sign to his shirt.'

'That's not funny.'

'I know. Look, droog, the chilly hours and minutes of uncertainty will pass. See you later.' Larry strode into the post office.

Gordon abandoned his letter to Grace and strolled to the British Council on Shakespeare Sarani to read the old newspapers from home. He was sticky from the afternoon sun so he walked close to the sprinklers on the Council's neatly cut lawn to cool himself. There was a Rover parked outside and men in 1950s lightweight suits and short-sleeved shirts chatting in the shade.

Inside the reading room, a queue of Indian students waited to read the *Daily Mirror*. *The Economist* and *The Times* remained untouched. Other students sat with copies of *Vogue* or the *Illustrated London News* on their laps. The news was old but Gordon read it anyway: six children had died in the Cairngorms in the snow. Manchester United were top and Heart of Midlothian third in their respective leagues. Edward Heath was about to do a deal on Rhodesia. It seemed remote and unimportant. A notice pinned to the wall said that the planned open-air screening of *Billy Liar* had been cancelled because of the blackout. He was disappointed. It was his favourite film. A man can loooooose himself in Calcuttttttaaaaa, he thought. He went outside when he saw Larry approach.

'Let's hit the museum, droog,' said Larry. 'Did you see Freddie here?'

'Nope.'

'I'm sure I saw him just before you came out.'

They had a routine constitutional now, which encompassed the British Council, the Museum of India, just round the corner from the Lux, the Victoria Monument and then some bhelpuri on a bench in the Maidan while they watched young men playing cricket.

'I wish I had studied archaeology, man, instead of cuisine,' said Larry after they had showed their bogus student cards and gained free admittance to the museum. 'For instance, look at this – Rajasaurus marmadensis. Is that for real? "India's own dinosaur." Is that right?'

'Why not?' said Gordon. They drifted into the almost empty room, Larry's favourite, where the South India bronzes were kept. Larry gazed at the statues of the goddesses.

'How come they all have tits like *Playboy* centrefolds?' he asked.

'Shhh,' said Gordon, looking round and catching a glance from a small family outing. 'Can't you just admire the handiwork?'

'It's a serious question. Why have they given them breasts like cannonballs?'

'Maybe that's the way they were then.'

'Well,' said Larry examining the label beneath one exhibit of a large-breasted goddess, 'I just wish I had been alive in Uttar Pradesh in the second century, man.'

'Maybe you were.'

'Christ, you're not into that reincarnation shit, are you? What do you think Remy will come back as?'

'Hey, let Remy rest in peace.'

Out on the street, they were debating whether to return to the Lux or take in the Victoria Memorial when they saw Karen. She seemed calmer now, sunny even. She was wearing her Rajasthani dress and a pair of pink sunglasses with heart-shaped lenses. She had washed her hair. She greeted them both with a soft kiss.

'Ever been to the Victoria Memorial?' asked Gordon. He wondered what Karen had been taking to be so calm.

'No, should I have been?' asked Karen.

'We'll take you. Part of your Calcutta education. You'll want to write a poem.'

The bogus student cards did their work once more.

'Wow,' said Karen, as she digested the memorial in all its gothic splendour: the marble statues of Lord Curzon, his mouth in a rictus of disdain, of Queen Mary and King George V, the pillar-box red uniforms of the regiments of the Raj, the haughty Empress herself surveying a post of the empire she never visited.

They sat in the grounds of the memorial, the three of

them, taking in the winter sun, watching crows and mynahs hopping sideways in search of snacks. There were a few courting couples, sitting chastely together, a trio of matrons on a 'ladies only' bench, their soft stomachs flopping out of the folds of their saris. Two middle-aged men were listening to a transistor radio which was interspersing martial music with news of surrenders and triumph. A young Bengali man introduced himself to them and spoke of the war. He said that he was a poet. Everyone in Bengal seemed to be a poet, Gordon thought, just like everyone in a pub in north London after 10 p.m. had once had a trial for Spurs or Arsenal.

'I'm going for a haircut,' Larry announced suddenly.

'Blimey, I thought that was the last thing you needed,' said Gordon, eyeing Larry's pate, already darkened to hazelnut by the Bengal sun.

'The beard has to go,' said Larry. 'They don't let you into Singapore with long hair and they give you a hard time in Bangkok. You'd better have a trim, too, if you want to get into Thailand. It's an unfriendly world out there.'

'You don't want to go to Singapore.'

'You kidding? Bugis Street? All those beautiful transvestites . . .'

'I'm staying here,' said Karen. 'If you see Kieran, tell him where he can find me.'

Twenty minutes later Gordon and Larry were sitting on adjoining seats in the barbers on Lindsay Street.

'Er, just down to here, please,' said Gordon nervously, indicating a line just above where his collar would have been. He was twelve again, trapped in a barber's chair in

Edinburgh, waiting for the fateful snip, snip, snip. 'And . . . er . . . the beard as well, please.'

The barber was solicitous without being fussy. He lathered Gordon's beard, produced a cut-throat razor, sharpened it on a handsome leather strop. The beard slid away with the first strokes. Gordon moved his head slightly to see how Larry's shave was going and jogged the barber's arm. He felt a slight nick to the left of his jaw and knew that blood had been drawn. The barber assessed the damage and glanced silently round, spotted what he was searching for and picked it up delicately. Gordon watched out of the corner of his eye as the barber placed a small spider on the wound.

'Draws the blood,' he explained. He was right. The wound dried almost immediately. Larry caught his eye.

'There are more things in heaven and earth, droog, than are dreamed of in your fucking philosophy . . . God, look at us. Freak flags at half-mast. We're just a couple of straights.'

Chapter Twenty-One

THE ROOF GARDEN of Anand's dreams would have had large parasols and tall cactuses – or was it, as Vanessa insisted, cacti? – a couple of flamingoes and a bar tended by a husky-voiced temptress with a name like Delphine who could make cocktails and salty jokes simultaneously. And on a night like tonight, as the whole country celebrated victory in Bangladesh, Delphine would have been serving Buck's Fizz and banana daiquiris to the guests, while musicians – a young guzzel singer, perhaps – performed in the background.

The reality was that Anand and Baba laboriously carried benches from the Lux's breeze-blocked garage on to the roof and arranged them in such a way that no party-goers would add to the casualty figures by tumbling to their deaths. He had invited all the hotel guests and told them to bring their friends – if they had any. There would be no Buck's Fizz or cocktails but he had four crates of Kingfisher, a large bag of bhelpuri and four dozen vegetable samosas from the corner café. They paused in reception to watch Mrs Gandhi on the snowy television.

'Dhaka is now the free capital of a free nation,' she announced.

'The goddess Durga,' said Baba with a wink to Anand.

'I thought she was meant to be Shakti,' said Anand.

Vivek and Deviani were the first to arrive. Deviani looked spectacular. She was wearing an eggshell-blue and silver sari and carrying a gift-wrapped bottle which she presented to Anand.

'To celebrate our glorious jawans' victory,' she said.

'This looks distinctly black market to me,' said Anand.

'My dear Anand, I am afraid it is much more bourgeois than that. It was in Papa's cellar where it has been since he won it in a bridge game about five years ago. When I told him it was to celebrate the victory, he was remarkably accepting. What do we call today? Liberation Day?'

'VB day? Victory for Bangladesh?' suggested Anand. He was tired. The previous night had been a bad one. Only two hours of proper sleep, the rest a fitful doze.

'Sounds terribly Western, Anand,' said Vivek. 'I knew you were away too long.'

'Where are the glasses?' asked Anand, fiddling with the cork as Baba hovered into view with a tray of assorted tumblers and wine glasses of varying thicknesses.

'Yes, where are your champagne flutes?' asked Vivek. 'Are we meant to drink out of these tumblers? Poor show. You'll never challenge the Hiltons at this rate, Anand.'

'Hi,' said a voice from the top of the stairs. 'Are we too early?'

The first wave of the hotel guests: Gordon, Larry,

Kieran and Freddie. Anand noted that they had done their best to smarten up. Some had clearly showered, had even cut their hair and shaved off their beards, others had been to the laundry. Freddie looked pale and even thinner than usual. Larry was carrying his guitar.

'Everyone is very smart,' said Anand. They looked like scruffy children who had been told by their parents to dress up for a family wedding.

'Well, we have to cut our hair to get into Thailand,' said Gordon. 'Can we help ourselves? This looks like great grub . . . Are you going to miss us all?'

'That is the burden of the hotelier,' said Anand. 'A life of constant partings.'

'Sounds like one of your English writers,' said Deviani, who, Anand noted, greeted Gordon rather warmly. 'Miss Constant Partings.'

'We've not been bad guests, have we?' asked Larry. 'At least none of us got murdered in the hotel which would have been a real hassle for you. All that blood on the sheets.' There was a brief silence. Kieran shot Larry an angry glance. Where, wondered Anand, was Kieran's girlfriend? And was Mr Mudd, the monk, going to come to the party? Did monks party?

Anand soon realised that the promptness of the guests was less to do with politeness than a desire to mount a swift assault on the free food and beverages. He remembered his first term at the London School of Economics and the party the professor of his faculty had thrown for new students. They all arrived on the dot of six and had scoffed all the nuts and crisps by 6.15 p.m., sticking around only long enough to empty a few dozen bottles of sweet sherry, poured out long-sufferingly by the professor's wife.

'A toast to free Bangladesh and to Remy – wherever his afterlife may take him,' said Larry. 'Drink up, droogs.'

They toasted the victory, their glasses raised by lucky chance just at the moment that a battery of fireworks exploded in the distance.

'And bon voyage to all of you,' said Anand. 'Wherever you may be travelling next.' He glanced at Larry whose guitar was slung over his shoulder, like a rifle. 'You don't play any Django Reinhart by any chance, do you?'

'Sorry. One of the many regrets in my life.'

'And where are you all going?' asked Deviani.

'Well, I'm off to Thailand, then Laos, I think,' said Gordon.

'And I to Atlantis,' said Freddie.

'Atlanta?' asked Vivek.

'No, he said Atlantis. The lost kingdom of Atlantis,' said Larry. 'Freddie, like many of his countrymen, harks back to a bygone mythical era. Is that not right, Freddie? You live in an alternative universe to the rest of us, where gods and dolphins frolic on the ocean bed and where all creatures are brighter than the brightest star.'

'Sounds like a lovely place,' said Deviani. 'How does one get there, Freddie?'

'Via Desolation Row,' said Larry.

'Let's drink to that,' said Gordon.

'Let's drink to anything,' said Larry.

Anand noticed Freddie whispering to Gordon who nodded with a grin and replied aloud, 'Left-hand pocket of my rucksack – my rucksack's the grey one, OK? Take two. At least.' Freddie departed.

'So what have you learned from this country of ours?' asked Deviani.

'Patience,' said Gordon.

'The patience of the cemetery,' said Vivek.

'The art of political discourse,' said Larry. 'I have had more decent political discussions in three weeks in Calcutta than in a lifetime in Nevada. Look at our political discourse – Nixon and Agnew accusing everyone of being commies. On the other hand, I miss being able to sit down on the can.'

'Thanks for that,' said Gordon.

'And you?' asked Deviani, looking at Kieran.

'Er . . . I learned how to meditate, how to fast . . . I'm sorry, I'm a bit distracted. I'm worried about Karen,' said Kieran. 'She's disappeared again.'

'I saw her earlier,' said Anand. 'She seemed a bit, er, abstracted.' When had he seen her? The day had been a blur.

'Well, she was missing for a while this morning and then she seemed to be OK and then, half an hour ago, she just took off again.' Kieran stared into his beer. 'I'm going to have to go and have another look for her.' He drained the bottle, placed it perilously on the roof garden wall and nodded his goodbyes. Anand watched him as he started down the fire escape stairs and saw him almost collide with a sweating figure in a safari suit, who could only be English. Who had invited him? Or was he a consular official?

'Christ, who's this? The British Ambassador?' asked Larry.

Gordon and Vivek both turned. Gordon greeted the new arrival without enthusiasm.

'This is, er, Hugh Dunn, someone who was at school with me,' said Gordon, introducing him. 'He's been covering the war. This is our esteemed host, Mr Bose.'

'So the old boy network is alive and well,' said Anand. He noted that the two old schoolmates did not seem very matey. 'That's very jolly. Are you going to sing us the old school song now? Look, Mr Anunziato is tuning up.'

Larry, now sitting cross-legged on the ground, started singing, with a delicacy that belied his bulk, to the tune of 'These Foolish Things'. It was a variation of what he and Gordon had been singing the other night.

A broken prayer-wheel that just keeps on spinning,
A junkie's story that has no beginning,
An ancient tape of Carole King's . . .
These foolish things
Remind me of you . . .

The guests applauded. Gordon stood beside him and they sang together a song about Benares being their kind of town. Anand caught Deviani's eye and she smiled back, a look of mixed puzzlement and pleasure. Larry handed the guitar to Gordon who tuned it for a moment or two before launching into the first bars of what turned out to be the Hallelujah chorus again. Anand had last heard it properly at the Proms in London into which he been press-ganged by Vanessa and one of her many aunts. He did not enjoy the experience. Too many Union Jacks and beefy, entitled-looking young men looking at him out of the corner of their eyes. No post-imperial guilt or self-examination there. Once again Larry and Gordon seemed to have come up with their own words.

> And we'll be ill
> For ever and ever.
> Hepatitis! Hepatitis!

Down on the streets, the crowds were gathering and there were cries of 'Jai Bangla!' everywhere. The noise of drums and fireworks almost drowned out Gordon's guitar playing. Out of the corner of his eye, Anand noted that Mudd the monk had now joined them, pressing his hands together in greeting before wolfing a couple of samosas.

'So you two gentlemen were at school together, is that right?' asked Anand, filling up Hugh Dunn's glass with the remains of a bottle of Kingfisher. He sighed inwardly as he saw Larry attempting to light a joint the size of a truncheon. Still, the police would be too busy tonight keeping the crowds under control to bother coming round again.

'Yes, we were,' said the Dunn fellow. 'Seems like a long time ago. We went our separate ways . . .'

'You to Fleet Street and he on the Road to Nirvana.'

'You could say that, I suppose,' said Dunn doubtfully.

'So you will be back in London in time to see the Christmas lights on Oxford Street?'

'You know London?'

'Oh, yes, I had four very happy – well, quite happy,' let's not exaggerate, thought Anand, 'years there. You have a loving wife waiting for you, no doubt?'

Dunn shot him a wary glance and reached his hand into the bhelpuri, pulling out a fistful and stuffing them unappealingly into his mouth. Deviani, who had joined them, realised that the question was not appreciated.

'Just ignore Anand, he is a nosy parker,' she said. 'What do people in Britain think about this war?'

'Well, I've been away since it started really so it's hard to say.'

Deviani looked unimpressed. 'You journalists are always so non-committal. Are you frightened to express your own opinions?'

This time Anand came to his rescue. 'Leave the man alone. This is party time. How were things looking in Bangladesh? Were the Pakistani army still there?'

'Lots of PoWs, yes,' said Dunn. 'In fact,' he reached into all four pockets of his jacket in turn, eventually pulling out two Pakistani army regimental cap badges which he displayed for the company as though they were rare butterflies. 'I have some souvenirs.'

Deviani examined them and placed them back in Hugh Dunn's hand. Freddie Braintree had returned to the roof and seemed even stranger than usual. He spotted the badges and picked one up, staring at it intently.

'Can I see this please?' he asked. 'In the light?'

'I don't think we've met,' said Hugh Dunn uncertainly.

'Freddie Braintree,' said Gordon with an exaggerated formality. 'Meet Hugh Dunn. Hugh – Freddie.'

'Spoils of war,' said Vivek with a hint of censoriousness in his voice as he looked at the regimental badge being examined by Freddie. Anand saw Hugh checking his watch, something the English did when they were ill at ease.

'Nice watch,' said Larry. 'Do you go diving?'

'Er, not much, these days, too busy with the job,' said Hugh.

'If you do, tell Freddie. He's looking for the lost kingdom of Atlantis which I think is somewhere on the bottom of the ocean.'

Hugh examined his watch again. 'Well, I must dash. I have a flight out tomorrow so I guess I had better pack up.'

'I'll come down with you,' said Anand. 'I have to see if Baba has any more food for our ravenous guests.'

They were halfway down the stairs when they collided with an agitated Karen. Her hair was sticking out wildly, her clothes looked muddy and there was a scratch on her face. She looked enormously distressed. She grabbed Anand.

'Don't leave me, don't leave me!' she cried.

'There, there, let's get you downstairs,' said Anand reassuringly. What should he do now? 'Deviani! Deviani, could you come down a moment?'

'Must dash,' said Hugh Dunn to Anand's retreating back. 'Very nice to meet you. I'll give your regards to

Oxford Street. By the way, do you know where that chap who took my regimental cap badge went?'

'I'm afraid I have no idea,' said Anand. He could see Deviani at the top of the stairs with Gordon.

'What's up?' said Gordon.

'She seems to be very unwell,' said Anand, indicating Karen, who was clinging to him. He could feel her nails in his arm. They made their way down to the darkened courtyard. The noise of the celebrating crowds in the neighbouring streets had grown; it sounded more agitated now. Anand gently detached himself from Karen.

'We need to find Kieran,' he said. 'And I think, maybe, a doctor.'

'You won't get a doctor at this time of night,' said Deviani. 'She needs a sedative. There is a chemist open on Lindsay Street. I will be back in five minutes.'

'I can go,' said Gordon.

'They won't give it to you, I'm afraid,' said Deviani. 'They will think it is for your personal pleasure.'

'DON'T LEAVE ME!' cried Karen, clutching frantically at Anand.

'Could you hold her a minute,' said Anand, 'while I phone and see if I can find a doctor?' Gordon took her gently in his arms.

'It's OK, Karen. It's me, Gordon. Mr Bose is going to find Kieran and Deviani is going to get you some medicine.'

'You won't leave me, you won't leave me?'

'Don't worry, I won't leave you.' Gordon rocked her backwards and forwards in his arms as she clung to him like a drowning woman. He caught Anand's eye over the top of her head and raised his eyebrows in what Anand recognised as a peculiarly British complicit gesture of mild despair. 'I won't leave you. I won't ever leave you.'

Chapter Twenty-Two

I T IS THE COLOUR of port, was Anand's first thought. The dark, treacly, seductive, ancient, plum colour of port, seeping through the dirty pillowcase beneath Freddie Braintree's head. He had seen dead bodies before. His grandmother's. His grandfather's. But never one so – fresh. He touched Freddie's forehead with his forefinger. It seemed warm. He couldn't possibly still be alive, could he? He placed two fingers gently on Freddie's lips. No breath.

'Baba!' he called. 'Baba!'

Where were all the other guests? The main room, with its six beds, was empty. The two Australians, Karen and Kieran, had fled for the airport in the middle of the night, spurred on by rumours that all flights out of Calcutta had been double-booked and it was first come, first served. Anand had been glad to see them go after Karen's hysterics; she had calmed down after being persuaded by Deviani to take a hefty sedative but was still wide-eyed and erratic. Dum Dum airport would be a nightmare. But where was Gordon? And Larry? Their haversacks were gone but they had not said goodbye. Had they, as they said in England, done a runner? He looked at his watch – 6.35 a.m. – and again at Freddie. Oh, Freddie, what a mess.

In the 'reception area' – he still put inverted commas round it when he thought about it – Anand picked up the phone and rang the police. After a dozen rings, a voice answered and took his details. The voice seemed untroubled and did not even ask for the sex of the dead person. After all, there was a war barely over, hundreds of thousands had died not so far away. What was one more? Particularly someone who may have been recklessly courting his own death. Was it Freddie who had asked him to treat his death as suspicious?

Anand returned to the room. The pillowcase seemed even thicker with blood. Was it still coming out? He knew better than to move the body and anyway Freddie seemed at ease, that familiar half-smile on his face, the blue eyes not quite focused. Anand looked closer. There was a gash on the forehead, partly hidden by Freddie's curly hair, but the blood seemed to be coming from the back of his head. Had he been shot or bludgeoned? He started to push Freddie's hair back and felt blood on his finger. It was sticky. Freddie was dressed in his usual kurta, patchwork waistcoat and frayed bell-bottom jeans. There was a string of coloured beads round his neck. Was that a brooch – with what looked like a little insignia of crossed rifles – pinned to his kurta? No, it was the Pakistani regimental badge that the English journalist had been showing off at the party. Freddie must have kept it. His hands were neatly folded in front of him as though he had just been lying down for a nap. He sighed. Poor Freddie, he thought, and then, unworthily, what a bloody nuisance this is all going to be.

He looked at Freddie's small pile of belongings. A stack of books by his bed. His cheap leather wallet, with its embossed Taj Mahal design, was half out of his pocket. Anand reached over for it and, after a brief pause, opened it. A student card. 'Leeds' written in the section marked 'college/univercity', spelled wrongly. A roll of $20 bills. A roll of £5 notes. A photo of a smiling young girl. He heard the sound of the police car drawing up outside. As he went into the courtyard to greet them, he was overtaken by the tall figure of the silent monk.

'Ah, Mr Mudd, I'm glad you're still here,' said Anand, as he opened the front gate. 'We need to talk.'

Mudd paused, pressed his hands together, granted him a gentle, beatific smile and walked smartly off. By the time Anand had greeted the police, Mudd had vanished into the Calcutta morning mist.

Chapter Twenty-Three

'"DON'T WORRY, I won't leave you. I won't leave you. I won't ever leave you." That's what he was saying to her,' said Britt, staring out of the car window at the familiar landmarks as her father drove her home from San Francisco airport.

A panhandler stood in the middle of the road, tapping on car windows for 'spare change'. These were 'panhandlers' rather than 'beggars', she thought, with their knowing signs – 'Why lie – it's for beer!' and 'Smile if you masturbate!' No one suggested that they were dropped off there in the mornings by crime syndicates or that their bandaged wrists or scarred eyebrows had been inflicted to make them more pitiable and marketable. There were joggers in brightly coloured T-shirts and sweatpants jostling each other as they ran towards the Golden Gate Bridge and, as they entered Marin County, the familiar rainbow painted round the entrance to the tunnel. The gateway always made her feel like a little girl again, with its hint that travellers were now about to enter the place where the rainbow ended, Shangri-la, Brigadoon.

Marin County had seemed like that to Britt when they

had first moved there from Ohio and her parents were still together. The deer on Mount Tamalpais, the view over the water to Alcatraz, which looked to a ten-year-old like a Transylvanian castle rather than a place of hellish incarceration, the music stores painted in psychedelic swirls and twirls, the crates of fresh oranges given free to customers who spent over $25 a week at the wholefood store. 'Mellow' and 'laid back' were words that people used without irony. Now it was changing. Her father and his friends complained about wealthy young things – 'straights' – from San Francisco moving in and pushing up house prices. There were BMWs and Mercedes in driveways instead of battered Volkswagen vans with dreamcatchers in their side windows and Beetles with anti-war decals.

She had dozed for most of the flight home from Delhi but the sleep had been in that odd no-man's-land where dreams slid into reality as you were awakened by the pilot's voice over the loudspeaker or a sudden slash of sunlight through the window. The dreams had been scrambled with the events of the past couple of weeks: the lost photos, Gordon, Josh – and that final night.

'And was this his old girlfriend or what?' asked her dad, keeping half an eye on the road and half on his daughter, her knees up against the dashboard despite his pleadings that she would be snapped in half if he had a tail-ender.

'I dunno, Dad. It was dark. I didn't feel like tapping her on the shoulder and asking her fucking name.' She stared out of the window again. 'I suppose it was funny in a way.

Josh had just gone crazy with rage when I told him it was over. Boy, you should have seen him.'

'I always thought there was something a bit creepy about that guy.'

'Well, you should have seen him. He had his hands round my neck and his face was all red and contorted. He wanted to know who this guy was I had met and where he could find him. He wanted to go and punch his lights out. God, it was heavy, Dad. He was like a psycho. I didn't know what he was going to do. Then after all that shit from him I go round to tell Gordon, this British guy, that I'm going to go off with him to wherever – and I find him in the arms of another woman.'

'Well, sweetpea, he sounds like a dumb bastard to me.'

'Oh, he wasn't like that, Dad. It seemed . . . I dunno, it seemed all the things that it isn't with Josh. Maybe there's no one that's really right for me. What was weird was that he seemed so keen.'

'Sounds like it's your pride that's bruised, not your heart, sweetpea.' He patted her knee. 'Just another guy who can't keep his pecker in his pants.'

'Just please don't tell me there are lots of fish in the sea.' She paused. Should she tell him about what else had happened that last night? That scream for help? Freddie's panicked, staring eyes in the crowd? It was easier to talk about being dumped by a guy than—

Her father broke the silence. 'Well, Josh rang me. I think he was still kind of hoping . . .'

'He must be crazy. I don't want to see him ever again.

He's got a real problem, Dad, and I'd never really seen it before. So I guess it was good that I found that out in time. You'll have to take me to the apartment when he's at work so I can pick up my things. I think I get custody of half the albums. And if I'm living with you, that'll mean no more porn shoots in the house.'

They drove on in silence, slowing down as the battered Buick in front of them pulled off the road to pick up a young woman hitch-hiker in a cheesecloth top and denim cut-offs.

'OK? I mean it.'

'OK – if you let me know how to pay the bills.'

'Oh, you can do weddings again, Dad.'

'No one's getting married any more – you know that better than anyone.'

'Commitment ceremonies, then. Bar mitzvahs.'

They drove past San Quentin prison.

'How's Mom?'

'Oh, pretty good, I guess. She worries about your brother. We haven't heard from him for a while. I hope he hasn't come back into the States because they're jailing a lot of draft evaders these days. Still, your mom seems to have found quite a lot of what she was looking for. She sent me some stuff that Krishnamurti had written – you know, "truth is a pathless land", the kind of thing people put up on their fridges when they want people to think they're profound.'

'Oh, Dad, it's more than that. And you know it. That's why she left, because you always mocked everything she ever tried to do. Truth is a pathless land, anyway. You should be a fan of Krishnamurti, he was always telling people not to follow leaders but to work things out for themselves.'

He took the Larkspur turning and wiped the condensation from the inside of the windscreen.

'So how was it, being in combat? Are you going to become Martha Gellhorn now?'

'Oh, I wasn't in combat. It was more taking pictures of the dead and the dying and the celebrations and – was there much stuff about it in the papers here?' She did not want to talk about the photos she had lost.

'Not a lot but then I haven't really been getting the papers that much. I guess one war is all that people feel they can handle at one time. I think there was more about the guy who was killing hippies there. I think there was even something about one just being killed in Calcutta. Oh, and your friend, George McGovern, has been getting into trouble for saying that every senator who voted for the war in Vietnam has to take part of the blame for sending fifty thousand Americans to an early grave. Looks like he's serious about trying to get the nomination next year. You should hear what the Republicans say about him – that he stands for the three As – acid, amnesty and abortion. I'd vote for that! So what was it like, honeybunch?'

'Well, there's some stuff I'm not sure I want to talk about right now . . .'

'All those bodies?'

'Well, that was part of it but, well, there was something that went down on my last night in Calcutta – not just this guy going off with someone else.' Did she want to tell her father when she had still, as it were, to tell herself what had happened? Did anyone know she had been there that night? 'Anyway, I'm just so tired. I seem to have been travelling for a year and I have so much stuff I still have to print. And I have to tell Mok he's not getting his hippy trail feature . . . God, how neat and ordered and new everything seems here.'

She could not tell whether her father was listening. His concentration was directed towards extracting the remains of a joint from the car's ashtray. He lit it up, inhaled and passed it to her, coughing. Her friends at school had always said that what was really cool about having sleep-overs at her house was that they got to smoke weed with her parents. They drove through San Anselmo, past the College of Marin, where she had modelled for the life drawing class for $15 a time during her student vacations. It had been fun. She liked to see how the students saw her: the men usually made her breasts more voluptuous than thcy really were and the women made her belly larger, more Rubenesque. It was flat now, though. She had lost weight in India. That was one plus. She sighed.

They hit Sir Francis Drake Boulevard and drove into Fairfax. She declined the joint. She saw two of her father's friends, his drinking buddies, heading into Nave's bar, shoulders hunched against the damp December afternoon. He did not acknowledge them.

He pulled the car into the drive as the rain and mist settled over Mount Tam. He hoisted her cases from the back of the pick-up and placed them on the bottom step leading to her old family home. She looked up at the familiar steps. He turned towards her and kissed her on the forehead, pulling her towards him with her saffron scarf.

'Nice scarf, where did you get that? Hey, what's up?'

Chapter Twenty-Four

'TRUST NOT THE drooping signal,' said the sign on the station platform. Anand noted it. It was the sort of notice that Vanessa would like, confirming, as it did, her views about the eccentric ways of the subcontinent.

It was dawn. The war was over now and Anand was travelling south to meet up with Vivek and his family for a break by the sea in Puri. Anand's first holiday since he had taken over the Lux. He knew he should have stayed in Calcutta to sort out the aftermath of Freddie's and Remy's deaths but he also knew he had to leave the city, leave the hotel, leave the room where Freddie had lain so peacefully in his own blood.

Almost all of the Lux's guests who had been stuck in Calcutta had now left – for Thailand, for Burma or back to their homes in the United States, Europe and Australia, leaving behind their tattered paperbacks, empty tubes of toothpaste, a razor and a pocket chess set with a knight and a bishop missing.

He told the police where they could find him, if need be, but he had answered their questions many times already.

He had given them the hotel register, told them about Freddie's weird behaviour, explained that the other guests in the room had departed in the night, left them to interview Baba. The British Consul had already visited, taking away some of Freddie's belongings with him.

Initially, the police seemed to be working on the theory that this was another 'hippy trail' murder. They wanted to know who had left so suddenly. They had taken finger-prints from the wall and the toilets where they found a bloodstained handkerchief. They interviewed the travel agent who hung around the Lux to ascertain the destin-ations of all the departing guests. Then the focus of their investigation seemed to shift. They were monosyllabic when he asked how it was going. When he told them of his plans for a few days' break by the sea, they had been non-committal.

Anand had been to Puri once before, as a child, with his grandparents, for the Car festival. His grandfather had taken him to the Sri Jaganath Temple and solemnly told him that it had been built by the old King of Orissa nearly eight hundred years ago. His parents had been part of the independence generation, proudly secular, but his grandparents had been devout Hindus and he remembered their pleasure when he was first able to recite the Gayatri mantra for them.

He climbed back on to the train as it left for the final stretch for Puri and made his way to the pantry car. He pounced on a discarded newspaper. The war was still on the front pages.

He booked into the Puri Royale, a slightly dilapidated

colonial hotel, dumped his luggage and strolled down the beach. Most of the people sitting in the sun seemed to be Russians, probably from the Soviet Consulate and Trade Mission in Calcutta. Large white thighs and bellies, faces sunburned red, unflattering bathing costumes. They looked like alien sea creatures.

A smattering of hippies, too, already engaged in their morning chillum rituals. There was an establishment in Puri, Fakir's, that catered to the long-haired wastrels as the Lux did.

He watched a Western girl with long dark hair stand up, peel off her kurta and run into the sea wearing only her bikini bottom. With a casual gesture of her right hand as she stepped into the water, she slipped the elasticated part of her bikini bottom to cover her right buttock. A couple of Russians followed her sprint into the ocean with their gazes. A group of fishermen, wearing only loincloths, were bringing their nets in, singing as they did so. Calcutta seemed a long way away. He found a rock to lean against, took out his ringed notebook and started writing.

My dear Nii,

Thank you for your postcard. War is over. That much is good. It took only 13 days. If only all our conflicts could be resolved so swiftly. They say that around 30,000 died during the actual fighting although, of course, hundreds of thousands had already been killed in the uprising before the war. Poor Bangladesh.

I have given myself a holiday down in Orissa, a beautiful part of the world although it, too, is just recovering from a cyclone in which 20,000 died. Death everywhere, it seems, even in my little hotel. But that is another story.

How has the war been covered in Ghana? I realise now that you are there how little I read of Africa in our papers. I am sitting on a beach watching young Europeans and Americans disport themselves with few clothes on while older Russians with slightly more clothes on look on in bewilderment. Are they attracted or repelled by the decadent West?

Vanessa has written to say that she is getting bored with Nottinghamshire and may be paying a visit. I think she still half believes that my hotel will be like the George V in Paris and we will spend our time sitting on silk cushions talking about mysticism.

What happens now in India is anybody's guess. Mrs Gandhi's hand is immeasurably strengthened by the victory in Bangladesh and one cannot see her being ousted by anything other than a Lee Harvey Oswald figure. She has certainly irritated the Americans with what she has said about Pakistan – she called it 'fascistic' – but I think they will soon calm down. I imagine Nixon is more concerned about what is happening to the east of us anyway – and getting re-elected.

What else the war may mean is hard to tell. I fear

that it has helped to water the seeds of Hindu fundamentalism and triumphalism and who knows where that may lead. I read about what is happening in Northern Ireland and remember our late-night discussions about religion. Is a blind belief in ideology – communism, fascism – any better or any worse than a blind belief in religion? I still think religion is more dangerous because a justification can be found in it for anything, whether crusades or inquisition or slaughters of infidels or adulterers. To be resumed?

Voltaire said that countries were either for sweating or thinking . . .

Your friend, Anand

The fishermen were departing the beach. What a straightforward and enviable life. No worrying about guests who ran off without paying. No balancing the books and bribing the building inspector and filling in tax dockets. And no one would be mysteriously beaten to death on your properties. No, you made your catch in the clear blue ocean, you brought it ashore, you sold it and you went home. You were helping to feed people and living in the open air, not in some crummy cubbyhole of a hotel where the smell of sewage was now starting to smother the scent of the guests' joss sticks. But would he really have relished the rough, salty waves, the daily hardship, the slim rewards? The sand in his underpants?

He started another page of the exercise book.

Dear Vanessa,

He tore it up and started again.

My dear Vanessa,
    It was lovely to hear from you again. War is over. I have to tell you about something awful that has happened. It is hard to explain and I find it difficult to put down on paper but I need to tell someone. Four nights ago . . .

He crumpled up the page and stuffed it into his trouser pocket, stood up and set off for his hotel. He wandered along the shore, fringed by tall palm trees, Tagore's 'single-legged giants'. The temple bells were ringing. By the seafront road there was a large water tank covered in nets. 'An experiment,' said the man tending it when Anand paused to ask. 'For mullet caviar.' Anand was not sure how to respond to this information. Were the Russians the intended market? He glanced at them as they folded away their blankets on the beach and brushed the sand from their mighty thighs and calves. Was India a great treat for them? Or was it regarded as what Narendra, his old school friend now in the foreign service, would describe as a 'hardship posting'? Would they rather be in Washington or in Paris or Rome, buying shoes and eating well?

    The local Baptist church, which he passed on his way back to the hotel, was displaying its Christmas decorations. Strange to see the nativity scene, complete with shepherds, wise men and baby Jesus, portrayed so delicately in Orissa in the midst of such religious competition. It reminded him of London in December when the West End stores would put the scenes of Bethlehem in the shopfronts. London, in turn, reminded him of his guests and threw him back to the night of the party. He re-ran the events in his head. Could leaving for Puri in some ways be seen as a sign of guilt? Can the mind ever bury such events? Would he look back at what happened that night for the rest of his life, as one did with defining moments – the first day at school, the loss of virginity, the death of parents? He missed his father and mother still. His sister's phone calls from India to him in London to announce first the death of his father through a botched operation and then, a year later, to say that his mother and uncle had perished in a car accident on the Delhi–Jaipur road, still cast a shadow. And now Freddie. I will always have Freddie's face staring at me, even when I close my eyes. Was that a hint of puzzlement, of disappointment in Freddie's dead eyes?

At the almost-empty hotel he took his hip-flask of Sandemans – the hip-flask Vanessa's father had given him that New Year – poured its contents into a pink plastic mug beside his bed, finished it, lay down and closed his eyes. He did not sleep.

Chapter Twenty-Five

GORDON HAD SLICKED his hair down with some Brylcreem from an ancient jar which looked as though it must have been in the Lux bathroom since the days of the Raj. A growing number of countries were now turning back long-haired travellers at their borders. Thailand had just started doing so, following the lead of Singapore, the strictest nation in the region. Travel agents now insisted that their hairier clients should try to look as respectable as possible. He had taken his clothes to the laundry the previous day to wash out any hints of dope.

Dum Dum airport had been crowded with people catching the first planes out of Calcutta after flying had resumed. He had left Larry still arguing for a ticket at the check-in desk. On the Thai Airlines flight to Bangkok, Gordon had his first Western meal since he had left London: egg mayonnaise, roast beef and sauté potatoes, trifle. The young Bengali beside him was travelling abroad for the first time and watched Gordon to see in which order he ate the items on the tray. Gordon was hungry. He had left the Lux before it was fully light.

Sometimes Gordon's nightmares seemed so real that it

took him a few minutes from waking to realise that they were illusions. Perhaps – perhaps – if he slept on the plane and woke only as they came in to land at Bangkok, Freddie Braintree's bloodied body would be a passing nightmare like all the others. But he knew in his heart that it was not. Oh, God, what use was all his meditation and study now? How had it happened? What had he done – or not done? Why had he fled?

Bangkok offered some temporary diversion. It seemed sleek and modern after Calcutta. Neon lights and flyovers. The pace was faster, more impersonal, as though the West, with its films and its hamburgers, its flashing advertisements and its miniskirts, had somehow vaulted over India and landed on both feet in Thailand. The smells – peanutty, coconutty, garlicky – were different. Yet it felt colder, less hospitable than Calcutta. Less of a hum. He felt suddenly lonely.

The motorcycle rickshaw dropped him at the Atlanta Hotel which seemed luxurious after the decrepit charm of the Lux. Hot and cold running water in the tiled showers, a fridge with cold Coca-Colas for sale, a shiny, black-and-white chequered floor in the reception area. Even a small swimming pool, for God's sake! The hotel had been catering to the American armed forces on rest-and-recreation breaks from Vietnam but, as the troops now opted for Japan, it had to rely on the hippy trail trade. It was almost full. In reception, two cadaverous young American men were having an argument about room rates with the manager, a young Thai in dark glasses and a Washington Redskins T-shirt. Gordon took an instant dislike to them, to their bullying manner and their short, service haircuts. There were a few familiar faces, fellow travellers whom he had seen in – where? Benares? A genial Dane with whom he had shared a meal in – where? Kabul? The Pudding Shop in Istanbul? They greeted each other as warmly as people can who both know they have forgotten the other's name. There were only a couple of beds left and Gordon took one of them, in a dormitory room. He slung his haversack down and looked at the warning array of mosquito netting over the other beds. Some travellers heading westwards for India had been waiting at the Atlanta until the war was over. Others looked as if they had been installed in the hotel for months or even years. Neat little bookshelves, carved Buddhas on their dressers, clothes carefully arranged on wire coat hangers.

Where would Britt and I have stayed? he wondered. He felt the ache of her absence again. She must have gone back to the States with whatsisname. Should he have tried to reach her again, fight for her instead of pathetically giving up? Should he have gone back the following morning to the Oberoi Grand just to be sure? Would he spend the rest of his life regretting that he had not made one more effort? Was she the dream woman that he had been too slow or too indecisive to win? Is this what life is – an endless series of regrets, of missed opportunities? Or was he, as his teacher in Kathmandu had warned against, merely watering the seeds of self-pity? Was there anything to be done? Fly to San Francisco? Or was it just that it had been the first sex he had had for ages? Yet it had seemed so perfect.

Back in reception, the two rangy Americans were

arguing about which was the better area to visit in search of bar girls. Gordon walked with the Dane to the end of the lane and the corner of Sukumvit. The ice-cream seller, explained the Dane, had a sideline in Buddha grass. Gordon drifted into his own thoughts and that last night in Calcutta. I blacked out, he thought. I bloody blacked out again. Oh, Freddie. Did I let you down?

The Dane pulled a packet of Zig Zags out of his tapestry shoulder bag and made a joint.

'Is it cool to smoke here?' asked Gordon. 'I thought the police were a bit heavy.'

'If you don't do it in their face, it's cool,' said the Dane. He lit the joint and passed it to Gordon. They contemplated the street in silence for a few moments.

'Why does time always go forward and never back?' asked Gordon.

'Been in India a long time?' asked the Dane.

They strolled back down the road to the hotel, swapping the joint and a mango ice-cream cone between them. Hope he hasn't got hepatitis, thought Gordon. As they arrived back, a motorcycle rickshaw pulled in and out jumped a familiar, yet unfamiliar, figure.

'Larry?' inquired Gordon, as the rickshaw driver was paid off. He gazed in puzzlement at the man in the well-cut dark blue silk suit, his shoes black and shiny, his open-neck shirt as white as one of the egrets Gordon had spent a whole day watching land off Colva beach a month or two ago.

'Hey, droog,' said Larry, showing little surprise at the encounter. 'It's Marvin now. Larry is . . . in the past.'

'You got here quick,' said Gordon. 'I didn't think I'd see you for days.'

'Everything has its price. Things got a little hotter. I have some shit to tell you later.'

Larry/Marvin – which was the real one? – raised one eyebrow as he registered with the hotel manager. Gordon noted that Larry's passport was now Canadian and looked new. He craned over Larry's shoulder to see what his new last name was but could not make it out from the scrawled handwriting. Gordon wanted to know about Freddie but knew that he should not be asking.

'Is there any news about . . .'

Larry checked out the other travellers in the lobby.

'Later, droog. What happened to that woman?'

'I told you, her bloke showed up—'

'But I saw her at the hotel the night of the party,' said Larry as he picked up his guitar case and what looked like a new rucksack. 'She was looking for you.'

'You're kidding?'

'No. She was pretty recognisable, droog – that body . . .'

'Oh, shut up.'

'I'm sure she was there, man. Still, it was a pretty crazy night, I guess.' He swung his stuff on to the bed beside Gordon's – the very last one in the hotel – and fiddled with the fan.

'What have you got to tell me?'

'Later, man.'

They sat by the pool in the moonlight that night. Larry played the tune of 'Me and My Shadow' and Gordon sang the song they had half written together – 'Me and My Sadhu' – which won a round of applause from a group of young, healthy-looking Australians and Scandinavians sitting in the white plastic moulded seats under a parasol. They tried out 'Hepatitis!' to the Hallelujah chorus and that went down even better. A tall Swede said that it wasn't very funny making a joke of a disease that was such a bummer. They sang 'Me and Bobby McGee' and the 'Fixing to Die Rag'. 'And it's one, two, three, what are we fighting for . . .'

Mosquitoes mounted attacks only partially deterred by the array of joss sticks and cigarettes, the ground-to-air defence system of the guests.

The two Americans appeared, flushed with alcohol and sex. 'You should have come with us, man,' they said to the assembled Australians, ignoring the two women in their midst. 'There was a chick that could fire a ping-pong ball out of her pussy. They really like Americans, too.'

'They like what you have in your wallet,' said one of the Australian women. 'That's all.'

'What do you know about American pricks, lady?' said one of the Americans.

'Only that there's about half a million of them in Vietnam and they've dragged us into it too,' said the Australian woman. 'Those girls you just paid for don't have any choice, they get kidnapped from the villages and brought down here. They're kids.'

'She's calling us all pricks, man,' said the American.

'You started it, man,' said one of the Australian men.

'Who the fuck are you, man?' asked the taller of the two

Americans, getting to his feet and pushing his chair back so violently that it crashed into the table and sent drinks and ashtrays flying.

'Who the fuck are you?' responded the Australian, also getting to his feet, a movement that showed him to be at least as tall as, if not taller than, his antagonist.

'Boys, boys!' said Larry, putting his guitar back in its case.

'OK, Oz,' said the first American. 'Let's fucking have you!'

The Australian woman tried to move in between them but without success. The two men locked each other in an inelegant hug, circling the pool like dancing bears until the American broke free and smacked the Australian hard under the chin. There was a cracking sound, a scream from the Australian woman and the Australian man fell to the ground, moaning and clutching his jaw. Two other Australians leapt up and grabbed the flailing American, one smacking him on the side of the head with a bottle of Tiger beer which amazingly did not shatter on impact. A slim trickle of blood ran down the shaven head of the American.

'For fuck's sake, cool it, man, we'll all get thrown out of here,' said Larry to no one in particular. 'This is a decent hotel and this is meant to be the time of peace on earth and goodwill to all fucking men.'

'You tell that to your fellow countrymen, fucking child molesters,' said one of the still-standing Australians. Two bodies tumbled into the pool as the wounded Australian combatant was tended to by his girlfriend. The hotel's night manager emerged and said something about 'no fights' and 'I call police'. Other guests had been woken or alerted by the noise and a trio of young Englishmen emerged at the poolside. They were short-haired and clean, with freshly pressed jeans and T-shirts, all of which carried messages or names of some sort on them. One was a Chelsea football club shirt, one a souvenir from Malaga and the third had a legend which looked strangely familiar to Gordon.

'What's happening?' said one of the trio.

'Just some fucked-up guys who've had too much to drink,' said Larry. 'Where you from?'

'London,' said the chattiest of the three. Gordon stared at the man's T-shirt. It showed a slice of bread with a smiling cartoon face on it and the slogan 'Got any bread, man?' My slogan, thought Gordon, the slogan that Adrian said was no good. Adrian had been right.

'Can I ask where you got the T-shirt, man?' said Gordon.

'My girlfriend got it – they give 'em away free with every six loaves of bread you buy at the supermarket,' said the Londoner. 'It's shit, isn't it?'

Why do people wander around with advertisements on their chests? wondered Gordon. They don't get paid for it. But then again, only six months ago I was getting paid to invent slogans that people would walk around with on their chests. Larry picked up his guitar and headed to a far-off table where he started strumming again. Gordon joined him.

'Let's get the fuck out of here tomorrow,' said Larry. 'There's heavy stuff going down. We'll go up into Vientiane, place I know, and we'll just play some music. This is bad karma here, wouldn't you say, O enlightened one? Here, what do you think of this:

> Dropped some O, snorted some smack,
> Feel so good, 'cos I'm going back,
> To Goa, that's G-O-A, Goa . . .'

He looked towards Gordon for reaction.

'Larry,' said Gordon, 'I think I blacked out that last night in Calcutta.'

'There was a war on,' said Larry. 'Don't you remember? Everything was blacked out. Things happen in blackouts that are nobody's fault. But I told you, man. Freddie's a casualty of war. It's just that if we'd stuck around, who knows what the fuck would have gone down. They'd have busted everyone in the Lux and I can't afford to have people messing with my life. I don't know what the cops are like there and I don't want to spend five years in some hellhole finding out. Nor do you. It was an accident. OK? Christ, I liked Freddie.'

'You would tell me if I had done something when I blacked out, wouldn't you? Something . . . something I should know about?' There was a pause. Was there something Larry wasn't telling him? Or – had Larry flipped and killed Freddie? Of course not. But how could he be so calm?

'Sure,' said Larry, picking up the guitar again and cocking his ear as he strummed it. 'This mother's out of tune. And so's my fucking stomach. Got any of your magic anti-shit medicine, droog?'

Chapter Twenty-Six

LONDON WAS COLD and bleak and unwelcoming. Everybody seemed to be dressed in brown or grey or black and had a drip on the end of their nose. The airport bus from Heathrow took Hugh to the Gloucester Road terminal. Why didn't they build the tube the whole bloody way? he wondered.

He had rung Jackie just before he left the hotel in Calcutta but, as usual, there was no answer. They would shortly be having Christmas at her parents' place in Gloucester, a prospect that filled him with gloom. Jackie's father, Arthur, also a teacher and a proudly prominent member of the National Union of Teachers, was, after a couple of bottles of Newcastle Brown, more than happy to expound on his theories about the British press. Although he affected not to read Hugh's paper, finding it 'too right-wing for me, mate', he always seemed to have spotted some story Hugh had written in which a union leader or leftie had been misrepresented.

Christmas was worse than other times of the year because Arthur's puritanical 'three-pints-and-that's-my-limit' rule was abandoned for the festivities. This meant that he would help himself to the bottle of brandy that sat untouched on the sideboard for the rest of the year. Then Hugh had to listen to diatribes about all the British governments for the last fifty years, from the current Heath administration ('pigs with snouts in the trough and chinless wonders'), the Wilson government ('sell-outs and fancy dans'), the Macmillan government ('adulterers and in-bred aristocracy'), the Eden government ('neo-imperialist adventurers and fops'), all the way back to Ramsay MacDonald's time ('quislings and placemen').

He would have asked the newsdesk to put him on Christmas duty – a task normally allotted to single men but, in fact, secretly much sought after by the married male reporters – but that would have meant talking to Linda. He was not sure he wanted to strike out in that direction quite yet.

It was less than three weeks since he had set off with a hangover for Calcutta and now, here he was returning with one. That last night in Calcutta was still a blur. How had it all happened? How had he found himself round at that grim little hippy hotel with Low Grady and his pals?

'We're 'ere, mate,' said the driver. Hugh pulled his case and portable Olivetti from the front of the cab and pondered for a moment telling the driver to take him back to Heathrow. He could fly away to – anywhere, anywhere that would get him away from recriminations from Jackie, from demands from Linda, from hints from the newsdesk that his copy had not been quite as hot as some of his rivals', and away from his own demons that had been awakened that last night in Calcutta. Three weeks ago, he had been a young war correspondent with a loving wife and admiring colleagues, his dream achieved at the age of twenty-seven, and now . . .

'Been hunting big game, have you, mate?' asked the cab driver as Hugh foraged through his wallet for another fiver.

'What?'

'Safari jacket – isn't it, like . . . er . . . *Born Free*.'

'Oh, that,' said Hugh, trying to hide his irritation as he calculated the smallest tip he could get away with. 'No, been covering the war in Bangladesh, actually.'

'Yeah, looks like you've got some blood on your sleeve, mate.'

Hugh glanced surreptitiously down. 'You should have seen the other guy,' he said.

'Is that war still going on?' said the cab driver. 'Didn't George Harrison do a concert for it?'

'That was last summer. No, the war only just finished. All over in two weeks – India beat Pakistan so there's a new country called Bangladesh now.' It was hard to tell with taxi drivers, thought Hugh, exactly what they did know and didn't know. You had to be so careful because they took such offence at being patronised. 'Just got back now.'

'Get any trophies? My grandad brought back a German helmet from Belgium in the First World War and sold it for two hundred quid forty years later.'

'Really. How interesting.' The cab U-turned and departed. That was a point. Where had he put the Pakistani regimental cap badges?

Hugh fished out his keys, opened the door and called out, 'Jackie? Hello?' The flat was chilly after the warm air of

Calcutta. The transistor radio was on. Jackie had not yet left for school. Or maybe they were already on holiday. It always seemed to be holiday or half-term at her school. No wonder the children were all illiterate nowadays.

'Hello, darling,' he called out.

Jackie came downstairs. She had her coat on and was stuffing exercise books into a leather briefcase.

'Oh, hi. I thought you weren't coming back till tomorrow.' She kissed him but without much warmth. 'How was it? Must have been interesting.'

'Yes, yes . . . I suppose so,' said Hugh, unzipping his case and rummaging in the top of it amongst the underpants and shirts that he had forgotten to give to laundry service at the Oberoi Grand. 'Got something for you. I hope it fits.'

He pulled out the sari he had bought at Dum Dum airport. The carpets had been ridiculously expensive. Jackie examined it with a frown.

'Is this for me?'

'I thought you'd like it – you could wear it to school,' he said in what was meant to be a jovial fashion.

'You're joking, aren't you? Anyway, it was a nice thought. It can go in the fancy dress box at school. Look, I must go in a minute. Do you want some tea? I'll put the kettle on.'

'OK. I'll dump this and run a bath, I think. Everything OK at school, is it?'

'Sure, it's holidays but they're having the end of term carol service. Oh, that Linda rang from the paper to tell you about the newsroom party tonight.'

Hugh feigned ignorance and indifference in what he

hoped was a convincing way and went upstairs to the bathroom. The hot tap made an ominous rumbling noise. He noticed, as he undressed, 'body oils' and a fat candle in a saucer at the end of the bath. Where had they come from? He heard Jackie call out from below. He could not hear her above the bath water so he hopped downstairs with a towel round his waist. She paused at the front door.

'I said I was heading off and I'll – what's that mark on your shoulder?'

Hugh glanced down. Fuck. The bite mark that Linda had inflicted on him nearly three weeks ago was still just visible.

'Shrapnel.'

'Shrapnel? You didn't say that you got hit! God, that's awful! They didn't tell me . . .'

She bent closer to examine it.

'It looks more like . . . like a bite mark . . .'

'Ricochet. Not a direct hit. The main force got caught by a wall, I guess, so . . . It was nothing, really, compared to what was happening to those poor beggars. God, my bath will be running over. I'd better –' and he headed up the stairs. 'See you tonight, darling. I'll try not to be late but I suppose I'll have to put in an appearance at the party. May have to check in for a medical, too.'

He climbed gratefully into a bath now nearly overflowing. He did not hear Jackie leave immediately but, five minutes later, was it his imagination or did the door slam?

Hot baths had been one of the treats at school, a sanctuary from the sheeting Highland rain and the rugby

289

played on pitches that could have been used for growing rice, cross-country races across potato fields. Unasked, a vague memory entered his brain, that memory again of the business with Farquar-Fox being held under the water for perhaps just a moment too long. Could he have done something? McGrady had been there at the time. Hugh soaped himself and thought of Linda. This led to an erection which he dealt with swiftly in the bath with eyes half closed. He scrubbed his nails and noticed a long, thin scratch across his left forearm which he had not spotted before.

He had been so keen to get out of Calcutta that he had flung all his possessions into his case and rushed for a taxi to Dum Dum. He had ignored the calls from the receptionist as he left the hotel that there was someone on the line for him from London. Probably either Linda or the newsdesk asking another inane question, he had reckoned.

He dozed in the comforting warm water.

Hugh awoke. He had fallen asleep in the bath. The skin on his fingers was unappealingly wrinkled. The water was lukewarm and the results of his ejaculation floated forlornly on the surface in a long, elegant swirl. It reminded him of the interiors of those lamps in the Habitat window. He dressed in fresh clothes and went downstairs. On the table was a neatly written note.

Dear Hugh,

I have been thinking a lot about our relationship while you were away and I feel that it would be a good idea to have a break from seeing each other for a while. I feel you have changed – perhaps I've changed, too – over the last year or so and that sometimes it's only really your work that matters to you. I know you are going to work later so I will come back and collect my things after school. I can stay with Nora and then I will be at my parents' over Christmas. We can speak in the New Year.

By the way, I may be just a silly comprehensive schoolteacher but I can still tell what a bite mark looks like. Jackie.

PS Can you give the milkman his Christmas tip? I think a pound should do it. And the dustman.

Hugh looked in the fridge and ferreted out a can of Tennant's lager from behind Jackie's massed ranks of yogurts. He studied the photo of the featured wholesome beauty – Maggie was her name, apparently – on the side of the can and then plunged the opener in. It was not yet 11 a.m. but, given the time difference with India, this was essentially like having an afternoon beer, he told himself.

He opened a tin of baked beans and searched for some bread to toast. There was a loaf of sliced brown bread – it had to be brown now, at Jackie's insistence – with a ridiculous cartoon character in the shape of a slice holding out its hand and saying, 'Got any bread, man?' He popped two slices in the toaster that had been given to them by Henry as a wedding present – 'You can never have too many toasters,' Henry had said – and checked his mail. By the second can of beer – Doreen, a brunette dressed in an unflattering ruffled cream blouse – everything was looking up: he would miss the hell of Christmas with Jackie's family and being lectured by her father on the imperial role of the United States in Bangladesh and he would be able to go to the office Christmas party at the Bell without worrying about getting back at 1 a.m. and listening to Jackie's theatrical sighs as he staggered into bed and had to get up half an hour later to empty his bladder. ('You don't buy beer, you rent it,' as Henry always, always said when they bumped into each other in the gents.) And, as he was reminded by a copy of *Time Out*, still open at the Theatre section, on the kitchen table, he would not have to spend a fortune on tickets taking Jackie's parents out for what had become their annual outing to the London theatre in that period between Christmas and the New Year. Jackie had circled four plays and scrawled a question mark by each, presumably in anticipation of offering her parents the final choice. *Sleuth*. *Hair*. *The Secretary Bird*. *Oh, Calcutta!* He noted that a line had been drawn through *The Secretary Bird*. Well, Jackie would have to foot the bill this year. He knew that her father would plump for *Oh, Calcutta!* because he would be able to look at naked women without having to compromise himself by going to a strip club. Hypocrite.

The office seemed remarkably unexcited when he rang to say that he was home and would be coming in for the Christmas party. 'Oh, are you back?' was the response from Max, as though he had not been out risking his life for the bloody paper. 'Someone will be pleased – Hughie.'

He took the tube to Blackfriars and walked across Ludgate Circus towards the office. He had shaved, splashed on some Old Spice and put on that Take Six suit that Jackie had helped him choose in the days when she still seemed to care what he looked like. The trousers seemed a bit tight, must have shrunk at the dry-cleaners.

The office had been decorated in the usual half-hearted fashion. Cut-out cardboard sleigh bells and a few strings of fairy lights. In the newsroom, a Christmas drink-up was already under way. Cheap wine, cans of beer, plastic cups, crisps, bottles of supermarket whisky and gin. Someone had already been at the gin. ('Gin is like a woman's breasts,' Henry would intone whenever anyone ordered a gin at the Bell. 'One is too few and three is too many.')

'Welcome home,' said Henry from behind his typewriter. 'Good job you did there. Great stuff. You must be knackered.'

Hugh gave Henry one of the Pakistani regimental badges which he had found at the bottom of his case. He wondered where the other one was now, the one that the weirdo – Freddie, was that his name? – had taken off him in Calcutta at that strange little party before, well, before all that business. Henry, looking slightly silly in a sort of *Man From UNCLE* polo neck, was a tiny bit too enthusiastic in his thanks. Over Henry's shoulder he could see Linda. She was wearing a very tight black sweater that accentuated her breasts, a black miniskirt, black lacy tights and very high heels. She smiled at him, winked and came towards him.

'Late,' she said, with a conspiratorial nod.

'I don't think so,' he said, looking at his diver's watch. It glowed luminously at him. 'Max said that it wouldn't kick off before half past six.'

'No,' she said, lowering her voice and her eyelashes. 'I am.'

Noticing that Max was coming towards him with a copy of the *Evening News* in his hand, Hugh swallowed and said nothing.

'Hello, mate,' said Max. 'We just missed you in Calcutta. They said you'd left. We were trying to get you to stay on for a day or two.'

'The war's over, Max,' said Hugh defensively. 'I didn't think there was much more interest in it.'

'I know, I know,' said Max, thrusting the front page of the *News* at him. 'It was just this – interesting tale, eh?'

Hugh looked at the paper.

'UNDERCOVER DRUGS SQUAD OFFICER FOUND DEAD IN INDIA,' said the strapline. Beneath it was the headline 'YARD MAN SLAIN' and a picture of a policeman in uniform. 'Could be serial killer's latest victim,' said the sub-head. The opening paragraph told how the body of Detective Sergeant Lewis King, 30, had been found with severe head injuries on a bed in a hotel used by hippies in Calcutta.

There was a large photograph of DS King. The hair was short and neatly trimmed and the man was clean-shaven but the photograph was, quite unmistakably, of the person who had been introduced to Hugh at the Lux as Freddie Braintree.

Chapter Twenty-Seven

5 January 1972

FROM THE MINUTES of the National Security Council's Special Action Group meeting in the Situation Room of the White House, 6 December 1971, leaked to the *Washington Post*:

> Ambassador Johnson added that Bangladesh will be 'an international basket case'. Dr Kissinger said: 'However, it will not necessarily be our basket case.'

13 January 1972
The new flag of Bangladesh is adopted. It consists of a red circle, to signify the rising sun and the sacrifice of the people, and a bottle-green background, to represent the youth and vitality of the country.

13 March 1972
Headline: YARD DRAWS BLANK IN CALCUTTA: Undercover officer's death remains mystery, say detectives returning from India.

Duncan Campbell

April 1972
Press release: The Pulitzer Prize for best news photograph for 1971 has been awarded to Horst Fass and Michel Laurent of the Associated Press for their photo, Death in Dhaka, taken during the Bangladesh war last year.

July 1972
Agency snap: George McGovern wins Democratic Party presidential nomination. Promises to bring troops home from Vietnam on first day of office.

November 1972
Agency snap: Nixon wins by landslide. McGovern concedes defeat.

August 1975
Headline: SHEIKH MUJIB, WIFE, RELATIVES KILLED IN BANGLADESH MILITARY COUP. TWO DAUGHTERS, ABROAD, SURVIVE HIM.

19 December 1981
   Mystery death officer remembered
   by Terry Tendler, crime correspondent

   The Commissioner of the Metropolitan Police yesterday joined family members in recalling Detective Sergeant Lewis King, who died ten years ago yesterday in mysterious circumstances in Calcutta. A service of remembrance, officiated by the Right Reverend Marcus Edney, took place

296

at the King family's local parish church in Epping.

Mr King, 30, was on an undercover assignment for a joint British-American drugs intelligence operation at the time of his death. His body, with severe head wounds, was found in a bed in a hotel used by Western backpackers on the day after the India-Pakistan war over Bangladesh had ended.

Despite an investigation, carried out jointly at the time by a team from Scotland Yard and the Calcutta Criminal Investigation Division, it has never been established exactly how Mr King died. His daughter, Sandra, fifteen, said in a short address during the service that she intended to become a police officer too, 'so that one day I can find out what happened to Dad'.

December 1981
Deluxe Hotel, Bahrain

My dear Vanessa,

I always think of you at this time, recalling the days we spent with your parents all those years ago. And, yes, I still remember your father's marvellous charade of 'She'll be coming round the mountain'!

I was very sorry to hear about you and Desmond. What can I say? I did warn you never to trust a barrister, especially one with the initials QC after his name. As you will see from the letterhead –

embossed, I hope you noticed – I am now installed at the Deluxe in Bahrain. My little cousin, BK, has taken over the Lux in Calcutta. With Uncle Framji finally dying last summer, there was enough money to renovate it. It now services a tour company called Jewel in the Crown, which runs architectural and archaeological tours of India and Sri Lanka. I was there only last month and it really is spectacularly changed – I even felt a tiny bit nostalgic for the travellers. I am not sure where they go now.

This hotel I think you would like and this time of year is the best to come. Bahrain has just had a visit from the Scottish comedian, Billy Connolly. The audience consisted mainly of oil workers from Saudi Arabia, many of whom had bought tickets for both nights of the show because they knew that they would be too drunk to remember any of the jokes from the first night – Saudi is dry, my dear, very dry, which is why Bahrain is so popular with Scottish expats. He made a rude joke about the Queen Mother after which some of the audience booed. 'F*ck off,' he replied. 'I'm one of these people who like Britain so much I live there.' That went down very well, as did a joke about a man with holes in his willy and a clarinet teacher which would take too long to explain.

I have to do a stocktaking now – you will not be surprised that we have the finest selection of Sandemans east of Cairo – but this was just to tell you to come and visit. Now that you are a single woman again, let the hot Arabian sun heal the wounds inflicted by the cold English psyche.

Your loving friend,

Anand

20 December 1981

Hughie,

I have gone to my sister's with the boys for Christmas. You are a complete shit and that business with the work experience girl – and she was a girl! – was the last straw. Your story about just trying to show her how the hostages in Teheran were confined was just plain insulting. And you know you promised Gavin you would take him to see *Chariots of Fire*.

For some time I have felt that you regard your job as more important than me and the boys. And I heard from Max that you actually got back two days before you said you did after the Reagan shooting. Where were you? What were you doing?

Ring me at Fran's if you want to speak to the boys. I have told them that you are going to be away on a story for a very long time and Godfrey said, 'So what else is new?' Henry rang to invite us to a Tarts and Vicars party. I am sure you know just who to take. I am not prepared to put up with things any longer unless you are willing to go to a marriage guidance counsellor which I very much doubt you will be.

Linda

PS Tip the milkman. Five quid should do it.

20 December 1981
Barcelona

Darling Dad,

As I am sure you have gathered, I will not be making it home for Christmas. Bumped into an old friend from film school – Hendrika, maybe you remember her, she came and stayed once in Fairfax, with her girlfriend. She's great fun and she's working on a documentary here and needs someone to take the stills. I should head home in the spring. You'd like it here, just your kind of place. Must run!

Lots of love,
Britt xxxx

25 January 1982
HEPATITIS IS CATCHING!
by our show business correspondent, Roddy de Vries

If you thought that a rock opera with a title like *Hepatitis!* and a theme of hippies in India would never make it to the West End – think again, man! Yes, the brainchild of former advertising copywriter Gordon McGrady – he wrote the irritating 'Got any bread, man?' slogan for the Flour Promotion Board in the early seventies – and his American co-composer, Lawrence Anunziato, got the same sort of reception that its big sister *Hair!* received more than a decade ago.

Critics have been mainly warm in their response

to the show, although a few have accused it of being derivative and slight. The audience on the first night gave the young cast four standing ovations and the planned three-month run has already been extended to six. Two of the songs from the show, 'Benares', and 'Me and My Sadhu', are already on the edges of the hit parade.

At the after-show party, McGrady and his glamorous girlfriend, Diana Scott, the 'socialist socialite', glad-handed guests from the world of show business. McGrady said his only disappointment was that Anunziato was not able to attend the premiere because he is in a jail in the US. Sing Sing, perhaps?!

5 February 1982

Obituaries

Henry Cyril Blakestock, who has died suddenly aged 64, was a 'journalist's journalist'. Mr Blakestock, who was born in Torquay, the son of a brigadier and a concert pianist, had worked for most of the newspapers in Fleet Street before going freelance last year on health grounds. A spokesman for the Middlesex Hospital said that Mr Blakestock had suffered a brain haemorrhage after an accidental fall during New Year's Eve celebrations at the Perseverance public house in Putney.

After starting his career with the *Liverpool Echo*, Mr Blakestock joined *The Times*, the first of many national newspapers he represented. He covered conflicts in Korea, Suez, Cyprus, Biafra and Vietnam.

Mr Blakestock was famous for his forthright manner on foreign assignments. On one occasion he was said to have commandeered an army jeep in Aden in order to 'get to the NAAFI before last orders', as he put it. He was also famous in Saigon for refusing to take cover during mortar attacks, claiming that he had a 'lucky sixpence' in his pocket which guaranteed his safety. His memoir, *War, War and Jaw, Jaw* was published in 1977 to mixed reviews.

Mr Blakestock is survived by his ex-wives, Claudia and Gwendolen, and by his daughters from the first of these marriages, Lucy and Maud.

As one former newsroom colleague, Hugh Dunn, said: 'He died as he lived – buying his round. He would have wished for no other epitaph.'

A memorial service will be held at St Bride's Church on Friday at 12 noon with a reception afterwards in the Snug Bar of the Bell, Ludgate Lane.

8 March 1982
Weddings: BOSE–PARTINGTON: at Nottingham register office, Anand Bose, son of the late Mr and Mrs Bose of Calcutta, Bengal, and Vanessa Partington, nee Balcombe, of Pheasant Manor, near Gidminster, Notts.

12 March 1982
Parole Board Ruling
Re: Prisoner number 1222288 Anunziato L

Lawrence (Larry) Anunziato applied for parole having completed nine years of his 20-year sentence for importing twenty-eight pounds of Cannabis sativa from Asia to the United States in the period 1970–72.

Anunziato pointed to his exemplary prison record and the fact that he now had an alternative career (see newspaper cuttings attached) as co-author of a successful musical, *Hepatitis!*, recently opened in London. Federal authorities argued against his release on the grounds that it would send the wrong message in the wake of President Reagan's 'war on drugs'.

Parole denied. Date for next parole entitlement application: March 11, 1984.

2 April 1982
From the home editor's desk:

Hugh – re your request to join the task force on its way to the Falklands, I am afraid we have already, as I think you know, asked Martin de Courcey to go. Without wanting to get into the whys and wherefores, can I just say that the incident with Magdalena at closing time in the Bell the other night did not exactly enhance your status at the paper. As a result, following a meeting of heads of department, a decision has been made to take you off reporting duties and appoint you deputy night news editor effective the end of the month.

Yours, Max

October 1984
Arts Diary, *Sydney Morning Herald*:

Poetry reading: Karen Chisholm will read from her new collection of poems entitled *Please Treat My Death As Suspicious*, based on her travels in Asia in the seventies. Downstairs at Gleebooks, Glebe Point Road, 7 p.m. Wine and finger food will be served.

2 April 1986
HEPATITIS! FOR BIG SCREEN
by our arts and heritage correspondent, Roderick de Vries

The musical *Hepatitis!*, now in its fourth year at the Adelphi Theatre in the West End and playing in twelve other countries, is to become a film, according to *Variety*. Negotiations are already under way to start casting the hit show which tells the story of hippies in India and Nepal.

The agent for Gordon McGrady, one of the two composers of the show, who will co-write the screenplay, said that it would be shot in Nepal and at Shepperton Studios. Rights to the film are understood to have been sold to Universal for $2.5

million. McGrady has also been contracted to write two further scripts for the Hollywood studio.

29 April 1991
Headline: CYCLONE KILLS 139,000 IN BANGLADESH

10 October 1993
Port-of-Spain, Trinidad

Hi, Dad! Sorry about the terrible picture on the other side but there are no decent postcards for sale. I'm here with Lori. She's that friend of Hendrika's I told you about, the interior designer. We're having such a good time. A lot of laughs! I feel really happy these days. We'd both like to come and stay with you for Christmas so you'd better start cleaning! Big kisses, B xxxxxxxxxxxxxxxxx

23 June 1996
Headline: SHEIKH HASIMA, DAUGHTER OF MURDERED SHEIKH MUJIB, BECOMES FIRST BANGLADESHI WOMAN PRIME MINISTER

9 November 1996
Via e-mail

Darling Dad,
    So sorry to hear about heart attack. Don't say I didn't warn you – and I thought your doctor had told you there would be risks from it. There is even a

Viagra ward in one hospital in Miami Beach! Lori
and I will come up at the weekend. We have exciting
news. Love, B xx

6 April 1997

Kieran and Karen Chisholm would like to invite you to
celebrate their 25th wedding anniversary which will be held
at the Star of India restaurant, Darling Street, Sydney on
April 6 at 8 p.m. No presents please but donations may be
made to the New South Wales Manic Depressive
Fellowship.

22 June 1998

From the home editor's desk:

Hugh,

As you may have heard, we have decided to open
a bureau in California, the better to cover both
Hollywood and the dot-com boom which is
obviously going to be the coming story of the next
decade. In light of what happened the other night
on the desk, it seems that it will not be possible for
you to continue working in the office so we are
prepared to offer you one last chance in LA. This, I
am afraid, is very much the last chance saloon and
any further problems will definitely mean closing
time. Don't blow it, Hugh – no pun intended.

Yours, Max

10 September 2001
Via e-mail

To foreign desk:
As all is so quiet – only shark attacks in Florida and the boring congressman-and-missing-intern story – have decided to take a four-day trip to Death Valley, something the travel pages have been asking me to do for ages. Apparently, there is even a golf course there! It may be difficult to reach me on my cell phone but I will be back by Sunday. Wish me well!
Hugh

28 February 2002
UNSOLVED: HBO launches new series on murder mysteries of the twentieth century, entitled *Unsolved*. Tonight: The Yin-yang Killer ... Bruce Montagne investigates the so-called 'hippy trail' deaths in India in the seventies in which two Americans and three Europeans, including an undercover detective, died. Their killer or killers were never found. Next week: the Zodiac murders.

April 2002
Press release: Bob Dylan to advertise Victoria's Secret lingerie.

Duncan Campbell

SERIAL KILLER MYSTERY
Hugh Dunn in Los Angeles

Police in Orange County, California, are investigating two deaths which bear a remarkable similarity to unsolved murders carried out on the 'hippy trail' in India in the seventies. In both incidents, the victims have been found with a 'yin and yang' sign with a line drawn through it pinned to their bodies.

The two victims were described as white males in their thirties. One was said by police to be a known vagrant.

In India and Nepal in the early seventies, the so-called 'Hippy Killer' is believed to have carried out at least five murders, usually leaving the yin-yang sign (see graphic) as a calling card. The most notorious of the killings was of an undercover British policeman, Lewis King, whose body was found in a backpackers' hotel in Calcutta in December 1971. No one has ever been arrested for the crime.

Sheriff Joe Dikerdem said that they were examining the possibility that the original killer was someone who had been in prison for a number of years and was now resuming his activities. 'Of course, we can't rule out a copy-cat killer,' he told reporters.

22 March 2003

Invitation to the opening of Lancers, a new experience in accommodation and cuisine.

Anand and Vanessa Bose invite you to join them at the opening in West Hollywood of the newest branch of the Lux-DeLuxe hotel and restaurant company.

Champagne cocktails, vintage port, Bengali snacks.
6–8 p.m.
Parking by Valet Girls.   RSVP.

Chapter Twenty-Eight

'**W**HAT CAN I get you?' said Deputy Assistant Commissioner Ian Mulgrew. 'Mineral water? Are you sure? Crisps or nuts? No? Let's get a table in the corner before the crowds arrive.'

As a humble detective constable, Sandra King had never bumped into DAC Mulgrew before, although she knew his nickname – Ginger – and his reputation as 'one of the old school'. He must have long since completed the thirty years he needed to pick up his police pension. Why did he stay on? She could feel his eyes checking her out, looking her up and down. She was in good shape at the moment, she knew – she wanted to be fit for her first marathon in May – but she still resented his attentions. Her male contemporaries in the police now, 'a twenty-first-century service for a twenty-first-century nation', as the commissioner liked to say, might still be wondering how they could get her into bed but at least they knew how to disguise their intentions. Some of the older women in the service still talked of times in the 1970s when they were called 'burglar's dogs' but no one would dare do that now. There was even an officer of Mulgrew's rank who was openly gay.

She asked for a still mineral water with no ice.

'Can't I get you something a little stronger? Not even a spritzer?'

'No, thanks,' said Sandra. 'I'm in training.'

He seemed to accept this.

'I knew your dad, you know,' said Mulgrew, as he sipped his pint of bitter. His hair was grey and thinning. She could see gingery strands in his moustache; possibly nicotine stains. The only people she knew with moustaches now were senior police officers or gay friends. 'Not well, but we were in the Drugs Squad together for about six months.'

'Yes, I know,' said DC King. She remembered the day she had been made a detective, the quiet pleasure in repeating the words 'DC King' to herself. 'Mum said you were at the memorial service when I made that embarrassing speech about becoming a policewoman so I could find out what happened to Dad.'

'How long is it now since he . . . er . . . since the death? It must be nearly thirty years.'

'More than that. But I still want to find out. You must have seen all the pieces in the papers about the "hippy killer" in California. Someone using that same yin and yang . . .'

'Calling card?'

'Yes – but I hate that term. It makes it sound so nice and neat. "Calling card". Bloody psycho. Anyway, I suppose I'm half resigned to discovering nothing new. It's just that I know it will keep nagging at me until I have, well, explored every avenue, as they say.'

'So, let's get it straight,' said Mulgrew. She noticed his eyes sliding down as she crossed her legs and her skirt slid up her thigh. She had dressed carefully for the meeting, white blouse and navy blue suit, heels not too high. Reflexively, she pulled her skirt down and Mulgrew tried to pretend he had been staring at a Scottish terrier sitting at its master's feet in the next booth.

'Dreadful noise, isn't it?' he said. 'Almost impossible to find a pub these days that doesn't have loud music or a football game on. Anyway, where were we? Yes, you want to go on unpaid leave for three months to try and find out what exactly happened to Lewis – to your dad. Well, I have spoken to Detective Superintendent Guttenburg and he is very happy with your work and is prepared to give you leave and then take you back to the unit when you return. So that's no problem. I also spoke to Brian O'Grogan, who led the original re-investigation – he's retired now, of course – and I've got clearance to give you the rest of the case papers.'

He reached into his briefcase, with its logo commemorating the Association of Chief Police Officers conference, in Torquay, the previous year. Two fat files, one the final report of the Scotland Yard team who had investigated the death with the Calcutta police, the other stuffed with contemporaneous press clippings; five battered paperback books and some dusty flotsam. Someone had scrawled 'Lewis King/Freddie Braintree' on the cover of the files in red Biro. Sandra felt a sudden jab of pain.

'I don't know how much of this you've seen, Sandra, but some of it is quite, well, explicit,' said Mulgrew. 'Photos of the body and stuff.'

She nodded in acceptance. 'I grew up with it. Mum told me everything, about how he'd decided that the best way to avoid ever having to explain his cover was just to play daft, like he'd been tripping too much. I think he had every Bob Dylan record and a whole lot of other stuff I've never heard of – Buffalo Springfield, Byrds, Turtles, oh, and the Incredible String Band, I think – and Mum said he would just spout stuff from the lyrics. I'd never heard of the Incredible String Band before. Had you?'

'Er . . . I don't think so. Not my cup of tea.'

'Really?' She fixed him with a piercing gaze which seemed to disconcert him. 'My mum said that he hadn't really wanted to go but that they reckoned he was the most suitable officer because he didn't look like a policeman.'

'He certainly didn't. If I can say so, you have inherited his, er, good looks.'

'You mean I've got freckles too.' He seemed embarrassed. Sandra wondered if she was being too hard. He would change the subject, she thought. He did.

'Another round? No? I'll just get myself one. Have a look at the files.'

At the bar, he exchanged banter with a couple of middle-aged men in tweed jackets whom she vaguely recognised as Scotland Yard press officers. She studied the thirty-odd black-and-white prints that had been made from the roll of film found in the pocket of her father's jeans.

'Did anyone ever work out what this was?' she asked when Mulgrew returned.

'I think you'll find that there's a note about it in the folder,' said Mulgrew. 'It's hard to tell what's happening, isn't it? There. "Photos appear to show man being attacked by mob who seem to be dropping stone slabs on head. No member of Calcutta police division able to recognise location. Could have been taken elsewhere on King's travels although he never used this type of film (Agfa 400) on any other occasion. Possibly film he acquired from elsewhere or passed to him by informant? In two photos (numbers 16 and 17), to right of frame with bushy hair, appears to be Western man. Not identified by Bengal authorities or European or American consulates. Too blurred to identify from CRO files. King notified bureau he feared photos had been taken of him." That doesn't really help us much, does it?'

Out of the corner of her eye she saw the two members of the press bureau ordering drinks at the bar. One of them nudged the other, who turned to stare. By lunchtime tomorrow, she thought, there will be a rumour in the canteen that I'm having it off with Mulgrew. She could not help noticing the bristle of stiff white and ginger hairs emerging from his nostrils. Yeugh.

'Now here's the passage that seemed most interesting to me,' said Mulgrew. He pulled a bundle from the second folder. 'UNDERCOVER DRUGS SQUAD OFFICER FOUND DEAD IN CALCUTTA,' said the newspaper clipping at the top of the pile. 'YARD MAN SLAIN.' There were typed notes stapled together beneath the news clippings from which he read.

' "King had informed liaison officer at consulate (see

consulate bundle, pp 2–6) the previous week that he suspected his cover was blown. Said he had been caught looking through other Lux guests' belongings and had been challenged. Did not say by whom."

'Have a look at this,' Mulgrew continued. 'It's a Pakistani regimental cap badge. No one seems to know why he would have that. It was pinned to his . . . er . . . shirt thing. Pakistani authorities have always denied any knowledge or contact with him. And you, er, saw the pathologist's report . . .'

'Drugs in his bloodstream . . . hallucinogens,' she said. 'Yes, I found that odd because my mum said that he avoided taking drugs by acting out of his head all the time. You don't think there's a possibility that . . .'

'He experimented?' Mulgrew shook his head. 'More likely he was given a spiked drink or something.'

'They never found the murder weapon, did they?'

'No. It's all a bit strange. His body was found in his bed in the hotel and it seemed . . . there's the report that he had been hit very savagely twice on the head, back and front, but there was no sign of blood on the walls which might have been expected. So perhaps he was killed somewhere else and then placed there. But why? As a warning? Surely it would have been much safer not to take the body there but leave it where it all happened. They did find blood on a handkerchief below the bed where one of the guests – McGrady – had been sleeping. And McGrady had already done a runner to Bangkok. He was interviewed a few months later when he was tracked down in Japan but he said he knew nothing about it till Anunziato – you'll come to him later on, the American bloke – told him about it in Thailand. Said he'd been at the airport all that night, as soon as the party had finished. They reckoned he was lying but they couldn't prove it. That handkerchief has been DNAed now – which they weren't able to do at the time – and it's not your dad's blood. It's all still a puzzle. The problem is that there was such chaos at the time that the investigation was, well – no disrespect to the Indians – very patchy, to say the least. By the time it was reopened by our chaps, lots of the evidence was missing.'

He pulled a bundle of stapled lined paper from the folder. 'This is what they had on the so-called hippy serial killer,' he said. 'Total of five unsolved murders with the yin-yang sign, all believed to be with the sign close to the body – "with the exception of King". It would seem that there were no more victims after your dad.'

There was a brief silence.

'Until now,' said Sandra. 'Until what's happening now in California.'

Mulgrew did not respond but looked in the folder again. 'And then there's your dad's notes and this.'

He handed her a student card and notebook. Then he waved over to the two press officers, who flushed slightly at having been spotted staring. They declined his mimed offer of a drink and went off to chalk their names beside the dartboard.

Sandra looked at the student card with its photo of her father, his hair a blond halo, gazing back at her. The name 'F. Braintree' was typed in beside it, with 'Leeds' written in his handwriting on the line marked 'College/Univercity'.

Duncan Campbell

You were a lovely young man, she thought, but I hardly remember you. What were you thinking then? Was it exciting or terrifying? Did you know someone wanted to kill you? She felt the tears coming but she was not going to cry in front of Mulgrew. She finished her mineral water, extracted the slice of lemon from the bottom of the glass and sucked it.

'Why did he have this?' she asked. 'He never went to university.'

'Oh, apparently they all had bogus student cards, got them reductions on the trains and so on. I expect he had it as part of his cover,' said Mulgrew. 'The books – they were beside his bed. There's some writing in them, your dad's handwriting. That's why they were kept as part of the evidence and not given back to the family – to you and your mum.'

Sandra stroked the old paperbacks. Jean Genet. Rabindranath Tagore. Herman Hesse. V. S. Naipaul. Joseph Heller. Some of the names were familiar but she had read none of them.

'That's his handwriting too, I think, in the notebook. It's been transcribed. Bit difficult to understand.'

'Yes,' said Sandra. 'He's sort of saying that he's sure there's an outside agency involved . . . I don't know . . . that he's on to something suspicious. He's written "Agency" with a question mark. Who was that? CIA? Travel agency?'

'There was certainly something going on involving somebody's intelligence services. He told us he was looking at it but he was never very specific. He said it was very hush-hush, need-to-know type of thing and it would need him to stay there, lying low, for a while.'

'Maybe he was afraid.'

'Maybe. Our chaps did make inquiries of the other team – of Six – at the time, but no go.'

Sandra looked again at her father's notes.

'It's got his assessments of all the people who were staying there,' she said, half to herself, half to Mulgrew. 'The owner, Mr Bose, he doesn't reckon was involved in drugs at all. Says that he turned a blind eye to smoking but discouraged dealers from coming in. Then, let's see, there's Ramesh Bannerjee, the one known to guests as Baba – again not seen as suspicious. Interviewed. Member of Christian missionary group. Kieran Chisholm and Karen Pitt, "address Sydney, believed to be sending drugs back to Australia". My dad says: "Karen mentally unstable, writes morbid haikus and hands it to people to read." What did my dad ever know about Japanese poetry? Then there's McGrady – is he really the same one who wrote that silly rock opera? I got taken to it on a date. God, what a waste of time, terribly derivative.'

'Never saw it myself,' said Mulgrew. 'What did your dad say about him?'

'Hmmm . . . "Frequent user, not seen as having sufficient nerve to traffic. Expresses standard anti-establishment views (anti-Vietnam war etc.). Spends time with Anunziato." Then there's this – I can hardly read his writing. Oh, look, they've put "indecipherable" in the margin. What does it say?'

'Looks just like a doodle to me,' said Mulgrew.

'No, he's written something. I've looked at so many of his letters to my mum that I can pretty much tell. That's an

R and that's a T, I think. It's something like "Photog . . . Brit? Tk pic at rst". I guess that's took picture at, I don't know, restaurant? Post restante? "Not dv." I dunno. I guess he must mean that one of the Brits there took his picture, which would mean McGrady or someone else who isn't mentioned at all. What's this? "Advtsng?" That must be advertising. Wasn't that what McGrady used to do? God, it could mean anything. "Remy Duval. French. French Foreign Legion." I thought you had to be foreign to be in the Foreign Legion?'

'Well, apparently quite a lot of French people lie about their nationality to get in. He had dual Swiss citizenship, I think. He was the one found in the cemetery with his throat cut a few days earlier with the sign on his body, and this,' he held up an identical sign, 'is what they found in your dad's pocket.'

'Not pinned to his body?'

'Er, no. Maybe whoever did it couldn't find a pin.'

Sandra emptied a large brown envelope in the bundle.

'Look at this,' she said, holding up a photocopy of the Lux Hotel register with comments attached, presumably by the investigating officers. ' "Bobby McGee – not traced. Frank Mills – not traced. Henry Chinaski – not traced. S. Paradiso – not traced. Major Major – not traced, believed to be fictitious name. Mr Mudd, believed to be pseudonym of man described by other guests as 'the silent monk'. Not traced." If it's all right with you, sir, I'd quite like to take all this home and have a proper look at it. Would that be OK?'

'Of course. I don't think anyone's had them out for years. It was pretty well established at the time that, well, it would just be one of those bloody frustrating unsolved jobs, although, of course, I appreciate that it means something very different to you. Oh, there's another letter here from the parole board in America about Anunziato applying for release.'

'Is he still inside?'

'Oh, yes, but I don't think he'll be much use to you.'

'Do we know where he is?'

'I think it's in there somewhere – there you are: US Federal Penitentiary, Terre Haute, Indiana. That's where our old friend Howard Marks, Mr Nice, "the sultan of weed", was, if I remember correctly.'

'And now Marks is performing at the Shepherd's Bush Empire, telling his dope tales. Crime pays, eh?'

'Don't tell me – my son went to see him with his pals from college. A great time was had by all. What a world. A bloke can make a living talking about his greatest drug deals. Sure you won't have one for the road? No? OK, then. Let me know if you need any more. Good luck! Now I'd better go and buy those press office chaps a pint or they'll be having you and me as an item by the end of the week.'

Mulgrew made a point of shaking her by the hand before striding through the now crowded, smoky pub to the dartboard. She looked down again at the folder in front of her and picked up one of the books, *Our Lady of the Flowers*, that her father had been reading perhaps, touching, turning over the pages, on the day of his death.

Chapter Twenty-Nine

'I'M YEVGENY AND I'm your waiter today,' said the young man with the Tin-Tin haircut and the sweet smile, as he steered Gordon across the floor of Pelicans, newly anointed by *Los Angeles Magazine* as one of the city's finest seafood restaurants and the best place to eat in Venice. Gordon noted that the sign had been changed since the restaurant first opened from 'Pelican's' to 'Pelicans'. Had someone – a pedantic English screenwriter of a certain age, perhaps, like him – drawn the owner's attention to the shoddy punctuation? he wondered.

The two studio executives were both already at the table, looking as buffed and shiny as a pair of fresh nectarines in a Bel Air deli. Gordon marvelled at the whiteness of their matching T-shirts, the snappy cut of their lightweight suits. Such whiteness took him back to his advertising days and the strangely fascinating secrets of lighting washing powder commercials, to which he had been privy as a young copywriter. Both men, he noted, as they studied their menus like earnest students sizing up an exam paper, had immaculately manicured nails.

Rob and Austin were their names. He had memorised

them from the e-mail advising him of the appointment. Both rose, beamed and shook hands as he reached their table on the beachfront terrace. Their manners were impeccable. When was it, he wondered, that Americans took over from Britons as exemplars of politeness? Gordon was gratified to see a pair of pelicans glide past, skimming the surface of the Pacific, as he took his seat.

'We have as starters – not on the menu – crab cakes with a lemon grass sauce, a Senegalese soup . . .' Yevgeny launched into the comforting litany which had the same familiar cadences as the chapel service which had started each day at Gordon's school. As with the old school prayers, the words passed in a blur. Instead of a conclusion giving thanks to the Lord and a firm 'Amen', there was a reference to snapdragon pastry.

It had been two years since Gordon had moved to California and more than thirty since he had been sitting on a seething mattress in the Lux, listening to Larry play the guitar. The events of the final night at the hotel he had never managed to obliterate from his memory, but it was like an old bereavement now, forgotten for weeks and then suddenly propelled into his thoughts by a smell – sandalwood incense, perhaps – an old Dylan number on his car radio, or even the glimpse of some curly-headed, barefooted drifter on the Venice boardwalk.

After his sojourn with Larry in Laos, Gordon had travelled for nearly two years, picking up odd jobs: playing guitar in a hotel bar in Manila; writing training manuals in Hong Kong; teaching English in South Korea and Japan. He flew home from Tokyo to London at the end of 1973.

The squat was long since dissolved, its members scattered into different worlds. Grace was living in Manchester with a companionable Chilean exile called Jorge and was pregnant. Gordon returned to his parents' home in Edinburgh to find that his father had suffered a mild stroke. He stayed for a dutiful while, playing piano for a ballet troupe rehearsing for the Edinburgh festival before heading south again and getting a job as an assistant administrator with one of the new fringe theatres blossoming in London in the mid-seventies.

One night, at a party for the end of the run of *Good Soldier Schweik* and with a bottle of the theatre's cheap red wine inside him, he took over the piano and performed from memory all the songs of the 'opera', *Hepatitis!*, that he and Larry had written during the month they had been lying low in Madame Lao's guest house in Vientiane. It brought the house down. In fact, the reception was much more enthusiastic than for *Good Soldier Schweik*. The theatre director immediately made him promise to allow them to stage it, setting in motion an eighteen-month chain of events that led to a premiere in the Little Upstairs Theatre in Holloway, then to the West End and, beyond anyone's expectations, to a run that had lasted for four years, with touring companies taking it around the world.

Once he realised that *Hepatitis!* really was going to be performed commercially, he had gone in search of Larry. What had happened to him? They had lost touch when they parted in Vientiane, Gordon to head east, Larry to do a little business, as he described it. Gordon tried every Anunziato in the phone book in Nevada, tried New York,

San Francisco, Seattle, Portland, Santa Fe and Eugene directories, guessing where Larry might have settled. Finally, the producer, fearful of some late copyright hang-up, hired a private detective. A week later, he came back with the news: Larry had been arrested in 1973 trying to cross the United States/Canada border using a false Canadian passport in the name of Marvin Smith.

'Hi, droog,' Larry said when they finally saw each other through the two-inch-thick bulletproof Plexiglas at Terre Haute Federal Penitentiary. Almost ten years had passed since their previous meeting but Larry had aged well beneath the prison pallor. He looked as though he was working out. He talked more or less non-stop. The only hint he gave of the hellishness of it all was when Gordon asked about what life was like and Larry replied, 'Well, let's put it this way – the most satisfying moment of my day yesterday was having a successful dump.'

'You look well,' Gordon had said.

'So do you,' Larry replied. 'No more blackouts?'

'Not for years.'

And that was true. They had looked at each other. They had spoken again awkwardly about Freddie's death. That morning, Larry told him that Freddie had died in an accident that had been nobody's fault but, when pressed, his description seemed vague and unconvincing. How come Freddie was lying there so neatly? A few months later, in mid-1972, Gordon had been tracked down by Scotland Yard detectives to his teaching job in Tokyo. He could still remember his heart thumping when they arrived at the language school and said they wanted to interview him at the British Embassy. The interrogation lasted all day. He told them he had been at the airport all night and had not known Freddie was dead till he was in Thailand. Could they tell he was lying? Two days later they wanted to see him again. They repeated almost the same questions and seemed unconvinced by his answers. Then they were gone.

'Who would have thought that Freddie was a policeman?' Gordon had said. 'Although when you think about it, remember how he always used to refuse to take the chillum? How he would say he'd just put one out or he had a bad throat?'

'And how he kept writing things in his little diary. And looking through other people's stuff. Remember what you used to say? All that second-hand Buddhist shit you used to lay on people but one thing was right – "never assume".'

'Larry, was there stuff about Freddie's death that we didn't go into at the time?'

'What d'you mean?'

'Just that.'

'Dreadful accident . . . I don't go back there in my head, man.'

A silence between them. It was Gordon who decided to break it.

'You know, I never realised that those elephants you had were full of dope. I honestly thought you had some little business selling Indian artefacts.'

'I know. I knew you weren't the narc, you weren't smart enough.'

'Never assume.'

'Time to finish up your visit, folks,' came a uniformed voice.

It was only then that they had had a hurried conversation about the musical. Gordon still assumed – never assume – that it would not be a success and that the most Larry would get from it would be a souvenir programme. Even so, Larry had seemed remarkably unconcerned about it as Gordon told him of the casting taking place, the plans to stage it.

'You are not innarested in this lousy production, are you?' Gordon had said.

Larry had smiled and wiped the sweat away from his upper lip with an orange jumpsuit sleeve.

'I'm here for a while, droog,' he had said. 'What's to be interested in?'

'By the way,' Rob was saying, as he soaked another piece of Pelicans' freshly baked bread in olive oil, 'I have to tell you I loved *Hepatitis!*. I saw it as a kid. We all thought, that's what we're going to do when we leave school, go backpacking on that Eastern trail. Course, we never did. Whatever happened to the guy you wrote it with? Didn't he end up in jail? Is he still there?'

'Yeah, I'm afraid he is. He got twenty years for the cannabis smuggling and then there was some fight with a prison officer and they added on another twelve for good measure,' said Gordon. He gestured at Yevgeny. 'Some mineral water, please?'

'Ever see him?' asked Austin.

'Yeah, I've seen him a couple of times. He looks after himself. I saw him last year. He was in pretty good shape.'

'What happens to his royalties?'

'Some went to his folks in Las Vegas until they died. To be honest, I don't know any more. Maybe he'll come out a rich man. But I think he'd swap it all to have had the last thirty years of his life.'

'Did he ever write anything else?'

'There was something called *Busted!* which – I dunno, it didn't quite work.'

'And you went on to . . . ?' asked Rob.

Did he really want to know? Or was he just asking to see if there was some discrepancy between his Wikipedia entry and reality? After the success of the stage version of *Hepatitis!*, at the suggestion of his agent Gordon attended a script-writing course given by a sardonic American dressed entirely in black. This was meant to equip him to write the film script for the musical, which had had moderate success, a couple of BAFTAs for costume and cinematography and three unrequited Oscar nominations. He wrote a treatment for a biopic of Robert Louis Stevenson, optioned for a year or two but never made. A comedy thriller about money laundering set in the Cayman Islands had not negotiated the journey from page to screen. A detective story set in the London of Hogarth and Gin Lane, also still unmade, had led to the invitation to come to Hollywood. Deciding to leave London for Los Angeles had been easy.

His relationship with Diana had ended when she had met a young Argentinian sculptor. Gordon was also being sued for breach of copyright over two of the songs in *Hepatitis!* in what had become a long and expensive legal action. The idea of an endless summer in southern California appealed. Now he had his green card, his Californian driver's licence and a house in an orange grove in Ojai, a couple of hours north of Los Angeles. Grace, long since married to her Chilean, came out with her family every summer, to sit by the pool, listen to the coyotes at night and occasionally talk of their days in Clapham. He even played the odd game of cricket for a Hollywood team of British and Australian expats and this had led to a reunion with none other than Anand Bose, the manager of the Lux Hotel, who played for a team of Indian and Bangladeshi expats called the Bengal Tigers. Mr Bose, who now had a hotel and restaurant in West Hollywood, had recognised him first.

'Aha,' he had called out. 'The star bowler from Calcutta!' For a few weeks after their reacquaintance, they had seen a lot of each other. He met Anand's wife, Vanessa, and their droll young daughter, Clara. They came up to Ojai to stay with him for the weekend. But the gaps between their meetings had grown longer, Gordon's troublesome back led to his retirement from cricket and it had been at least six months since they had met.

He lived alone, his six-month affair with the American actress and singer, Faye Fado, having come to an end when she announced that she was quitting show business entirely and moving to a desert ranch. Since she had been due to star in two major productions at the time, Faye's decision had excited the media enormously and there was a hunt on to find where she was now living, not least because she was said to have shaved off all her hair. For a few weeks after their split, Gordon noticed paparazzi, a combination of grizzled old English and shiny young Latino, hanging around at the bottom of the gated drive to his house.

'I'll start with the crab cakes but with no sauce,' said Gordon. 'And I'll have the sole as a main course with the spinach and arugula salad.'

'Good choice,' said the waiter.

'So,' said Austin, who was obviously going to chair the meeting. 'To cut to the chase, what we wanted to talk about was this: *Ill Met by Moonlight*. Does that ring a bell?'

'The film?' said Gordon. 'Sure. I saw it when I was a boy. Powell and Pressburger's last film, wasn't it? Dirk Bogarde as the hero. Great movie. That's what we grew up on. Those war films. *Reach for the Sky* – Douglas Bader, fighter pilot, war hero, lost his legs when he was shot down, taken prisoner but carried on flying, doing missions against the Germans. Kenneth More. I remember it – one nurse telling another not to make a noise when he's lying in hospital – "There's a boy in there dying", something like that. *Ill Met* was about kidnapping a German general on – where was it? Rhodes?'

'Crete,' said Austin. 'We're not sure about the title. It was called *Night Ambush* when it played here in the fifties but at the moment we're sticking with *Ill Met* if we can secure the rights.'

'I would have thought it's a bit British, isn't it?' said Gordon. 'Not exactly *Saving Private Ryan*. Is there much of an appetite for that now? I thought that the vogue had passed.'

'Well, that's where you may be wrong,' said Austin,

picking up another piece of bread and preparing to dip it into the tempting saucer of Napa Valley's finest extra virgin olive oil before a hidden voice seemed to still his manicured hand. 'There is a taste at the moment for great war tales, the "greatest generation" wind hasn't blown out yet, and there's a feeling that this has everything. We are possibly entering another war, there will be an interest in the heroics of battle. And *Ill Met* was practically fifty years ago. Think what we can do with special effects that you couldn't do then.'

'It's still a very British story. I'm not sure that an American audience would be that interested.'

'Well, that's where you come in. You see, in the version we're talking about, it turns out that this is a joint American–British operation.'

'You're kidding,' said Gordon.

'No. It's no great stretch to have some of the special forces as American. In *Pearl Harbor*, there was an American pilot in the Battle of Britain.'

'But that was a film,' said Gordon, feeling, for the first time since he had written the Flour Promotion Board's campaign, a frisson of guilty embarrassment running down his spine.

'Pearl Harbor wasn't a film, Gordon. It happened.'

'*Pearl Harbor*, the film, was a film.'

'Look, at the moment we're just kicking something around,' said Austin. 'What we want you to do is just come to the table with a treatment. At the moment, the idea is to have a British guy, an American and an Australian. What we need is the camaraderie between the American and the

Brit, like you had with the characters, the American and British hippies, in *Hepatitis!*. They start off as hostile, bit of resentment, distrust, loud American, uptight Brit, but then, in the course of the kidnap—'

'They fall in love?' said Gordon.

Austin gave him another look as their waiter placed their starters in front of them with a flourish. 'Gordon, we felt you were the right person for this project but if you can't see yourself committed to it in any way, I quite understand.'

'No, sorry,' said Gordon, calculating that around $250,000 was on offer, which would pay off the latest tranche of legal bills. 'Are we making the German general a nice guy or a nasty Nazi?'

'Up to you,' said Rob. 'People aren't wild about the Germans here at the moment because they won't back us over Iraq. Although, of course, by the time this comes out, things may have changed.'

'Well, I could certainly think about it,' said Gordon. 'How soon do you need to know?'

'End of the week, next Monday at the latest,' said Austin.

'Blimey, you're in a hurry,' said Gordon. 'What else have you got up your sleeve? Bonnie Prince Charlie as a Californian who comes back to free Scotland?'

'How did you guess?' asked Rob with a smile.

Austin paid the bill with one hand and checked his messages on his cellphone with the other. I will have a long swim in the pool when I get home, thought Gordon. And smell the oranges.

Outside the restaurant, he handed his ticket to the valet parker who was dressed in the standard red waistcoat, white shirt and black pants – good God, thought Gordon, did I think of trousers as 'pants'? I've been away from Britain too long. As the young Latino – Guatemalan? Salvadoran? – went off to fetch Gordon's Prius from down the street, an emaciated, bare-chested, middle-aged man, dressed only in a pair of filthy jeans hanging perilously over his protruding hips and with ugly open sores on his bare feet, approached.

'Spare change.' The words were a demand, not a request. He stared Gordon straight in the eye. Gordon placed a couple of quarters in the man's calloused hand. He scrutinised them for what seemed like almost a minute. Gordon gave him one of the dollar bills with which he was planning to tip the valet parker. The man stared at him again, as if gazing deep into his soul. Beautiful clear green eyes, thought Gordon. Should he share with him what Nietzsche had said about beggars? Maybe not. The man turned slowly and strolled down the street, towards Venice Boulevard, limping.

Chapter Thirty

HUGH HAD BEEN looking at his driving licence renewal form for nearly ten minutes. The height was the same, five foot ten inches; the weight, he had to admit, was now 210 pounds – just over that ominous 200 barrier, not bad for someone nearing sixty. He realised that he no longer converted the pounds into stones. Going native. Even although he still objected to the height in his British passport being translated into metres. But what about hair? Hard enough five years ago when he had had to put 'grey' down for the first time, although 'white' would, even then, have been more accurate. Now should he, in all honesty, insert 'bald'? Or 'bald with a tiny sprig of springy hair on top and white sides'? But by its very nature, he thought, you cannot have 'bald' hair.

This had been one of the most painful of reminders of age. He remembered the first tiny sign that he no longer looked like a young man. It was that period, more than thirty years ago now, when he had just come back from Calcutta. Jackie had left him, Linda had told him she was pregnant, there had been the worry – it seemed so remote now – over what had happened on the last night in Calcutta and he had ended up getting very drunk every evening in Soho, hanging out with Henry until they were thrown out of Muriel's and then looking for whatever joint was open – usually Maltese-run strip clubs where a pint of non-alcoholic lager cost ten pounds – to make the night last longer. In those days, young people, mainly Italians or Spaniards, handed out flyers to clubs on Oxford Street and Hugh had been made painfully aware, when they ignored him, that his receding hairline and expanding girth made him, at the age of twenty-seven, too old to be considered a potential raver.

He remembered how livid Henry had been once, not long before his death, when a young woman offered him her seat on the tube. So far, nothing as disturbing as that had happened to Hugh, not least because he never travelled by public transport, unless it was airborne. Except out at Lone Pine on the way to Death Valley on that September weekend eighteen months ago for what his fourth wife, Helena, had planned as a romantic weekend under the pretext of doing a travel feature, when a cheerful waitress asked him if he wanted to see the 'senior diner's menu'. That had, initially, been the weekend's low point. Immediately forgotten, of course, when they emerged from their romantic retreat at the inn that offered 'no distractions from the outside world – no phones, no TV, no problems!' – late on 12 September 2001 and saw, when they paused in Parumph for a burger on what was planned as a leisurely drive home, the banner headlines of every newspaper.

There had been recriminations from the foreign desk –

'For fuck's sake, Hugh, you know you should always, always make sure the desk can reach you.' Worse were the constant sly innuendoes.

Apart from that, the job of LA correspondent suited him, even if he had been miffed when he was turned down first as home editor, then as foreign editor, in favour of two young women who had not even been born when Kennedy was assassinated (thus ending that particular line of conversation in the pub; not that they deigned to visit it very often).

His third marriage had been coming to an end – another sign of age, he felt, since Lysette (head of classified ads, West Country girl, lovely bone structure) had left him for another man with whom she turned out to have been having a two-year affair – so a move had been welcome. Linda had made a bit of a fuss, since their second son was having drug problems, but, as Henry had always said, 'a man's got to do what a man wants to do'. Relations with Linda had been frosty since the divorce and she had undoubtedly turned the boys against him. Both young men now, with neither girlfriends nor jobs, they came out for a two-week holiday every year and he saw them when he went back to London to check in at the office, have his teeth done and see his mother, now in a nursing home in Hove, a depressing departure lounge full of confused people in their eighties and nineties asking when lunch was. His mother would call him by his father's name and hold his hand while he surreptitiously looked at his watch and calculated the train times back to London. The 'care assistants', mainly Belarusian and Nigerian, called her by her first name which

Duncan Campbell

irritated him. She seemed to spend her days watching wild-life programmes on television and eating mashed vegetables and trifle. His sons were tall, diffident creatures who spoke as though they were football players who had not had the benefits of an expensive education and wore their underpants above their waistbands like Latino gang members in East LA. The younger one, Gavin, had claimed to be on his 'gap year' on both of his last annual visits. More like a bloody gap decade. He sent them money for their birthdays; they sent him text messages: 'hpy bdy dd!' Attempts to interest them in any of his pursuits (a season of Gilbert and Sullivan revivals at UCLA, a few jars at the Queen Bess in Santa Monica) were unsuccessful. All parties were always relieved when the final day of the holiday arrived.

He had been married to Helena for just over a year. Number four. Had he really gone down the aisle four times? Actually only once, the others had all been civil ceremonies. Still. Number one, Jackie, had long since remarried and moved to Wales where she was a headmistress – although she would probably insist on being called a head teacher. Number two, Linda, he had to keep in touch with because of the boys. He exchanged occasional e-mails with number three, Lysette, to sort out loose ends over the house which, for reasons understood only by her lawyer and militants of the feminist persuasion, she had been allowed to keep.

Helena never asked about his previous wives. He liked that about her. She did her best to make the boys feel at home when they visited. He did not really deserve her.

338

They had met three years ago at a press conference where she was handling the PR for some over-ranked American novelist who wrote in verse. She was divorced with two well-behaved teenage daughters who said that Hugh sounded like Anthony Hopkins, nicknamed him 'Hannibal' and seemed to accept him as their new stepfather with equanimity. He actually preferred them and their easy affection to his own stiff sons, who would search his fridge and ask, 'Any beverages here? Got any Stella?' or would want him to drive them, not for some fresh air at Mount Baldy but to the nearest Gap or Urban Outfitters.

The work itself was fairly simple, if the events of 11 September could be forgotten. His patch was mainly show business – 'something to take our minds off all the doom and gloom elsewhere in the world', Max suggested – so he found himself lifting stories off the front pages of *Variety* or interviewing directors and actors at the Four Seasons Hotel, waiting patiently with earnest Chinese journalists or large, louche Dutch reporters to share a table for thirty minutes and perhaps three questions each with Quentin Tarantino or Jewel or whoever the studio had strong-armed into making an appearance for the media.

For the first few weeks, he wrote a weekly picture byline column on film which had been sub-headed 'The man the stars trust'; the description had been meant as a joke but had been dropped when it turned out that too many readers took it literally and started sending him e-mailed requests: 'Dear Mr Dunn, could you please ask Tom Cruise the next time you see him whether he would be interested in looking at a script about a gay astronaut? . . . Could you ask Meg Ryan if she could open our newly refurbished local theatre? We would, of course, pay her air fare and arrange suitable accommodation. Best weekends for us would be . . .'

Initially, he lived in a beachfront condo in Santa Monica, overlooking the Pacific and the cycle path that ran from Marina del Rey through Venice and nearly all the way to Malibu. He used the Joan Rivers line about Malibu – 'where you can lie on the sand and gaze at the stars or, if you're lucky, vice versa' – so many times in his stories that a pushy sub-editor asked him the last time if he was sure he wanted to use it again. Then he met Helena, whose admirable divorce settlement had left her with a house in Pacific Palisades, where they now lived. He missed being able to walk to the faux-Irish pub (and being able to use his binoculars to gaze at the honeyed bodies of the rollerbladers with their peach-shaped bottoms swishing by in the late afternoon sun) but there were compensations. The pool, the barbecues at sundown, the absence of police sirens at night, no rent.

'What are you doing, darling?' asked Helena, coming into what she called his 'den' to say goodbye before she went to work.

'Killing spam e-mails from people who want to increase the length of my penis,' he said. 'Is that coffee I smell in the background?'

'Fresh pot,' she said. 'Decaf.'

'Oh, God.'

'You know what the doctor said.'

'That's what I miss about the National Health Service,

at least the doctors didn't feel that they had to deliver a moral lecture every time they saw you.'

'Did you get that message from the English woman?'

'Who? Pru?'

'No, Sandra something, Sandra King, I think. She left a number. She said you wouldn't know her. It's on the fridge door under one of the Shrek magnets. Bye, darling.' She kissed the top of his head. 'Love you.'

'Likewise,' he said.

Helena was much less, well, judgemental than his previous three wives. She did not make a fuss if he had to go off for a story. In fact, she seemed quite pleased when he did.

He had a few friends amongst the other foreign correspondents. They were mostly a fairly tame and conscientious bunch these days, anxious to get to bed early so that they could file another thousand words or 'blog' about Arnold Schwarzenegger's governorship or whatever ancient actor or record producer was on trial for murder that week. The American journalists tended to be even more serious and none of them drank. He had a couple of muckers, one British, one Canadian, with whom he could go out for a drink or a decent lobster dinner and talk about Americans. But there was no colony of foreign correspondents, no watering hole where you could go and complain about your newsdesks and the local bureaucracies.

Even at the Oscars, the one event that all foreign correspondents were obliged to cover, there were few familiar faces. Many British papers parachuted in their showbusiness editors – people like Roddy, or Roderick, as he liked to call himself now, de Vries who would ask superfluous questions of the occasional British winners in the hope that the flattered thesp would say, 'Hi, nice to see you here, Roddy!' in response, thus guaranteeing themselves favourable mentions – 'that very parfit theatre knight . . . the always alluring . . .' – from Roddy for the next year.

Hugh had covered three Academy awards ceremonies now. He was already weary of them, having to dress up in his dinner jacket, which had shrunk apparently in the heat of southern California so that the trousers now looked like tights with a silk stripe down them. The *Vanity Fair* post-Oscar do, supposedly the party of the night, was a tiresome affair where journalists like Hugh were treated like trade, told they could only attend for forty-five minutes and then bullied afterwards if they failed to mention the event in their paper. The party itself was like a nouveau riche wedding, full of vaguely familiar people who spent their time looking over the shoulders of whoever they were talking to in case someone shinier had arrived, while fat English paparazzi with pasty faces and bad teeth patrolled the red carpet outside, barking, 'Brad! Brad! Pamela! Pamela!' as the stars entered past fans who looked as if they had walked out of the pages of *The Day of the Locust*.

His latest assignment was a rum one. He had to interview Gordon McGrady. Yes, that same Gordon McGrady who had been a drop-out in Calcutta all those years ago. Who would have thought that ten years later his picture would appear in the paper as the co-author of some dire 'rock opera' with no plot and dreadful lyrics. He had gone to see it with Linda – or was it Lysette? – and Henry (who fell asleep and snored) and Henry's then girlfriend, a spectacular Latvian dentist. They all agreed it was unbelievable that it was such a hit. There had been a film of it and Hugh had a vague feeling of having seen McGrady occasionally in the papers since then when some film or other opened, even recently going out with the very loopy American actress and singer, Faye Fado. Now the arts desk had asked him to get an interview with him, something to do with a story in *Variety* that McGrady was rewriting *Ill Met by Moonlight* and turning it from a British operation into an American one.

'Poor show, if true,' as Greg, the shaven-headed arts editor, said. Anyway, they wanted an interview with McGrady, photo and everything. The usual snappers were all busy so Hugh had been told to come up with someone local, anything to save the picture desk from doing their job.

Hugh thought of saying he was too busy to do the interview but there had been a few recent suggestions that one of the young 'colour writers' on the paper, a woman who could not have been much more than twenty-five, was keen to work in LA. Was this a hint? Voluntary redundancy had yet to be mentioned but he knew that some of his contemporaries back in London were being subtly leaned on to take early retirement. He dreaded returning to England. On his last visit, London seemed to have been taken over by drunk young people barking inanities and obscenities into mobile phones and sullen eastern Europeans who jumped the queue at bus stops. The streets were covered with dog shit, nothing worked and everyone seemed in a bad mood. Anything to avoid going back.

So he had contacted McGrady through his agent. They arranged to meet at some fancified new place in West Hollywood called Lancers, probably a gay hangout. He wondered whether to mention in his article that he had been to school with McGrady, that he had been a bit of a guitar-playing poser who wore mohair sweaters. Or would McGrady, if he did this, possibly tip off *Private Eye* that he had been called Bogbrush, just the sort of thing that the *Eye*, who still gleefully mentioned his 11 September mishap every now and then, would love.

The girls, his two stepdaughters, were out riding. Helena was arranging a silent auction for a charity do to be held in Palm Springs ('where the average age is the same as the average Fahrenheit temperature', as he put it every time the place cropped up in a story, until that same snooty sub-editor asked him if he thought the joke was, just possibly, a bit tired). He reached for his Filofax and ran his finger down to P for Photographers. All four names were busy. He helped himself to a Pacifico beer from the fridge, which was the size and temperature of a morgue, went out on to the deck and settled down on the sun lounger to read the *Los Angeles Times* magazine to look for feature ideas to appropriate.

He was half reading, half dozing in the sun when his eye was caught by one of the names attached to a photo spread about a new Marina del Rey building, some place that was supposedly the most original design since Frank Gehry's Venice beach house. Britt Pedersen. The name Britt had rung a bell from the moment he had seen it in the register at the Oberoi Grand in Calcutta more than thirty years ago. Britt. Still taking pictures. He dialled 411 and told the impressively accommodating operator the person he was seeking. Refuelling in the kitchen, he plucked the number for Sandra King from the fridge door and headed back outside. Who the hell was Sandra King?

A hummingbird was hovering over one of the deckchairs. It deposited a tiny, elegant dropping, the size of grain of corn, before flying off.

Chapter Thirty-One

THERE WAS THE Queen of the Rodeo on the white Arab, carrying the star-spangled banner. There were the bull riders and the clowns and the steer wrestlers and the barrel racers and the women's formation riding team from Bakersfield, all in sparkly lilac outfits with their matching Stetsons at a jaunty angle. There was the sun over the Kern Mountains, directly behind the parade. It was not going to be the easiest of shots.

Britt started shooting from her position on the top of the stand, conscious that every time the composition seemed right, one of the riders would shift in his or her saddle and turn into the sunlight or one of the horses would buck. Still, her close-ups were fine: the Rodeo Queen with her little button WASP nose and adolescent zits only half obscured by the shadow thrown from the brim of her Stetson; the rodeo riders with their pinched faces, prematurely lined by the pain of cracked ribs and pinned ankles; the kids that rode the bucking sheep, little replicas of their tough-guy dads, from their bow-legged swagger to the who-the-hell-are-you expressions when you asked them if it was OK to take their picture.

Beside her in the stand, Lori pulled a bottle of water from their cooler and gave her hand an imperceptible squeeze. They were used to walking through Venice hand in hand, along the boardwalk with their arms round each other, but here, four hours from Los Angeles, where Lori seemed to be the only black person and where the police log in the local paper suggested that the main crimes were 'spousal abuse' and methamphetamine manufacturing, they limited their public expressions of affection.

A few years ago, up in the Bay Area to visit her dad, they had bumped into Josh. He had eventually taken his revenge by going off with Patti (two children, unpleasant divorce) and was now a sleek architect living in an ugly house he had designed himself near Point Reyes. His expression, when he saw them together, had registered about six different emotions: surprise, curiosity, desire, resentment and a couple of other things she couldn't put her finger on. She soon realised that some men, some old high school friends, found the whole idea of her being a lesbian a bit of a turn-on at first and then a relief. Her father laughed out loud when she told him she had a girlfriend: 'Great! I always wanted another daughter.' Her mother's reaction had been more nuanced, an unarticulated calculation about grandchildren hovering behind her tanned, patrician brow as she was introduced to Lori for the first time in a laid-back Ojai eatery. Brother Brad, now the owner of a little coffee bar called AWOL in Vancouver, had been thrilled. Patti, of whom she saw more after her divorce from Josh, asked sideways questions about the sex.

Britt was doing a lot of work for European publications

these days as well as her regular stuff for the *LA Times*. She made extra money taking portraits of the children of dentists and plastic surgeons and some occasional work for women's magazines, illustrating such articles as 'What men think of your orgasm face' and 'How many ships would your smile launch – if it's only a couple of kayaks, here's some tips!' There were features on the LA gangs, on the polygamists of Utah and on women in the military for *Paris Match* now that a war in Iraq looked inevitable. And then, two days ago, this very strange call.

'Hello,' said the voice, with its quaint English accent. 'Bit of a blast from the past here. This is Hugh Dunn. I'm sure you don't remember me but I was a British journalist in Calcutta for the Bangladesh war in '71. We shared an army van a couple of times . . .'

'Bogbrush!' she had exclaimed before she could stop herself, startling Lori who was reading on the sofa beside her and drawing a quizzical look from Luz, their adopted Guatemalan daughter, who was doing her geography homework. 'Sorry, yes, of course I remember you.'

A slight pause at the other end. 'Well, anyway, the reason I rang is that I'm still, God knows how, with the same paper and I'm their man in LA. I've got to do an interview with someone called Gordon McGrady – whom you may also just remember.'

Gordon. Of course. That Gordon. Back then. Gordon, who acted as an unintentional catalyst, who had helped to make up her mind to say farewell to Josh. Gordon of the Lux Hotel, that hotel from which she had fled on that night that she had never quite unscrambled in her brain: the mob, the cry for help, the firecrackers, the fusion of the memory with that body in the ditch in Khulna, a body that did not cry for help, the dying face she had photographed only to lose the film that same night, a film never recovered and never mentioned to Mok, not then and certainly not when a similar photo – other collaborators pleading with the Mukti Bahini just before they were bayoneted to death – had won lots of prizes.

That Gordon, with whom she had made love in a Calcutta hotel room, who had laid his head between her thighs, gently curled her hair around his fingers and told her that he could not remember when he had been happier. The Gordon who gave her his saffron scarf. There had been a postcard, or two. She had been half tempted to respond but probably he was sending them to all the women he met on his travels – like the one in whose arms she had found him that final night in Calcutta, whom he was promising never to leave. She had run from the hotel, turned and seen Freddie, sweet-natured Freddie, in the midst of an angry crowd. Was he being chased by someone? She had never found out. He was screaming, he was in panic but she had not stopped, she had run and run until she reached the safety of her hotel room. A week later, back in the safety of Marin County, she had read in the *Chronicle* of the British undercover cop who had been killed and stared and stared at the fuzzy newsprint photo to reconcile it with the dreamy Freddie. *Newsweek* had run an item too, linking it to the other hippy trail deaths. She never mentioned it to anyone, not even Lori.

After Calcutta, there had been the new men. Josh had

been replaced by passive-aggressive Dick and Dick by passive-passive Hassan and so on until she had met Hendrika again and a new world had opened up in front of her. Why did I wait so long? she wondered. Why didn't I remember that feeling of thrilling anticipation in the hot tub with Louisa all those years ago? After Hendrika, there had been Lori, a Trinidadian interior designer. They ended up in bed, much as she and Gordon had, after a night of wine and laughter in Barcelona. Only this time there had been no backdrop of war and no blackouts and no parting, only spectacular sex and the tipsy pleasure of love in a foreign country.

Lori had meant a feeling of having come home, as eventually she did after a spring season taking fashion pictures in Rome. There was a mad year in San Francisco launching 'brittlorimages.com', an internet photo agency – Lori always said the name was too long – and losing all their savings as dot-com boom turned to crash. They moved south to Venice – 'THE Venice, not the wet one in Italy', as she described it to annoy her European friends – adopted Luz from a Guatemalan orphanage, after much hustle and many dollars, and then Dad had his stroke.

That had been the darkest cloud in her sky since her parents parted. She had not recognised his voice when he called her from the hospital. By the time she and Lori reached him, he seemed to have shrunk in size. His self-confidence had evaporated. Her big, swashbuckling, chuckling father had become a little old man with a peevish view on life, dependent on nurses and relatives. Her mother came to care for him, hold his feeble hand while she wiped the dribble from his lips. Brad, pardoned for his draft evasion during the Carter years, had returned briefly from Vancouver where he had just become a grandfather. When her mother phoned late one night last summer to say that her father had died, her first emotion was relief. The mention of Gordon took her back to the time when her dad had picked her up from San Francisco airport all those years ago, told her not to worry and admired her saffron scarf.

That Gordon. The 'blast from the past' carried on talking. She had to ask him to repeat himself because her mind had immediately flown to Calcutta and that night.

'So tell me about this guy, Gordon,' said Lori as they drove home from the rodeo shoot in their VW convertible. 'You had a scene with him, right?'

'Well, hardly.' She cast a glance into the rear-view mirror and saw that Luz was asleep. 'A couple of nights of passion in Calcutta. I'm sure I told you about it.'

'Was that when that guy, the cop, got killed?'

'Yeah, that time.'

'That was that hippy killer thing, wasn't it? How do you feel about seeing him again? Maybe he's the killer. Isn't he still around? Wasn't there another couple of murders in Orange County last year?'

'Were there? I'm kind of curious, I guess. It's always interesting to see how people have aged, don't you think?'

'Can be a bit depressing. You look at them and think, God, they must be thinking the same about me, about all the weight I've put on.'

'You haven't put on weight.'

'You didn't know me when I was eighteen. I was nearly Miss Port-of-Spain. Why have you got to take his photo?'

It turned out that Gordon McGrady, who had had a hit with a musical called *Hepatitis!* – she vaguely remembered seeing the name and wondering if it was the same person – was now a screenwriter in LA. He was writing a screenplay based on a much-loved British film called *Ill Met by Moonlight*, something which had caused a furore in Britain because it apparently intended to substitute Americans for British. There had been a 'major national hoo-ha', said Hugh at the end of the phone, a petition to studio heads. Upshot of it all, said that voice that was now starting to sound familiar again, was that Gordon McGrady had agreed to an interview. A photo was needed. She checked her diary. Although the fee was pretty cheeky, it would pay for Luz's soccer camp week. She was to meet him at Lancers, a South Asian boutique hotel and restaurant in West Hollywood.

They hit the 5 freeway just before Bakersfield – 'Bikersfield', as a gnarled Hell's Angel with a voice box had told her, when she did a feature the previous year on a bikers' reunion there – and Lori put her head on Britt's shoulder as she drove into the sunset. The sky was darkening and Luz stirred in the back seat.

'This is the moment when girls of your age are supposed to ask are we nearly there yet?' said Britt, glancing at Luz again in the rear-view mirror. Lori laughed.

'Why is that funny?' asked Luz.

Britt flipped through the CDs in the rack. Mainly old favourites taken from her father's house after he died. She found the one she was looking for and slid it into the player.

'I used to ride the rodeo,' sang the soft cowboy voice. She sang along with him. I'm like you, she thought, I only ride wild horses in my dreams.

Chapter Thirty-Two

'THAT'S ABOUT THE third time you've read that letter,' said Vanessa over breakfast on the terrace of Lancers. It was their habit to eat the first meal of the day on the roof before the day staff arrived to prepare the tables for lunch. Most of the hotel guests had already left for script meetings or auditions. 'What are those photos? Is it a blackmail demand or something?'

'Not exactly,' said Anand, stroking his beard, an impressive, patriarchal, metallic grey.

'Not exactly?' said Vanessa, dipping a sliver of toast into the baked egg that she had taught the young sous-chef, Alfonso, how to prepare and pushing her thick red hair from her face. 'Pray tell us what that means.'

When they had first met, thirty-five years ago now, Vanessa would tease Anand about what she told him was his old-fashioned English usage, which she suggested came from reading too much Kipling and Hardy as a boy in Bengal. She would mimic some of his more arcane expressions. Those old bantering phrases had become their conjugal shorthand.

'Many years ago . . .' said Anand, pushing the *New York Times* away from his plate. He had subscribed to the paper since he first arrived in Los Angeles after Vic had told him that all he needed to retain his sanity in California were subscriptions to anything with the words 'New York' in the title; the *New Yorker* and the *New York Review of Books* also arrived regularly. Vic, now a neo-con academic who wrote abrasive op-ed pieces for the *Washington Times*, still sent Christmas cards, as did Nii, now with the UN in – where was it? – Somalia? Sudan? Something with an S. He felt guilty that he could not remember.

'Many years ago,' Vanessa mimicked him, using the strangled, upper-crusty voice with which they used to tease each other.

'Many years ago, in 1971, when I was still running the Lux –'

'Of blessed memory,' said Vanessa.

'– something happened,' said Anand, pausing to let the sound of a passing police helicopter die down. 'It was the night the Bangladesh war was over and there were lots of celebrations and confusion. We had a little party on the roof. Deviani and Vivek came and all of the guests.'

'The great unwashed.'

'That's a little unfair. As far as I recall, they spent quite a lot of time on their ablutions that night. Anyway, there was one guest there, a chap called Freddie Braintree, who we all thought was a bit mad, touched by the sun or too much LSD. You could never have a straight conversation with him, he would always answer obliquely, quoting Bob Dylan or somesuch.'

'Or somesuch,' she mimicked.

'Anyway, there were odd things about him. Baba – who really ran the establishment – said he'd seen him looking through other people's belongings and Baba also said that his student card – all the hippies had bogus student cards to get them discounts – did not match his passport. Odd stuff. Anyway, on this particular night, he was in an agitated mood. We thought it was just the noise and the confusion and quite a few people had found the blackout a strain. Well, that night one of the people at our little soiree was an English journalist, Hugh Someone, who had been at school with Gordon McGrady. And, I don't know exactly what happened but I think there was some sort of confrontation between Freddie and either this Hugh character or Gordon about who knows what. I asked Gordon about it when we met up again here but he said those days were all a bit of a hazy time and we never really had the conversation. Anyway—'

'Anyway.'

'To cut a long story short, we heard this noise on the street, not far from the hotel. There were big crowds out celebrating. I remember looking out and seeing something going on. There was a hubbub, raised voices. I have to confess I did see Freddie and he was in some sort of bother, looked like he was being chased by someone. Part of me thought I should go down and investigate but, well, I left it and when I did think about it again, the crowd had moved on and all was quiet so I never went down. The following morning, I found Freddie dead on his bed, head all bashed in, poor chap. I can still see it.'

He could, too. He paused. The blood, like port, that was the image that stuck. 'It was awful. Only his name wasn't Freddie Braintree at all. He was a British undercover drugs squad officer called Lewis King who had been living in all the hippy hotels from Benares to Kathmandu, supposedly gathering information on who was sending drugs back to Britain and America. He was working for some Anglo-American drugs task force thing. The dotty behaviour was all part of his cover.'

'So?' said Vanessa, pouring coffee from the pot into her Lancers logo china cup.

'Well there had been this "hippy killer" supposedly going around bumping people off in India at the time. So it looked like Freddie must have been one of his victims, but they never found out who killed him. Never even found a weapon. They interviewed all the people there at the time and me and Baba, of course. But a lot of the hippies had already flown out that morning. Then they sent out chaps from Scotland Yard and they went through the whole thing again. Every now and then some journalist or television crew would come out to do something on the "Lewis King mystery" or the "hippy killer" – in fact, there was a documentary on one of the cable channels about it a year or two ago which I caught the end of. A few Americans and Europeans are killed in India and there are lots and lots of investigations. What about the mass murder taking place at the same time in Bangladesh? Not too many documentaries about that. Anyway, the murders stopped until – well, that thing in the papers about the chaps who were murdered in Orange County by someone who left the same sign. As though the murderer was back in business and over here.'

'So? The letter?'

'Well, what do you make of this?

Dear Mr Bose,

I was given your address by your cousin who now runs the Lux Hotel in Calcutta. I hope you will forgive this intrusion after so long but I promise not to take up much of your time.

I have been given leave from my job as a detective constable with the Metropolitan Police to look into the death of my father, Detective Sergeant Lewis King, in Calcutta, in December 1971.

I understand that at that time you were running the Lux Hotel where my father was staying under the name of Freddie Braintree. There was, as you may know, an investigation at the time into the circumstances of my father's death but no conclusions as to what had happened and, as I am sure you can imagine, it has been on my mind as I grew up, not least now in the light of the two murders in California carried out in similar fashion. For this reason, I am trying to talk to as many as possible of the people who may have met my father in his 'Freddie Braintree' days to see if I can learn from them, even after this passage of time, what happened. I have a roll of film which was by my father's body when he died and hope you may be able to identify some of the people in it. I enclose prints.

I am flying to Los Angeles this week and will ring on my arrival.

Yours,

Sandra King, Detective Constable

'Well, well,' said Vanessa. She paused to let the noise of another helicopter, this one from a television news station, pass.

'Well, well, indeed. Now I know what you think about fate and serendipity—'

'Serendipity is just what unimaginative people name their gift shops,' said Vanessa. She gave her husband a loving look.

That morning, after receiving the letter, Anand had stared at himself in the mirror, looking for the young man who ran the Lux. The hair was still intact, if a different colour. A few more ounces of flesh on his face. Dark bags beneath his eyes. The insomnia continued, his lifelong companion. A week at Insomniacs Boot Camp at Newport Beach, which he had attended unwillingly at Vanessa's insistence, had had no noticeable effect. He was intrigued by the way that Americans believed that everything – obesity, insubordination, addiction – could be solved by a week or two in a boot camp. He had been instructed at the camp that he must not watch television, listen to the radio or speak on the telephone from 9 p.m. onwards but found these instructions impossible to follow when running a hotel and restaurant. The joy of the United States was that at any hour of the night there was something on television, whether it was tractor-trailer racing, re-runs of *M*A*S*H* or manic preachers. Age also gave him the ability and licence to snooze in the afternoons.

'So what are you going to do about it?' asked Vanessa.

'Well, as it happens, Gordon is coming here to be interviewed by that same journalist, Hugh Someone.'

'Is Gordon with anyone these days?'

'I don't think so. I think that thing with Faye Thingy came to an end. He doesn't seem to have much luck in that department.'

'Why have you never mentioned all this about the dead policeman before?'

'It was so long ago, you were with your dreadful barrister husband . . .'

'Judge, please.'

'God, is he a judge now? How depressing. Poor criminals. Anyway, back then, there was a suggestion that Freddie – King – was in the intelligence services, possibly a double agent – he did have a Pakistani regimental badge on him, as far as I remember, or something like that. We are out of marmalade.'

A second television news helicopter swept past. The day staff had now arrived to clear up the debris from the night before and to set the tables for lunch.

'Gordon is coming here to meet this journalist chap so I was going to read them the letter and see what they remembered of the night. I know Gordon got very irritated with Freddie for misquoting Bob Dylan –'

'How egregious.'

'– and I have a feeling something was going on that day.'

Maybe they had all rumbled that he was a copper.'

'I don't exactly see Gordon exacting vengeance for the crime of misquoting Dylan.'

'Well, no, he would have been a bit too soft-hearted to do anything about it but there were others in the hotel—'

'Soft-headed,' said Vanessa.

'The others might not have taken too kindly to an undercover officer sharing their lodgings and fooling them – ah, Ramon, good morning. Can we keep that table in the corner reserved this afternoon? Someone needs it for an interview. It's all right, it is a British journalist but not the one who called you "amigo" all the time.'

A fourth helicopter flew past and when Anand turned on the television to see if anything was happening, there was live coverage of a police chase down the Harbor freeway. It was being reported on all the local news channels, which had interrupted their discussions on the probability of a war in Iraq to follow the pursuit. Anand took a secret pleasure in following police chases on television; usually some Latino youth would stumble out of the car forty minutes later with his hands in the air, be made to lie on the ground while he was handcuffed and then turn out not to be an Al Qaeda member but someone who had driven illegally in the car-pool lane or jumped a stop sign in Long Beach. Sometimes the fugitives would wave at the television crews or make a run for it over the back walls of houses. A couple of times they had been shot dead after they had appeared to aim weapons – which would later transpire to be a cellphone or a bottle of beer – at the police.

California had never been part of Anand's long-term plan but, after his success in Bahrain, his cousin shared his dream for a hotel chain that would encircle the world and announced that a property in West Hollywood had been made available as part of a debt owed by an old business associate. So Anand and Vanessa arrived in Los Angeles with their daughter, the adorable Clara, and created Lancers, 'the boutique hotel with the rooftop Indian brasserie'.

He found LA strangely comforting. Calcutta might be the city of 'dreadful night' but Aldous Huxley had called LA the city of 'dreadful joy'. He had been intrigued to see on television one evening a black civil rights lawyer tell an interviewer that the city came fourth after Calcutta in the world's 'wealth disparity' league. Twin cities, one wrapped in darkness, the other in the slanting light that made dark glasses as much a necessity as an umbrella in London. There was even a Skid Row in downtown LA quite as desperate as any beggars' quarter in Calcutta. He liked the Beverly Hills architecture, the palm trees, the fact that the city did not keep telling itself how marvellous it was, like New York and Paris. It was an oddly puritanical place, he thought, where a madam like Heidi Fleiss could go to jail for 'pandering' while every week women offered their bodies in the back pages of the *LA Weekly*.

'Penny ha'penny for your thoughts,' said Vanessa.

'Why is it that, every time you say that, I am thinking about something I would be ashamed to admit?'

Vanessa got up. As she left the terrace, she ruffled the

flop of grey hair that hung over his forehead and straightened the tiny gold pendant of Ganesh that hung round his neck.

Chapter Thirty-Three

'YOU LOOK VERY distinguished,' Gordon was informed by Anand when he greeted him at the entrance to Lancers. 'Distinguished is the word people use when they mean "God, you've gone really grey",' said Gordon. Anand did not demur. 'How's things? Still playing cricket?'

'What do they say in London – "can't complain"? And, yes, still the odd game,' said Anand. 'By the way, I received a strange letter this morning. A piece of our mutual past.'

'Is this about Freddie Braintree?'

'How did you know?'

'My agent in London said that the police had been in touch. Freddie's daughter or something. Pretty weird after all this time, *n'est-ce pas?*' Gordon tried to make it all seem as casual and inconsequential as possible. Since he had renewed acquaintance with Anand, Freddie's death had cropped up only once. 'Ah, hi, Vanessa, you look great. You've lost weight – not that you needed to, of course.'

'My revolutionary diet.'

'What is it?'

'Silk Cut and still water.'

'Sounds like a song.'

'How are you anyway? Can I get you a drink? What are you going to tell thingamabob's daughter? I thought the whole business was lost in the mists of time.'

'Yes, it was very sad. All a long time ago. I'll have an Ame, please, if you've got one.'

'God, that mouthwash. You're not "recovering" too, are you?'

'No, just too early in the day for me.'

'Half our friends are in AA now,' said Vanessa.

'And how's . . .' Gordon searched for the name of Vanessa and Anand's daughter, who had arrived late in their lives, now a darkly humorous young student. Gordon, quietly envious, reckoned she would be a stand-up comedienne one day.

'Clara's well,' said Anand. 'She's rollerblading in Venice with some unworthy young man.'

'Any rollerblading in Calcutta these days?' said Gordon.

'You would be surprised,' said Anand. 'It's a lot different since you were there. All the old colonial names of streets have been changed to Bengali ones. And it's Kolkata now.'

'Jai Bangla.'

'Jai Bangla indeed.'

'It was a magical moment, though, wasn't it? Liberation, all that optimism.'

'Such optimism,' said Anand. 'And now look at it – corruption, crime, poverty, people in Chittagong dismantling Western ships for a dollar a day and as much toxic waste as they can inhale. The dream doesn't last too long. The rest of the world forgets and moves on. But yes, you are right, it all seemed very magical then. "Our true paradises are the paradises we have lost", isn't it? And now it looks like we've got another little war coming along. They think this one will also be over in two weeks. No one seems to take it very seriously.'

'Oh, that's not true,' said Vanessa. 'We were meant to go and see that anti-war version of *Lysistrata* in Venice tonight. And I think there's some "hands off Iraq" demo in MacArthur Park at the weekend.'

'Did someone leave the cake out in the rain?' asked Gordon.

'What?' said Vanessa.

'Never mind,' said Gordon. Did no one remember the old songs? Was the darkest hour still just before dawn? 'This place looks great. Business humming?'

'Oh, it's not bad,' said Vanessa. 'One works all the time . . . So what's this interview you're doing?'

'It's all a bit tedious. It would take too long to explain but, funnily enough, Hugh, the guy who is doing the interview, was in Calcutta at that time. In fact, you may remember, Anand, he came to the party that . . . that night. That's why I suggested we do it here. I wonder if Freddie's daughter knows he was there that night too.'

'Oh, lovely, this is going to be like an Agatha Christie,' said Vanessa, lighting a cigarette. 'Can I be Miss Marple?' There must have been something unintended in Gordon's expression. 'I know, I know, I'm the last woman smoking in California.'

'Not at all, I love it. It reminds me of Faye.' It did.

'Poor Faye.'

'Oh, I think she's fine. If the press would leave her alone she would be perfectly happy down in Borego Springs – oh, don't mention to anyone she's there now, please.'

'Of course not,' said Vanessa, squeezing his arm. 'Is it just this Hugh character you're expecting?'

'There's a photographer,' said Gordon. 'He said it would be a surprise.'

'And here,' said a voice, 'is that surprise.'

And there at the entrance to the roof terrace was Hugh, accompanied by a tall, blonde woman with dark eyebrows. Hugh and Gordon took in each other for a moment, old stags on a Highland hillside, weighing each other up to see which one still had the fight left in them.

He has aged a lot, thought Gordon, noting the beach-ball belly and the saggy jowls above the open-necked striped shirt, the bald head, darkened and reddened by southern California sun to the texture of an old crab apple, the scarlet cross-hatching on the cheeks, tufts of white hair in nostrils, ears, the sides of the neck where they had survived the lazy stroke of the latest triple – or was it quadruple by now? – razor blade sensation. He's probably thinking the same about me, thought Gordon, sucking in his stomach and wondering if the remaining strands of his long grey hair had been blown aside by the breeze.

'You must remember Britt,' said Hugh, with just a hint of triumph in his voice, as he gestured towards her.

'Britt,' said Gordon. He stood up. Gulping like a teenager. Light-headed. Romantic vertigo. 'Well, you look terrific,' he managed once he was confident his voice would not crack. 'Why do women age so much better than men?

Are you living here now? You used to live in the . . . the Bay Area, didn't you?' He was gabbling now, he knew, talking too fast, giving the game away. Was she married now? She must be. But maybe divorced? Was that look on her face one of curiosity or something more? Should he kiss her?

He moved closer to her, took her by the arm. He could detect a few hints that she was not quite the same person that had lain beside him in the Oberoi Grand. The hands, the neck, the upper arms – and the knees, if you could see them – were the giveaways, his old girlfriend, Diana, had once told him. But the body was as slim as in Calcutta and the smile – rueful, conspiratorial – was the same. He could not help thinking of that white triangle of flesh in the darkness of the hotel room.

'Old school reunion, eh?' said Hugh.

'And you realise,' said Gordon, 'that this – Anand, Anand, come over here a sec – this is the man who ran that hotel where you came that final night, Hugh.'

'Indeed,' said Anand, who had been pottering at a table on the far corner of the terrace. 'And Gordon and I were just talking about that final night, Hugh.'

'Any chance of a beer?' asked Hugh, changing the subject abruptly and not catching Anand's eye. 'I hate to push things along but I have to pick up the wife in a couple of hours because her car's at the garage.' He took out a tape recorder and a spiral notepad and gave Anand only the briefest of acknowledgements.

Gordon had been interviewed many times, although only rarely in the last few years, now that his star had waned. Not that he minded the obscurity. He was not looking forward too much to the interview. He knew the journalist's technique well: the soft, amiable opening questions; the quotes, usually hostile or disparaging, from other journalists that one was given the chance to rebut, 'to set the record straight'; then the 'anything you particularly want to say?' question and, finally, almost as an afterthought, just when it seemed that the interview was over and the journalist was half closing his notebook and checking the 'time left' panel on his tape recorder, would come the killer question, the prosecutorial knife below the ribcage.

Hugh's technique was pretty standard. He read from printouts the angry editorials about taking the much-loved British story and Americanising it. Gordon already had his answers ready: that he was keeping the main characters British, that Americans had often served alongside them in the Second World War, that it was a way of retelling a great story, and that if he felt that the British were in some way being excluded from the plot, he would remove himself from the project.

'And how much, can I ask –' the familiar journalistic weasel words 'can I ask?' – 'would they be paying you for this?'

'Oh, that's all up in the air at the moment,' said Gordon. He knew that $250,000 would be more than Hugh or his readers could stomach. He gave him some snappy quotes about the state of the British film industry and told a harmless anecdote about Peter O'Toole and the Oscars.

'By the way,' said Hugh, putting his notebook away and fiddling with his tape recorder.

This is when the killer question comes, thought Gordon.

'Um . . . Faye Fado . . . she's in the Mojave desert now, they say. You still in touch?'

'No,' said Gordon sharply.

'Just so I get the record straight. There've been some things in the tabs about her . . . Just really to make sure I've got it right . . . Has she joined the—'

'Hey, guys, can I get a picture of Gordon now?' said Britt. Had she come to his rescue or was it accidental? Gordon wondered. He stood up, aware of the frostiness in the air caused by his snub of Hugh. Britt had rigged up one of the Lancers' hotel rooms as a mini studio, complete with white umbrella and lights. She took his hand and led him to it. Hugh ordered another beer, surveyed the skyline and pretended to check his notes.

'So,' said Gordon, closing the door. 'Long time since we were alone in a hotel room together.'

'Long time,' said Britt.

'I . . . I used to write you postcards from, well, everywhere. Did you . . . did you ever get them?'

'I did. But you hardly ever put a return address on them. And then they stopped.'

They looked at each other. Gordon wanted to put his arms round her. So was she with someone? Bound to be. Oh, God, if only it had worked out that night, if she had come with him to Thailand, if . . . if . . .

'So . . . what happened with you and – what was his name?'

'Josh?' She laughed. 'Oh, I told him it was all over as

soon as he arrived. I told him I had met you. He went crazy. I thought for a moment he was going to kill me. I think he was pissed that he had spent all that money getting into India and I didn't want to see him any more. Boy, he was mad. He ran out into the street, he wanted to punch your lights out.'

'You broke up with him right away? So – why didn't you come round to the hotel that night?'

'Perhaps I did.'

'Perhaps?'

'I did come round.'

'But – but what happened?'

'You were in the arms of another woman.'

'Never!'

'You were. She was that Australian, I think, and you were murmuring something about never leaving her and—'

'God, who was that?'

'She had hennaed hair, as far as I remember, centre parting, I'd seen her before. She was one of your gang. She was certainly clinging on to you real tight.'

'Oh, no, oh, no,' said Gordon, shaking his head. 'Not Karen. Not Karen! She was freaking out, Britt, she was asking everyone to hold her and not leave her. The next morning she was on a plane out of there with her boyfriend – what was he called? Kevin? Kieran? – and she's now probably a grandmother in Sydney. Oh, God, Britt, did we part because of that? For me, I have to say, it was quite magical . . .' He searched her face for some reaction. Surely this odd meeting must mean something?

'I enjoyed it, too. I really did. Look, I broke up with Josh because of you, if it's any consolation.' Britt looked busily into her steel equipment box. 'How about you? Are you married? With anyone?'

'No,' said Gordon. 'I was with someone for a long time and then with someone else for a short time but now I'm not. So I just Google ex-girlfriends and read a lot. Bit sad, eh?'

'Children?'

'No. How about you?'

'Yeah, I am with someone,' said Britt. 'You'd like her.'

They looked at each other. Did this make it all easier? Gordon wondered.

'We have an adopted daughter,' added Britt.

'Well . . . that's great,' said Gordon. 'Now you'd better take my picture in the most flattering way you can and then let's get back before Hugh falls off the roof.'

'Bogbrush, you mean.'

'Bogbrush.'

She took his photograph.

'Did you ever get to go to bed with someone taller than you?' she asked.

'God, you remember that. No, I never did – unless you count high heels. Did you do any more wars?'

She shook her head. 'That was it. It's hard to explain now but it sort of slipped away from me. Now I do magazine stuff, portraits, that sort of thing, you know. I wouldn't be able to be away now anyway, being a mom.'

'Yeah,' said Gordon, taking a deep breath. 'You still wear rose water . . .'

'Don't look so wistful,' she said. 'It wouldn't have worked out. In those days we thought everything was as neat as a line in a song. It was all much more complicated than that.'

'I'm not so sure it was. If we had—'

'Oh, Gordon, if, if, if . . . It's a waste of time, I've found. If I'd had those photos of the guy being killed in Bangladesh – remember, the ones I lost in the café? – maybe I would have won a prize and then maybe I would have become a world-famous photographer and then maybe I would have got killed and, if we had gone travelling together, maybe you and – what was his name? Larry? – would never have written your musical. We all thought everything could be fixed instantly. War. Desire. Pain. Do you still smoke dope?'

'Too strong for me now.'

'I miss it but I can't afford to get busted. They'd take Luz, our daughter, away. You know, I still have that saffron scarf you gave me somewhere.'

'Oh, Britt,' he sighed.

She returned his gaze.

'Come on,' she said. 'It's Americans who get sentimental. You guys aren't meant to.'

They embraced. She pulled away first but stroked his face as she did. They went back to the roof terrace.

'Now,' she said before they rejoined the others. 'Tell me what that smell is.'

Gordon inhaled the night air.

'Dunno. Car fumes? Vanessa's cigarette?'

'Sandalwood incense,' she said. 'You never did quite get in touch with all your senses, did you?'

Hugh had a fresh Kingfisher in front of him and was trying to reach his wife on the phone to explain that the interview was taking longer than expected and she should call a taxi to take her home. His wife rang back. Hugh's cellphone played the opening bars from 'Three Little Maids' from *The Mikado*, which Gordon recognised from an old St Gregory's school production. There was a mumbled conversation which appeared to end in mid-sentence.

Anand rejoined them, having just glad-handed a table full of Asian television executives. He carried a bottle of champagne with him.

'Since this is one of the most improbable of reunions, I think champagne is called for,' he said.

'On the house, I hope,' said Hugh, under his breath, to Gordon. 'I'm having all sorts of trouble with my exes, these days.'

'Your ex-wives?' said Gordon, genuinely puzzled.

Hugh looked irritated. 'My ex-pen-ses.'

Anand pulled up a chair between Gordon and Hugh as Britt packed up her camera gear and made a cellphone call to Lori.

'Gordon and I were talking earlier about that night in Calcutta,' said Anand. He reached a hand into his jacket pocket and pulled out the letter from Sandra King and placed it on the table.

'Sounds like a film,' said Hugh. 'That Night in Calcutta.' He looked at the now open champagne bottle in its ice bucket and helped himself, filling his flute with precision.

'Well, Freddie Braintree's daughter, Sandra, is now a

police officer,' said Anand. 'She wants to know what happened to her papa. Do you remember that night, that party, Hugh?'

'Well,' said Hugh, checking his watch. 'All a bit lost in the past, isn't it? She's been leaving messages for me, too.'

'Yeah,' said Gordon. 'My agent said there was a re-investigation going on. It's all a bit of a blur to me. It was more than thirty years ago, after all. I don't really see what she hopes to find out.'

'That horrible word "closure" probably,' said Vanessa.

'Is she interviewing people?' said Gordon.

'That's what the letter seemed to indicate,' said Anand. 'Said she was coming out to LA. Due here this week, I think. I won't be able to help her too much. I saw a bit of a kerfuffle from the roof that night but, well, I never went down to investigate, I'm afraid, until it was all too late. Sin of omission.'

'They said in the post-mortem, as far as I remember, that there had been traces of drugs in his bloodstream,' said Hugh. 'Hadn't he gone native – begging your pardon, er, Anand – been taking drugs and stuff?'

'So?' asked Britt.

'So maybe he was out of his head and who knows what might have happened. Maybe he thought he could fly,' said Hugh.

'There was that American chap, Larry, who turned out to be a drug dealer, I think,' said Anand. 'I had the FBI round after him for weeks afterwards. Oh, Gordon, he was the chap you did the musical with, wasn't he? You never thought that Larry might have—'

'Larry wasn't like that,' said Gordon. 'There were other people doing drugs there too, you know, and anyway it was when that "hippy killer" guy was around in India, leaving his little calling cards. In fact, there was one on Freddie's body—'

'In his pocket, I think,' said Hugh.

'Blimey, you've got a good memory,' said Gordon. 'I thought the killer pinned the sign to his victims' bodies.'

'Maybe he was taking drugs all the time,' said Britt. 'Like vice squad cops go with hookers.'

'The other puzzle seems to be that he had a roll of film.' Anand produced the photos that Sandra King had sent him. He spread them out on the table. The others gathered round him.

'Jeeeeez!' said Britt. 'That's my film! That's the missing film, Gordon! You remember? He took my film, the bastard! The bastard! Why did he do that?'

'He was an undercover cop, you were taking his picture,' said Hugh.

'But his picture wasn't on that film, those were the pictures I took of that guy being killed in front of us in Bangladesh,' said Britt, pointing at the film. 'Can't you see? Look, that's you, Hugh, isn't it?'

'Had a bit more hair then,' said Hugh, putting his spectacles on and holding a photo up to the light.

'What's going on in the photo?' asked Anand.

'An informer, being killed, lynched, really,' said Britt. 'God, I never thought I would . . . How did he – God, he must have taken it off me in that restaurant. You remember, Gordon, that night we . . . Those pictures, they could have changed my life. I could have won a Pulitzer, man! God, you remember, Gordon, don't you?'

'Yeah, I remember that night,' said Gordon, not catching her eye. 'And you were taking pictures in the restaurant. He must have thought you'd taken one of him so he must have nicked the film from your pocket when you weren't looking. They are amazing pictures, Britt. I can see why you were so upset. So that's what happened to them. Freddie must have thought his cover had been blown.'

'Was that why he was running away that night he was killed?' asked Anand. 'Hugh, you must have seen him in the crowd. I thought I saw the two of you together from the roof. I couldn't exactly tell what was going on but it seemed like you were having a row.'

'No, I think you must have got something wrong there. We may have bumped into each other in the street but, God, it was so long ago and I didn't know that anything had happened to him until I got back to London the next day. I think the cops at the time reckoned that he must have been another of the victims of that yingy-yangy killer – who looks like he's up to his old tricks again in California. What are you going to tell the daughter?'

A silence fell over the group.

'Poor Freddie,' said Britt.

'Poor Freddie,' said Gordon.

Anand filled everyone's glasses.

'To Freddie Braintree,' he said. 'A casualty of war.'

They clinked glasses.

'I guess the old hippy trail's completely finished now

anyway,' said Hugh. 'You certainly can't go through Afghanistan and all those places like you used to. Who knows, perhaps all those hippies coming through, wearing hardly any clothes and taking drugs, is what brought the Taliban in there – you know, a revulsion against what they saw as Western culture, all that decadence.'

'Oh, I think that's a little unfair,' said Anand. 'I think there just may be one or two other things about the West that people in the East might find . . . unappealing. The hippies were hardly the first Westerners to arrive with a rather different culture.'

Gordon was wondering whether to engage in all this – was it worth it? – when Hugh's cellphone rang again and he announced to the table, 'In the best traditions of British journalism, I am making my excuses and leaving.' After he had speedily shaken hands with everyone, signed for the bill – minus the champagne, on Anand's insistence – he walked, slightly unsteadily, towards the lift.

The group of Indian and Sri Lankan television executives came over to the table to say hello to Anand.

'So, it's war,' said one, conversationally. 'They have just announced it on the news.'

'It's really happening then, is it?' said Anand.

'They are bombing Iraq as we speak,' said the executive, who was dressed formally for LA, suit, matching tie and shirt. 'There is a blackout in Baghdad.'

Anand, Vanessa, Britt and Gordon rose from the table in coincidental unison. Britt said she must rush. Anand was wanted by his receptionist. The night was over.

Chapter Thirty-Four

'So . . . Freddie Braintree, eh?' said Hugh as he and Gordon stood together on the sidewalk waiting for the Valet Girl parkers to bring their cars round. They had said their farewells to Anand and Vanessa and seen Britt into her VW convertible. Hugh checked his watch, the one he'd bought – when was it now? – ten years ago, at least, at the duty-free in Heathrow after his old diver's watch had finally packed in. 'The plot thickens.'

'How do you mean?'

'Do you really not remember?'

'Well, as I said just now, it's all a blur to me.'

'Yes, but . . .'

'But what?'

'Do you not remember him that night on his way out of the hotel, when I was leaving? He was out of his head.'

'Was he?'

'You must remember, he was being really irritating.'

'He was always being a bit irritating.'

They paused to let a police car, siren wailing, speed past them. Hugh could sense Gordon's unease. He seems quite shifty, he thought. Did he really not remember what happened?

'Well, he kept plucking your sleeve and asking who he was.'

'Yeah?'

'And you told him that he was Freddie Braintree.'

'That's who I thought he was then. I didn't find out he was a cop until much later. I left for Bangkok the morning after the party. First plane out.'

'Really? But on that night,' said Hugh looking hard at Gordon, 'he went on and on asking who he was and you got irritated with him and eventually you told him he was Tiger Niazi.'

'Tiger Niazi?'

'He was the head of the Pakistani army, probably the most hated man in Calcutta at that time.'

'So?'

Hugh looked down the street to see if his Valet Girl was approaching with Helena's Mercedes. How should he play this?

'So he goes into that crowd grabbing people and shouting that he's Tiger Niazi. What do you think might happen? It's like someone running round Trafalgar Square on VE day saying they're Hitler.'

'Christ, I didn't think he was going to . . . I just . . . Did I really say that?'

'You certainly did. I scribbled it down in my notebook on the plane home.'

'And?' Gordon was wriggling a bit. Hugh recognised the dry-throated response from the times when he'd cornered a guilty quarry. Their bodies always gave them away, whether they were politicians having affairs or film stars not wanting to talk about coke habits.

'Well, we were always told to keep our notebooks. Part of the old training – always keep the notebooks, always let the desk know where you are, always buy your round. I had been thinking of doing a book about war reporting so I still have it somewhere. I suppose I shall have to dig it out now if his daughter—'

'What? You're not going to tell her about all this? What's the point? You know I didn't mean Freddie any harm. I was fond of him.'

'But if he hadn't told people he was Tiger Niazi – if you hadn't put the idea in his head – he would never have been attacked, perhaps never have been killed. Because, to be frank, I don't think he was killed by serial killers or drug dealers at all, it looks like he must have been attacked by the mob and chased back to that fleapit where you were staying. I know you had no idea, of course, and I'm not suggesting—'

'Why didn't you say so just now, when we were all talking about it? Anyway, if you saw him in trouble, why didn't you try and help him?'

'I couldn't get near him, it was all a bit of a scramble, got into a bit of a dust-up myself.'

'So why didn't you say all this just now when everyone was there?'

'Didn't want to embarrass you, old man.'

'Oh, come on, Bog— Dunn . . . you . . . How do you know that's what happened to him? All that playing the crazy guy was a cover, don't you see? He was just acting mad. He was in control. Anyway, he was found in the hotel – Anand would have noticed if a crowd had chased him in there. You're not saying that I'm responsible for his death?'

'Well, not intentionally, of course, but—'

'Are you going to tell his daughter this?'

'Well, I suppose, in a way, I should give her the basic facts. As I remember them.'

'Why?'

'Set the record straight. But I'll certainly think about what you've said. Maybe best let sleeping dogs lie – "lie" being the operative word.'

Hugh watched Gordon. What an unctuous creature he was, anxious that no one should think ill of him. Still feeling guilty, probably. Of course he could remember what he had done.

'The other thing is,' said Hugh, 'I'm having a bit of a hard time with the desk back in London at the mo. They think I'm not coming up with enough stories, you know, about Hollywood and so on. I want to stay here, Helena wants to stay here, the girls are happy here. I don't want to go back to bloody London . . . and . . . I could really do with a good story and if you . . .'

Two tall, young white men with the easy entitlement of wealth in their gait, diners from Lancers presumably, joined them in the valet parking line, handing their tickets over to a smiling blonde Amazon in white shirt, maroon waistcoat and high-waisted black trousers. Hugh heard the words 'Baghdad' and 'walk in the park'.

Gordon was staring at him, nodding slowly.

'And if, say,' said Gordon, 'I was to tell you where Faye was living now, what she's up to, just maybe you would tell Freddie's daughter that you couldn't remember a damn thing about that night. Is that what you're trying to say?'

God, thought Hugh, he's smarter than I thought. And he's starting to break already.

'Oh, God, you don't really believe that I'm that much of a shit, do you?' said Hugh. 'I'm teasing, for heaven's sake. Christ, you really must imagine that I'm that much of an arsehole. How depressing. Don't worry. I'm not going to shop you. But if you happen to—'

The valet parker had arrived with the Mercedes. Hugh pulled a business card out of his wallet and thrust it into Gordon's hand. 'Give us a ring, some time, eh?' He paused, waiting for a response from Gordon. 'You probably think I was partly to blame for Farquar-Fox killing himself at school, don't you? You were one of Farquar-Fox's "avengers", weren't you? We all fuck up, McGrady, and we all have to live with it. Perhaps we both understand that now. You chose your direction – one might ask now what all that stuff achieved, all the drugs and free sex. Anyway, here we are.' Hugh saw the Valet Girl hovering and nodded at her.

'I got the impression you weren't too averse to the fruits of all that sexual liberation yourself,' said Gordon.

Oh, the worm was turning. Who rattled your cage? thought Hugh. He pressed a $2 tip into the hand of the Amazon who had parked his car. She seemed unimpressed.

'No hard feelings, McGrady,' he said. He felt ever so slightly pissed and made a mental note to drive carefully and stop off for some peppermints at Vons on the way home. 'Ciao. Floreat St Gregory's!' His exit was slightly marred when he banged his knee on the car door as he closed it while trying to catch the eye of the Valet Girl.

He accelerated a little too fiercely and caught a brief glimpse in his rear-view mirror of Gordon McGrady climbing into one of those silly-looking fuel efficiency cars that self-righteous Hollywood stars boasted about driving. God, I'm knackered, he thought. Even with the air conditioning on full blast, he was sweating.

Chapter Thirty-Five

SANDRA KING HAD visited many English prisons since she joined the police. She had taken statements there from nervous young men who had decided to give evidence against former friends and interviewed surly old lags about crimes from their past which they had hoped were long forgotten. None had anything like the security procedures at Terre Haute Federal Penitentiary, Indiana.

As she stepped out of her two-door rental car on to the wide expanse of tarmac outside the prison, a disembodied voice instructed her: 'Lock. Your. Vehicle. Proceed. To. Entrance. Have. Your. Picture. ID. Ready.' The staff inside in the first bullet-proof reception booth were expecting her.

'Good day, ma'am,' said the genial correctional officer in charge. 'Come to see Mr Anunziato, is that correct?'

'Yes,' said Sandra. 'Here's my passport and the letter from the FBI and ... the one from the Justice Department.'

'And how is England?'

'It was OK when I left.'

'My wife and I had a very fine holiday in Cheltenham.

Do you know Cheltenham?' He pronounced every syllable of the name.

'I've been there, yes, once or twice, for the races – the horse races.'

'You don't know people there called Harrison by any chance, do you, Bill and Dorothy Harrison?'

'No, I'm afraid not.'

'Fine people,' he told her, pushing her documents back across the counter. Sandra had only ever been to the States once before when her mother took her to Disneyworld many years ago but she felt she liked Americans. They seemed more open, more optimistic than English people. 'Now if you just go through that door there, someone will take your photo and escort you to the visiting room.'

When she had been photographed twice – 'one for us and one for you, in case there is a hostage-taking situation and we have to evacuate; it means you can prove to us who you are' – pat-searched and had passed through the metal detector, she was led into an empty, sunlit room. Ten minutes later, a tall, handsome, shaven-headed man, tanned and fit, entered. His handshake was iron firm.

'Larry Anunziato,' he told her. 'So, the Hangman's Beautiful Daughter. How are you?'

'Fine, thanks.' What did he mean? 'Well, you know why I'm here.' She pulled out her black Metropolitan Police notebook.

'You're not wired up, are you?' he asked.

'No, I'm not.'

'It's OK. I'm not going to ask to frisk you.'

'I wouldn't let you anyway.'

He paused and stared at her for almost a full minute. 'I can see Freddie there for sure.'

Sandra looked away. She felt his eyes boring into her.

'How is this – as a jail?' she asked.

'What do you think? Pascal said that all human evil comes from man's being unable to sit still in a room. I have accomplished that, if you count a cell as a room, but it took me about ten years . . . So what's the deal?' asked Larry.

It was Sandra's turn to pause. She looked over her shoulder. In the corner of the room, standing beside a neat pile of plastic toys for children visitors, were two guards. Both nodded at her as she turned.

'Well, as I think you know, my father was part of a joint US/UK drugs task force, that's what he was doing when he . . . died. Anyway, the Justice Department here have been very helpful. I've been told that, if you give me what I consider to be genuine material details as to what happened to . . . my father . . . then I am at liberty to put you forward as a recommended person for early release . . .'

'Meaning?'

'That you could be out of here in a month or so if you help me.' She smiled at him. He looked intently at her again.

'You do look just like Freddie. He was a beautiful man.' There was a long pause as they both stared at each other.

'So. Can you tell me what happened that night?'

Another long pause. Larry took a deep breath and, staring straight at Sandra, told her, 'OK. The first thing you should know is that I knew your dad was a fed – was a cop. OK? At first, I didn't know for sure but there were a lot of tells, a lot of things that didn't add up. Then one night we were sitting on the roof of that hotel, the Lux, and I told him that I knew.'

'What did he say?'

'He laughed. He said that he knew I was sending dope back to the States and that everyone in the DEA must know that stuffed elephants were being used for smuggling. He told me to wise up and get out while I was ahead.'

'So?'

'Look, I don't know how to put this but I promise you I'm not bullshitting you.'

'Yes?'

'You see, Freddie – your dad – he didn't want to bust people any more. He said that he had worked in a police station in London somewhere – I can't remember which one. Began with a W, I think. Yes? And they used to bust people and then keep some of the gear for themselves – that was what Freddie called it, "gear" – and use it to plant on other people. He said he wasn't happy about it but the other guys told him to keep quiet. Anyway, he went to the anti-corruption guys. I don't know what you call them. We call them Internal Affairs . . .'

Larry's eyes drifted over her shoulder towards the two guards. 'Hey, droogs,' he said, 'is it OK if we get a soda here?' Both guards nodded and he asked her for any quarters she had on her, took four from her purse, strolled over to a massive drinks dispensing machine and returned with two frosty Dr Peppers. 'I would have asked you what you wanted but that's all it has – it used to be a polling booth in Russia. Don't feel you have to drink it.' He opened his own can and took a swig.

'But the anti-corruption guys told him not to make any waves and – this is what Freddie told me – they passed the news back to the bad guys at his station that he was snitching on them. They weren't happy. He didn't know what they were going to do to him. He was kind of scared.'

Sandra gazed at him without blinking. All this was new.

'You married?' he asked suddenly.

She shook her head.

'Engaged? Boyfriend? . . . Girlfriend?'

She laughed. 'I had a boyfriend, he was in the job too. It didn't work out. Don't keep changing the subject.'

'Well, that's when he volunteered for the undercover thing in India. He wanted to get out of his police station, out of London, away from all the bad guys – they all had these nicknames. What were they? Tonto and Ginger and . . . Why do English people like to give each other nicknames all the time?'

'Ginger?'

'Yeah, Tonto and Ginger and – God, I can't remember. Anyway, he wanted to get out before he got framed for something. Or worse. He knew they were on his case.'

'Are you saying that he was frightened of the other officers?'

'Look, Freddie wanted to get out of town. They were looking for volunteers who didn't mind being away for six months or so.'

'Yes, I remember,' she said. Say goodbye to Daddy, Sandra.

'So he comes to India, he starts hanging around with all of the outlaws in Delhi and Benares and Goa and so on. Well, it was like taking candy from a baby to spot traffickers there. Mostly they were small fry, amateurs. But everyone liked him, you see, because there was something magical about Freddie . . .'

'And? Don't tell me he found you all so sweet and charming that he couldn't bear to see any of you locked up.'

Larry smiled back at her. 'Well, you would be surprised. You see, people really liked Freddie, they looked out for him. When he got the shits, someone would get him medicine. I know that a lot of the people on the road in those days – probably the same now – were pretty fucked-up, unworked-out sort of people but they were quite sweet-natured and Freddie brought that out in people. To cut to the chase, Freddie told me he'd decided he wasn't going to stay in the police but he didn't know how to get out of it. He said that he had to provide for his family – you, I guess – and he didn't know what he would do when he went back. So he was kind of sussing things out in India, seeing if he could get a job teaching or something. I know he went to – what do you call it, not the British Consul but—'

'The British Council?'

'That's it. I used to go with Gordon to read the newspapers. I even saw your dad there just before we left. And he was spinning it out, trying to work out what to do and all the time telling the people back in London and Washington that he was on to something really, really big, hinting that it involved governments and the intelligence services and international trafficking and stuff.'

'And?'

'It was all bullshit. He was buying time, Sandra. There was no big conspiracy. He didn't really have anything on anybody beyond all the small-time guys.'

'But what happened to him that night, Larry?'

Larry emptied the Dr Pepper down his throat.

'There was a party at our hotel, if you can call it that, some beers, some samosas, probably the last time I was a bit drunk in thirty or so years. Gordon was there, the Australians—'

'Kieran and Karen?'

'Yeah, that's right. You spoken to them?'

'Kieran's dead. Karen sent me a long e-mail saying she couldn't remember a thing, but she did say that it was her who wrote that note, "Please treat my death as suspicious", that she pushed under Mr Bose's door.'

'Why would she do that?'

'Said she was suffering from panic attacks. She wrote lots of little notes like that, turned them into a volume of poetry. Not my cup of tea exactly but – whatever gets you through the night.'

There was a silence.

'So Kieran's dead,' said Larry, nodding slowly. 'How did he die?'

'Hepatitis.'

'Of course.' They shared a dark smile. 'And then there was that schmuck of a British journalist whose hair stuck up like a toilet brush. I think that's what Gordon called him. "Bogbrush", is that right? My memory's pretty good, eh?'

'Hugh Dunn.'

'You seen him?'

'Haven't actually spoken to him as such. I rang him a couple of days ago and I think he hung up on me. I've left about three messages. I'm going to try again when I get to LA. I've got an appointment with McGrady on Tuesday.'

'Anyway, to get back to that night: Freddie's got the runs again – that's what you call it, isn't it, the runs? He asks me if I've got any medicine. I don't but I know Gordon always had some so I point him over there. And Gordon tells him that he's got some pills in the side pocket of his backpack. Off goes Freddie.'

'And?'

Larry shook his head.

'You see, Gordon did have some anti-diarrhoea tablets in his backpack but Freddie must have gone to the wrong one. I guess he wasn't listening to what Gordon said – because Gordon was quite specific. He goes into someone else's backpack – people were all getting packed up and there were a lot of them around. Freddie goes into the wrong backpack and the pills he takes must have been acid – LSD. I guess he must have gone into Remy's backpack – it was like a drugs store and he sure had lots of acid. He'd been killed a couple of days before and his stuff was all packed up in the room.' He peered at her notebook. 'You getting this down? Anyway, when I got to Bangkok and hooked up with Gordon again, I had the runs and I asked him for his pills and they were all still there in the side pocket of his backpack. That's when I realised what must have happened, why Freddie was so damn crazy that night.

I used to trip a long time ago. Most of the time it's cool but sometimes it can do strange things to your head. There was a lot of bullshit about what acid could do to you but some of the stories were true. Freddie took the acid by mistake. Two tabs, man. Strong stuff. Owsley's best, I think. Ever heard of Owsley?'

'I'm a cop.'

'I know you are but most people your age have no history. Strong acid, man. Freddie takes them both. He goes on a trip. He's never been on a trip before. Baba, the guy who worked at the hotel – have you spoken to him?'

'He died a long time ago.'

'I'm sorry. He was a good guy. Baba tells me that Freddie's out on the street making an idiot of himself so I go down. There's Freddie on the street, making a nuisance of himself all right. Now he's got a Pakistani army badge he's wearing – he took it off that English journalist guy – and he's telling people that he's Tiger Niazi, the head of the Pakistani army. Why, I don't know. Crazy stuff. He's out of his head. Some of the people in the crowd take a swipe at him and he reacts. He's trained in unarmed combat, I guess.'

She nodded and returned his gaze.

'And he was a fit guy, Freddie, that was one of the reasons I thought he was a cop. But there are ten, twenty of them. Baba and I are shouting at him and telling the people that he's crazy and to ignore him.'

'They killed him?'

'No, they didn't. They roughed him up a bit but they were celebrating. They didn't want trouble. That's all. It's night. He's dazed. There's a blackout still in place. We lose him for a minute in the crowd. I call out to him and we've almost got him back with us. Then we see him running across the street like a crazy guy. He gets side-swiped by a big army truck full of celebrating soldiers. Hit on the back of the head by a big wing mirror. The driver didn't even see him. Crack – on the back of the head. He gets spun around. I see him staggering. We look everywhere for him but, like I say, there's the blackout still on. We reckon he can't have been hit as hard as it looked, must have run off in shock. We head down the street, look everywhere. We walk across the Maidan – the big park where we all used to hang out together. Look everywhere. No go. Remember, the city is still full of refugees. Go back to the hotel. Wait for Freddie to come back.'

'Yes?'

'Well, in the morning, first light, I see that he's still not back. I can't wake Gordon. He's out of it. He sometimes got that way. I go out again. There, not very far from the hotel, not very far from where we last saw him, in fact, under the lip of a ditch, near where the army truck hit him, there's Freddie. He's dead.'

'He's dead,' echoed Sandra. She felt her eyes filling with tears. Larry put his large hands across the table and grasped hers. She did not pull them away. The guards looked across and exchanged glances.

'He must have been killed by that whack to the back of the head from the lorry and then the fall into the pothole. There's blood at the back and the front . . . I'm sorry . . . Well, I couldn't leave him there. There's a few guys on the street, just waking up. One of them, old guy, comes over to see what's happening. We carry Freddie back into the hotel, me and this old guy. There's only Gordon in the room, still passed out. Almost everyone else has already left. They took cabs out in the middle of the night so they wouldn't miss the flights. We put Freddie in his own bed. I was going to tell the cops and everything but then I realise, they may have stuff on me already, I may find myself charged with killing a cop. I try and wake Gordon but he's well out of it. It takes a while to wake him. I tell him that he'll be in the frame too. That there's nothing we can do for Freddie by staying. We go to the airport, Dum Dum. It's chaos but Gordon picks up his flight and I bribe my way on to another, get to Bangkok. Had another identity up my sleeve . . .'

'But who was the "hippy killer"? Who was leaving all those signs? Who's doing it now?'

'God, Sandra, you're meant to be the cop, not me. I guess whoever it was got tired of it – or died. As for this stuff that's happening now, who the hell knows? If it's the same guy, he must be in his sixties at least. That should help them eliminate some suspects.'

Is he lying? Sandra tried to read his body language. People think cops can tell when someone's not telling the truth and usually her instinct was right. That's why no one in the section house would take her on at poker when they were training. But Larry? Who knew? She was tired and she wanted to believe him. She didn't want those demons skipping through her head any more.

He took her hands more firmly. 'Your father was an OK

guy, Sandra. He loved his wife, he loved you. And he had total recall of Bob Dylan and the Incredible String Band. That's not such a bad legacy.' She laughed, which made her cry more. She took a deep breath to try to stop the tears. She was glad she wasn't wearing mascara.

'Another way to look at things,' he went on. 'Aldous Huxley, when he was dying, he took acid, he wanted to cross over to the other side with his headlights on. Maybe it was the same for your dad.'

'Is that meant to be comforting?' she asked. He returned her gaze. 'So how did you get busted then, if Freddie – Dad – told you that they knew about you?'

'That was my fault. I reckoned I was untouchable. Gordon and I went up to Laos and did that damn musical together as a joke. Neither of us ever thought anything would come of it. We sang it for a few travellers up there, that was it. Anyway, I'd bought another phoney passport in Thailand, reckoned I could shift some Thai grass and some opium and set myself up with a restaurant somewhere in the desert in Nevada. I trained as a chef, you see – I do the best soufflés in the federal penitentiary system. Stupid, I guess. They busted me crossing the border from Canada. I was already on their radar as a draft evader. I should have taken Freddie's advice.' There was another silence between them which lasted long enough for the guards to look up and see what was going on.

'Is this all frustrating for you? Did you have an idea that you were going to catch your dad's killer? See them busted? Isn't it better to know that he wasn't killed in anger?'

'Is it?' said Sandra, asking herself as well as Larry. There was a long pause. 'Why do you think there were no more of those murders?'

'Beats me.'

'You don't think . . .'

'What are you saying?'

'The killings did stop after Dad died.'

'Well, until now they did.'

'Yes. That was one of the reasons I got back into this whole thing. One of the people at the Lux was never traced. Do you remember a monk called Mudd?'

'Oh, Mudd – the silent monk.'

'No one ever tracked him down. He disappeared without trace.'

'Sandra, did you ever read a book called *Catch-22*?'

One of the books in her father's little pile. Sandra shook her head.

'There's a guy in it called Mudd, the "dead man" in Yossarian's tent, who never speaks. Lots of us signed in with bogus names in those days and so did that monk guy. I guess that's why he chose the name. Who was he? He wasn't talking then. Then – amazing thing, this – one day, quite early on in my stretch, oh, about twenty years ago now when I was in another jail in Colorado, I was killing some time in the chaplaincy and in comes this guy in robes. It's Mudd, hardly changed at all. He's the Buddhist chaplain for the western states' penitentiary system. He's talking now all right. He'd been in Vietnam, seen a lot of shit and went off and studied in Nepal, then hit the road. That's when we came across him in Calcutta. We had a laugh about it all.'

'A laugh?'

'I'm sorry, I've been here a long time. Not a laugh about Freddie, a laugh about our own foolishness. Look, if you can help me get out of here . . . It's about thirty years too late but I appreciate it all the same. Your dad wasn't murdered, Sandra, he died in a road accident. I hope that's easier to take. It happens. He wouldn't have known a thing. And Sandra . . .'

'Yes?'

'Did you keep your father's records?'

'Of course.'

'Play that Incredibles track, "Air". Close your eyes and think of your dad smiling on the roof of a hotel surrounded by people who dug him. "Dreaming . . . all creatures are. Brighter than the brightest star",' he sang. The guards looked across at them. 'Although I have to say that was their only decent song.'

'I don't have a record player. Things have changed. They've got something called CD players now, you know.' She turned away. Larry laid a large hand on her shoulder.

'I heard,' he said. He called to the two guards. 'Take me back to my dungeon. But as Dick said, you're not going to have me to kick around for much longer . . .'

Outside the jail, Sandra sat in her hired car and took half a dozen very deep breaths before she turned on the engine. She turned it off again. Her hands were shaking.

Chapter Thirty-Six

THEY WANTED SIX hundred words on American reaction to the first days of the war in Iraq so Hugh drove down to the coffee bar at the bottom of Sunset Boulevard, just where it hit the coast, and asked the first three people he saw. That was the nice thing about working in America: everyone was happy to share their thoughts. In England, a similar request would have been greeted with suspicion – 'Why do you want to know?' – or sometimes even a request for money. Here people were instantly and often surprisingly quotable.

'George Bush is an Oedipal fool who is going to make the rest of the world despise us and stoke the fires of hatred against us,' said a man with grey hair in a ponytail, wearing camouflage trousers and a tank top. Why are they called tank tops? Hugh wondered. Do tank commanders wear them because of the heat?

'Edible?' he asked.

'Yeah, that's right. O-E-D-I-P—'

'Oh, EE-dipal,' said Hugh.

'You say Eedipal, I say Edipal,' said the man with a smile, as Hugh scribbled the quote down in the shorthand he had learned more than thirty-five years earlier. 'He's doing this for his daddy.'

'Well, if you were a Kurd or a marsh Arab, you would be celebrating today,' said the woman behind him in the queue. An Iranian expat. Hugh scribbled on. She, irritatingly, would not give her name to be quoted. After a giggling teen had declined to say anything, he found a middle-aged Russian immigrant – called Boris, of course – who thought the war was a 'good idea' and said it would be over 'in five minutes, no problem. Sometimes a country has to invade – like Vietnam had to invade Cambodia to stop Pol Pot, and yes, like Soviet Union in Afghanistan and India in Bangladesh. What paper you write for? Hmmm. Have not heard of that one. You have website?' This was a good quote. Hugh's paper favoured the war, arguing the same line.

He climbed back into the Mercedes and drove up the hill to his house. He had overslept again that morning and felt a little rough. In fact, he had felt a little rough, a little breathless, since that night at Lancers a few days earlier. The policewoman, Sandra King, Freddie Whatsit's daughter, had phoned again just after he had left, wanting to meet up. He would, he supposed, have to see her. What would he say? Should he tell her about that prig, Gordon, and how he had told her father that his name was Tiger Niazi? But could he describe the night without mentioning how he himself had had to push Freddie Braintree away from him? How her panic-stricken father had spotted him in the crowd and grabbed him so violently that he had drawn blood? Would she understand how alarming her father had been and how he could not possibly have stayed to help him out in such a volatile crowd?

He tapped out the 600 words – 615 as it happened, always give the sub-editors something to cut – and tried to send it. The screen of his computer froze. He tried again. It froze again. He spoke to someone in the IT department in the London office who sounded about fourteen years old and could not understand why Hugh was having a problem. The newsdesk rang and asked when the copy was arriving. They needed it for an early page. Should they just take agency copy? they asked annoyingly. He tried again. The newsdesk rang again and suggested that he file the old-fashioned way. Phone it over. All the paper's copy-takers had been long since made redundant but the Press Association had a general service still, based in the north of England somewhere.

A male voice answered and asked for a catchline and subject matter. 'HDIRAQ,' said Hugh. 'War.'

He read it through. 'Open quotes. George Bush is an Oedipal fool—'

'Edible?'

'No, Oedipal. O for Oscar, E for Echo, D for Delta—'

'Oedipal?'

'Yes, Oedipal, that's what I said . . . fool.'

'What did you just say?'

'Fool . . . Oh, God, not you, the copy. "George Bush is an Oedipal fool",' cried Hugh. His cellphone was ringing now. 'Hang on a sec, someone on the other line.' He picked up the cellphone.

'Hello,' said an Englishwoman's voice. 'My name is

Sandra King, Detective Constable Sandra King. I wondered if I could have a word with you. It's about my father, Lewis King . . .'

The connection was perfect. 'Hello? Hello? I, er,' said Hugh. 'I'm losing you, I'm afraid . . . Terrible line. Sorry.' He switched off the cellphone.

He felt suddenly very cold and noticed that he was breathing heavily. He picked up the main phone and started talking to the copy-taker again. There was a stabbing pain in his arm. He ran through the Russian's quotes, making up a surname – Vitaliev, Boris Vitaliev – after he realised he had forgotten to ask for one. He was just about to launch into the quotes from the Iranian woman when the voice at the end of the line said, in a strangely familiar Welsh accent, 'Is there much more of this?'

Chapter Thirty-Seven

(Can we get this in on page two? I think there's a decent picture of him when he joined the paper before he put on so much weight. Thanks. Max.)

Journalist Dies

Hugh Dunn, our Los Angeles correspondent and one of the paper's most experienced reporters, has died suddenly, aged 58. He suffered a heart attack at his home in Pacific Palisades, Los Angeles, and did not recover. He is survived by his wife, Helena, his ex-wives, Jackie, Linda and Lysette (SUBS, PLEASE CHECK) and his sons, Gavin and Godfrey. The editor, Dale Box, said last night: 'Hugh will be remembered in many, many ways. We would like to express our deepest sympathy to his family.' An obituary will appear in tomorrow's paper.

Chapter Thirty-Eight

ANAND TREASURED HIS Saturday mornings in bed. Vanessa would bring him a cup of tea and the *Los Angeles Times* and *New York Times* and he would sip and read and doze, able to ignore the responsibilities of Lancers for a few hours. He was reluctant to give up this weekly treat when Gordon rang and suggested that they meet at the Queen Bess in Santa Monica for breakfast.

The pub, as Anand knew from his one previous experience of it, showed live televised English football games beamed in by satellite. Crowds of British expats, many of them in replica football shirts, bearing the names and numbers of their heroes, and unflattering shorts which exposed their hairless, alabaster legs, would gather for a weekly ritual throughout the English football season. Anand had watched the Cup Final with Gordon there the previous year; they had had a reasonably jolly time but he had managed to turn down all subsequent invitations. This time, however, Gordon was very insistent. Vanessa told him to be firm and say no, his weekends were for his family, but Clara was staying with friends in San Diego and there was something in Gordon's voice that made him feel he should make the effort.

It was only seven in the morning but, because the west coast of the United States was eight hours behind the time of the kick-off in England, the pub was already full to overflowing with Englishmen, Australians and a few Anglophiliac Americans. A huddle of smokers stood outside, in the sharp LA sun, drawing heavily on Marlboros and American Spirits, before crushing the butts beneath their trainers, paying the manager the $10 entrance fee and entering the dark womb of the pub.

Gordon was outside the pub when Anand arrived. He was clutching a copy of *Expat Express*, a free-sheet aimed at the million or so Britons in the United States, which could be found in the British pubs and Tea Shoppes of Los Angeles and New York, San Francisco and Miami. It had a Union flag logo and carried all the football league tables, some rehashed old news from Britain and a few items about the 'British community', as if such a thing existed. Anand had advertised in it a couple of times when Lancers first opened.

'Hi,' said Gordon. 'Sorry to drag you away from the bosom of your family but – did you see this?'

Anand studied the paper. There was an old photo of Hugh Dunn, the English journalist, slimmer and hair still bushy, and a small headline: 'Hugh Dunn – a gentleman and a scholar.' Anand read the fulsome obituary, clearly written by a friendly former colleague, extolling Dunn: '. . . he dodged many a bullet and reported with great courage from Bangladesh during the war in 1971 and went on to become one of his paper's most experienced correspondents . . . Iran . . . attempted assassination of Ronald Reagan . . . four marriages . . . happily settled with his good lady, Helena . . . heart attack . . . a man who always bought his round.' Anand digested it. He looked up at Gordon.

'So, was the reunion bad for his ticker, do you think?' he asked.

'I wished him dead,' said Gordon. 'I watched him drive away that night and hoped his car would crash. I wished him dead and now he is dead. D'you think I have some responsibility for his death?'

'This is very early in the morning for an existential conversation,' said Anand. He tried to decode Gordon's expression. Was he serious? Was he joking? He felt a sudden wave of tiredness. The previous night had been a bad one. The thought of the drive back along the freeway depressed him. Did they serve a decent coffee here, he wondered, or would it be that walnutty filter stuff they sold in gas stations?

'Why did you wish him dead?' he asked.

Gordon gazed westwards across Lincoln Boulevard.

'Was it about Freddie?'

Gordon nodded but did not return Anand's gaze.

'He sort of hinted that . . . he was going to tell Freddie's daughter . . . that I was . . .' Gordon paused and turned towards Anand. 'Do you know if she had interviewed him?'

Anand shrugged. He had seen Sandra King, told her of his regrets that he had not gone down on the street when he had seen the kerfuffle and had been slightly surprised that she did not press him for more details. She had not said who she had spoken to or who she was planning to see.

'I don't think so,' said Anand.

Gordon nodded at this and took a deep breath as though about to make a statement. Anand sensed that Gordon wanted to tell him something. Why else this early-morning summons? Did he know more than he had said about Freddie's death? Was there something confessional about his mood?

'Have you seen her?' Anand asked.

'Saw her on Tuesday,' said Gordon. 'That's what I wanted to talk to you about.'

The noise from inside indicated that the game had begun. They fought their way to a table with a bad view of the giant screen and ordered a 'full English breakfast' from an elderly Scottish waitress. Arsenal were playing Manchester United. The referee blew his whistle for some foul. 'You wanker! You fucking tosser!' shouted a voice from the back of the pub. The crowd bayed, in a way that Anand still found intimidating even though, looking round, he realised that most of the fans here were soft-faced, soft-bellied, middle-aged screenwriters, gaffers and cameramen, rather than the skinny teenage ruffians with whom he associated that sound.

Halfway through the first half, just after the waitress had plonked down a platter of bacon, egg, fried bread and baked beans in front of him, Anand felt his cellphone throbbing in his pocket. He took the call outside. It was Vanessa. He nodded as he took in what she was saying.

Back inside the pub, he distracted Gordon's attention from a disputed corner.

'Gordon, do you remember Deviani?'

'Er, sure. Vivek's friend, who was at the cricket . . . and the party?'

'Yes, that's her.'

'Didn't you say that she and Vivek lived in the Bay Area now?'

'They did, they did, but they split up a year or so ago,' said Anand, ignoring the scowls from a fat Englishman in a Manchester United shirt in front of them. 'She teaches South Asian studies at USC now.'

'And?' said Gordon.

'She needs help,' said Anand.

Chapter Thirty-Nine

THE YOUNG MAN at the information desk in the Virgin Megastore in Oxford Street that Saturday afternoon could not have been more than twenty-two, thought Sandra. He had a white boy's dreadlocks, a sweet face and interesting piercings. She pulled the folded sheet of paper out of her handbag, making sure that she concealed her warrant card and badge as she did so.

'I'm looking for these CDs,' she said, handing over her neat list. 'I know they're all a bit . . . old.' She looked again at the text message that Mulgrew – 'Ginger' Mulgrew – had sent her the night she returned to England. 'Any joy?' it said. It was the third such message he had left her. She had not yet replied. She would let him stew a little longer.

The young assistant studied her list and frowned. 'The Incredible String Band, the Velvet Underground . . . the Mamas and the Papas . . . Yes, I think we have most of them,' he said as he tapped the titles into his computer. 'Having a theme party, are you?'

Sandra could not stop the tears. The young man was solicitous.

'Hey, are you OK? Was it something I said?'

She shook her head, paid and hurried on to the crowded street where no one would notice she was crying.

Chapter Forty

GORDON HAD NEVER stood bail for anyone before but he was happy to be there in the waiting room in LA's downtown jail, the Twin Towers, as they were known, sitting alongside a keen young lawyer called Jay Rosenfeld. Even if it meant that he had missed the rest of the match.

'It's good of you to do this,' Rosenfeld was telling him.

'Well, I'm happy to. I didn't have too much on and anyway I knew Miss, er, Chaudhury many years ago.'

'Is that so? Normally for something as minor as this, unlawful assembly and trespass, they wouldn't need a bail bond but perhaps because it was an anti-war demo and because she took the officer's hat in front of all the cameras – and she's a university lecturer – I guess they wanted to make an example of her.'

Gordon glanced along the bench at the stout mothers from Compton, waiting to bail out their feckless sons. Am I better off with no kids and none of these worries, he wondered, recalling the twinge he felt when Grace's children called out, 'Hey, Dad, look!' to Jorge as they dived in the pool at Ojai? He knew the mothers would not think so. Beside them were the languid Latino girlfriends from Boyle Heights with their intricate tattoos and low-slung jeans, showing the tops of their crimson thongs, as they waited for the bail bonds to be processed. Good material, he thought. But should he make more of an effort to live in the present and not regard everything as potential 'good material' for some screenplay that would probably never be a film? He was still pondering this, still sipping on his latte in its 'please-recycle-me!' cardboard container, when he saw Deviani behind the locked glass door.

She had not seen him and was talking to someone – a guard? a fellow prisoner? – beside her. Something her companion said made her laugh and Gordon immediately recognised that flashing smile. Like Britt, she seemed remarkably little changed by the thirty-odd years. There was one defiant streak of grey in her swept-back hair, a hint of thickness round the hips and the skin under her eyes seemed darker, as though someone sketching her had absent-mindedly carried on shading for too long, but she was undeniably the same person who had teased him on the boundary in Calcutta. She was dressed in a dark blue sari with golden edges. After much unlocking, both old-fashioned keys and new-fashioned electronic, she was ushered into the waiting room and gave her lawyer a broad and semi-apologetic smile.

'Thanks, Jay, sorry you had to do this,' she said as she shook hands with the guard and signed for a small plastic bag of her belongings.

'Don't thank me,' said Rosenfeld. 'This is the guy who put up the money.'

She stared at Gordon for a moment.

'You won't remember,' he said. 'Gordon McGrady. We met about thirty years ago in Calcutta during the Bangladesh war when I was—'

She took his hand. 'Of course I remember you. I read an article about you once that Vivek showed me. Don't you live in some fancy house in . . . where? Santa Barbara?'

'Ojai.'

'That's right, where Annie Besant and Krishnamurti were,' said Deviani. 'I remember thinking that.'

Rosenfeld put his arms behind Gordon and Deviani and gently steered them towards the door.

'Let's get out of here before they change their minds,' he said. 'Deviani, I've got to pick the boys up from basketball practice. Can I get you a cab?'

'Oh, I can give you a lift,' said Gordon as they walked out into the bright morning light. 'Just tell me where to.' His Prius was in the car park beneath Frank Gehry's new Disney Concert Hall, blazing in the midday sun. Jay Rosenfeld dropped them off nearby. The harsh brightness from the hall's shimmering walls made Gordon reach for his sunglasses. 'So – do you go back to Calcutta much?'

'Oh, yes, every year,' said Deviani. 'My mother and sisters are still there. And it's Kolkata now and Chandra Bose airport – although everyone still calls it Calcutta and Dum Dum.'

'Has it changed much?' he asked, as they walked into the grey bowels of the parking lot.

'Oh, we've got our own metro now – and there's a flyover at Chowringhee – but not much has changed really.

They still have rickshaw wallahs, although they're trying to get rid of them because they say it's demeaning for people to pull passengers by foot. They think it's bad for the city's modern image. We rather lost out to Bangalore and Delhi with all the IT stuff and the call centres. But it's still one of the few places on earth where you can see trade unionists on a bandh – a strike, you know – marching behind a red flag with a hammer and sickle on it. So that's nice. At least, I think it is. The Naxalites have spread to lots of other states now. They're everywhere, as are the reasons for their existence. Some things have changed. You know, mobile phones and Domino's Pizzas everywhere. Flurry's has gone a bit upmarket and you can get lattes in the Oxford Bookshop – d'you remember it, in Park Street? But, apart from that, life is much the same.'

'And are there still lots of, well, travellers?'

'Mmm, Sudder Street is much the same although all the young people look much more together than your lot. They wear "Free Tibet" T-shirts and have the Lonely Planet guide in one hand and a bottle of mineral water in the other.' Deviani smiled. 'They probably know a hell of a lot more about India than your crew did. "Backpackers" now, aren't they? You wouldn't recognise Goa either.'

'Why, what's happened?'

'Full of foreign tourists, all jet-skis and paedophiles.'

'And Bangladesh?'

'Poor Bangladesh. I went to Dhaka a couple of years ago for a conference. So many of those collaborators came back and now some of them are in politics. It's as if they forgot why the war was fought. It's . . . sad. Terrible corruption in all the public services. And the fundamentalists are cashing in on all that disillusionment. Some people say it'll be the next Afghanistan. The end of the war is celebrated every year there and in India, they have some ceremony at Fort William and fly the Bangladesh flag, but it means less and less. They hate India now – they see us as big brother – and you can't really blame them. We've even started evicting some of that first wave of refugees, the ones who ended up in the Gobindapur railway colony. Do you remember them? No? But everyone's forgotten, haven't they? Three million people died there; three thousand die in New York and the world is about to be at war without end.'

She smiled at him, that same half-mocking, half-flirtatious smile that he had last seen on the roof of the Lux on the night after the war had ended. She climbed into the car and he closed the door gently behind her. As Gordon drove, frowning in concentration to find the right freeway entrance, she shifted her position in the front seat so she could study him.

'Do tell me,' she said. 'Did you ever find what your purpose was?'

Gordon looked at her out of the corner of his eye.

'What do you think?' he replied, as he swung the car up the ramp and on to the 10 going west. 'By the way, where on earth are we going?'

'You never did find out, did you?'

Chapter Forty-One

ANAND AND VANESSA lay in bed together beneath a crisp white sheet in their penthouse flat at the top of Lancers. Vanessa took her afternoon nap naked. Anand still felt more comfortable in his pyjamas, silk and midnight blue now, rather than the old striped cotton of his student and Lux days. The television was on but the sound was off. It was a news channel and an earnest male newscaster with too much pancake make-up on was wearing his 'this is serious' face. Anand vaguely tried to lip-read but could not decipher what was being said. He still could not sleep.

On his last trip to Calcutta, he had bought, from a pharmacy in Ballygunge, two packets of Powergra, a local version of Viagra, for which one did not need a prescription. It had been Vanessa's idea. Was she trying to tell him something? Looking at her as she slumbered, sleep erasing the lines in her forehead and a tiny drop of sweat slowly sliding between her breasts, he felt no need of any chemical assistance. He smiled.

'What are you smiling at?' she asked.

'I thought you were asleep,' he said.

'You're the one that's meant to be asleep,' she said, pushing the hair out of his eyes. 'So was Gordon OK about bailing out Deviani?'

'Oh, yes, I think he probably welcomed it, having something to do. Redemption, that sort of thing.'

'Why does he need redemption?'

'I don't know but I sense he does, something to do with Freddie Braintree, perhaps,' said Anand. He kissed her on the forehead. There was a silence. He could tell that Vanessa was still awake.

'Do you remember in London when we were students, in the Aldwych, there was a place called the India Club where we used to go for a curry?'

'Mm, you always said the food was a bit bland.'

'It was, it was. But do you remember there was a waitress there, Austrian, I think, maybe German. She had her hair in a bun and she used to keep her pencils stuck in it and she would pull them out to write your order down.'

'Yesss . . .'

'They used to say that Krishna Menon, the old Defence Secretary, was in love with her.'

'And?'

'I was just looking at you and wondering how many people who come to Lancers must be in love with you.'

'What a strange thought. I don't have my hair in a bun. Yet. Try and sleep.'

Anand stared at the ceiling and tried to sleep. Perhaps, if he ran through the names of his top twenty Indian batsmen of all time – no, he was bored with that. What had Gordon wanted to tell him? The television was still flickering silently on the dressing table. There were some young American soldiers with crew cuts kissing women who he presumed were their wives or mothers. Was it the news or a trailer for a movie?

'Close your eyes and go to sleep,' said Vanessa firmly.

Chapter Forty-Two

'SO WHAT WAS she like?' asked Lori as Britt slipped their VW through Malibu on the northbound Pacific Coast Highway.

'Who?' said Britt.

'The policewoman.'

'Quite sweet. Very English. Freckles.'

'Did you tell her . . . that you thought you'd heard . . .'

'Did I confess that I may have heard her father cry for help but was too lost in myself to do anything about it?'

'Oh, Britt, I didn't mean that.'

'I know you didn't. No, she didn't ask. She just wanted to know what her dad had been like so I could tell her, quite honestly, that I hardly met him but he seemed very sweet.'

'Like her.'

'Like her. She said that she now knew what happened that night,' said Britt. She went over in her head what she had told Sandra King. Had she been honest? She had planned to tell her the truth – that she had heard Freddie's scream but had not turned to help him. Would she have understood that? Or, as a tough policewoman trained to confront her fears, would she have despised her for it? In the end, the words had not come. She had minimised her role, excusing herself from a full confession because Sandra King did not press her too heavily. 'I wish I had—'

'There's a hitch-hiker, Mom,' said Luz from the back seat where she had settled with her arm round Ahimsa, their bull terrier. 'Can we stop for him?'

'There's not much room, darling,' said Britt as she slowed in the traffic. It was a glorious day, pelicans were skimming the ocean like prehistoric stealth bombers.

'Please,' said Luz. 'Please. You always say we should help people who have no money.'

Britt and Lori exchanged glances.

'Oh, all right. He doesn't look too bad. He's pretty old anyway. As long as he doesn't smell.'

They pulled off the road and on to the gravel. The cadaverous figure trotted towards them. He was travelling light. He had the once-handsome, weatherbeaten face and faraway gaze of a hobo. The skin was drawn tightly over his cheekbones, giving him a thirties, dustbowl look or what Britt, through growing up with her father's books of Dorothea Lange photographs, automatically associated with that period. It was a face you did not often see nowadays. A black-and-white face in a technicolour world.

'I'm headed for San Francisco,' he said with a slow drawl.

'Hop in,' said Britt. 'This is your lucky day. We're going all the way. We're getting married.'

'Well, congratulations, ma'am,' said the hitch-hiker. He opened the back door and climbed in beside Luz, who greeted him with a grin.

'How about you?' Britt liked the fact that he did not ask who the lucky guy was. 'Have you come far today?'

'Nope. It's been a long, strange trip so far. No one picks up hitch-hikers these days. Guess everyone's kind of afraid of strangers, what with the . . . murders and such . . . Been standing there since before dawn.'

'That's too bad,' said Britt. 'It's a sign of the times. I can remember when everyone hitch-hiked everywhere. You stood on the road with your thumb out and a smile on your face. I like that – that jacket you're wearing. Haven't seen one of those for a while.'

'Yup, got it at a thrift shop in the last place I stopped, back in Pacific Palisades,' said the hitch-hiker. 'Two bucks. There was a stack of good clothes there. Someone must have been moving house or something.'

'There's a mess on your pocket, sir,' said Luz. 'Your pen must be leaking . . . Hey, Mom, keep your eyes on the road!'

The hitch-hiker gazed contentedly out of the window as four pelicans, flying in formation, granted them an escort up the coastline.

Epilogue

THIS IS LARRY HERE. After thirty years in jail, I get to do the epilogue.

Freddie Braintree's daughter kept her side of the bargain, although it all took a little longer than I'd hoped. Anyway, I've been out for more than three years now. Apart from being pulled over one time by the highway patrol for speeding on my Harley – pathetic and predictable purchase, I know – I have not been in any kind of trouble with the law.

My folks both died while I was inside. Their visits had drifted away long before they did so I can't pretend the deaths hit me too hard. I tried to get them to spend some of the money I made from *Hepatitis!* but, apart from a couple of vacations in Hawaii and a new RV that some Vegas dealer overcharged them for, they hardly used any of it. It was nice to come out to some money in the bank but the whole success of *Hepatitis!* was a mixed blessing for me. Once the news got out in jail, word went round that I was some wealthy guy. So both cons and guards hit on me for money in exchange for favours and protection. One of the guards got too pushy and I finally flipped one day and whacked him in the exercise yard. It was more of a cuff than a real blow but he was fat and unfit and lost his footing, cracked his head on a steel bench and fractured his skull. That added another twelve years to my sentence. So be it.

Gordon kept in touch while I was inside. A few postcards, that sort of thing, and he was pretty honorable about making sure the royalties got through. He visited a couple of times but it was kind of awkward and, when I first got out, I didn't bother getting hold of him.

Then a few weeks ago, I saw his name in the papers. Some Second World War film that he had written the script for called *Moonlit Kidnap*. I wondered if he remembered that conversation we had somewhere in Calcutta about moths being drawn to flames because they thought it was the moonlight. Probably not. The film got trashed. 'Ludicrous' and 'risible' were two of the kindest words used about it. It got 'two thumbs down' from the guys who do that. Everyone said the old original version was better, why do a remake, why do another war movie?

Then there was the arrest of California's own 'hippy killer'. The guy who killed two people in Orange County and left the yin-yang sign on them like in India all those years ago. So who was the big, bad serial killer who came out of hiding after all those years and got the press so hyped up?

Just a messed-up punk of eighteen who had seen a TV doc about the 'hippy trail killer' on some cable channel and must have thought – hey, this would be cool. His dad, some big business guy, appeared on all the news programmes blaming his mom and his teachers. Then his mom appeared blaming his dad and violent video games. His lawyer is trying to negotiate a deal so that he'll do life rather than take his chances on death row because it looks like Arnie is not too bothered about people going for the long walk. I reckoned this was all a sign to get hold of Gordon.

Tracked him down easily enough through his agent. He was living in a place called Ojai. I called him up. A woman with an Indian accent and a kind of friendly voice answered the phone. I almost got the impression she knew who I was.

Gordon sounded a bit surprised to hear from me. He asked me over to stay but I didn't fancy that so I said I would be heading by on my way up to Big Sur and maybe we could meet somewhere on the road. He suggested a place on the Pacific Coast Highway called Neptune's Net, a sort of fish restaurant where bikers stop for coffee and to check that their leathers are still looking as cute as when they left Brentwood. It's right on the coast, by a little bay on the Ventura county line. We met last week, both pulling in at the same time, him in his hybrid Prius, me on the bike. Here's how the meeting went.

Me: 'Hi, droog.'

Gordon: 'Hi, Larry, you look great. What's your secret?'

Me: 'Weed, whites and wine.'

Gordon: 'Seriously, though.'

Me: 'Reds, vitamin C and cocaine – I wish. I have to

Duncan Campbell

abide by the terms of my parole: it's all boring grains and juices and pulses.'

A hug – British guys find that hard, however often they try it; you can feel their little spines stiffen.

Me: 'You look OK yourself.' To be honest, he looked a bit ragged.

He pointed out a sign that the Highway Patrol had posted saying, 'Please Ride Quiet. Stop Road Thunder or Be Cited,' and told me to make sure I didn't rev my bike on the way out. He was joking. The restaurant had signs saying, 'No shoes, no service.' Is it just me or did the world get a whole lot more prohibitive while I was inside?

We order. He has a Diet Pepsi and crab cake. I had the double combo of clam, shrimp and french fries. I tell him about the little spa hotel I've opened in Desert Hot Springs which caters to a lot of Hollywood types. I serve the best breakfast in the Mojave. He tells me about his film and how bad it was and I nod as though I haven't read that it was a load of crap. I tell him I'm on my own so that he doesn't have to ask that sort of question sideways. (There have been a couple of women but they didn't work out; my fault entirely with the first one and the second was a bit too excited about my prison past, telling her friends about it all the time, so I checked out.)

We have a bit of shared small talk – stuff about Bush, prostates, Afghanistan, the new Dylan CD and an article we both spotted in that morning's paper about some research that shows that marijuana can slow down the onset of Alzheimer's. That all takes us pretty much through to the end of our meal, at which point we stroll outside because I'm the last person left in California who still smokes and I fancy lighting up. Gordon suggests we cross the road to the little stretch of beach and that takes us to this exchange. I offer Gordon a cigarette. He shakes his head. I light up.

Me: 'One cigarette closer to Jesus . . .'

Gordon: 'Freddie's daughter came to see you, didn't she?'

Me: 'Sure. Nice-looking woman, reminded me of Freddie.'

Gordon: 'She wanted to know what happened that night?'

Me: 'Yeah.'

Gordon: 'What . . . what did you tell her?'

Me: 'Well, that it was an accident, that no one was to blame.'

Gordon: 'You lied, didn't you?'

Me: 'What do you mean?'

Gordon: 'I saw her just after she interviewed you. She told me that she now knew how her dad – Freddie – had died and why he had traces of LSD in his body. She said that he misheard my instructions about where my anti-runs pills were and took two tabs of acid from Remy's backpack, the wrong backpack.'

Me: 'Where would she get that idea?'

Gordon: 'You must have told her that.'

Me: 'Isn't that what you told me back in Bangkok?'

Gordon: 'I never said anything. And anyway, Remy had a kitbag, that old army thing.'

I could tell what he was about to say was hard for him. I

433

let him take his time. After a couple of minutes of looking out over the Pacific, he came out with it.

'Larry, I realised before I left Calcutta that I told Freddie the wrong pocket to look in. I realised when I was looking for the acid so I could dump it before I went through customs in Bangkok. I'd told him the wrong pocket and that meant that he took the acid. I kind of think you knew that all along. On top of that, I now know that Freddie kept asking me who he was and I got fed up and told him he was Tiger Niazi – the Pakistani general – and that can't have helped him out there in the crowd. Hugh, you know, that journalist guy, he was probably going to tell Freddie's daughter that. Can I tell you something? I wished Hugh dead and the next day he died.'

'Cool,' I said. 'I sell some weed and get thirty years, you kill two guys and get off scot-free. What's your problem?'

Well, we were both looking out to sea so I couldn't see his expression. But he was right, I knew back in Bangkok that he'd told Freddie the wrong pocket but I never brought it up. His little mistake probably led to Freddie's death. If he wanted to 'fess up to it now, who was I to argue with that? I had plenty experience of guys wanting to admit to much worse shit than that. It wasn't like he had meant to harm him.

So there was a long silence.

Me: 'But you weren't the hippy killer, were you, droog?'

Gordon: 'Christ, Larry! You never thought that, did you? I couldn't even kill a fish. I tried once but I had to throw it back in the lake – those big eyes.'

Me: 'All those murders stopped after that night. Did you ever wonder why?'

Gordon: 'What are you saying?'

Me (enjoying this bit of tension, I'd had a lot of time to think about it inside): 'I know who the hippy killer was.'

Gordon: 'Fuck! Why did you never say? God, Larry, you're not going to say that—'

Me: 'Don't worry, droog. I'm not going to slit your throat. It ain't me.'

Gordon: 'Oh, God, it was Freddie – wasn't it? If he hadn't been hit by the van he would have gone on and on killing people . . . Was he just a psychopath? Was that why he talked in nonsense all the time? God, did you know all this and—'

Me: 'Hey, hey! Wrong again.'

So I told him what happened.

'One night, just before the war kicked off in India, I got stoned with Remy on the roof of the Lux. He told me why he came out to India in the first place: his little sister, a kid of seventeen, had become a junkie in Bombay so he went to find her, bring her back to France. He found her all right – with a couple of American junkies who were fucking her and giving her lots of smack. Remy got into a fight with them one night – he really was ex-Foreign Legion – and he slit their throats, said he'd once done the same thing to a guy in Algeria and it was easier the second and third times. The yin-yang thing wasn't planned – there was just some scribbled sign in the hotel room where he offed them and he put a line through it. Then the press turned it into something bigger. But his sister's not so keen on coming home with big brother so she runs off again. He tracks her down again – in Benares. She's with another dealer. German guy, I think. So he offs him, too. This time he deliberately leaves a little sign behind him. But little sister has had enough of this and she heads off again. He catches up with her one final time in Kerala. Too late – she's ODed and she's gone.'

Gordon: 'Wait a minute. Remy was a junkie. Why should he be so bothered about his little sister taking smack?'

Me: 'Ah, he wasn't a junkie when he arrived. But you remember the moths looking for the moon? He had to try. And it really suited him. By the time we met him, he was a paid-up smack-head. His brain was scrambled. He sees Kieran and Karen and he knows that they were in Bombay too, that time when he killed the junkies. He recognises them, OK, but he doesn't know if they recognise him. So when Karen goes to the cemetery – you remember that graveyard where we used to go? – he follows her to find out. He pulls a blade on her. Now Kieran arrives on the scene. He takes the blade off Remy – and remember Kieran was in the Australian army in Vietnam – and he kills him. That's why the killing stopped. I came across them just after the deed was done, while you were getting out of your head round the corner. Remy had that yin-yang sign in his pocket so we just shoved it on his chest.'

Gordon: 'But . . . but . . . why did you never tell me this? All that time . . .'

Me: 'I'm not a snitch, man. I knew if I told you, there would always be a chance that you would tell the police. Then what would have happened? Kieran gets arrested? Kieran tells the cops about me? Fuck that.'

Gordon: 'So why are you telling me now?'

Me: 'Kieran's dead – I only found that out from Freddie's daughter. Hepatitis. Of course. Nothing can happen to him now. And nothing can happen to Freddie either.'

Gordon: 'Jeez. But I'm still to blame for—'

Me: 'Oh, come on, there's too much blame around, droog. "Be here now" – isn't that what you used to say all the damn time? So why are you doing all this "being there then" shit? You think the truth will set you free? The truth didn't set me free. It got me locked up for half my life. What happened to Freddie was no one's fault. Or, if it was, it was everyone's.

'You can blame that journalist friend of yours for giving him the Pakistani badge he had on him or blame the folks who saw him in trouble on the street and didn't help out – or blame the Pakistani government for the war and the blackout, or the crazy drug laws for sending Freddie out there in the first place, or the Bengal government for not fixing the roads in Calcutta or international capitalism for keeping the Bengalis so poor that they didn't have the money to fix the roads or the inventor of wing mirrors – or even the damn British empire for carving India into bits which led to the war in the first place or . . .'

I was looking for someone to blame for Freddie's digestive problems when I noticed that Gordon was smiling, that old two-chillum smile I remembered from Calcutta and from the places where we hung out together all those years ago, Kathmandu, Delhi, wherever. He was still looking out to sea but smiling, the way he had smiled when he was playing the guitar or we were having one of our pointless stoner discussions about whether the darkest hour was just before dawn or which lowlands the sad-eyed lady came from and it reminded me of that time when it seemed to us that anything and everything was possible. Maybe it was just nostalgie de la bong. Perhaps everyone has a period in their lives like that. Perhaps not. Perhaps the truth did finally set him free. Who knows.

A couple of kids in wetsuits ran past us, heading for the sea with their surfboards under their arms even though there wasn't that much surf. They were laughing and joshing each other. I don't know what they made of us, who they thought we were. Two old surfers with knee issues? Two methamphetamine dealers? A couple of sad old guys?

They probably didn't even notice us.

Acknowledgements

MANY THANKS FOR different reasons to: Pankaj Mishra, Pat Kavanagh, Nur Laiq, Penny Tweedie, Chris Burrill, Mary Mount, Jawid Laiq, Bharati Bhargava, Ralph Edney, Alistair McClure, the late Nick Tomalin, the late Jim McClure, Lorna Macfarlane, Anne Dowie, Gus Mok Chiu-yu, Fionna Macleod, Anand Patwardhan, Bonnie Swift-Langbehn, Larry Becker, Martin Fletcher, Jo Matthews, Jane Heller, Clare Toynbee, Fran D'Abreu, Alex McGregor, Ruby Crystal and particularly David Jenkins, co-author of the original *Hepatitis!* (which remains, puzzlingly, still unperformed).

THALASSA ALI

Companions of Paradise

In 1838, Mariana Givens came to India to find a husband, but instead rescued a neglected Indian baby. Now, after three years of political upheaval and personal danger, and a reckless marriage to an Indian Muslim, she finds herself exiled to the vulnerable British cantonment at Kabul. Forced to make a final choice between her English upbringing and her husband's fascinating, mystical family, Mariana enters the roiling, dangerous city of Kabul in search of a seer who holds the answers she seeks. But the mystic's help comes with a price.

Meanwhile, the British colonials enjoy the fruits of Kabul, oblivious to the resentment their occupation has caused among the Afghan chiefs. As the chiefs' anger turns to violence, and the British cantonment comes under siege, Mariana must make a terrible choice in order to save those she loves from unimaginable horror . . .

Companions of Paradise is the unforgettable finale to Thalassa Ali's extraordinary tale of Mariana Givens. Her first two novels, *A Singular Hostage* and *A Beggar at the Gate*, have been richly praised:

'A thrilling read, alive to cultural difference, awake to the scents and sounds of a distant epoch' *Sunday Herald*

'A story of love and understanding, of duty and honour, of spirituality and redemption, painted beautifully and vividly with deft soul-strokes' *The Big Issue in the North*

'Eminently readable' M M Kaye, author of *The Far Pavilions*

978 0 7553 6774 4

headline
review

PAUL DOHERTY

The Poisoner of Ptah

Pharaoh-Queen Hatusu's Egypt is in a new and glorious ascendancy. But for all its prosperity and power it is not without its weaknesses – or enemies.

At a peace treaty signing between Egypt and Libya in Thebes, three of Egypt's leading scribes die violently on the Temple forecourt, the victims of poisoning. And when a prosperous merchant and his wife are found drowned, rumours sweep the imperial city. The Poisoner of Ptah has returned.

Pharaoh Hatusu orders Amerotke, Chief Judge of the Halls of Two Truths, to find the perpetrator of these abominations. His hunt for the Poisoner uncovers a seething mass of suspicion and danger. Now Amerotke must pit his wits against a cunning opponent intent on vengeance and survive the twilight world of Thebes where life can be so rich and yet death so swift and brutal . . .

Praise for Paul Doherty's novels:

'Doherty dazzles with his knowledge and intimate feel for ancient Egypt' *Time Out*

'Doherty has woven a delightfully dark tale around what must have been the most remarkable period of Egyptian history' *Historical Novels Review*

'Resurrectionist magic' *New York Times*

978 0 7553 2887 1

headline

Now you can buy any of these other bestselling Headline books from your bookshop or *direct from the publisher*.

FREE P&P AND UK DELIVERY
(Overseas and Ireland £3.50 per book)

Towelhead	Alicia Erian	£7.99
The Cruellest Month	Louise Penny	£6.99
The Pirate's Daughter	Margaret Cezair-Thompson	£6.99
The Good Thief	Hannah Tinti	£6.99
The Poison Maiden	Paul Doherty	£6.99
I Predict A Riot	Bateman	£7.99
In A Far Country	Linda Holeman	£6.99
A Small Part of History	Peggy Elliott	£6.99
Pretty Dead Things	Barbara Nadel	£7.99

TO ORDER SIMPLY CALL THIS NUMBER

01235 400 414

or visit our website: www.headline.co.uk

Prices and availability subject to change without notice.